AWAKENING OF HANNAH GRANT

THE PERCEPTIONS SAGA BOOK FOUR

DAVID PARKER-ROSS

TAIRIS ANDERS MEDIA, LLC

Editor

Tegan Bourke

ALSO BY DAVID PARKER-ROSS

ALL BOOKS AVAILABLE ON AUDIO

Perceptions – The Jenna Plural Saga
Jenna Plural Wants You
That Girl from Wagga
Walking in Her Shadow
Awakening of Hannah Grant

Perceptions – Prequel Novella
Force 10 from Wagga (A Stacey Grant Novella)

Writing as DS Parker
The Rise of Artemis

Coming soon...

Perceptions – The Jenna Plural Saga
The Angel of Phobos
Memoir of a Martian

The Bloodline Chronicles
The House of Maine
Escape from Jilrir
The Rise of the Shieldmaidens
The Age of Commech
Banner of the Hawk

iii

DAVID PARKER-ROSS

Dedication

For my shiny new niece
You are not due to be born until one month after this book is published.
As I write this, you still reside within your mother's tummy. Personally, given the state of the world, I would stay there.
However, I am really looking forward to meeting you. Unfortunately, I do not yet know your name, and I don't think your parents even know, for sure, how the world will know you.
So at this point, I will just call you Miss Collins and assure you that you will have an amazing life with a wonderful family.
I am really glad that you're a girl because I recently dedicated one of my books to your cousin Jaxson naming him the best nephew. I am soon to have the best niece.
I have suggested that they call you Davina after me, but, alas, your parents have no taste. Of course, they could call you Jenna or Stacey after the greatest characters ever created, but again, I doubt they will listen to my pearls of wisdom.
Well, Miss Collins, like I told your cousin, you really need to be an adult before you read this book, but I hope one day you will and that I will still be around to find out what you think of it. I can't wait to meet you and look forward to the fun we'll have together.
As for my readers, I will, of course, reveal the answer to this naming cliffhanger in book five, The Angel of Phobos, later this year....
Tons of hugs from your Uncle David xxx

AUTHOR'S NOTE

Perceptions is a series that tells tales from different characters' perspectives. Each has their own ideas, their own values, their own beliefs, and their own memories.

The characters, including the narrator, have their own perception of the events that took place at the time of the stories. They may very well have political, religious, and social opinions. Those opinions do not necessarily reflect this author or anyone involved with the creation of this work. Indeed, I have very much tried to keep my personal opinions out of the stories.

The whole idea is to leave it to you, the reader, to make up your mind on the rights and wrongs of the characters within the tales.

Memory is a fickle beast; not everyone will remember events similarly. One should not assume that a narrator is either accurate or, for that matter, even truthful.

Perceptions... It's all about who you believe.

Clear Skies to You,
David Parker-Ross

3

THE AWAKENING OF HANNAH GRANT

BY HANNAH GRANT

Dedication
For my most beloved Harper Grant

**From the Office of Hannah Grant
C.E.O., Grant Industries**

There was once a time when my name was better known than my sister's.

Stacey has become a legend throughout the Solar System, almost as well known as Jenna Plural herself. Her maneuver in the Battle of Deep Space, where she took out a frigate with the Lady Liberty, is the stuff movies are made of.

Although we are sisters, we led and still lead very different lives. Our mother was Marcia Grant, one of the richest women in the Solar System, if not the richest.

Stacey's father and our mother broke up, and he spent the rest of his life in virtual poverty in Wagga, while I was born eight years later to our mother's third husband, but not her last. While Stacey barely had enough to eat, I rarely wore the same outfit twice.

5

It was many years before I felt any guilt for this, for I never even thought of Stacey throughout my youth. I'm not even sure when I first became aware she existed. She was that unimportant to me.

This is not Stacey's story.

I am often asked to tell my experiences of Last Day, as we Australians call it, and what befell me during the invasion of my country. It is not a story I have told often, if at all. Mr. Phelkar is choosing to make this part of Jenna's saga because he believes I have affected the war's course. I'm not sure I agree. I'll let you make up your mind. Indeed, Jenna barely appears in this tale.

My life before Last Day was very different, and like every Australian, it changed in that single day, and it truly was the start of my awakening.

My name is Hannah Edith Grant, and this is my story.

CHAPTER ONE

THE DAY BEFORE

I am a GenMod.

It is bizarre that I can say that, as it is something that has been hidden for all of my life. The reason? I am not just a GenMod. I am an illegally manufactured GenMod. I was programmed and grown in a tank with a mixture of D.N.A. from my mother and unknown donors who were considered genetically superior to the man I thought was my biological father.

Of course, my mother used her financial and political clout to ensure all the appropriate paperwork was done. If it had been known, I would have been refused Australian citizenship.

It seems strange that I can even talk about it now.

However, with Jenna Plural as our leader, genetic modification is no longer the stigma it once was. Indeed, if we hold her up as an example, it is evidence that genetic modification is a pretty neat idea.

I kind of became aware that I was different at a very early age. My family was very much in the public eye, and a scandal broke when pictures of me appeared in one of those trashy celebrity magazines that pried into the private lives of the well-to-do. Someone had questioned how I looked so perfect. Even with copious amounts of plastic surgery, my mother was no model, and my father, or rather the man I thought to be my father, was not exactly on a list of beauty.

Of course, my mother provided evidence that I was not genetically modified and paid off anyone official likely to investigate me any further, and eventually, the story became boring and went away.

Leading up to my eighteenth birthday, the story began to emerge again. It was getting harder to hide what society considered my flawless features, not that I particularly tried. I am incredibly vain

and completely aware that I am considered exceptionally attractive. In my youth, I positively relished it and took full advantage of the opportunities it afforded me.

I don't know how the story would have played out because, as you know, the day after my birthday, my world ended. At least the world as I had known it from my ivory tower of privilege.

However, today I can say I am a GenMod. I will never age, and I will never die, barring a violent act. Do I say it with arrogance and pride? No. I say it as a matter of fact. I understand AntiGen bigotry may color your judgment of me, but I assure you that you find much more to dislike me for within these pages than petty prejudice against my D.N.A.

So let me take you back to my eighteenth birthday and how, unbeknown to me, I was to play a part in the life of Jenna Plural.

That morning, I was in a bad mood as I drove my new Jaguar to school. I was seriously pissed off because I wanted a Bugatti, and my mother had adamantly refused to buy me a French car. Such things were illegal to import, but since when had that stopped us? The European black market was the backbone of Australian commerce. I had to settle for the Jaguar, and I was not very happy about it at all. I was eighteen today, and it was supposed to be my special day, and she had absolutely ruined it.

I drove dangerously at high speed and without due care and attention, almost hoping that I would mangle this piece of British shit around some lamppost even if it killed me. Death was a better choice than the humiliation of driving this embarrassment.

I cursed and punched the steering wheel as a siren went off, and the flashing blue lights above me indicated for me to pull over. The police drone hovered over me, instructing me to await the rival of an officer of the law. I waited impatiently, knowing a copper could take up to an hour to arrive. I wanted to drive off, but I knew the drone would land upon me and hold me in place, and instead of a fine that I could easily pay off with the contents of my purse, I would face possible jail time. By the time the cop car pulled up next to me, it was about thirty-five minutes later, and my mood had not improved. However, I hitched up my already too-short dress and puffed out my chest, undoing the top few buttons on my dress.

To make matters worse, the cop that arrived was so pleasant and smiled at me as he asked for my license. I could hate an arsehole so much easier. I handed him my phone, having already brought it up on the screen. "In a hurry, Miss Grant?" he asked as he scanned it and handed it back to me.

"Yes, I am, so write me the bloody ticket and let me get out of here, would you?" I snapped, keeping my hands on the wheel to ensure he remained at ease.

"Well, there's no need to be like that, Miss," he said most pleasantly. "Especially as this is your twelfth speeding violation, and by rights, I should arrest you and impound your car. Which will be followed by some jail time, probably about three months, and the loss of your license until your twenty-first birthday."

This had the desired effect. I did not only just become nice; I immediately burst into tears. Something I have had a talent for ever since childhood. This had the desired effect, and he looked quite concerned. "I'm so sorry, sir, I'm late for school; if I'm late again, my mother is going to positively kill me. Honestly, I'd rather go to jail than face her."

He looked flustered. Like most men, he could not deal with a crying woman. "Look, I still have to write you this ticket, you've been caught on the drone, but I'll let you off with a warning for the rest of it. Please try to drive more carefully. I strongly recommend that you switch on the auto driver and let the car do it for you."

I wiped away the crocodile tears and smiled warmly up at him. "Yes, sir. I'll do just that. Thank you for being so understanding."

"It's not a problem, young lady," he said, smiling back at me. "You have a g'day now."

Amazingly as I pulled away, the tears dried up, and I stuffed the ticket in the glove compartment with the rest. I had a few choice names

9

for the cop as I headed to school, only speeding up again once I was out of his sight.

As I pulled into the car park of Melbourne Grammar, I was twenty minutes late for class. This did not improve my mood. I usually got myself something to eat in the cafeteria before class started rather than breakfast with my family and listening to my mother lecture me once more on whatever was on her mind that day. Being my birthday and tonight apparently the social event of the year, I would no doubt get lectures on presenting myself as a socially responsible lady. I did not realize that my moods were part of my genetic design. Jenna would explain it to me much later, but it was my body switching on defense systems working overtime to prepare to fight the degeneration of my cells. Around twenty-five, I would stop aging, which took a lot of work on the part of my system. It was almost like a form of puberty, having the side effect of mood swings. Jenna would joke that it was God's payback for us not menstruating like regular women. However, at the time, all I knew was the world, and everything in it, pissed me off. I slammed my car door and did not bother to lock it. Let some fucker steal that piece of shit. I thought.

I ran up the stairs of the age-old school and then through the double doors hearing the beep as the camera marked me as delinquent. No doubt I'd have another lecture on that too. I headed over to my locker and placed my hand upon the picture of my absolute crush, rockstar Philip Morgan as I did every morning. I then proceeded to pull out my tablet. I didn't carry a schoolbag as I always thought they spoiled the look of my outfits. Today I wore a Perdan dress a couple of inches above the dress code. No doubt I'd be written up on that too.

I heard Josh's voice behind me as I shut the locker door. I rolled my eyes. The last thing I needed right now was that pathetic little loser who had become my personal stalker. "G'day, Hannah."

I turned to face him, "Oh my God! Do you always sneak up on girls like that? Do you even have the remotest clue how creepy that is?" I said, sneeringly at him.

The boy shifted uncomfortably before he spoke again. "I'm sorry, Hannah. I just wanted to wish you a happy birthday." He said, his eyes lingering too long on my legs which disappeared into the ankle boots that matched the color of my turquoise dress.

"Oh my God, Josh, stop undressing me with your eyes, you little pervert," I said, looking at him in disgust.

He flashed bright red and stammered, "I wasn't. I promise you I wasn't."

"Just get out of my way before I start screaming."

"I'm sorry." He said, scampering away. By the time I reached my class, he was the furthest thing from my mind.

However, thoughts of him came back to me during the lunch hour. We sat outside in the hot February sun with my three best mates, Isla, Sarah, and Bronwyn.

I was eating a sandwich that my nanny had made for me. Of course, I was too old for a nanny now, but old Amberline had become part of the family and remained with us in her retirement.

"Oh, my God!" Sarah said with indignation. "That creepy Josh boy is watching us again."

"Oh, you wish he was watching you," Bron said with wide eyes and a cruel smirk. "He only has eyes for Han here."

"Oh, don't be gross. I have better guys than that watching me." Sarah was quite the plain girl and barely fit in with the rest of us. Her entire cool factor came from being the daughter of a prestigious singer from the Eighties. Otherwise, she would not have got a look in with our group, which was quite exclusive.

I looked over to where Josh sat at another table, eating some sort of salad and staring at us or, as Bron had pointed out, me. I suddenly felt hands upon my shoulders, and my head whipped around to see Patrick. Unlike Josh, Patrick was a real guy. Captain of the football team and all-around jock. Nothing helps break the rules more than money, and he was pumped up with steroids, but as he won most of our games against other schools, everyone turned a blind eye. I smiled up at him as he leaned in to kiss me, and I went with it.

Unbeknownst to my mother, we had been dating for about three months. She seemed to think she had a say in who I had relationships with. She eventually wanted to find me a publicly acceptable partner who would fit in with the Grant ethos.

11

"Happy birthday, babe," he said caringly. "How's it going?"

"Pretty shit so far." I muttered and then, looking over at Josh, added, "and it's not helping that that creep keeps watching me." Patrick looked up and scowled as he saw Josh looking over, and the little weasel quickly looked away.

"Well, you're the one who won't let me do anything about him. I keep telling you I'll have a quiet word in his ear to leave you alone," Pat said, irritated.

I sighed wearily. It was true I did stop him, but only because I didn't want the creep to become important enough to have Patrick do something about it. But my mood that day was ready for some trouble, and as I watched Josh eat his lunch and occasionally glance over at me, I said softly, "I think I've changed my mind, but I want to watch whatever you do."

Bron, an even bigger bitch than me, grinned widely. "Oh, so do I. Please tell me I can."

So, at the end of the school day, we waited in the corridor until Josh came out of his class. The little nerd was always the last to leave. He actually took school seriously. Patrick patiently waited until Josh passed the door of the boys' bathroom. "Hey Josh!" he said quite pleasantly, making the young lad stop and look up. At that point, Patrick shoved him through the boys' bathroom door, and grinning, Bron and I followed them inside. A startled kid was taking a piss at the urinal as Josh came

flying in, followed by Patrick and us girls. "Zip it up and get out, or you're gonna get some, too," I said softly, and the chubby little kid hastily fastened himself up while running out the front door.

Patrick grabbed Josh by the collar and slammed him against the sinks causing him to cry out as his back hit the porcelain. "We have a little problem, Josh. You really don't know your place." Patrick sounded like a schoolteacher reprimanding a young child. "You see, girls like this are out of your league. They really aren't interested in creepy little nerds like you, and frankly, you scare them. Do you enjoy scaring girls, my little freak?" Patrick sounded so gentle and kind that it made it all the funnier. Bron giggled. I don't think there was anything she was ever scared of.

12

Josh looked up at me with hurt and fear, but all he got from me was an amused grin. Hell, he'd been asking for this for a long time.

"Don't look at her." Still holding his collar with one hand, Patrick slapped his face hard. "You don't even deserve to be in her presence. From now on, I don't want to hear of you even looking her in the eye." Josh quickly turned his head away from me. Patrick's own words gave him an idea. He pulled Josh away from the sink and turned him to face me. "In fact, Josh, the only place you should be in Hannah's presence is on your knees." He brought his ankle around Josh's and brought him down to his knees in front of me. The terrified boy stayed down, staring at my heeled turquoise boots, saying nothing. Patrick pushed his head down until his face almost touched my feet. I could not help but laugh. My birthday had suddenly become quite entertaining. "Say, 'I'm sorry for being a pervert, Miss Hannah,'" Patrick instructed. Josh didn't move, and he certainly did not speak. That annoyed me, so I lifted my boot and pushed the pointed heel into his shoulder, and he gasped in pain.

"Come on, where's my apology," I demanded. Behind me, Bron was cracking up with laughter.

"I'm sorry for being a pervert, Miss Hannah." He muttered barely audibly, and for good measure, I pushed the sole of my shoe onto his face and slid it down with a chuckle.

"There you go," Patrick said pleasantly, pulling him back up to his feet. Josh's eyes met with mine briefly. Pain and hurt where in his eyes, and I enjoyed it. That feeling of power over another human being is like an aphrodisiac, and I can't explain it better than that. I still struggle with it to this day. Patrick spun him around and shoved him into a cubicle, and Bron and I rushed around to see what we knew would happen next. Patrick shoved Josh's head into the toilet, and we could hear him gasping and spluttering as Patrick flushed it. Then he let him go, and he just lay there, his head soaking wet, his morale crushed, and his dignity in tatters. "This, my friend, is just a friendly warning," Patrick said ever so sweetly. "If I ever hear you are bothering my girlfriend again, I promise you it will be a whole lot worse." Josh did not reply. He didn't even move. He just lay there staring at the bathroom floor. Patrick stepped out of the cubicle, and I stepped in,

13

clearing my throat until I got a good amount of spittle in my mouth and launched it at Josh's face. As it hit his cheek, he barely blinked. I admit I was amused and even a little turned on as we left the bathroom.

CHAPTER TWO

EIGHTEEN

I can't say I was looking forward to my Eighteenth birthday event. My mother and my twenty-three-year-old sister Annabelle had arranged everything. No one asked me for my input or what I wanted. My mother had selected even the dress I was to wear from a range displayed for her in a private fashion show. I wasn't even invited.

As I looked in the mirror at the wavy five-thousand-dollar hair my hairdresser had just finished according to my mother's instructions. I sighed with considerable disappointment. It may have been the height of the latest fashion, but I liked my hair straight and simple. No, my eighteenth birthday was not about me. It was once more about my mother showing off. The paparazzi were going to be out in full force, and she was going to milk the limelight.

As I walked down the long stairway to the front door, a maid ran up and started fastening a corsage to my wrist. I stopped and waited impatiently, and when she was finished, I headed out the door without so much as a thank you. It was dusk as I stepped out of the house and into the waiting limousine, where Pearson, the driver, had the door open for me. My sister Annabelle was already inside, and my mother had obviously gone in her car so that she could drive alone and get all the attention from the press without being upstaged by me.

"You look good, Han," my sister said, and I responded with a grunt. Unlike me, my sister was not genetically modified, and the moment I reached puberty, I had already started to upstage her. She didn't mind. She was quite a sweetie and the sort of girl a guy should want to date,

15

but would usually prefer a beautiful bitch to a beautiful soul. She was smart like my mother but with a conscience. She was the eldest, once you exclude Stacey and our brother, as my mother did, and was in line to take over when mother retired. Which would probably be the day she died since Mother loved her power

and influence so much. Anna tilted her head to one side at my grunt. "What's the matter, Han? This is supposed to be your moment."

I snorted at this and pulled the hem of my dress into the car so the chauffeur could close the door. "This whole thing is a crock, Annabelle. This is not my moment. It's just another way for my mother to show off."

Annabelle sighed and didn't say anything for a moment. She looked down at the ground and then back up at me. "She just wants the best for you, sis."

I snorted again. "Bullshit," I said as the car pulled out of the long driveway and onto the highway.

"Must you use that language? It's so unbecoming of you."

I rolled my eyes, then glared at her. "Every day, you sound more and more like Mother." I looked over at the liquor cabinet and then up at the back of the head of the driver. "Hey, Pearson," he slightly inclined his head toward me. "Can I assume my mother made sure there was no liquor left in here?"

"That would be an accurate assumption, Miss Grant," he replied.

"And I guess I can assume you have been instructed not to let us stop at a bottle-o?"

"Again, that is a very astute observation, Miss Grant." He chuckled.

I shrugged that off and started to hitch up my ugly orange dress. Much to my sister's horror, I pulled it up to my undies and reached down to the garter on my thigh. It was not there to hold up my stockings for wore I a suspender belt. Instead, it was holding a half bottle of whiskey, which I pulled out. Annabelle made to take it away from me, looking aghast. I slapped her hand away. "Annabelle, you know I can beat the shit out of you, so I really wouldn't try that," I growled.

Annabelle knew that I could beat her arse in an instant. It wasn't like we were superhuman, but we were at the pinnacle of possible human development. "You know I'll tell mother," she said snippily.

"You know I'ill tell mother," I repeated in an imitation of a whiny voice as I started to open the bottle. "You're a complete shit, Annabelle. I don't even want you at my party tonight." I took a deep swig of the drink as my sister just sat there and sighed.

We rode the rest of the way in silence. By the time we arrived, I had drunk a third of the bottle and returned it to the garter under my dress. Now I know you're what you are thinking. GenMods can't get drunk. However, we can if they take metabolism inhibitors, which are available to those with a generous expense account, although they are highly illegal. I planned to get well and truly munted tonight, and if I humiliated my mother and sister, all the better.

As we pulled up outside the Crown Towers where the function was to be held, Pearson opened the door, and the flashing lights of paparazzi cameras lit up as I stepped out onto the red carpet as if I was going to the Oscars. I beamed the fake smile my mother had told me I had to display. I waved to the cameras, and I waved to the onlookers. They were sad, pathetic people who had such boring lives that they wanted to follow mine. Annabelle stepped out behind me but was mostly ignored. Everyone wanted to see the girl that was known as Australia's Princess. And that was me.

As we got halfway up the carpet, we stopped for the obligatory posing for photographs, and then it went to shit. Something hit me in the face and splattered. It went into my eyes and mouth, and I spluttered about and wiped my eyes as cries of shock went up, and someone shouted, "hang the damn GenMod. It shouldn't be allowed to live." I felt Annabelle's arm around me, trying to hustle me into the building, and suddenly security surrounded us, and the doorman whisked the door open. Inside I burst into tears as I looked down and saw red paint covering me. Within minutes, my mother took control of the situation as she did with everything. "Did they get whoever did this?" she snapped at her security man, who always followed her.

"Yes, ma'am, the police have him in custody."

"Well, make sure he gets a damn good beating while in jail." She snapped, and he stepped away to make a call on his radio.

Mother turned to me. "Come on, Hannah, let's get you cleaned up."

"For fuck's sake, mother, do you really think I'm going now?" I cried.

She slapped me hard on the arm, for it wouldn't look good to mark my face. "You can cut out that language for a start, young lady," she snapped at me. "And, of course, you are going. We will not let some protesters stop you from making this appearance. It would mean they would get the better of us, and no one gets the better of a Grant."

She took me to her room, and after I had showered and cleaned everything off, I stepped out to find a hairdresser and style consultant waiting for me. As I was made to sit down, they worked on my hair as the designer bought out different clothes to choose from. Well, for my mother to choose from, for, once again, I had no say in the matter. It was barely forty-five minutes after the incident, and I was once more in a long evening gown with what was considered perfect hair.

"You look absolutely delightful, my dear." Mother said with a smile. "Now come on, we must get going. We are already late, and gossip needs to be silenced."

So it was that I made my appearance. Everyone of any importance in the city of Melbourne and beyond was there. And I didn't know any damn one of them except, of course, my three amigos, Bronwyn, Isla, and Sarah. All three upstaged me in the outfits chosen by themselves with a greater sense of teen fashion than my aging mother.

Of course, I couldn't hang out with them as my mother paraded me along to meet all the VIPs she considered influential in my future career as a ... I don't know what.

I had no plans or ambitions. I was certainly not going to join the family business and hoped my mother would keep up my expense account, so I could travel and have fun. But that was a couple of years away. After about an hour of smiling politely at people, everyone went into the dining room, and I excused myself to the bathroom, where I sat and finished the bottle of whiskey with my girls squashed into one cubicle.

18

"That was really fun today," Bron said as she pulled out a spliff and lit it.

"What was?" I asked as I took the spliff out of her lips, placed it between mine, and drew hard. I genuinely had no idea what she was talking about.

"Watching Patrick beat on Josh. Perhaps next time, we could get more involved."

"What next time?" I asked as I passed the spliff to Sarah. "That was supposed to be a punishment, not an entertainment." I giggled as the relaxing wave started to seep into my brain.

"Oh, bullshit, Han." Bron giggled. "I saw your face. It was making you horny."

Now that I couldn't deny but, I did anyway. "Oh, fuck you," I said dismissively, although I couldn'tt hide the grin that might have been down to the cannabis winding its way through my veins. I pondered how I was going to get out of eating. The metabolism inhibitors would mean I could not digest food for at least twenty-four hours. And I'm warning you out there. Those pills are dangerous shit, and I was an idiot to have been using them.

I checked the time. I could only remain so long before mother sent someone looking for me. If she caught me smoking weed, I would still be in the shit. It that she was exactly going to be bothered about me doing drugs. On the contrary, she was prone to the odd pill or two herself. If the wrong person saw me, it would simply give the Grant name a bad rep. Seeing how much time had passed, I snatched the spliff. I took another long drag. "For fuck's sake, this is my shit, and I haven't got any yet," Bron complained.

"I have to get back out there. You can stay and finish it," I rasped out and ended in a coughing fit. I checked myself in the mirror as I stepped out of the cubicle. I cleaned myself up a bit and washed my hands before going back out to my public. The rest of the evening was as dull as I had expected. I sat by my mother and played with my food, ignoring the gaze of people that had come to be seen with me. I looked over to the table where my three friends sat, laughing and joking and having a good time, and I hated them for it. When the music and

19

dancing started, I blamed the new shoes for not joining and soon. I found myself left alone at the table.

"Happy birthday, Hannah." I looked up to see Emilio Baalbek, the nineteen-year-old son of my mother's biggest rival. He was tall and had handsome indigenous features. He took a seat at the table. I had met him several times but only at social functions like this. I didn't really know him.

"Is it?" I said sullenly.

He looked confused as he sat back in the chair and studied me. "Is it what?"

"A happy birthday," I replied, toying with a cocktail stick and staring at the dancing idiots.

Emilio laughed lightly. "Poor little rich girl." He grinned at me.

I shot him a look. "Oh, fuck off," I said with genuine contempt in my voice

He was completely unfazed and laughed some more. "We all have to do this, you know. It's payback for our privileges." I looked at him, confused. He could see that, so he elaborated. "You're not the only one who must go to some event supposedly in your honor that is actually a public relations stunt. So, suck it up and get what you can out of it."

I cannot explain it, but that made me feel somewhat better. It did't fix my situation, but simply knowing that I was not the only one who had to suffer this indignation made me feel better. I smiled at him. "Are we supposed to be even talking to each other? After all, you are only invited because public relations demanded it. It is not like our parents are friends. More like the Capulets and Montagues, if you ask me."

A wicked green crossed his face, and a twinkle in his eye, "wouldn't that make us Romeo and Juliet?"

A wicked thought crossed my mind. Nothing would destroy my mother more than me being with the son of her worst enemy. I rested my elbow on the table, placed my chin in my hand, and gave him the sultriest look I could. "I guess it would." To make matters worse for my mother, this young man of aboriginal descent would tear at the heart of her racial bigotry.

He smiled back at me, and to my surprise, I felt his hand on my knee, slowly caressing it and moving up my thigh. "I think you need the bathroom," I whispered. He looked at me questioningly, not understanding the inference, but the penny dropped when I added, "I think I will need it in a couple of minutes."

A wide grin crossed his face, "I look forward to seeing you there."

As he walked off, I looked out at the crowd to see where my mother was, and she was deeply engaged in a conversation with some politician or other and paying me no heed. I double-checked around the room and I slipped out of my seat and headed to the men's room.

I was not exactly a virgin, but this was not something I often did. Sure, I had my share of one-night stands but never in such a public place.

As I closed the cubicle door behind me, he pushed me up against it, his hands all over me as he kissed me deeply and started to lift my dress. I never worried about protection. Only another GenMod could get me pregnant, and should he have any diseases, my immune system would soon clear any of that up.

He was clearly less experienced than me, although that is embarrassing to say at only eighteen. It proved quite unsatisfying other than knowing if my mother knew, she would be beside herself. I was not exactly going to tell her. Even though this was an act of vengeance against her, it was enough that I knew.

He pushed up against me, fumbling to unfasten his pants as I awkwardly hitched up the long ankle-length dress. I reached down and gave him a quick hand to turn his semi to full mast. It was most uncomfortable as I slipped aside my undies and allowed him to enter me. He grunted as he pushed his way back and forth, and as I looked at him, he had this nerdy gormless look on his face, like the nerd who had just got the cheerleader. It made me think of Josh. Oh, how gross.

The reality of what I was doing overcame me. I thought of Patrick, my boyfriend, who I thought I was almost sure I was maybe possibly in love with.

"Stop," I said softly and gently pushed him back. He didn't listen. He looked annoyed and just thrust harder, and once more, I said, "stop." I was more insistent this time, and I pushed a little harder.

"Are you playing with me?" he said frustratedly as he fell out of me.

21

"No," I shook my head. "I just changed my mind, that's all," I said, pushing my skirt back down.

"Is this just a game to you?" He snapped at me, and I must admit I was a little scared as anger entered his beautiful brown eyes.

"I'm sorry...I didn't...." I sighed, looked away, and said weakly. "Would you just let me out of here, please?"

He sighed, but it was not one of resignation. It was irritation bordering on anger. "It was you who asked me to come in here," he said bitterly.

I fidgeted uncomfortably, "and now I'm asking you to let me out, please."

He suddenly poked me hard in the shoulder blade with two fingers. I made to step back, but I was already pushed up against the door. "You're a prick-teasing little slut. It doesn't surprise me. Now give me what I came in here for. It's all Grant women are good for, anyway."

GenMods are not superhuman. However, we are at the peak of human ability, which makes us better at most things than the average person. As he pushed himself against me, I easily pushed him back. I even held back a bit out of a lifelong habit of hiding my true nature. Or rather the lack of nature. "I just want to get out of here."

He was startled and looked at me suspiciously about how easily I had managed to move him back against the cysten. Everything was going wrong. "If you think this makes you any better than you really are, I'll show you it doesn't. You came in here with a guy you didn't know. Everybody will know that you're a dirty little slut."

I felt cheapened. And I had done it to myself, but I now had room to open the door. Without another word, I rushed out of the stall. I hastily checked my dress and stepped back into the dance hall, wishing this ghastly night was over.

My act of vengeance turned into one of utter humiliation. My hatred for the world turned into hatred for myself, and I felt disgusted and dirty, and I prayed to God that he wouldn't tell anyone. As it turned out, it wouldn't matter one iota the following day.

CHAPTER THREE

—·—

LAST DAY

When I got home that night, I showered three times, but I could not wash out the filth I felt, and going to bed, I cried myself to sleep. When I woke up the next day, I convinced myself it was a bad dream and somehow managed to push it from my mind as I headed to school again.

I arrived on time while other kids were entering the old building. I saw Josh standing by his car. I thought I saw a long canvas bag in his hand, which he quickly dropped back into the trunk and shut as he saw me watching him. He took great care not to meet my eyes. I pushed back the desire to take out my frustrations on him.

I parked my car, ignored him, and headed into the building. I took my tablet from the locker, grabbed a couple of croissants from the cafeteria, and headed into class. It was a dull, ordinary day, and I spoke to no one until lunchtime, and it became unavoidable. I joined my three amigos and let them chat about how much fun they had at my party without contributing as I ate my sandwich.

Isla noticed it first.

We were used to hearing the Australian Air Force fighter planes going overhead. It may have been peaceful in Melbourne, but there was still a war going on out there. Isla, however, was quite the military nerd, and she noticed something different about the noise of this one. She looked up and tensed. "What the fuck?" she murmured. The others stopped talking, and I stopped eating. We all looked up, but it was already gone.

"What's the matter?" Sarah asked nervously.

"That wasn't one of ours. It was a Peon scout interceptor."

"Bullshit," I said, returning to my sandwich. It had been over a year since we had an air raid.

"I'm telling you guys, that is not one of our aircraft. Trust me on this." Isla said nervously.

We all looked back up into the sky, and as if to prove her right, the klaxons and sirens came on. We had drilled for this on many occasions, but when they did not announce this was a drill, everyone knew it was real, and panic started to ensue. Chairs were tipped, food was dropped, and bags were left behind as everyone started to race towards the air-raid shelter built under the school. Kids pushed past each other in a panic as teachers tried to maintain order but were just as knocked over as where are the students. Before we even got there, the first wave of aircraft was overhead, and explosions from around the city had begun. When I finally managed to squeeze through the entrance through the mass of students and into the shelter, I didn't notice that Isla was not with us.

Of course, being at such an exclusive private school, even the bomb shelter was luxurious and had plenty of room. Still, that claustro-phobic feeling overcame me as the teacher sealed the doors, and the pounding overhead began.

There were still shouts and screams of terrified students. We all stood in that crowded reception area until Mr. Collins took control. He was a portly elderly math teacher but, clearly, the calmest of all the staff. "Calm down, everybody. It's probably just an air raid. It will be over soon, and everyone is perfectly safe in here. Please move back to the rooms you were allocated in the drills. We can't all stand in here. Come on, let's move."

"Isla didn't make it in. She's still out there." Bron said with incred-ible stress in her voice. To be honest, I didn't give a shit. I was terrified. My level of self-preservation is extremely high.

We returned to our allocated rooms, which meant separating from my besties. Rooms have been allocated by grade and alphabetically. I found myself alone in a room with Josh Green. The discomfort was intense, and even the sound of bombs exploding overhead did not detract from what had happened the day before. Josh was sitting on the side of a bunk and looked up at me as I entered but immediately averted his eyes, looking downwards. I sighed and bounced on my heels as I

pondered, turning around and finding another room despite the rules. I then looked back at him, "I hope you're not gonna make this difficult for us."

He shrugged, not looking up. I looked down the corridor to see if I could see Patrick, but I couldn't even recall if he had been around and had come in. I knew he would protect me from this dork and whatever was going on outside. I bit my lower lip and glanced back at the nervous-looking Josh, who kept his head down and eyes averted from me. I stepped in and sat down on the bunk opposite him. He shifted uncomfortably in his seat, still not looking up as he turned to face further away from me. I felt intensely uncomfortable, and I blamed him for it. "Yesterday wasn't my fault. You asked for it." but he didn't respond and kept staring at the ground. I was not used to sitting in silence. Especially now when hell was raining overhead. I sighed and stood up, and he flinched. "You can cut that out. What we did wasn't that bad." I began to pace the room up and down, but it made him so nervous, and I gave up and sat back down with a wumpf. I laid back with my head against the wall but immediately sat up again as I noticed the canvas bag I had seen him getting from his trunk was just under his bunk. "What is that?" I asked.

"Nothing," he said, kicking his heel back and knocking the bag out of my sight.

Our protocol in the drills was not to leave the room without a teacher or responsible adult instructing, and I looked toward the door, hopefully, desperately wanting to get away from this freak.

But no one came, and the bombing continued. I lay down on the bunk, and turning on my side, I hugged my knees up to my chest, ensuring I was facing him and could see him. I don't know what I expected him to do, for he was far too scared of me now to ever mess with me. In some way, I must have been assured of that because, despite the bombing, I fell asleep.

When I awoke several hours later, the only sound was talking outside, coming from various places. Josh was no longer in the room, and I sat up and rubbed my eyes. I climbed up to my feet and headed towards the doorway, but I remembered the bag under the bunk, and I turned back and knelt

on the ground to look. Just as I was about to reach under and pull it out, there was a sharp slap on my backside, and I spun around. "If that's not a genetically modified arse, I don't know what is," Sarah said as she stood over me, grinning.

"That's not very funny, Sarah," I said, standing up and turning to face her.

"Come on. They're dishing up some grub." She told me.

"The bombing has stopped." I frowned at her. "Why aren't they letting us out?"

Sarah shrugged, "I don't honestly know."

I followed her out and returned to the reception, where Mr. Collins and Mrs. Crumpton handed out foil-wrapped packets of post-apocalyptic meals. I was certainly not hungry. Many people are stress eaters, but I can go whole days without eating when under stress. It wasn't healthy since GenMods required a much higher calorie count than the average person. However, I was not exactly an expert on genetic modification, considering it was taboo for me to talk about. "You need to eat, Hannah," Mr. Collins chided me. "You don't know where your next meal may be coming from."

"Thank you, Sir, but I'll have it in a few minutes. Have you seen Patrick Johnson anywhere?" I knew if I could find Patrick, everything would be alright. He would surely take care of me and make sure I was safe. Mr. Collins narrowed his eyes at me. "Why do you want to know about Patrick?"

It was a strange question, and it took me by surprise. "Well, he's a friend of mine, and I want to know he made it safely."

"I see. Well, the young Patrick made it inside all right. But he's with the nurse at the moment." My genetically enhanced vision and ability to take in detail made it easier for me to detect deceptions, and in the case of Mr. Collins, he was clearly holding something back from me.

26

This startled me, "Oh no, I hope he's okay and not injured or something."

Mr. Collins hesitated before replying, "no, he's not injured but don't worry, Hannah, he's been well taken care of."

After all, I took the offered food and followed Sarah back to her bunkroom, where we found Bronwyn sitting and eating her food. Bron could eat even if the gunfire was going off in the room, and I had never known her to miss a meal. She was one of those annoying people who could overeat but never put on weight. So was I, for that matter, but I never realized it, for my mother always had me on some sort of diet. It surprises me how little she seemed to know about GenMods, considering she was the one who had me created. I guess when buying hooky made-to-order kids, we don't come with an instruction manual. I looked at the processed food that Bron was shoveling into her mouth. It looked disgusting, and I tossed mine onto the little table beside one of the bunks.

"Don't you want it?" Bron asked with a mouthful of food.

"I'm not hungry," I responded, unsure whether I was or not. Bron pointed to my food with her fork and then at herself. "Have at it." It would be the last time I would ever give away my food in my life.

All I wanted to do was leave. I didn't understand why we were still here when clearly the bombing had stopped. I was scared and wanted Patrick, but I sat down on the bank next to Bron and hugged my knees up to my chest.

The chimes of a tannoy system coming on startled me in my already fragile state. The confident-sounding voice of Mr. Collins rang out throughout the complex. "Good evening, ladies and gentlemen. I understand you all want to go home and are probably very afraid. However, we are going to have to stay here a little longer. Just while they sort everything out upstairs. I suggest you get ready for bed and settle down for the night. Everything will be sorted out in the morning." As the line went dead, the chattering of voices could be heard coming from all the surrounding rooms.

I was about to protest to my friends when Mrs. Crumpton appeared in the doorway. "Come on, ladies, time to get ready for bed. It will be lights out in fifteen minutes."

"Excuse me, Miss," I said, stretching out my legs and climbing off the bunk. "Is there a way I can call my mother? There is absolutely service on my phone down here."

"Oh, my dear, don't worry. Your parents are aware of what's happening, and it will all be sorted out in the morning."

Again, my acute vision told me a different story. As I saw her pupils dilate, I knew that she was lying to me. "Don't bullshit me, Mrs. Crumpton. What is really going on?"

The elderly teacher looked quite taken aback by how I spoke to her, as were my companions. "Hannah Grant. The situation is already bad enough without you wanting to let your imagination get carried away. I will let you off because I understand the stress of this situation but don't talk to me like that again." She looked at my two companions and then back at me. "This is not your allocated room. I must ask you to stay in the room assigned to you. We must know where everyone is at all times."

This immediately distracted me from my concerns. "Please, can I just stay here? I don't want to go back in that room with that creepy kid."

Mrs. Crumpton's reaction was like I had personally insulted her. "Joshua is a fine young man and very hardworking. You could take a leaf out of his book, young lady." And without answering my request, she turned away and headed down the corridor shouting at a couple of other kids to get into their rooms.

I looked back at Bron and Sarah, who had nothing to say and merely shrugged at me. I frustratedly muttered some profanity under my breath and strode out of the room. When I returned to mine, Josh was sitting there in the same position he was in earlier, as if he'd never moved. "Oh my God, you are such fucking creepy retard," I said, not stepping beyond the door's threshold. Screw this; I was not going to stay there. I turned back and headed towards the reception area, determined that I was going out that front door one way or another. It was heavy and locked with several bolts

but no key or other type of lock. I started pulling back the bolts, and as I pulled back the last one, the door forced me back as it opened from the pressure of something outside. Dirt and debris started piling in. I screamed and jumped back as it started to cover me. Others came running into the reception area. I barely noticed them, for as I looked out of that door, I was staring into the face of a surprised-looking man in the light blue uniform of the European army.

The soldier quickly raised his rifle and shouted to someone who was up the steps and out of my field of vision. Soon he was headed down the steps toward me, with more troops coming in behind him.

Mr. Collins suddenly appeared and stepped between him and me, protesting futilely to a man who could not understand a word he said. However, as Mr. Collins tried to stop them from entering, he received the rifle butt around his head and went down to the ground. I don't know what happened to him after that, for everything happened so fast. Screams started going up around the room, and the soldier fired into the air to bring silence; however, it only increased the panic as students started running back down the corridors away from the troops.

Suddenly a gunshot rang out again, but it was a different sound this time, and it came from behind me. The soldier in front of me went down. His shirt was now stained red. For a moment, I stood there rigid unable to move, and then another shot rang out, and another soldier went down, and I threw myself to the floor. I looked behind me as a third shot fired, and I saw Josh standing there with a rifle in his hand and that green canvas bag lying on the floor in front of him. Why the fuck did he have a rifle?

I didn't have time to think about it, for by now, one of the soldiers fired back, and Josh ducked into the hallway out of sight. The three remaining soldiers ignored me and chased after him, but the first one to turn the corner came flying back with a hole in his chest. They hit the ground. I   started to crawl away, my heart racing and trying to make sense of everything around me. There was

another gunshot that I recognized as Josh's, then two more that weren't. I clambered to my feet and ran down a different corridor, having not even considered my best option may have been to go out the front door. My herd instinct, I guess.

I started looking around to try and find the nurse's station and Patrick. He would know what to do. I pushed past the panicking students, looking desperately. Bron and Sarah joined me, and I found the nurse's room and pulled open the door. Patrick was alone, seated upon a gurney with his knees hugged to his chest, slowly rocking back and forward. It did not register at the time that anything was wrong. I was in such a panic myself. I ran and hugged him, but he flinched and pulled himself away from me, mumbling incoherently. "What's wrong, Pat? Come on. I need you." But he just stared ahead, rocking back and forward. I didn't understand it then, but fear had broken him. "Come on, Pat. Talk to me." With Bron and Sarah behind me, more aware of the situation than I was, we were suddenly interrupted. "If you wanna get out of here, come with me." I looked up to see Josh standing in the doorway, casually reloading his rifle.

"Are you fucking crazy? You're going to bring them here." I shouted.

He looked at me without emotion in his eyes and calmly said, "it's okay. They're all dead."

"You are some fucking mental case," Sarah said to him in disbelief.

Josh just looked at her. "Don't be stupid, Sarah. This is clearly not just a bombing raid. This is a damned invasion, and we must fight to stay alive."

I turned back to Patrick and slapped him hard, but the only effect it had was to have him grab the covers of the gurney, pull them up over his head, and lie down sobbing quietly. "Leave him. Come on. We need to get out of here." Josh said quite coldly.

"I hate to say it, Han," said Bron. "But I think he's right."

But I was just frozen there. I didn't move until Sarah laid an arm on my shoulder, and I jumped as if a spider had just landed upon me. I took one last look at the inert form lying under the blanket before turning away.

Josh disappeared down the corridor, and like frightened sheep, we followed him. It still had not clicked in my head why he had brought a gun to high school. I didn't even take time to think about the people we were leaving behind. Fear is a funny thing. Everyone stayed hunkered down in their rooms while I, Bron, and Sarah followed Josh out of the front door.

As of the time I'm writing this, I have not been back to Australia, and I do not know what fate befell the rest of my schoolmates, but I hope I will one day.

CHAPTER FOUR

JUDGMENT DAY

Leaving that bunker is hazy in my memory. I have basic images of us scrabbling out through the debris and up the steps to see the devastation of what was once one of the greatest cities in the world lying in ruins and looking up to see the tall buildings that still stood aflame. I recall the stench of the smoke in the air. Burning oil, wood, and, what I would later realize, was burning flesh. The school was completely gone, and we could see for miles where before, all we would have been able to see was the buildings across the street. Now we couldn't even see the street. "Come on," Josh said, and he led the way across the devastation, and we just blindly followed him without question. Our minds were lost in the horror of the situation.

We continued this way for several minutes with no one speaking until finally, Sarah said, "where are we going?"

"To get out of the city, of course," Josh said as if it was just a normal routine activity, like a walk in the park.

"I need to go home," I said desperately.

Josh smirked at me and looked around, waving his arm out. "Sure. And where exactly do you think that is?"

I looked at the devastation again, and he had a point. I couldn't recognize any landmarks, and there were no streets to speak of. We scrambled over the debris. We passed burnt-out cars, some still a flame. The night sky was lit with orange fire, and a weird twilight was all around us. As the panic within me began to subside, my acute senses again became aware of my surroundings. I could hear the distant

33

sound of gunfire, and the occasional plane went streaking past over-head. Completely unknown to me at the time, my sister had been part of those air defenses but by now already had been defeated. She was struggling for life with Harper Davis in a distant forest somewhere in Japan.

"You said we're leaving the city, but where exactly are we going, and what about our families?" Sarah demanded. I had moved up next to Josh.

He didn't say anything at first, just pressing on, but she stopped and grabbed him by the arm. "Get off of me." He pulled his arm away. "At this time, all I know is getting out of the city is going to be the best idea. "

Sarah turned to look at me, then at Bron. "I'm not just gonna go off without my family."

"I understand that, but how long is it since this bombing started?" Bron said. "Ten or twelve hours. It is feasible that your family has already been evacuated."

"Your family may have left without you, but mine wouldn't have." Sarah snapped.

"Oh, fuck you, Sar," Bron responded bitterly and turned away.

I was always the arbiter when it came to disagreements between these two. I looked over to Josh, who was scanning the horizon and pretty much ignoring us. "You must have some idea where we're head-ed."

He looked back at me and paused a moment. He had confidence in himself that I had not seen before, and it was almost as if this was what he was born for. "I'm taking the shortest distance out of the city. We need to get away from here. We have no resources, and the Peons are most likely to occupy the cities rather than the farmlands."

"This is fucking Melbourne, mate," Bron said curtly. "It could take us a day or more to walk out of this city."

"Which is why we are wasting time standing around here talking." He replied quite calmly, in fact, unnervingly calmly.

"Screw this. I'm going home. I will find it somehow and will find my family." Sarah turned to head off in a different direction.

"Sar, hang on. We shouldn't split up." I called after her, but she waved a dismissive hand at me without looking back, and it was the last time I saw her.

"I think we'd better keep moving," Josh said coldly.

I looked up at him and nodded. I don't know why I was following him like a sheep. I guess I had no confidence in those days, and the guy with the gun who had taken out some Peon soldiers was the closest thing to security I knew at the time.

We continued onwards, and I don't remember much about it. I think my brain has blocked out the constant fear we were under. We came across an area still fairly built up and had missed most of the bombing. It had been abandoned in what I would later learn became known as the Great Australian Exodus. Thousands of Australians fled from the cities into the harsher depths of the country.

We were growing tired, for it had been several hours since we left the bunker. We broke into a house to stay for the rest of the night. Josh perched himself by the window, seemingly on constant alert for trouble. Bron and I went into the kitchen to see if we could find some food, but it had been cleaned out. It was around now I wished I'd eaten that last meal in the bunker.

We then move mattresses from the beds into the living room. There was something odd about sleeping in someone's bed, and as Bron pointed out, we needed to stay together and on the ground floor with an easy exit. I can't believe I managed to sleep that night. I guess I was exhausted from the walking and the stress of everything. When I awoke in the morning, I thought it was still night. I could not immediately tell the time for my watch nor my phone as both were connected to the internet, and neither had been working since the bombing started. It looks strange not having simple access to something such as the time.

Sitting up and rubbing my eyes, I saw Josh sitting by the window. He was looking out, ever alert. "Did you get any sleep?" I asked him.

He glanced back at me, then turned to the window before saying, "meh! I don't sleep much."

"You really should get some sleep before the morning if we are going to continue walking out of here," I said, trying to sound casual.

35

He glanced at me again with a smirk. "It is morning."

"But it's still dark," I said with a bewildered frown

He turned and looked at me, and then a wide grin crossed his face. "Did they only genetically modify that body and leave the brain alone."

The mention of my genetic modifications startled me so much that the insult went over my head "I'm not genetically modified." I said defensively.

Looking back out of the window, he laughed and muttered, "and I'm the president of Australia."

"No. That's just a media rumor." It seems funny now that I was worried about this, considering everything that was going on.

"Will the two of you shut up? I'm trying to get some sleep here." Bron murmured sleepily next to me on the mattress.

"No," Josh said firmly. "It's time we were moving on."

"Just ten more minutes, Mum," Bron murmured.

Josh grinned and looked down at his rifle that rested on his lap. "Fine, just ten more minutes." He said.

"Where did you get that?" I asked, and when he looked at me, I nodded toward the firearm.

"From my dad." He said, now sounding a little bit sullen.

This rang hollow to me. Strict gun control legislation meant such weapons were very hard to come by outside a club or a range. Any normal parent would not exactly hand over a weapon to their child and risk multiple years in prison. "He just gave you a gun, did he?" I asked disbelievingly.

"Of course not," he said as if the question was simply dumb. "I took it."

"What did he need firearms for?"

He looked at me sneeringly, "All of a sudden, you're interested in my life! That was hardly the case yesterday."

"Oh, don't even go there, Joshua." I snapped back. "You were bloody stalking me."

His grim expression faltered, and an expression that looked more in line with what I was used to appeared on his face. However, it quickly

36

returned to the grim, determined man of today. "Is liking someone such a crime?"

"When that liking becomes an obsession, then yes," I said rather harshly.

He turned and fixed his eyes upon me, his gaze intense. "Well, you no longer need to worry, Hannah Grant, because, after yesterday, I don't like you anymore."

I don't know why that affected me. I guess no one likes to be told that they don't like you. At the time, I still didn't comprehend that what we had done to him the previous day was particularly wrong. Of course, I certainly would have thought it was wrong if it had been done to me, but I had been raised with the belief of my social superiority over most people. Not because I was a GenMod but simply because, financially, I was considered to be of the highest class.

"Why did you bring that gun to school?" I asked as it suddenly occurred to me what an odd thing that was to do. His grim expression turned to unease, and he muttered, "that's not important. Not anymore, anyway."

I let it go at that for the time being, for it occurred to me that he had been planning something bat shit crazy, and I didn't want to know what it was. Instead, I elbowed Bron. "Get up. We have to get moving."

She grunted back at me but sat up. We had not changed out of our clothes, and I felt most uncomfortable having slept in my own grime. The journey so far had been beyond the limit of what I

considered filthy. I went to the bathroom and was quite put out when I realized it didn't flush despite several attempts. Josh heard me and came and knocked on the door. "What's going on, Hannah?" he asked from the other side.

"Bloody thing won't flush," I replied impatiently. I gave up and went to wash my hands, but no water came out of the taps. "Oh, for fucks sake, there's no water either," I said, slapping the taps as if I was punishing them for their insolence.

"Fuck!" Josh cursed outside of the door.

I pulled it open, wondering why he was so upset about what I considered to be, although an extreme inconvenience, just an annoying turn of events in an already shitty situation. "What's the matter?"

"It means no fresh water." He muttered.

"I don't drink tap water anyway," I responded.

He looked at me with wide eyes and said, "fair enough. You wait here while I run to the store and pick up your favorite mineral water."

I glared at him. "Fuck you, Josh. The last thing I need is you patronizing me. You may be bigging it up with your gun and everything, but don't forget, under all of that, you are still the retarded little loser you always were."

He stared at me, and I was unable to read his expression. He turned back into the living room.

It's strange the things you take for granted, like food and running water. The bare necessities were handed to you on a plate without you even having to think about it.

Before we left, I had an idea, and while Josh headed off to the garage to see if there was any equipment worth looting, I went upstairs to search the wardrobes. I wore a very short dress, and my legs were scratched to pieces climbing over the debris during our exodus. I wanted to find something

more fitting to our situation. In the first room, I found your typical working-class mum clothes, which alludes to my arrogance that I turned my nose up at this and went to another room.

It was clearly that of a teenage girl, and my hopes were raised that I'd find something attractive, but it turned out she was a couple of sizes bigger than me. With a reluctant sigh, I returned to the mum clothes and pulled out some ghastly store-brand jeans that were only one size bigger than me and would do in a pinch. I pulled them on underneath my dress. I then took out a button-up shirt which was also too big for me but wearable.

I looked around for some runners, but there was nothing that would fit. Josh called from downstairs, and I went back down. Bron laughed at me in my new outfit. However, she, too, went up to grab some clothes while Josh went outside to check if it was safe to move on. By the time he came back in, Bron had also returned. Although her jeans and tee shirt were hardly designer, she looked better than me because she had fitted into the teenager's clothing. "Look around to see if you can find any keys for a car. There is a Jeep in the garage that they've left behind."

We began to search. Stealing a car had become virtually impossible, so unless we found them, the undamaged vehicle was completely useless to us. Bron searched the living room, and Josh and I took the kitchen. I had my eureka moment when I opened the catch-all draw that every kitchen has. There were two sets of key fobs. One I assumed was the spare for the car they had taken, and the other I hoped was for the Jeep. Josh immediately put his hand out to take them. I pulled them back and held them behind me. "Do you have your license?"

He dared to laugh at me. "Are you worried that the cops will come and get us?"

I rolled my eyes at him. "No, you loser, it's just I've been taught how to drive, and you haven't. With the roads damaged as they are, there's no way the automated navigation system will get us out of here." Even with the typical self-driving car, you still needed a license if that ever failed or

lost signal with a satellite navigation system. With the phones out, it was most likely the sat NAV was out too.

"I've been taking lessons," he replied defensively, putting his hand out again.

"I'm driving." I said defiantly, and before he could respond, I added, "anyway, you need to ride shotgun, literally."

"I guess you have a point there," he replied, sounding quite disappointed.

We headed out to the garage, and I saw an almost brand-new Jeep Avenger, all shiny and black. I tried the first fob, and they didn't work, so I tossed them onto a shelf. However, the second set immediately unlocked the doors, and I smiled triumphantly. "Pop the trunk, would you, Hannah?"

I did as Josh asked, and he picked up a duffel bag he'd found. It looked heavy, and he clearly stocked it with some hardware that he thought might come in handy. He tossed it into the back, closed the trunk, and headed around to the front passenger seat as I climbed into the front. As expected, the automated systems were out, and there was not even the typical warning for us to put on our seatbelts, although instinctively, we all did. Bron was sitting in the back, and to my disbelief, she was already asleep again as I pulled out of the garage. I had always driven the car without automated support. I just love the feeling of being in personal control of my vehicle. Plus, safety laws did not allow such systems to break the speed limit or rules of the road.

However, this journey would be far more difficult than avoiding a police drone. Driving through the relatively undamaged suburb proved quite easy. However, things got more difficult about an hour later when we started to reach the borders of central Melbourne. Navigating around the older neighborhoods proved difficult and slowed our progress. Rubble, debris, and even burned-out cars littered the main highways, and I quickly realized the back roads could possibly be better. Even then, we would reach a dead-end from a fallen building now and then. I was getting increasingly frustrated as we kept going back on ourselves and trying a different direction.

The most disturbing thing, however, was not seeing anyone. No, no, I'll take that back. The dead bodies were most disturbing, especially when it was children. I had always been too busy to be worried about the war. Most people my age were worried about impending national service at eighteen, where one would have to serve an obligatory two years with pressure to stay longer. I knew full well my mother would use her influence with the government to ensure my national service would not have been in the military. I was going to be safe, and that was as far as my concerns about the war reached.

I don't think anyone really believed an attempt would be made to invade Australia. The sheer logistics of it made such a concept frankly impossible. Despite being one of the largest countries in the world, our population did not exceed around seventy-five million, and we were scattered all over the place even though the vast majority still dominantly inhabited the coastlines. We had communities all over the place, and one thing's for sure, even in the event of Canberra surrendering, the Australian people wouldn't. However, as it would turn out, the Peons did not believe they could subdue Australia any more than we did. Taking out the government at the military high command was all they needed to take us out of the war beyond our borders. Instead of sending troops to the front, the Australian people would be forced to fight for their lives and freedoms.

As I drove that Jeep around the ruins of Melbourne, all I considered was when everything was going to get back to normal. My naivete did not come from stupidity but simply a lack of education about the world around me. I had lived like Rapunzel in an ivory tower distant from the proletariat and the real Australians who were my country's lifeblood.

CHAPTER FIVE

— • —

EXODUS

Josh did not relax for one moment, and his anxiety was infectious. I don't mean anxious in a scared way, but tense and alert, ready for trouble. I was surprised we did not encounter any of the enemy, but I would later find out it was simply because they were still securing their beachhead, and our school was as far inland as they had come. We did get passed by an enemy drone occasionally. They would follow us down the road and eventually veer off. I can only assume they did not consider a single car with some kids in it a target worthy of their resources.

After several hours, I was almost surprised when we made it out of the city unharmed. But that was as far as we got in the Jeep. As we reached the suburbs, we started to see people. Desperate people were all trying to put what belongings they could on the roofs of their cars. Again, in my naivete, I thought how stupid this was as they could all buy new stuff. I was clueless about the lives of people who did not have multiple noughts on the end of their bank balance. I was oblivious that the Australian dollar was now valueless, and I had no more money than they did.

"I don't like this," Josh said quietly as traffic ahead of us built up, and we had to slow down. I glanced at him questioningly, and he said, "if everybody is on the road, the traffic ahead will stop. We may have to abandon the car."

"And then what?" I asked with a mixture of bemusement and irritation.

43

He shrugged. "We keep going. We keep going until we put as much distance between the Peons and us as possible."

I had been so busy navigating the roads that I hadn't had time to think about the situation, but now I was hungry and thirsty. I believe I was looking out to see if a diner was open. I was so dumb.

Josh proved right, for traffic stopped as soon as we got onto the highway. All I heard were the horns of the cars and frustrated shouts. "Pull over," Josh ordered. There wasn't anywhere to pull over unless I took the car off the road. Even the hard shoulder was packed with traffic. As I stopped, I saw other abandoned cars on the grass by the road.

"This is bullshit," Bron said as we climbed out of the car.

Josh glanced back at her. "Do you have a better idea?"

"No, of course, I don't." Bron snapped back. "Obviously, there's nothing else we can do, but it doesn't mean it doesn't piss me off."

Josh did not respond to that as he had me open the trunk and pull out the duffel bag. "One of you will need to carry this as I have to carry the gun."

"Give it to me," I said, taking the bag from him. A wide grin crossed his face, and it took me a moment or two to realize why. I had completely forgotten to pretend it was heavy, as my genetically enhanced muscles had no problem with it. I then tried to fake it, but that only made it worse, and I believe I colored slightly as I slipped my arms into the straps and pulled them onto my shoulders like a backpack. Josh didn't say anything about it, but his grin lasted for quite a while as we began to walk across the grass down the side of the road.

People looked out of their cars at us as we walked past them, mostly fixating on the rifle in Josh's hands. "I think we should probably move away from the road." He said carefully. "I think people will find this exceedingly useful, and I'm not going to put it past them to try and get it from me. I have no problem shooting Peons, but I don't want to have to shoot an Australian."

So, we headed down the embankment until we were out of sight of most of the road and continued northwards.

The day drew on, and the hot February sun finally came out, beating down on us. I grew more and more thirsty and hungry. I noticed both Bron and Josh start to go red in the face. I became self-conscious as I knew that would not happen to me.

I was so self-absorbed with this that I did not notice anything wrong with Josh, but his breathing was becoming labored, and he was slowing down, with Bron and me now taking the lead. I got into some conversation about, I don't know what, with Bron, and after not hearing anything from Josh for a while, I glanced back. To my shock, he was lying on the ground. I ran back to him, but Bron could not do that by then. "I can't go on." His mouth was so dry he could barely get the words out. I knew I had to get him out of the baking sun and looked around. I saw a small clump of trees in the distance. But to get him there, I had to do something I didn't want to. I looked back at Bron. "You're about to see something that's gonna make you ask questions, but you're one of my best friends, and I want you to ignore it."

Her response surprised me, for she rolled her eyes and hoarsely said, "everyone knows you're a fucking GenMod, Han. Just pick him up, and let's go." I was about to vehemently deny that out of sheer habit, but she waved a dismissive hand at me, picked up the gun, and walked to the trees herself. I turned Josh onto his back and easily lifted him. If I had put him over my shoulder, it might not have looked as odd as it did. But I'm not exactly a firefighter, and I didn't consider that. I carried him in my arms like a baby, aware his eyes were now closed and he was no longer speaking. Bron reached the shade first, fell to her knees, and lay down. I caught up about a minute later and lay Josh down beside her. I shook him, but he barely responded.

"It's either heatstroke or dehydration. I don't know which. I read about this stuff, but I haven't experienced it." Bron told me, rasping out her words. "Either way, you need to get us some water. We haven't had any since yesterday now."

I took the duffel bag from around my shoulders and let it drop to the floor before turning around and opening it. I hoped I would find some jug or bottle, but there was nothing like that. Then I noticed a tin of paraffin oil and realized I could use that. "Okay, I'm going to go see if I can find some water somewhere. Are you going to be okay to stay here?"

Bron smiled weakly at me. "It's not like I have any choice, Han."

I didn't reply but nodded and looked around before heading off away from the road, hoping to find some water. I must have walked for at least thirty minutes when I came across a razor wire fence. It was just three lines designed to keep critters in but not people out, for I easily passed through the top two wires carefully. Farmland. Even with my dumb worldly ignorance, I knew that water had to be around here somewhere. I walked along the fence and felt relief as I saw a trough and quickly ran up to it. It was half full, probably having been filled the day before. I cupped my hand and drank some of the liquid. Whatever bacteria was in this water would not harm me, but I knew I'd probably have to boil it for the other two. I then poured out the paraffin can, filled it, and poured the water onto the ground. I repeated this several times, sniffing the can to ensure I'd cleaned it before I filled it and resealed the lid. I then headed back the way I had come, hoping I was in time before any permanent damage to my companions occurred.

Bronwyn looked better for having taken the rest. I sat down by her and gathered up some dry grass. "Got your lighter on you, mate?" I asked her casually. She usually had some on her, along with an ounce of weed. She slipped her thumb and forefinger into her jeans pocket and pulled it out, handing it to me. I lit the dried grass, and it quickly took to a flame. I pondered how I was going to do this since I could not simply lay the can over the flame without putting it out. In the end, I simply held it with the tips of my fingers over the fire.

"For fuck sake, you're going to burn yourself." Bron snapped at me. I just turned and looked at her uncomfortably, and her eyes widened. I feel pain, sure, I do. It is just that our tolerance is much higher. After a few minutes, it began to hurt, but not enough that I could not hold on. The flames did, in fact, slightly burn my fingers, but the medical nanobots within my system would already be working on repairing that. In addition, my own physical defense systems were way beyond what was considered normal. It was smart for a couple of hours, but otherwise, I would go unharmed.

Eventually, even I could not tolerate it anymore.. The water was not exactly boiling, but it would have to do. I set it to one side to cool down. I then got up and started to stamp out to the fire. Even a city girl like me knew the dangers of bushfires springing up. I made absolutely sure there was not a single ember left lit.

I allowed them to cool, slapping Bron's hand as she tried to reach for it. You're going to have to be patient."

When I thought it was safe to do so, I handed the can to her, and she drank deeply from it. In fact, I had to take it away from her to save some for Josh. As I knelt beside him, I slapped his face a couple of times until his eyes blinked, and he looked up at me. "Come on, mate. I got some water for you."

He sat up, took the can from me, and drank it down fast. This seemed to help both a lot, but we all agreed it would probably be best if we waited until sunset to continue. So, we did. It also gave them time for their nanobots to work on restoring them.

Bronwyn was carrying the rifle when we set off again, and I once more had the duffel bag on my back. The temperature had cooled considerably, and the bright stars of the Milky Way shone brightly overhead. However, navigation without a line of sight is incredibly dangerous, as we found out.

As we continued for several hours, we were unaware that we were moving further and further away from the road. We reached another fence of razor wire. It was part of the same fence that I had encountered earlier. Farms can be bloody big in Australia. We didn't even think about it as we climbed through and continued walking. Eventually, I noticed a light ahead, and we decided it was our only hope, whatever the danger. As we got closer, I realized it was a farmhouse, but I didn't say anything at that moment, for I knew it would be a while before my companions could tell. Even

though both were clearly aware of what I was, it wasn't easy to overcome the defensive habit of a lifetime.

We stopped about a hundred meters out. "So, what do you wanna do?" It was Joshua that asked. He was no longer as confident as he had been when we started this endeavor.

"I guess we go up and knock." I shrugged.

"After you." Said Bron stretching out a palm to indicate the way.

I pondered a moment more before heading up to the front door. I could hear people talking inside, a man and a woman, but when

I knocked, they fell silent, yet no one came and opened the door. I knocked again, and suddenly, the door swung back as if by magic, and I found myself staring at an elderly man who stood in the middle of the room pointing a shotgun at me. I didn't move for a moment, for I was startled, and then I slowly raised my hands. "I'm sorry I didn't mean to disturb you. We have been out on the road all day, and you're the first sign of life we've come across."

"It's okay, Katie. It's just a couple of kids." He said, quickly lowering his weapon. And from behind the door, an elderly lady looked around at us. She had opened the door in a way to ensure her safety and her husband's ability to shoot a would-be intruder. He did not relax completely, asking Bron to lay down the rifle outside before inviting us in. Katie looked quite concerned when she saw the state of Josh and Bron, but this made the man, whose name was Bruce, relax. Yes, I know that sounds so cliché Australian, but that was his name, honestly.

Katie bustled us in and led us into a large kitchen with an old oak table. She made us sit down while she poured us glasses of water and started to heat some leftovers from their evening meal.

"How bad is it out there?" Bruce asked as he took his seat at the head of the table.

"It's pretty grim, to say the least," I told him. "Melbourne took an extreme pounding, and the city is in ruins."

Bruce sighed. "It's happening all over the country. I listened to it on the radio until it went out late last night." He looked at me curiously. "You look familiar."

His wife turned around from the stove, where she was stirring a pot the old-fashioned way without microwaves and hydrators. She studied me and smiled, "I know who it is, Bruce. She looks like that Hannah Grant we watched on the telly last night."

"I guess she does a bit," he said, but I said nothing. "Personally, I found watching an Australian acting like an American quite embarrassing."

"Oh, stuff and nonsense, Bruce, you're always putting down my reality TV shows."

"She is Hannah Grant." Said Josh, and I shot him a glare because I certainly wasn't going to reveal that information.

Bruce's eyes narrowed as he looked at me again, "Is that true?" I nodded sheepishly. And a slight smile crossed his face as he looked up at his wife and then back at me. "Then I guess you won't have a problem if we charge you for this meal."

"Oh, don't be so rude, Bruce. They're just kids, and they need our help," Katie said sharply as she started to dish up our food.

Bruce's face fell, and he muttered something under his breath, but clearly, he was not going to cross his wife.

I do not recall what we ate, but I do remember that it was very tasty. That could also be due to how hungry we were. Josh and Bron were already on their third glass of water before we even started eating. I cannot honestly say that, even today, I understand the limits of an unmodified person. Of course, eventually, I would feel the same effects as anyone in any situation, but it takes a lot before I ever feel desperate thirst or hunger, or even exhaustion. I was not concerned. Sympathy is an affliction I, fortunately, am rarely cursed with.

"Do you need a bed for the night?" Katie asked as we finished our food in silence.

"No," said Josh, handing her his plate. "We need to get moving and get more distance between the Peons and us. And to be honest, I suggest you do the same."

Bruce snorted at that. "This farm has been in my family for over five hundred years. My kids may have forgotten their heritage for life in the big city, but as the last Harrison of Cotton Hill Farm, I'll be damned if I give it up without a fight."

"We are talking about the military might of the European Union," Josh said, sneering. "Not a bunch of cattle rustlers."

"Oh, they'll be out of luck if they come here looking for cattle because I'm a pig farmer." Bruce laughed heartily. "But seriously, I'm an Australian, true blue, and this is Australia, and no damned Peon is gonna take my farm away from my family or me."

Josh shrugged, "I guess that's up to you, mate. But we have to leave."

"You leave if you want to, Josh," Bron said curtly. "But he's right. We are Australians, and this is Australia."

49

"Stay here and die if you want to, Bron. Makes no difference to me." Josh said casually. Then he looked over at me. "What do you have to say about it, Han?"

Honestly, I didn't give a shit about Australia at the time. All I cared about was getting my perfect arse out of there in any way possible. However, my view of Josh had not changed that much, and I did not wish to be left alone with him. "If Bron stays, then I'm staying with her," I said more curtly than I intended, and it was clear by his expression that Josh had not expected me to say this. He looked disappointed and creeped me out even more, for I now thought he was looking for an excuse to get me on my own. This convinced me all the more that I would stay near Bronwyn. I turned to Bruce. "If there was anything we can do to help you, we will," I said, totally unaware of what I was signing up for.

He was pleasantly surprised but smiled at us and said, "that's not something I could ask you to do or expect of you. Frankly, I don't think we're going to make it, but you youngsters have your lives ahead of you. Stay the night, and my wife and I will prepare some provisions for you. I'll even give you the keys to my truck because I'm not likely to need it again." It was a generous offer, although I didn't appreciate it at the time. Having seen the vehicle when we were approaching the house, I thought he was just trying to get rid of his old garbage.

When the meal things were cleared away, Katie took us to the back of the house where some quaint old bedrooms were. I finally had a shower and felt so much better for it, even though I had no clean clothes to put on.

It had been a long time since males and females were segregated, but the Harrisons were very much old school, much to my relief, and I found I was sharing a room with just Bron. To be completely honest, I was extremely relieved. I had two minds about Josh in these trying times. Part of me was pleased to have someone who knew how to use a firearm, but on the other hand, he still creeped the shit out of me to no end.

As we got ready for bed, I pondered sleeping naked, so I wouldn't have to wear those dirty clothes again. However, I thought about Josh again, and while I felt safer with him around when it came to the

Peons, I certainly did not feel safer with him in general. However, about three hours after I went to sleep that night, I was going to be very grateful that he was around.

CHAPTER SIX

THE BATTLE OF COTTON HILL FARM

The bed was uncomfortable. I didn't notice how comfortable the mattress I had slept on the previous night had been, but I was sure it was better than this. I had been so exhausted from the stress of everything that I would have slept on a rock. However, I missed using my smart bed, which was adjusted as required to my form to ensure a perfect night's sleep.

I lay awake listening to the nighttime critters outside, something else I was not used to in our house in the city.

It was even worse when Bron started snoring loudly in the bed beside me. Eventually, I gave up and climbed out of bed. I went outside of the house to sit on the porch. I was deep in my thoughts for some time, trying to find some semblance of sanity about everything. It still hadn't quite registered that things would never be the same. I believed that somehow all this would be cleared up, and we'd return to normal. Even when I noticed the light in the sky far away, it did not register as a potential problem. You can often see commercial and military aircraft, and the brain has a way of ignoring the normal unless you pay attention to it. I disregarded it for quite some time, but then I started to think, was it one of ours?

Gradually, it grew closer, but it was hard to judge how close. I could not hear it, but that could mean they were using the dark energy generators that nearly all air vehicles of every kind we're now fitted with. While it was coming in our direction, I did not realize it was coming straight at us until just before it landed. I was standing up by now watching it, and while I don't exactly have night vision like my sister Stacey and her artificial eye, I do see better in the dark than most. A pang of fear ran through me as I realized it was some dark energy transport, for it was certainly not aerodynamic. I saw men jumping out of it even before it even hit the ground. They were carrying rifles and coming in toward the farmhouse.

I ran back into the house screaming, "the Peons are coming." Bruce came out of his room first, dressed in nothing but his underwear, but was quickly followed by a fully dressed Josh.

At the time, I had no idea why the Peons would want to come to a little old farmhouse like this. Only later would I learn that taking control of local resources was a tactic of war. First, they would deprive their enemy of their resources and potentially gain those resources for their own men and women.

Bruce ran to the window, and Josh was quickly up by his side. "Well, it looks like I may need your help after all." He disappeared down into the basement. By this time, both Katie and Bron were up. Bron immediately headed for the front door, intent on grabbing the rifle we had left outside. However, when she opened it, someone called out something in French as she slammed it shut again.

Bruce reappeared carrying an array of rifles and ordered Josh to go down and bring up the ammunition boxes. Josh nodded and raced down as Bruce handed a rifle to Bron, then one to his wife, and then proffered one to me. I took it nervously, looking at him wide-eyed. "What am I supposed to do with this," I asked.

Bruce laughed. "Shoot the damned Peons, of course. Give it here." He quickly ran through with me how to point a modifier using the site on the top of the barrel. He then showed me how to pull out a clip and put a new one in. Another aspect of my nature was to be able to memorize instructions word for word. As he finished, I nodded and took the weapon back. "Go upstairs." He instructed me. "Find a window, and for god's sake, keep your bloody head down." I nodded again uneasily, then raced upstairs and entered what I assumed was Bruce and Katie's bedroom. I knelt by the window and peered out. I could see a dozen or so Peons fanning out around the house. Suddenly all the lights went out, and I started to panic until Bruce called up that he had done it. Josh appeared a minute later with a bunch of extra clips and placed them next to me. I looked up at him, then down   at the boxes. "Are you gonna be okay, Han?" he asked, placing a reassuring hand on my shoulder. At least if it had been anyone but Josh, it would be reassuring, but I flinched and pulled myself away from him.

"Please don't touch me," I said with an ice-cold voice that could have frozen the balls off of an elephant. Then, with a healthy dose of venom added a few moments later, "ever!"

He snapped his arm back and just stared expressionlessly at me for a few moments. It looked like he was about to say something in response, but ultimately he just sighed and went back downstairs.

He was gone from my thoughts moments later as I checked the loaded clip in my weapon. On the extremely rare times I talked about Josh later, some people would find him a sympathetic figure, but trust me, if you had met him, I am quite sure you would have found him the contemptible sleazebag that I did, especially if you are a girl. I was crouched below the window frame, too nervous to look up. I took a couple of breaths and steeled myself before slowly raising myself up to look out of the window like Chad looking over the wall.

They were now close enough that I could ensure these unexpected visitors were not Australian. I waited. I wasn't sure what to do. Well, apart from the obvious that I was going to shoot at Peons. I haven't really had time to think about the fact that I was about to attempt to kill someone. It seems like something very easy to do when you watch movies or read books, but the reality is very different. I really struggled with the concept of empathy for other people, but even I balked to the idea of actually taking a human life. They say it gets easier the more you do it, and I can truly testify, but that's the truth. However, it is also true that you never forget your first kill. I didn't have time to dwell on it; a few moments later, everything happened quickly.

A shot rang out from the ground floor, and one of the incoming troops went straight down. A couple more shots, possibly Bron and Josh. Only one went down, the other having clearly missed as already the troops had hit the ground. Someone was barking orders in a foreign language. I assume it was French, as that is the official language of the European Union, even though the other member states have their own.

I hesitated momentarily, wondering how I was supposed to shoot through the glass. Crouching out of sight once more, I reached up and tried to unfasten the window, but it had been years since it had ever been opened. Even out here, people would rely on air conditioning rather than the fresh air of open windows. I quickly jumped up and hit the window with the butt of my gun, which shattered into a thousand pieces causing me to step back to avoid being hit by the debris. Within seconds I was back down on the ground, crouched to one side of the window. "Go back to Europe, you Peon scum." I heard Bruce cry before he fired again.

I carefully peered over the edge of the window frame. The men and women of the European army were running for cover. I raised the rifle over the edge, resting it on the ledge, and I looked down the sight, my heart pounding into my chest. I found it hard to squeeze that trigger, but something suddenly zipped past me and hit the wall behind me. I realized it was a bullet that barely missed me. Anger and a severe desire for self-preservation welled up within me. Getting a Peon in my sight, I fired. She had been running to find a way to avoid the gunshots coming from us, but now instead, she flipped over, landing on the ground and not moving anymore. That day, I found my genetically enhanced abilities made me an excellent sniper. I fired twice more, and on both occasions, I found my target, sending both to whatever afterlife was reserved for Peons.

However, it was not all that easy. While we were shooting at them with our semi automatic rifles, they returned fire with fully automatic weapons.

The spray virtually obliterated my room as I lay flat on the ground, praying that none of the shots would hit me. Of course, they didn't, for I'm telling you this story. I waited for a break in the fire. As I heard more shots downstairs, I jumped up quickly. Bang. Bang. Two more dead Peons.

Something came flying through the window, and for a moment, I thought someone was throwing a brick or something, but as I turned around to look at it, I saw that it was a grenade. Once more, my genetically modified reflexes came into action and saved my life, for I had less than three seconds, I jumped over to the other side of the bed and let it absorb the blast.

However, I did not walk away uninjured. Splinters from the wooden bed hit me in my arms and legs, but with the adrenaline flowing through my body, I would not even notice it until afterward. I shimmied on my elbows to the door. For now, the front wall of the bedroom no longer existed and was open to the sky. Only then did I notice that Bron was calling down from below to see if I was alright. "I'm fine. I'm coming down." I shouted back. As I got to the top of the stairs, there was a loud crash of a door being busted open. The Peons had made it through the back door. As I looked down, I could see the kitchen area, and I saw Bruce shoot the first one that entered before he fell under a hail of bullets. His body jerked just like it did in the movies, and it was a surreal moment for me.

I did not waste any time, and my rifle was raised to my shoulder again. As soon as Bruce's attacker came into view, I shot him straight in the forehead. Whoever was with him backed out of the building. I jumped up and ran down the stairs, two or three steps at a time. I took a moment to duck down beside Bruce, and thanks to a high school first aid class, I was able to check for a pulse in his neck, but it was all too late. He was dead. Katie was standing there staring at him in disbelief, and it took both Bron and me to move her out of harm's way. Something suddenly rolled in from the back door. I thought it was another grenade, but it began to smoke. Within seconds, tears were streaming down the faces of everyone except me. They cried out in pain, trying to wipe their eyes but only making it worse. Smoke filled the room. My eyes started to sting, too, but not to the same degree, and I could still function. I looked down at the floor at the Peon I had shot, grabbed up his automatic

weapon, exchanged it for my single-shot rifle, and stood in the smoke-blanketed room facing the door and waited.

It did not take long, and the Peons came in faster this time. Their gas masks were in place, and they were not expecting any resistance. I squeezed the trigger. The recoil surprised me, and I almost lost control of the weapon, but I think you know by now I am no ordinary Aussie girl. I managed a steady spray of bullets from left to right, and bodies began to fall. I think I took out three, and the last two managed to get back out the door, to my disappointment. This time I did not wait or hide. The death of Bruce had stripped me of any qualms about killing these Peon bastard motherfuckers.

Stepping over the corpses, I made it to the doorway. The nearest Peon had his back to me as he ran away, and without hesitation, I put a single shot in the back of his head. The two ahead of him instinctively dove to the ground, but it didn't help them as I emptied the gun into their prone forms. I cannot deny it, but this was the most satisfying feeling in the world. As I have said, taking a life isn't easy, but it gets easier after the first and quite satisfying after the first half dozen.

To my left, I noticed the craft had come in closer and was starting to take off, and I smiled victoriously. However, I noticed the pilot still had his door open. I raised my weapon. It was a long shot, quite literally, in this case. I fired. It had been many years since gravity or wind resistance would inhibit the aim of a modern military-issued firearm. Nearly all bullets were jet-propelled and, in some cases, even had heat seekers that helped to ensure no one missed their target. I did not have heat-seeking rounds, but I did have the almost superhuman ability of perfect aim.

He was locked in my sights, and that meant a guaranteed kill. I think I actually grinned as I squeezed the trigger and saw him fall limply to one side. For a moment, the craft hung in the air like some alien spaceship before tipping, wobbling, and then slammed into the ground. I waited for a satisfying explosion, but sadly nothing came.

With the immediate danger passed, I became aware of Katie, Josh, and Bron, who had scrambled out of the house, coughing and choking. It was then the pain hit me. And I spent the next fifteen minutes pulling out splinters of wood for my left leg and arm. It took about thirty minutes for the effects of the tear gas to wear off to the degree that my companions could become functional again. Katie seemed remarkably well-composed for someone who had just lost her husband. There was a grim determination about her as she reloaded one of the rifles.

"We need to get out of here," I said curtly. "It won't be long before these guys are missing, and someone comes looking for them."

"Damn it," Josh muttered, and I turned to look at him. He stared back into the still smoke-filled house. "All the weapons are still back in there."

I sighed. I had given up worrying about displaying my abilities and said, "don't worry about it." And I reentered the house, picking up guns and throwing them out. I also unclipped hand grenades and tear gas canisters from their belts and tossed them out as well, only to have Josh shout out, "for fuck's sake, Hannah, be careful."

I ignored him as I went back out and watched as Katie talked to Bron and Josh stacked the weapons into the back of the truck. I turned to the old lady who had just stood at one side, watching us with her rifle resting on her arm.

"Is there anything you need to bring with you that I have to get from the house?" I asked her.

"Oh, my dear, I'm not coming with you," Katie said. "My duty is very clear. I'm going to kill the livestock, so the Peons don't get their hands on them, and then we will see what we will see."

I want to say that I've tried to persuade her to come with us, but honestly, I didn't care. It was her life, and if she wanted to throw it away, it was nothing to do with me. I just wanted us to get out of there so I could hide my arse and stay safe.

She had me go back into the house and pick up food and water supplies for several days. She did not once question how I was able to do this. I only guess that her fascination with watching me on the television made her well aware that the rumors of my genetic modifications were correct.

I eventually climbed into the truck with Josh next to me and Bron in the back. We bid farewell to Katie, and I put it in gear and headed away from Cotton Hill Farm. I will not keep you in suspense and tell you that Katie Harrison did indeed survive, and we would be reunited some years later. I will address the details of that at the appropriate point in this tale. However, as we drove away and I looked up at her in my rearview mirror, she stood resolutely up on her porch watching us leave, only turning away when we had made some considerable distance from her.

CHAPTER SEVEN

THE RAY OF HOPE

Over the next few days, there was a steady learning curve for us. The truck was solar-powered but old and faulty and consumed power faster than it could charge. The result was that most evenings, we broke down. However, we quickly worked out that if we left it sitting to charge during the day and drove it at night, we could make more distance. This also meant we could sleep in the front cabin with the air conditioning on during the day, and we wouldn't overheat the vehicle, or ourselves, driving in the summer sun. We drove for two days without seeing anyone. We took the vehicle off-road whenever we reached a town. We were simply too scared to encounter anybody else. We also stopped frequently. We still had no plan. We couldn't just keep going. Eventually, we'd hit the Outback, which was pretty much certain death.

On the third day after the Battle of Cotton Farm, dawn was coming up, and we pulled over so that we could prepare a meal and settle down for the day. By now, I was missing the uncomfortable bed in the farmhouse.

I climbed out to stretch my legs, having been sitting in that vehicle for eight hours without a break. I stood looking at the road ahead, my hands resting in my back pockets and trying to think what to do next. We had no idea what we were doing, where we were going, or what each day would bring. Bron wound down her window and called to me. "Hey Hannah, someone is calling on the radio."

I raced back to the front of the truck and immediately jumped into the driver's seat. The vehicle had a short-range communications device designed for use around a farm. We periodically checked it every day and had been met by nothing but static, just as the regular radio was, but now there was a man's voice. He kept repeating the same message. "This is the voice of Free Australia. Canberra has surrendered, but the fight goes on. Join the resistance. Call me if you can hear me."

I picked up a small wireless mic device and nervously said, "G'day, Free Australia, this is Hannah. Where are you?"

There was a pause, then the voice returned. "G'day, Hannah, good to hear you. I can't tell you where I am yet. This isn't a private line; I need to check your true-blue credentials."

"Do I sound like a fucking Peon, mate?" I responded indignantly.

"I don't give a shit what you sound like. Anyone could sound like an Aussie if they wanted to."

"How do we know that you're not the enemy?" said Josh curtly, and I waved a hand to hush him.

"Good question." Came the response over the radio. "You don't. However, as I am sitting here safely in a base drinking a beer and you're out there, probably lost, and alone and running out of resources. It makes a lot more sense that you take the risk than I do."

"He does have a point," said Bron grinning.

I pinched my lower lip, a habit I had when I was indecisive.

"Well, what's it gonna be? I don't have all day." And after a short pause, he added, "Well, I do. I'm just impatient."

I steeled myself with resolve that I didn't feel. "Okay, mate, what do you want us to do?"

"Do you have a satnav with you? Or even a mobile phone?"

"I have my phone, but it's not working," I replied.

"Your phone is working fine. It's the satellites up there the Peons took out. Turn it on and give me your identity profile, and I'll be able to locate you."

I reached into my pocket, pulled the device out, and turned it on. I was glad I had turned it off and still had a charge. "Hannah Grant ident 53BCV198."

"Hannah Grant, did you say? The girl from the TV shows? You're pulling my leg, right?"

I sighed and rolled my eyes. "It's just a coincidence, and what would be the point in giving you a fake ID?" I really didn't want to get into a discussion about who I was, although when I think about it now, I have no idea how many people in Australia had the name, Hannah Grant.

There was a long pause at the other end, and when he spoke next, there was a slight tension in his voice. "Okay, sweetheart, this is what I want you to do. I can see you on my system. I want you to keep driving north for two miles. You'll then park. Doesn't matter where, as I'll be able to find you. You wait there for three hours."

"Three hours!" Josh shouted indignantly.

"Just shut up and listen to me. Let that girl with the brain talk when I've finished." Josh looked quite put out, and he flushed slightly. "After the three hours is up, if it's safe, we'll contact you. If we don't, then it's not safe, and you're on your own. Do you understand me, Hannah Grant?" He said my name somewhat disbelievingly, but I replied that I did and started up the vehicle. I set my odometer back to zero.

As I drove, I glanced in my mirror to see Bron checking that the clip in her automatic rifle was full. I looked up at her, and she shrugged. "Just in case." And I nodded.

As I reached the distance, I just stopped, not even bothering to pull over, for there was nothing on this road either behind or ahead.

We sat in nervous silence for almost thirty minutes. Suddenly a voice boomed out from outside. "Step out of the car. Do not be carrying any weapons, and keep your hands in the air."

We froze in our seats until the radio came on again. "Okay, Hannah Grant, that's my people talking to you. Now, do exactly as they say. We can't take chances, and we won't take chances. They will open fire if you do not comply. Confirm that you understand me."

Infuriated, I replied. "Oh, I understand, alright, but this is bullshit."

"This isn't a game, Hannah Grant. Will you comply?" He replied, almost sounding extremely aggressive now.

"Yes, yes, we are getting out now." I snapped back. "Just be careful, and don't do anything stupid."

"And the same goes for you, Hannah Grant," He said once more, sounding quite pleasant.

"You know, just Hannah will do," I said, but I didn't hear any response. I turned off the radio, and slowly we climbed out. With our hands held high, we looked around. I saw nothing until I looked up and saw a small compact attack copter. The outline of the Australian Air Force emblem was still visible, although it had been removed, meaning this vehicle was now unarmed and in civilian ownership. Well, although its weaponry would have been disabled, hanging out of the door was a man with an automatic rifle trained upon us.

"Place your hands on the top of the vehicle, stay where you are and don't move." The amplified voice from the silent aircraft instructed. We complied even though the car's roof was still almost scalding hot from the day. As we did, the vehicle floated down but didn't quite touch the ground. The young guy with the automatic rifle jumped out and covered us. From the other side came a serious looking woman who didn't look much older than me. She looked into the back of the truck, raised her eyebrows at the weaponry we had stowed there, and then went round to look into the cab. She reached in, pulled out Bron's firearm, and tossed it into the back. It was only then that she looked up at us. "Okay, which one of you is it that can drive?"

I raised my hand, and she nodded at me. "Okay, these two get on the copter. Blondie, you're with me."

"Why are you separating us?" Bron asked.

"It's dangerous out here. But we're not going to abandon this truck. You'll go on ahead to the base, and we should be there in about an hour."

Certainly, I wouldn't say I liked this plan. Especially as it was me that was the one to remain. "I don't think we want to be separated," Josh said firmly.

The young woman, dressed in just jeans and a T-shirt with frizzy red hair that was tied back, tilted her head to one side and looked at him with a thin patronizing smile. "I didn't ask you what you wanted. I'm just telling you the way it's going to be." She looked back at her partner. "Get them out of here. I'll see you back at base."

With a final look back at me, Bron and Josh followed the young man and jumped onto the small aircraft.

I looked back at the woman who was now smiling at me and offering her hand. "Madison Grainger." I looked down at the hand, somewhat confused but took it all the same.

"Hannah Grant," I said softly.

"Yeah, I heard about that." She grinned. "I thought Ray was joking with me when he told me your name, but he also said you said it was a coincidence, which I can clearly see that it's not."

I shrugged. "It was an honest lie. I didn't think he'd believe me if I said who I really was."

"Fair enough. But I want you to realize, Hannah, Ray is a good bloke, but winning his trust isn't easy, and it certainly isn't a good way to start by deceiving him.

"Is there any reason why I should give a fuck what he thinks?" I responded snarkily, not at all liking in the way this woman was talking to me.

She stared at me for a long moment as if trying to wake me up, but eventually, she simply shrugged. "well, we'll just have to see about that now, won't we, mate." She moved to open the passenger door. "Come on. We better get going."

I climbed back into the driver's seat and powered up the vehicle again. "So, tell me, how come you didn't get out of here with all the other rich and powerful," Granger asked me.

"Well, for one, I didn't know it was an option, and for another, I was cut off from my family," I said with the clear implication prevalent in my tone that the question was stupid.

"Now that's disappointing," she said, sounding regretful.

Without looking away from the road ahead, I frowned, not understanding her response. "why would it matter to you if I got away or not?"

She shrugged and gazed out of her side window, resting her elbow on the sill and placing her chin upon her hand. "I was hoping that you hadn't left because you were gonna stay behind and join the fightback." I positively snorted at that incredibly preposterous idea.

65

She turned back to look at me. "So, you would have fled if you had the chance?" she sounded disappointed.

"Of course, I would. What do you expect me to do? You really expect me to stay here and the battle against the armed might of the European Union?" I laughed mirthlessly at this.

"Of course I do," Granger responded indignantly. "I would hope every Australian would want to stay and fight."

"Well, there is a big difference between the willingness to fight and the ability to fight. I'm not exactly trained in the art of warfare. My training ends up being able to walk in high heel shoes without tripping over my feet."

"Every Australian should be playing their part." She said curtly.

"Hey, if you need makeup tips, which you surely do from the look of you." She wasn't wearing any makeup, and I positively despised women who didn't take the trouble even to try to look good. I couldn't hold back the absolute annoyance which generated my sarcasm. "Or even a shoe-shopping buddy, then Hannah Grant is your girl. But if you wanna expect me to go taekwondo on a Peon with a machete, then no."

"Well, if you plan to join our resistance group, you'll have to play your part," she snapped at me quite aggressively. I watched her glaring at me in my peripheral vision. That was something else that I understood the unmodified couldn't do.

"Who said anything about joining a resistance group? I'm just looking for somewhere safe. Anyway, how could you possibly have a resistance group going and set up in just two days?"

"Oh, we've been preparing for this for years," she said proudly.

This did not make sense at first. Sure, a war was going on, but no one expected anyone to try and take over the country, and then it clicked. I found myself laughing patronizingly, and she looked confused, "Oh my God! You are a bunch of those crazy doomsday preppers, aren't you?" Even before the start of the war, groups had begun banding together as if the end of the world was coming. They would get ahold of equipment, nonperishable foodstuffs, and any weapons they could get their hands on. They were considered crazies.

She raised an eyebrow, and rather than take offense, she grinned. "Crazy, huh? and what is it exactly that's going on now?"

I stopped laughing and thought about that for a while before I smiled at her. "Now that's a good point," I said as she directed me to turn off the road. Moving off-road made us go significantly slower, and I had to navigate between trees and other foliage. Soon I could no longer see the road in the rearview mirror, and I realized that wherever we were going, it was well and truly hidden.

Eventually, we came out into a clearing, and I saw multiple military-looking tents scattered around and covered in foliage to hide them from aerial view. At the center was the helicopter that had taken Josh and Bron. As I pulled up, I noticed other vehicles and boxes of ordinance stacked up. Someone here clearly had military connections. As I climbed out of the car, I could hear the hum of generators powering this little encampment. A watchtower had been erected, and the man stood upon it with a full-size machine gun. He waved down at Grainger, and she waved back.

A tall, well-built man with a long black beard came out to one of the tents with Bron and Joshua on either side. They looked quite relaxed and even cheerful, which helped put me at ease.

"G'day love." He beamed at me with a big rosy-cheeked smile. "Hannah Grant, I presume." He extended a rather grubby hand, and I was momentarily loathed to take it until I realized it was no cleaner than my own.

"You presume correctly," I replied.

"Crocker, Ray Crocker, but everyone just calls me Croc."

"Nice to meet you, Mr. Croc."

"Just Croc'll do." He turned and smiled at Madison. "It appears we have a celebrity with us."

"Yes, it would appear that way," Madison said with less enthusiasm.

I rolled my eyes and looked at each of them in turn. "A celebrity courts the attention of the media. I don't."

"It doesn't appear that way on the telly," Madison said quite provocatively.

I was tired, and I was fed up. I was not about to get into it with her, and beyond a short glare, I let it go.

67

Croc looked down in the back of the truck and whistled appreciatively at our collection of weaponry. "My, my." He grinned and picked up one of the assault rifles. "French military issue. You kids have been busy."

"We're willing to trade some of them for other supplies," said Josh in a businesslike tone. My eyes widened, and I stared at him. Was he really thinking that we were going to leave and carry on? We've found a bunch of badasses in the Bush who could certainly keep me safer than he could. I still wasn't sure that he wasn't a danger himself.

"Whoa! Slow down there, young fella." He put the rifle back in the back of the truck. "Let's talk a bit before you start making up your mind about things." He nodded towards his tent. "Let's go

have some tucker and talk about the future." Josh glanced at me, apparently once more seeking my approval, and it was getting irritating, but I just nodded. Croc noticed this, and with what was previously discussed while in the car, he now took it that I was the decision maker of the group, and I guess I really was. Despite the recent bravado and his denial, when back at that house in the suburbs of Melbourne, Josh was still obviously obsessed with me. I think he would have walked into a lake of fire to follow me.

Bronwyn was just Bronwyn. Brave, feisty, and able to hold her own, but I believed she would always be a follower. However, she would certainly prove me wrong on that account later on. It was not that I found anything wrong with followers. Even now, I have an ego and enjoy the attention. I was raised to seek that attention, and it is hard to put it aside. Back then, in my immaturity, I was even worse.

Chapter Eight

In Our Own Way

The meal we were served looked like roadkill, but I was so famished that I didn't give a shit. The three of us new arrivals ate in silence as Croc told us about their setup. "We have been preparing for some time despite the government's constant bullshit reassurance that this would never happen, but some of us realized differently. So, we started prepping."

"How did you get your hands on all the military hardware?" Bron asked.

"Oh, there's a black market out there. I have contacts. Some of the stuff was purchased legally from the military, such as the 'copter. The armaments were removed, but owning nonlethal, surplus equipment is not illegal. The weaponry was obviously the hardest, but as I said, there's a black market. Not all of it is Australian. Some of it is from the United States, but the larger portion is from the Baltic states and even China."

This even surprised me, who was mostly ignorant about this stuff. China was famously neutral in this war, but as I was to learn, they were not so neutral that they didn't profit from selling weapons and equipment to both sides. Their biggest industry had become what was known as mercuranium. A resource that came from just one planet that we knew of. A toughened steel, almost as hard as diamond, lined many military vessels traversing the Solar System. The Chinese monopolized it, and that nation prospered like no other. Relations

69

with the Chinese were always cordial, for neither side wanted them to join the war against them. If ever they did, it would be game over.

"No, we don't lack equipment, but what we do lack is people. A gun is only as good as the person shooting it."

"How many of you are there currently?" I asked, hoping that somewhere around here, he had an army waiting to strike back at the heart of the enemy.

"There are presently only twelve of us, and if you choose to join us, we'ill train you to be Peon-killing machines. We'll grow in number. Hundreds out there are willing to fight back, maybe thousands."

I sighed and shook my head. "As I already explained to Madison, I'm not military. I don't know the first thing about waging war, especially guerrilla warfare."

Bron snorted. "Oh, and I suppose what you did back at Cotton Hill Farm doesn't count?"

I colored slightly. "I got lucky. And I don't think I want to go through that again."

"That'ss disappointing to hear," Croc said rather despondently. "Having a GenMod on our team would have been extremely useful."

I looked at Croc with a deepening frown, "I'm not a GenMod."

Croc almost belly laughed at this. "Bullshit!" he slapped the table. "I have fought alongside GenMods and know one when I see one."

"There are GenMods in the Australian army?" Bron asked, believing, as I've already told you, that genetic modification in Australia had been illegal since the practice first came into being.

Croc shook his head. "Maybe one or two went under the radar, but none that I know of. No, about fifteen years ago, I was attached to a United States Marine Corps unit. The officer in charge was a woman called Jenna Plural." He smiled whimsically at the memory. "I must admit she was so beautiful. I had a crush on her the entire time I served with her. However, it was her skill as the perfect fighting machine and her ability to win conflicts with the minimal loss of life of our own was where her talent truly lay."

"And she still serves?" I asked.

"No idea. The Americans don't exactly post details of their operations, and I've been out of the military for ten years now. For all I know, she's dead. More than likely, considering the types of insane missions they sent her on."

So that was the first time I heard of Jenna Plural, but by the time I met my sister four years later, I had completely forgotten the name and the fact she was a GenMod. When I recently talked to Jenna about my time with Croc, she mentioned knowing him, and that was when the memory returned to me. Truth be told, I wasn't paying that much attention. I was more concerned about him thinking I was a GenMod than anything else.

"That still doesn't relate to me," I said indignantly. Josh and Bron exchanged glances but said nothing.

"Calm down," Croc said, placing his hand upon mine. "No one here is going to judge you. At least not for your D.N.A.. But if you want to pretend you are not what you are, that's entirely your business."

I pulled my hand out from under his and looked down at my food, and for lack of response, I stuck my fork into my unidentifiable meat and took a mouthful.

"Well, I, for one, want to stay and fight back," Bron said, much to my annoyance. I would have much rather we discussed this issue in private before declaring our intentions.

Croc smiled at her but turned to look at Josh and me. Josh immediately looked at me to answer for him. Clearly, he was going to decide whatever I did.

I sighed frustratedly and threw my fork down onto my plate. "Look, Im really tired," I said coldly. "Can I just get a good night's sleep, and we discuss this in the morning?" I had already decided what it was that I was going to do.

I can honestly say I was not remotely tempted to stay. This was clearly not the sanctuary that I expected it to be. The idea of remaining with some guerrilla units in the Bush fighting back at the Peons was the last thing I wanted to do. I wanted to get the heck out of Dodge and get out fast. Maybe go to the United States or even the UK.

Bron had decided to stay, and hey, good luck to her. But I certainly didn't want to hang around Josh. So that night, I pretended to go to sleep on the uncomfortable cot in the tent and waited until I was sure the other two were asleep. I was unsure where I would go, but finding a way out of Australia felt like a good idea. I threw a few things into a pack and made my way back to the car. I knew Crock would have people patrolling around, so I moved very carefully, keeping in the dark. I then slowly opened the door and climbed in. That was when I realized I didn't have the ignition fob. I slapped my hands as quietly as possible on the steering wheel as a gesture of my frustration, then jumped out of my skin as a voice said, "if you're gonna leave, Miss Grant, you're gonna need this." He tossed the fob to me through the window, and I caught it in my hands. I looked at him uneasily and said, "there's nothing personal, Mr. Crocker, but I'm no fighter, and I just want to get the hell out of here."

"No one was forcing you to stay, Miss Grant." He shrugged. "So, I don't know why you feel the need to be sneaking off like this." At that moment, the passenger door opened, and Josh climbed in. Crocker saw the look on my face and said, "ah, now I know!" I sighed and rolled my eyes.

"Hey, why didn't you tell me we were leaving?" Josh said.

"I didn't want to pressure you into making a decision," I said weakly.

Crocker sighed. "Let me get you some food and some weapons."

He wandered off, and I just sat there staring out of the windscreen with my hands gripping the steering wheel in frustration.

"Where are we going?" but it wasn't Josh who spoke. Bron climbed into the back seat, dropping a little backpack beside her.

It gave me some relief that I was not going to be stuck with Josh on my own. However, as I looked in my rearview mirror at her, I raised an eyebrow. "I thought you were going to stay?"

She shrugged. "What can I say, Han? Sure, I wanted to stay, but we're besties. If you don't wanna stay, then I'm not staying either."

I managed a smile just as Crocker came back to the truck, chucked a couple of rifles into the back then passed a backpack of food to Bron.

"Where are you planning to go?"

"To tell you the honest truth, I have no idea," I said dejectedly. "Find a way to get the hell out of Australia."

"Well, don't head back to the coast. All you'll find there is death or worse."

"Worse than death?" Bron said with a snort.

"Oh, trust me, young lady, there is much worse out there than dying," he said ominously. He looked back at me. "If I were you, I would head inland. Less likely, the Peons have made it there yet. There are astrodomes out by Alice Springs, which is a good twenty-four hours away from here. Can't guarantee it hasn't been taken, but if anywhere is going to give you a chance to get out, that will be it."

"Thank you," I said softly. He patted the roof of the car, and I put it in gear. As I headed back down to the road, he stood watching us for a while before turning away.

"So, what made you change your mind?" Bron asked.

I looked at her in my rearview mirror. I shrugged and said, "I didn't. I wasn't going to get involved in this war before, and I'm certainly not going to now."

"It doesn't look like we have much of a choice."

I responded to that contemptuously. "If Alice Springs is still not taken, then I'm pretty sure we will have some of my family's resources there. We own hundreds of interplanetary commercial vessels. Something that would get us the hell out of here."

The drive to Alice Springs was uneventful. Occasionally, some aircraft would pass overhead, but I couldn't tell if it was Peon or Australian. It's not like I was some sort of military nerd beyond drooling over some musclebound stud in a uniform. We were crossing the Outback now, and I admit

to being a little nervous about breaking down. The last gas station we passed was closed; if we broke down, we could hardly call out to the RACV.

I also found it somewhat unnerving that Josh sat with the rifle between his legs, coming up and resting upon his shoulder. Seriously, there was nothing miles ahead, nothing miles behind us, and nothing to our left or right except desert. I think he felt that he was my personal security guard and had gone from nerd to macho overnight. I should tell you right now, if you think this will turn into some redeeming story where Josh went from utterly contemptuous to becoming my

73

boyfriend or something, you can think again. The guy was creepy as fuck, and nothing was going to change that.

He sat quietly for the most part, but I couldn't help but notice when he kept looking down at my legs. And I swear to God, on occasion, he pressed his hand against his crotch, thinking he was being very subtle. Seriously, he was not just grossing me out. He was scaring me. We were in the middle of nowhere, and he was the only one armed.

We spent a couple of hours in total silence, lost in our thoughts about everything happening. It was only broken when Bron said, "are we nearly there yet?"

I couldn't help but laugh and glanced at her in the mirror. "What? Are you like seven years old?"

She grinned back at me. "I'm just getting bored as fuck."

My amusement vanished quickly when I noticed Josh looking at me again and rubbing gently at his crotch, less subtly this time but oblivious to the fact I was aware. I frowned up in the mirror at Bron and indicated to him with my eyes without moving my head. She looked towards him, saw where he was staring, and could make out his slow, almost imperceptible arm movement. A look of revulsion crossed her face. She imitated a gagging reflex and looked at me with horror. We continued to drive on in silence. Bron was staring at him, horrified. Suddenly she said, "pull over. I need a piss." I did   pull over to the side of the road, which was quite stupid because I could have just stopped there in

the middle as I was hardly going to hamper any traffic. She jumped out of the vehicle on Josh's side, and I slowly got out on mine. Josh started to get out, but Bron snapped at him. "What the fuck Josh? You coming to watch me take a piss," he muttered something that sounded more like the old nerdy Josh I knew and loathed. He climbed back into the truck and shut the door as Bron and I met up around the rear. "What are we gonna do about him," Bron muttered.

"Don't look at me. I don't have any clue," I said irritably.

"What if he's some kind of rapist or something?"

I scowled at her. "Well, until just now I thought he was just a freak. I mean, who does that?"

"Exactly. The guy is literally masturbating next to you. Right in front of you, for fucks sake."

I sighed with frustration. "So, what should we do about it?"

"We should ditch him here. Get him out of the truck and drive off without him."

I looked at her wide-eyed and then at the expanse around us. "That's pretty much the same as killing him."

Without missing a beat, Bron said, "isn't that better than waking up in the night and finding him jerking over your face, ready to rape you?"

I crinkled up my face. "Oh, you're so gross."

Bron shrugged. "Only telling you as it is, mate."

I glanced through the truck's rear window and the back of his head and let out a long weary sigh. "Two days ago, I was happily pissed off that my mother had bought me a car I didn't want. Now I'm standing in the desert, talking about killing one of my schoolmates."

"He's not your mate, Han. He is the school freak who fucking stalked you for the last two years. He is now in a situation he can do something about it. The guy is literally wanking off in the car as you drive without thinking about the repercussions. If that's not a case of a guy knowing he's safe to do whatever the fuck he likes, I don't know what is."

I pondered this a moment as I stared at the back of his head, and then I steeled myself with resolve. I look squarely at Bron. "Okay, so what do we do?"

It was the only time I ever saw hesitation in her as she looked back at Josh and then back at me. "Okay, so we tell him that I'm going to take over the driving, you're going to get into the back of the truck and call him out. Once he is out, I will pull away, and bam, we lose him."

"Why are you gonna drive?" I asked curiously.

"Because, my dear Han," she grinned. "Your genetically designed ass can beat the shit out of him if it goes wrong."

I stared at her for a moment and then said sheepishly, "I am not a GenMod."

Her grin widened, "I'm not a retard, Hannah. Everyone knows you're a fucking GenMod."

75

"I'm not a GenMod," I stated firmly.

Bron chuckled. "Whatever! It's not like anyone can actually report you now."

I think that's when it truly hit me that nothing would be the same again. It would never really occur to me that Australia could lose this war. Australia had never lost one, and I didn't see that changing until now. Everything I understood as normal had gone up in the flames of Melbourne. I looked once more at the back of Josh and said very quietly, as if he could hear us, "Okay, let's do this."

Bron grinned, and I wondered who the real psycho was here, but I climbed into the back of the truck as she moved round to the side and climbed into the driver's seat. I made it look like I was sorting some stuff out and watched as Josh and Bron conversed for a moment or two. Then Josh climbed out and started heading around to the back where I was. I waited for the truck to move, but instead, it just kangarooed, and I almost lost my balance. Josh stopped and looked back to Bron, and the car kangarooed again. As I looked at her through the window, she waved her hands and banged   the steering wheel. Josh looked confused, but when the car kangarooed again, his eyes widened, and

he turned to me, standing there looking down at him. "Are you trying to leave me behind?" he said, sounding quite sad.

"I don't know what you're talking about." Usually, I'm a pretty good liar, but this was taking a turn I hadn't expected. He stared at me a moment, and as the car kangarooed yet again, he ran to the driver's door and pulled it open. I heard Bronwyn scream as he pulled her out of the vehicle dragging her onto the floor. "Let her go," I demanded, and when he looked up, he saw that I was now holding one of the rifles and had it pointed directly at him. He did as I commanded, raising his hands and stepping back from her. He looked so confused.

"Why?" was all he said.

"Because you're a fucking pervert, Josh," I screamed at him. "You have been sitting there jacking off to me for the last hour and scaring the shit out of us."

He looked quite embarrassed as he mumbled out an unconvincing denial. Bron had got to her feet. No longer afraid, she stepped up to

76

him and slapped him hard around the face, and he just stood there and took it. He stared blankly at me. I can't honestly say I knew what to do at that moment, and we just stood there in silence until he said, "I love you, Hannah. I have since the first day I saw you." I can't even tell you what was racing through my mind, fear, anger, utterly grossed out. I don't know what. They say self-defense is when you act in fear for your life. However, you can judge me for what I did next any way you like. I don't care, but I swear to you that I was in fear for my life.

CHAPTER NINE

THE ALICE

Unlesss you are a complete psychopath like Emma Dodgson, taking a human life is not easy. I could have made him walk away and got into the car with Bron, but at that moment, after he had just said what he said, I was more afraid of him than anyone I had ever been. I pulled the trigger. Bron jumped back at the loud bang. Josh stood there for a second, staring at me. His eyes opened wide as he looked at me. I had never seen such surprise on a person's face. I fired again, and he fell where he stood. Bron stepped over and looked down at him as I climbed out of the truck. "He's not dead," she said quite calmly, looking up at me as if waiting for me to fire again. But with my imminent fear no longer present, I found I couldn't do it. I pointed my firearm at him but could not pull the trigger again. He stared up at me, fear and confusion in his eyes. "What are you waiting for?" Bron said impatiently.

I looked at her with annoyance. "What the fuck happened, Bron? Why didn't you drive off?"

She just shrugged casually. To her, it seemed like this was just another day going through an old routine. "I didn't realize it was a stick shift. I've never driven one before. Come on, let's just get this over with. It would be shitty just to leave him here to bleed out." I looked back at Josh and raised the weapon again, but I still couldn't do it. "Please," he said in a quiet, raspy voice before Bron snatched the gun from me. It was totally weird that he didn't take his eyes off me even though she

79

now had the weapon pointed at him. She fired straight in his head. He was dead, and I could never take that back, even if I wanted to.

It's hard to believe that once upon a time, Alice Springs was this little town in the middle of nowhere. Since the development of dark energy generators revolutionized flight, it was Australia's central hub of commerce. Anything imported from overseas came through Alice Springs and then distributed countrywide.

For almost a century, it was the largest spaceport in the world. Hundreds of ships from the colonies and other nations would arrive and depart daily. It is now the third largest spaceport, with the second largest being just outside Frankfurt, Germany, and the largest in Dubai. However, I have to say I don't honestly know if it is even in operation today since news from Australia is very hard to come by. At least accurate news that isn't propaganda from the Peons.

We had continued that journey in silence. Leaving Josh dead on the side of the road left a sour taste in my mouth. It was not that I felt any particular guilt. I still don't. I honestly feel he gave me no choice. It was simply that the whole thing was just plain icky.

Our first sight of Alice Springs was the top of the Canberra Building. Three hundred floors of corporate offices made up the headquarters of eighty-three percent of the major corporations within the republic. I knew Grant Industries had offices there, exactly where I have no idea, but we had offices everywhere, although its headquarters was in Melbourne, or rather had been.

"Well, it doesn't seem to be under attack," Bron said hopefully.

"No, but something is clearly wrong," I replied, and she looked up at me questioningly. "Look up at the sky." She did, then she looked back at me again and shrugged. "No aircraft or ships," I said. "This is the busiest spaceport in the Pacific Alliance. There should be hundreds of ships coming and going." At that, she tensed, realizing that I was right.

"What does that mean?" She asked curiously.

"How the fuck do I know," I replied irritably. "It can't be good. You would think that ships would be getting the hell out of Oz even with commerce disrupted."

"Maybe we should turn back?" she said uneasily.

I look down at the power gauge. "We need a recharge; we'll be stranded and have to walk. Whatever is going on there, we are going to Alice Springs."

But as we drew close, everything started to become clear. The road was closed off, and there was a checkpoint. I saw it long before Bron, thanks to my enhanced eyesight. "Does the army ever wear blue uniforms?" I didn't think they did, but who was I to know? A few days ago, all I was concerned about was that I didn't turn up to a party in the same dress as someone else.

"Han, what are you talking about?" Bron asked nervously.

"Some sort of checkpoint up ahead. I can see men in blue uniforms."

"Oh fuck, Hannah, turn us around. Turn us around as fast as you can," she said urgently with a liberal helping of panic.

I did what she asked of me, but I asked, "what is it?"

"The French wear blue like at the farmhouse and in the bunker. We don't, Han. They're fucking Peons."

She didn't need to say it twice, and I floored the vehicle in the opposite direction. No clue where we would go or how we would even get there. However, it turned out not to be an issue, for as I looked in the mirror, I saw several cars leaving the checkpoint and heading in our direction at a very fast speed. There was no way I was going to outrun them. It didn't take long for them to catch up, and then, in a desperate act, I took us off the road and started to head out across the bush. It was pretty bloody hopeless. A voice shouted at us from some loud hailer, but it was in a foreign language which I believe was French. I assume they were asking us to pull over, and though I considered trying to outmaneuver them, I knew it was hopeless. I slammed on the brakes, kept my hands on the wheel where they could be seen, and waited.

One car pulled up in front of us, another behind, and one to the driver's side. Men and women in the French blue of the Peon army jumped out from their vehicles, raising rifles toward us. Both our doors were opened at the same time, and Bron was roughly pulled out and onto the ground. It was   a slightly harder job for me as the natural instinct to resist being thrown onto the floor is hard to hold

81

back. It's not easy moving a GenMod when they don't want to be moved. However, when a second soldier came to help, I let them drag me out, and I lay face down in the dust as they roughly cuffed my hands behind my back and then dragged me to my feet.

I heard Bron scream and looked over. I guess it was sheer panic rather than anything detrimental happening to her. They dragged her to one of the cars and then me to another. I was pushed into the back and seated next to a female soldier who spoke to me calmly yet coldly, but I did not understand what she said. The driver got back in, and another soldier was in the passenger seat. With no one being able to speak English, I was at a loss as to what was going to happen as first Bronwyn's car, then mine, went back onto the road.

As we reached Alice Springs, we stopped at the checkpoint, and the driver spoke to one of the guards. He glanced back at me and said something to the driver with a huge grin on his face, and the pair laughed lightly, and the woman at my side shook her head and said something reproachful to them. She then looked at me and said something gently that I assumed she thought would be reassuring.

It didn't reassure me.

As we entered the city, I was surprised about how vacant the streets were. All I saw were occasional Peon vehicles patrolling as my captors took us further into the city.

Alice Springs was the epitome of modern Australian architecture, with gleaming towers and exclusive shop fronts. It would have been a mecca for a girl like me in normal circumstances. However, I was unsure if I would see the end of the day alive. I tested the strength of my handcuffs, but there was no way that even I would be able to break them. People may think we're superhuman, but we are just people designed without genetic flaws. Anyone could be like us if they could overcome the natural tendency for errors in the D.N.A.. We were simply humanity at its best.

I don't know the full details of my genetic parentage. Being highly illegal, it was not something my mother chose to speak openly about. I have read my sister Stacey's book, and she does make a couple of mistakes. We don't have a shared father. My D.N.A. is about twenty-six percent of my mother's, albeit cleaned of her natural flaws. The rest of me is made up of the best traits of multiple men and women, of whom it has been deemed to have the most perfect D.N.A. compatibility. One mother. Numerous others. And that's the reason there is very little similarity between myself and my sister Stacey. However, I digress.

I had never been to Alice Springs before, and I don't count this as a visit since I didn't get to see much of it. We were taken to a police station that the Peons had commandeered. There was an Aussie cop there that appeared to be cooperating. I would guess it was under duress, considering the state of his face, which was bruised with a bloody nose and a split lip. As we entered, he stood behind the counter and looked up at us apologetically. Neither Bron nor I spoke as I was pushed up against the counter. The officer quietly asked, "name?"

"Hannah Grant." His eyes flashed up at me, and a look of recognition crossed his face.

"Address?" He asked, looking back down at his terminal.

"The third crater to the left as you enter Melbourne," I replied coldly.

The cop just sighed impatiently. "Ma'am, it's been a really shitty day, and I don't have any sense of humor left. Please just answer the question." I gave him the address, and he wrote it down. "Why are you in Alice Springs?"

"Well, I thought I was running away from the Peons, but clearly not," I said, glancing around at the Peons that stood close by.

"Do you have any family here?"

"Not that I am aware of, officer," I replied.

He stopped typing and looked up at me. "You are now a prisoner of war of the European Union, and the rights of the '24 Galle Convention apply to you. You will not talk unless spoken to by any of the European personnel. You will be expected to cooperate with all instructions, and I am to inform you that there will be serious repercussions if you fail to do so."

"Any news from Canberra?" I asked softly.

He looked back down at his terminal and just muttered, "government officially capitulated two hours ago. We surrendered."

His words didn't sink in as I was pushed away from the counter. Australia had never lost to war. It was unthinkable.

As I was roughly shoved out into a corridor, I looked back at Bron, who was now pushed up to the counter. Our eyes met briefly before I turned away at yet another shove.

I was taken down to a cell, pushed in, and the door locked behind me. I can't deny that I was near to having a total meltdown. I had never felt such fear in my short life. Even worse than when I was in the bunker. For all I knew, they would take me out and shoot me. It was, however, just a holding place before transport could be arranged to take us to one of the internment camps set up on the outskirts of the city.

Time passes slowly when you are in a bare room with just a bunk, a dunny, and nothing to keep your brain occupied except your dark thoughts. I thought about Josh and wondered if things would have been different if he had been with us. I felt no guilt about what we did but simply that he may have been useful in getting us out of the situation we had gotten into.

As it grew dark, I realized we had been there all afternoon and evening, and as time drew on, dawn eventually came. I did not sleep. Another aspect of my genetic makeup is that I need very little sleep. I can function with just a couple of hours a day. It doesn't mean we can't sleep longer, just   that we don't need to. I know that Jenna Plural enjoys getting in the full eight hours. I prefer to keep

it short. However, I find it highly unlikely that I would have slept even if I was a normal person. I wondered what Bron was doing and if she was as afraid as me. No food or drink was brought to us, and I was certain she was suffering. I could go longer without the ill effects, but she couldn't.

Shortly before dawn, the door opened, and I stood up nervously, wondering what to expect. I certainly did not expect what I saw. "G'day, Miss Grant." The cheerful guy standing in my doorway smiled at me. He was dressed in black pants and a collared shirt, but what stood out to me was the Grant Industries logo on his sleeve. "I'm Adam Blake. I'm here to get you out of here."

"Did my mother send you?" I asked uneasily. Considering she would have no idea where I was, it was most unlikely.

"No, Miss Grant. We haven't heard from your mother since this all began. However, most of the board of directors have managed to get off-world. They sent me to negotiate for your release when we discovered you were still alive."

"And the Peons agreed?" I found this unbelievable, thinking this was all some game.

The man smiled, "Well, not for nothing. We did have to transfer a considerable amount of assets to them in return for you."

"How much?" I asked, genuinely interested.

"I understand the amount was in the region of four hundred seventy-five million United States dollars," he replied.

Now that shocked me, but I didn't show it. I'd become used to hiding my feelings and reactions to surprising news. So instead, I said, "why in United States dollars?"

"Because Australian dollars are not worth the paper they're printed on now unless you want to use them for toilet paper." He replied with a shrug. "Now, I don't know about you, but I don't want to stand in a Peon prison cell for the rest of the day. Do you want to get out of here?" I nodded emphatically. He stepped back from the door, allowing me to exit, and confidently walked back out

to the front desk under the eyes of the Peons. I tried to stay stoic and confident and keep my heart from beating fast. I knew my family was powerful and influential, but I had no idea that extended to the enemy. A tall woman in a white skirt and matching jacket business suit was standing at the counter in front of the cop, signing some paperwork. When I say tall, I mean tall. She was clocking at least six foot three. She looked up at me, and those features screamed GenMod. She was flawless with tied-back platinum blond hair and bright green eyes.

"Miss Grant, please meet Emberlynn Stepanchikov. She's your security detail." Blake introduced her. She nodded to me, and I nodded back.

"You ready?" She asked with an accent I did not immediately recognize. She addressed Blake directly.

"Let's go before they change their minds," he muttered with a casual smile, trying to hide his unease as the Peons watched us.

As we reached the front door, a thought suddenly struck me. I couldn't believe that I had almost forgotten all about my friend. I looked up at Blake. "We can't leave without Bron."

He looked at me, confused, apparently unaware that I had not been picked up alone. "We either leave now, or we won't be leaving at all, Miss Grant."

I stopped, in turn, to face him. "Seriously! We're not leaving without Bron." I made to turn back into the room, but he grabbed me by the arm and tried to pull me toward the door. I immediately snatched my arm away from him, which for an ordinary girl may have been difficult. The Peons were now looking at us with concern. After all, they had as much to lose as me since they were complicit in my leaving.

"Miss Grant, we have to go now," Blake said urgently, his sunny disposition rapidly evaporating. He was one of those types who was clearly not used to not being in control of a situation.

One of the Peons stepped towards us and started talking to him in French. He replied, and the name Bron was mentioned, but the Peon shook his head. "Non monsieur."

"Miss Grant, there is nothing I can do, and you are starting to piss off the Peons. Please let me get you out of here. It won't do you or your friend any good for you to be detained again."

I nodded in response and made it look like I was about to turn and leave with him. As the Peon turned away, I swiftly slipped my hand down to his waist and pulled his handgun out of his holster. Once more, something the average person would probably not have done before the man reacted. I fired a shot into the back of his head before anyone knew what I was doing. Don't ask me why I did it. It was a stupid move, even though it worked out.

Chapter Ten

Goodbye Australia

Until then, the Peons had been quite relaxed as they watched us, but as their companion fell face forward onto the ground, they started scrabbling for their weapons. Beside me, I heard Blake shouting, "shit, fuck, and damn it." He reached inside his jacket to pull out his own handgun, but it was not in time for me as I was already staring down the barrel of a Peon rifle. I suddenly found myself going down to the ground with a weight on top of me. It was an odd sensation, as never in my life had anyone been able to move me with such ease.

When I heard the gunfire, I thought it was game over for me, but standing behind the counter, the Aussie cop from earlier had somehow managed to pick up a rifle and kill my assailant.

Stepanchikov, who was the one that knocked me down, was already up and firing two guns with unbelievable precision.

Blake fired off two rounds, taking out two more Peons as I managed to get to my knees to shoot a third, and the cop took down the final assailant. It was a massacre, and over in seconds.

"That was fucking stupid, Miss Grant," Blake said as the cop tossed me the keys to the cells, and I headed back to where I had come from. Bronwyn had heard the gunfire and had been hoping it was some form of rescue and was ready as soon as I opened the door. She came running out without asking questions. When we returned to the front desk, the cop had already done a runner, and the corporate guy was talking into some sort of wrist communicator. He looked up at us and

87

dropped his wrist back down to his side. "Walk out slowly and calmly, and don't look suspicious."

Stepanchikov said nothing but gave me a cold glance as she went ahead of us, stood by the grey company car parked outside, and looked up and down the street, assessing the situation.

It was kind of surreal to step out of the police station and see a Grant Industries company car sitting outside, waiting for me. My liberator opened the back door, but I just raised my eyebrows at

him. "Yeah, like I'm gonna drive around Alice Springs in a chauffeur-driven car while the Peons take it over," I said as I climbed in the front passenger seat.

"As you wish, Miss Grant," he said curtly, stepping around to the driver's seat, and climbing in. Bron and Stepanchikov climbed in behind. "Astrodome terminal twelve." He commanded the auto drive system.

My head snapped around to him as I fastened my seat belt. "Where are we going?"

"Off-world, Miss Grant," he said as the car engine fired up and pulled out into the empty street.

I frowned. "Off-world? I don't want to go off-world."

"You are the only member of the family that we know still to be alive. No, don't panic. We don't know if they're dead. We just don't know if they're alive. The board of directors wants to ensure you stay safe."

I certainly wasn't panicking and responded, "isn't Grant Industries pretty much finished now?"

Blake raised an eyebrow, glancing at me with surprise at my question. "Not at all. They're simply relocating their headquarters to the U.S.A. "

"But how could they do that without my mother's approval?"

"Your mother anticipated this possibility. It's also part of her plan that the first thing we did was search for her, you, and your sister. Should your mother or sister not have survived the attack on Melbourne, you are now the company's primary shareholder."

I frowned. "So, you're working on the basis that my entire family is dead. Thanks!"

"No, we are simply working on the possibility. However, I can confirm that your entire family isn't dead."

"Really? Who's survived?"

"Your sister, Stacefield Ellen, is in a hospital in Japan. She was part of the Air Force's last defense of the mainland but apparently got shot down. I can't tell you more than that because the Americans got to her before we could."

I shrugged. "She's not really part of the family. I've never even met her. I barely know much about her other than her name. The subject of Stacey was pretty persona non grata around my mother."

"Understood. However, she is still a legal relation and potential heir to your mother's estate."

"What do you know about her?" I asked with growing curiosity.

"Oh, she had quite an interesting life. She grew up in Wagga, headed down the wrong side of the tracks for a while, and gained a few juvenile convictions, which were expunged when she joined the military."

"That's kind of ironic." I laughed, and he looked at me with a raised eyebrow. "Mother was pretty much going to pay my way out of the military and allow me to avoid doing national service. Now I know I have a sister, who I don't know, who is out there doing it."

"Oh no, Stacey isn't doing national service. She signed up for it. She spent two years working for Air Force Intelligence before becoming a pilot. She is considered the best pilot in our Air Force and possibly the world."

"How do you know this?"

"Actually, it's Stepanchikov who's our family specialist."

I glanced over my shoulder at the blond GenMod. "Exactly who and what are you to my family?"

"I'm head of the corporate security personal division." She responded in that funny accent.

"And what exactly does that mean?" I asked impatiently.

"It is my job to keep your family alive and unharmed." She said, as if she filed papers in an office.

I couldn't help but retort, "pretty shit at your job, considering I'm the only one alive."

Stepanchikov responded, unfazed. "We all have off days, Miss Grant."

I couldn't help but grin as I turned back to face the front. "You could well be the new head of the company Miss Grant," Blake said.

"Well, to be quite honest, Mr. Blake, I don't really give a fuck about Grant Industries."

"If I could be as frank as you, Miss Grant? It's probably about time you did start giving a fuck." Blake responded curtly.

I chuckled mirthlessly at this, "I never intended to follow in my mother's footsteps, and I don't now. I see no reason why I should."

"Really? Are you aware that if your mother and sister are dead and no provision has been made for Stacey in her will? You now have a controlling interest in the company. You are now chairman in waiting, whether you like it or not."

"In waiting?" I frowned.

"You are a GenMod, Miss Grant. You can't legally control the company without government approval, and it can take up to a year to complete the application process. It's beholden to the board of directors to take care of you until then."

"You make me sound like I'm property," I snorted.

"We prefer to think of it as a corporate responsibility," he replied.

I fell silent as I allowed all this to ruminate around my addled brain. I can't explain what it feels like to have your entire world uprooted and transformed overnight. Of course, many of you reading this account have probably suffered similar upheaval. I thought back to Last Day and our time in the bunker. Then about the trek across the desert and what we did to Josh.

I can't honestly say I think about Josh often. Sure, I probably wouldn't have gotten out of Melbourne alive without him, but he served his purpose. It's not like he would have gone on to serve some greater good. The guy was a freak, and the only use he had or would ever have was keeping me alive. Beyond that, he's not worth thinking about. If you think I'm being callous, then ask yourself this... Why did he bring a rifle to school that day? It wasn't like he knew the Peons were coming. No, I did the world a favor by removing Josh from it, and to be honest, I'm now quite proud of it.

I remained silent for the rest of the journey. Blake was tense. We had no idea how long it would be before the bodies at the police station would be found.

As we pulled into the terminal, we were stopped by Peon security, and Blake spoke to them in fluent French and showed them some papers. After a cursory look around our vehicle, they waved us through. As we drove up to the hangar, the Grant Industries logos became more prevalent, and I realized we owned this particular terminal. However, we didn't drive up to the buildings, but instead went straight to a landing pad, where I could see techs prepping a ship for launch. I recognized it at once. It was my mother's personal yacht, although she never used it apart from the occasional trip to the moon and back.

"Are we leaving straight away?" Bron asked with concern.

"Paying off the military to get you out is not exactly legal," Blake replied. "And after Miss Grant's performance back there, we don't want to hang around for someone to become aware of what's going on and change their minds."

"Can't we find out what's happened to my family?" Bron asked insistently.

"With all due respect, I don't even know who you are, Ma'am. I can't find out if Marcia Grant is alive, let alone anyone else."

He pulled up by the passenger ramp leading into the craft, and a woman opened my door. She smiled at me as I climbed out. "Welcome to the Last Star." She said a bit too cheerfully, considering the situation.

"Last Star? I asked, noticing Stepanchikov had quickly joined me and was looking around at everyone with the alertness of a security pro.

The woman who greeted me smiled as she said, "it's the ship's name, ma'am." She indicated the steps that led up into the vessel. "I'm Emily Taylor, your board-appointed personal assistant. If you would go straight aboard, we can prepare for takeoff."

I had barely reached the ramp when a shout went up. I turned to see Peons running across the tarmac in our direction. "Detail to Last Star. Prepare to repel. I repeat, prepare to repel." Stepanchikov shouted into her wrist communicator, and men and women in black suits appeared from the hangar and the ship itself.

"Get aboard now," Stepanchikov shoved me onto the ramp and stood between the Peons and me, acting as a barrier to any incoming fire. Pulling out her two handguns from under her jacket, she began picking off targets with amazing skill, considering the distance.

The men in suits opened fire on the Peons with assault rifles. When I didn't move, Stepanchikov holstered her weapons and grabbed me by the arm, and she pulled me up the steps with Taylor and Bron close behind us.

Stepanchikov tried to make me sit in a seat as the door of the yacht shut, but I ran up to the cockpit, where the pilot started to fire up the engines. I stared out in horror as I watched the exchange of fire between the enemy troops, and what I would later find out, were simple company security officers. Bodies from both sides lay everywhere.

"Please take a seat." The pilot barked at me, and Stepanchikov pulled me back into the luxurious cabin, that looked more like a cocktail lounge, than a passenger area. I sank into a large caramel-colored seat by a window and fastened my seat belt. Bron sat next to Stepanchikov, and Taylor sat next to me. I looked out of the window again. I saw Blake lying in a pool of blood on the ground. I could see no living member of our security team, and the Peons were getting closer and opening fire upon the yacht.

Dozens of dead to save me? It was kind of surreal yet exciting at the same time, to realize how valuable my life was over that of others.

Then we shot off into the air at a speed that pushed me down into my seat. The pilot slammed on the dark energy compensators to full power. A fairly dangerous maneuver that could only be made by a highly skilled pilot. I watched the ground disappear rapidly, as we left Australia for what was to be the last time.

"Relax, Miss Grant," Taylor smiled at me. "Curtis is the best pilot money can buy."

"Funny you should say that, someone just told me my sister Stacey was the best pilot."

She chuckled. "I did say that money could buy. I don't believe your sister Stacey would be willing to leave the air force for any amount of money. However, she certainly does have an exemplary flight record."

Now that really gauged my interest, but I just shrugged. "So I just found out." I was startled when suddenly everything outside went dark, and it took me a moment to realize we had left Earth's atmosphere. I was in space for the first time in my life. "Where exactly are we going?" I asked.

"To the moon, Miss Grant." She replied.

"You can call me Hannah or Han," I responded, tired of being called Miss Grant.

"As you wish, Hannah."

"Why are we going to the moon?"

"Right now, it's the safest place. The moon is forever neutral territory, thanks to a treaty signed hundreds of years ago. There are both Peon and Pacific Alliance bases there residing in harmony."

"You expect me to live on the moon?" I said sneeringly. "Why can't we go to the US or even Britain?"

"Because we don't know the political ramifications of the fall of Oz. Refugees are fleeing the country and there are those who were already offworld. After all, more Australians live outside Australia than within."

I fixed my gaze on her with determination, "I don't give a shit what the government says, mate. We're talking about Australia, which will never surrender, whatever its official position."

"I absolutely agree. However, Grant Industries is an international concern, and we have to think outside Australia as well."

"You should know, and I ask you to excuse my language here, but I don't really give a fuck about anyone else right now. Australia should be our first priority." At this, I looked at Stepanchikov. "What's your stake in this?"

Stepanchikov frowned, then shrugged. "Stake? I just do my job, Miss Grant."

"You're not an Aussie. Where are you from?"

"I'm South African, Miss Grant. Is that a problem?" She responded.

I shrugged, "I dunno! Is it? I mean, where does your loyalty lie?

A thin smile crossed that perfectly chiseled high cheek-boned face. "I can assure you, Miss Grant. As long as my check hits my account at the end of each month, I will remain forever loyal to you and your family."

I grinned back at her. "I appreciate your honesty."

We fell into silence, and I stared out the window at the stars and the various pieces of space junk the pilot expertly navigated us through. Honestly, I had no clue how dangerous it was piloting through near-Earth orbit, but our pilot was clearly an expert at his craft.

"What's going to happen to me?" I'd almost forgotten Bron was there. She had been quiet for most of the time since we boarded the ship.

"Don't worry, mate," I told her. "We're in this together till the end." I hoped to reassure her, but she did't respond.

The journey to the moon was uneventful, and about four hours later, we started to descend toward it. It felt more like we were going on a vacation than a flight from chaos. We had been fed a freshly cooked meal and pampered by the ship's stewards. Although they always acted professionally, they, too, were clearly concerned about events back home.

Of course, I barely noticed this, being more concerned about my own welfare and what the future held for me. It was only later that it would concern me that I hadn't been worrying about the mother and sister I had left behind.

The moon was the birthplace of colonization, the first place mankind had settled, and it was covered in interconnected bases from almost every country on Earth. In a treaty signed hundreds of years ago, the moon remained independent, and a neutral zone even before Neil Armstrong had set foot on the world. Both Peon and Alliance nations worked side by side in a very uneasy peace. Weaponry was banned except for that carried by the security forces.

We came down into the Australian hub and then the docking bay. As I made to get out of my seat, Stepanchikov stopped me. "Due to the nature of this base, there is quite a procedure before we're allowed to disembark." We all sat there for the next thirty minutes as Luna security boarded the ship to search the cargo hold for contraband. It was quite a large team for such a small ship, and it was only later that I discovered this was due to internal politics, with most nations wanting one of their own to be part of any searches.

We eventually received the captain's order to disembark and getting out of my seat, I followed Taylor down the steps with Stepanchikov right behind me and took my first steps onto another world.

If it weren't for the fact that I had just stepped out of an apocalypse, maybe I would have one of the fond memories most people have of the first time they do such a thing. However, I was facing an unknown fate, and the idea that I was going to reside on this desolate desert of a world was all I was thinking about.

CHAPTER ELEVEN

— · —

CUSTOMS AND EXERCISE

I don't know if Samuel Herriot hated his job or was stressed about the situation Down Under. He was the head of security for the Australian base, and while true blue, he had to follow the regulations of the neutral world. Taylor went ahead of us and tried to speak on our behalf. Herriot was having none of it, and he beckoned Bron and me forward, telling Taylor to shut up when she kept trying to answer questions that he had addressed to us. "Please state your full name," he said to me first.

"Hannah Marcia Grant." A small device on his desk repeated it, and I realized he was taking a voiceprint. He then pushed a small device across his desk, which was about the size of a phone, and turned it sideways. "Place your thumb and then your four fingers up on this device."

For some reason, Stepanchikov stepped forward. "Why is this necessary?"

"Regulations!" Herriot said wearily. "You can comply or be arrested." Stepanchikov uneasily stepped back behind me. I complied with instructions. "Purpose in coming to the moon?" Herriot continued.

I looked at him incredulously and laughed. "Avoiding death back Down Under," I replied.

This seemed to affect the man, and he calmed himself down and became more pleasant. "Right!" he asked me to stand aside and repeated the process with Bron and Taylor. Not being Australian but in the Australian sector, Stepanchikov took longer to process.

"Welcome to the moon," Herriot said in the monotone voice of someone repeating something he'd said a million times. "You are re-minded that this is neutral territory and that the war is not waged here. You are not to be engaged in any overt or covert activity against any nation. You will understand that any crime is, at the least, punishable by expulsion from the moon at the discretion of the Superintendent. You are also not to act in any capacity against the interests of the Australian government." I had no idea at the time, that this line had been added to the instructions after an incident involving my sister Stacey and her friend Harper four years previously. "Are all these instructions understood, and are you willing to comply?"

We all said yes in unison. And without another word, Taylor led us out into the corridor. Two burly security men dressed in uniforms supplied by Grant Industries were awaiting us. Stepanchikov flashed her ID and was clearly of a superior rank as they instantly conceded to her.

We went in silence through a maze of corridors until we came out into an open area where there was a monorail with a small transit capsule waiting for us. I climbed in the front with Taylor next to me, Bron and Stepanchikov immediately behind us, and the two security men in the last two seats at the back. We took off immediately after the doors closed and quickly found ourselves exiting the base and traveling across the lunar desert.

I could describe to you in detail the view of the rugged lifeless terrain shimmering under a million stars, but nothing can relate to that feeling you get in your stomach when you see it. It is simply mind-blowingly amazing. I smiled as I heard Bron gasp behind me, but I became a little unnerved when we disappeared over the horizon, so there was nothing ahead except this desert. It only lasted two or three minutes before a vast dome started to appear ahead, and as we closed in on it, we saw the symbol of Grant Industries on the side. My eyes widened, and I looked at Taylor. "We have our own city on the moon?"

Taylor laughed at this. "It's not exactly a city, Hannah. It's a transit hub. Most of it is for warehousing the goods destined to ship out to or coming in from the colonies. Anything nonmilitary stops here before heading to Earth."

"Why only nonmilitary?" Bron asked.

"Because anything else would breach the convention of the moon. Nothing that can be used for warfare can be brought through here."

Suddenly, darkness surrounded us as we entered the large base, but it only lasted a few seconds before we came out into a brightly lit monorail station. Several official-looking people were already there to meet us. As I climbed out, a tall, good-looking man in a business suit approached me. "Good morning, Miss Grant. It's a pleasure to meet you." He proffered his hand, and I took it.

"Is it?" I asked casually.

He frowned quizzically, "I'm not sure what you mean."

"A good morning," I responded. Yeah, I was being a bitch, but I was tired, cranky and was fed up. "First, I see nothing good about it, having just watched my country blow up, and two, I have completely lost track of time and don't know if it's morning or not."

His annoying smile disappeared but quickly returned. "Yes, well. Day and night are completely different here, but we operate by the convention of Greenwich Mean Time, so although it is nighttime in Australia, it's morning here."

"It's been over a hundred years since we were in the Commonwealth, mate. Why on Earth are we operating in the British time zone and not AEST or the like?"

"Because we're not on Earth, Miss Grant. The moon has nations from all over the world, and GMT has been the central point at which time has been measured since records began."

I merely shrugged at that and said nothing more, and after a brief silence, he continued, "I'm Matthew Barton, director of Grant Industries Public Affairs. The board would like to extend its welcome to you, and the C.E.O. would like to meet you at once."

"If it's all the same to you, I'd like to shower and get a fresh change of clothes before meeting anyone. And I wouldn't say no to a bite to eat."

"And is it possible to find out what's happening back home and to our families?" Bron added.

"Yeah, that too." I agreed, although noncommittally.

"Of course. At least I can help with the first of those requests." He smiled at each of us in turn. "Let me take you up to the executive suite."

The executive suite looked like the penthouse of an exclusive hotel, all cream-colored marble-looking walls with ornate trims and expensive furniture imported from Earth. It probably cost more than their value to have them shipped here. I would soon learn nearly everything else was basic and functional, but here was a place where Marcia Grant would have been in her element. There were two bathrooms, so Bron and I could shower at the same time, and it was good to feel the hot water on my body and get out days of grime and filth. By the time I came out, an outfit was waiting, laid out on the bed. As I put on the button-up shirt and black slacks, I could not help but wonder how they knew my sizes, and the fact that they had them. We were certainly not expected guests here.

I met up with Bron again in the lounge, and she flopped down on the couch, clearly exhausted. I was tired too, but as I have already stated, the need for sleep was not a priority.

When a meal was sent up to us, I discovered that Stepanchikov had been standing guard outside the door, and she looked surprised when I invited her in. "Is it necessary for you to stand out there?" I asked.

"Under current circumstances, it's best I maintain a constant guard." She responded, not getting my meaning.

"I understand that. But couldn't you do it just as easily but more comfortably inside?" I asked.

Her eyes widened, "Actually, it makes my job easier to always have eyes on you."

I grinned. "Take a seat and make yourself comfortable." I was used to having security around but never had someone personally assigned to me. It was pretty cool.

When Taylor arrived, Bron was snoring peacefully. We left her to sleep and headed down to the conference room for my meeting with the C.E.O. of Grant Industries.

Drake Tanner was a man in his forties and had served on the board of directors for nine years, but only three in the capacity of being the chief operating officer.

As I entered, it was clear that he had just moved into the office. Boxes lay around unpacked, and it would turn out that he'd only beaten us here by a day, having escaped Melbourne immediately when things went pear-shaped. He smiled upon me but didn't rise from his desk as manners would dictate, and while I was not immediately concerned, I did find it unusual. "Welcome to the moon, Hannah." He looked over at Stepanchikov. "You can wait outside."

She turned to leave, but I interposed, "I'd prefer her to stay, Mr. Drake." I had no good reason for this, but he rankled me, and I wanted to be difficult.

"As you wish, Hannah." He said, looking quite confused.

"And do you really think it's appropriate to call me Hannah?"

"My apologies. I understood from Miss Taylor it was your preference."

"It is, but I don't like that you assumed that I afforded you the same courtesy as I did Emily and Emberlynn." I smiled sweetly.

Drake shook his head, grinning patronizingly at me. "We find ourselves in quite a predicament."

I took the seat opposite him without invitation, crossed my legs, and folded my arms. "When do I go back to Earth?" I asked sharply.

"We'll come to that, Miss Grant," he responded. "But there are some other matters we need to discuss."

"Seriously, mate." I shook my head. "I am so not interested. I never intended to participate in this company, and I still don't."

"And that may well be the outcome of our conversation, Miss Grant. However, some legal formalities need to be dealt with."

"Fine!" I responded irritably.

"We haven't heard from your mother, and the presumption is, she didn't survive the attack on Melbourne, nor did your sister." He paused and looked at me for a reaction, but I gave him none, other than a bored look. "This leaves you as the sole heir to your mother's estate."

"I thought I just made it clear, mate, I'm not interested."

"Well, that will certainly make things easier because, under the convention, the genetically modified are not allowed to hold controlling interests in companies with congressional approval."

Now that meeting changed everything. My not being interested in something was very different from someone else taking it away from me. Although Taylor had told me this, his attitude seemed pleased about it. However, there was first the automatic denial. "What exactly does that have to do with me?" I replied.

"Miss Grant. We can play games as much as you like, but you know you're a GenMod, and I know I know you're a GenMod."

I narrowed my eyes at him. "Considering Grant Industries has devoted itself and plenty of resources to hide that fact, it's ironically convenient that you now find that revealing that information is in your interest."

"Your profile is different now. You are Marcia Grant's successor, whether you like it or not. Hiding your D.N.A. will be impossible. As such, we are compelled to make you a ward of the company."

Now that raised my hackles. I even noticed Stepanchikov tense in my perfect peripheral vision. "I am not property, Mr. Drake."

"Miss Grant, you're an illegal GenMod, which makes your status dubious at best. As a ward of the board, we can protect you."

"Bullshit. As a ward of the board, you get to make all my decisions. You want to take over Grant Industries and throw me under the bus to do it, Drake. It's you who is playing games." I said coldly.

It amuses me that, with some hindsight, I would probably have let him have whatever he wanted. As I have said, I had no interest in running the company. However, behind that veil of corporate professionalism, he pretty much started to threaten me. "Don't worry. I have absolutely no interest in running this company. Here's my deal. Set me up a nice little trust fund account and keep paying me, and I'll leave you the fuck alone." I was going to finish with that, but suddenly, a thought occurred to me, and I added, "at least for the next five years."

"Why five years?"

I shrugged in response. "I might change my mind about wanting to run the company."

He paused as he mulled this over. "I think we can do business here, Miss Grant. If you agree for me to retain my seat as chairman, then I'll have the board withdraw its claim on you."

"You realize you're seriously fucked up?" He looked startled again and waited for me to elaborate. "Our nation just went up in flames, and you're still worried about this damn company."

"Miss Grant. This company is spread across the Solar System with one million, two hundred and twenty million employees from all nations. Even if the board was to give up on the company, we have hundreds of ships out there with no home to go to and operations on over a dozen planets. Do you suggest we just give up and abandon them?"

I looked embarrassed and shook my head, but I simply said, "I just want to go back to Earth, even if it's not in Australia."

"That can be arranged. We can find you accommodation in any Pacific Alliance country." He stopped then added with a grin, "Actually, we could find you a home in a Peon country too, but I doubt you would want that."

This seemed to amuse him, but it certainly didn't amuse me. "Are we done here?" I asked with annoyance.

He nodded. "For now, Miss Grant. Please make full use of the facilities here to make yourself comfortable, and as soon as we have more news of what's going on, I'll be in touch."

"Ooh, I just can't wait." I didn't even attempt to hide the sarcasm in my voice as I got up out of my seat. As I returned to the suite, I had no idea we would not be meeting again for a very long time.

"Miss Grant." Stepanchikov moved from her usual position just behind me to walk next to me. Her voice was low, almost conspiratorial. "I may be out of place here, but that conversation concerned me."

We were walking back to the suite alone, Taylor having remained with Drake. "What's up?" I responded, curious at this changed demeanor in the security officer.

"I take it as a personal affront that the company is targeting you for your genetic status." She said, and the irritation in her voice was apparent.

"Yeah, I'm not exactly overjoyed by it," I muttered.

"I want you to know, I'm not about to participate in anything the company does in relation to that." She sounded genuine.

103

"Is this some sort of GenMod bonding thing?" I replied sarcastically.

She stopped walking, and I did the same. "Miss Grant. I grew up during the Grozny crisis over seventy years ago. I lived through the oppression of the genetically modified. Call it a bond if you like, but we are in the same situation with limited rights."

"Oh, we have one major difference, mate." I snorted. "If you were born before Grozny, you're not illegal."

"Even more reason you need protection, Miss Grant."

"You are already protecting me, Stepanchikov," I replied, wondering where she was going with this.

"Drake just moved the goalposts, Miss Grant. You are now at risk beyond being some little rich girl. I just want you to know, as a fellow GenMod, I can move the goalposts too."

I smiled, "Glad you have my back, Stepanchikov." Although I had no idea what she meant, I would soon find out.

CHAPTER TWELVE

GOODNIGHT MOON

Bronwyn was still asleep when we returned to the suite. I told Stepanchikov to take one of the bedrooms and stay with us, and she took time to shower. A small bar was in the room, and I firmly wished I had my metabolism inhibitors. But I did not. I switched on the large telly to see if I could see some news about what was happening back in Australia. However, the lunar news network appeared more concerned about maintaining neutrality, and I couldn't get an accurate picture of what was happening. Indeed, over the next few years, the Peons controlled all media output from my homeland, and it wouldn't be for some time before I could start getting accurate news through my own sources.

"When are we going back home?" I turned to see Bron had woken up and was now sitting, looking at me questioningly with folded arms and a grim expression.

I snorted. "Home is a cluster fuck. They're going to see if they can get us into the UK or the U.S.A."

"Who is 'they'?"

I shrugged. "The bigwigs in my mum's company. Oz may be down, but the corporate wankers are still doing their thing."

"Any way we can find anything about my family?" she asked, sounding more bitter than upset.

I shook my head and nodded to the telly I had turned off. "Can't get anything on that thing, and to be honest, I think it's too early to know anything anyway."

105

"I don't like admitting that I'm scared. You have people out here, I don't. Can you assure me I won't be forgotten or pushed aside?"

I turned to look at her. "They're not my people, Bron. They're my mother's people, and while it might say on paper that I'm now responsible for them, honestly, I don't give two shits about it. Grant Industries can go fuck itself as long I get what I want."

"And just what do you want, Hannah?"

I finally grinned, "I have no fucking clue, Bron. But I will tell you, I plan to survive this, and no one better get in my fucking way."

Bron returned my grin. "Isn't that our group's motto back at Melbourne Grammar?"

My grin widened. "Too right, mate, too right."

Before we could say anything else, we were startled as the door burst open, and Taylor came running in with about four or five security men. "Sorry, ladies, but we must get out of here," she spoke rapidly. We just stared at her, startled. She looked straight at me. "When they ran your prints, they also did a D.N.A. test from the sweat on your fingers. You've been flagged as a GenMod."

"That's not possible," Stepanchikov said sharply, coming out of her room. "I checked specifically for what they were sampling when we came in. It was a standard fingerprint scanner."

I simply said, "I'm not a GenMod."

Taylor just shook her head. "Seriously, Hannah, we don't have time for this. GenMods are banned from the moon, even the legal ones. As of now, you have no legal rights here and will be shot on sight. Now, do you want to come with me, or do you wanna stand here and debate the structure of your D.N.A.?"

I stared at her wide-eyed. "No worries. I think you just made a convincing argument."

Bron was already up and at my side. However, to my utter surprise, Stepanchikov withdrew her dual pistols and trained them on Taylor and the guards. "Back off!" She demanded.

"What the fuck, Stepanchikov?" I snapped.

"They didn't take your D.N.A., Miss Grant. If Lunar control knows you're a GenMod, someone damn well told them." Stepanchikov stated.

"You are out of line, Stepanchikov," Taylor shouted at her, and chaos was unleashed as one of the guards went for his weapon, and Stepanchikov fired directly into his chest. He staggered back. His flak jacket took the brunt, but otherwise not harming him. "That was a warning," Stepanchikov growled.

"Stop!" Taylor cried nervously. "You may be right. I don't know. I swear I'm just here to help!"

"Fine!" I replied. "Get us the fuck out of here, but hey, any funny business and I will be more than happy to let Stepanchikov here blow your brains out."

Taylor took the lead, and with security personnel flanking us from all sides, we headed out into the corridor and half walked/half ran down the corridors until we came through to a docking bay. "I'm sorry, but we only have cargo transit vessels here, and it won't be as comfortable as your last ride," Taylor said, turning to face me.

"For fuck's sake, do I look like I give a shit?" I snapped back. "Can we just get aboard and get out of here." she nodded, and we continued on.

Unlike the docking bay we landed on, which could only hold one craft, multiple ships ranged from large cargo vessels to the smaller planet hoppers that were intended for carrying personnel, rather than cargo. We headed straight for one, which they had already powered up. I turned to Bron as we reached the entrance. "Bron, I really want you to come with me, but you know you don't have to. It's me they're after."

Bron hesitated but then shook her head. "Get on board, Hannah. We're wasting time."

As she said this, Taylor's radio burst into life. "Security has arrived on the base. They will be at your location within minutes." We needed no other encouragement and raced aboard the old planet hopper.

Indeed, it was not like the luxury yacht that had taken us to the moon, but the seats were comfortable, and I could not help but wonder at the size of the vessel. It was an interplanetary craft; traveling to other worlds took weeks, if not months, and there were no quarters aboard. I didn't have time to discuss it. Stepanchikov didn't allow the guards to board and almost stopped Taylor, but relented after seeing true fear in her eyes.

I strapped myself into the seat, with Bron next to Taylor, and me behind them with Stepanchikov. When we launched with thrusters and D.E. compensators, the lock had barely clicked on my safety strap. Something that would not normally be necessary on the moon, but accelerated us fast enough that we could feel the pressure even with the inertial dampeners on. This this time, I had no window to look out of, and I had no idea what was happening, but very quickly, our upward momentum changed to a forward thrust, and I knew that we had left the moon behind us.

"This is your captain." A voice boomed from the speakers in each corner of the passenger cabin. "We will soon be exiting neutral space and expect pursuit. Please stay strapped into your seats."

Both Bron and I remained quiet as we continued onward with full thrust. Everything seemed to be going well until suddenly, the ship began to jerk. "What the fuck is going on," Bron blurted out with fear in her voice.

"We're under fire," Stepanchikov shouted above the noise of the grinding of the ship's bulkheads.

I looked up at the mercuranium lined walls, and I swear I saw them buckle, but it would turn out to be my imagination, caused by the terror of the moment. We began to lurch left and right and forward and back as the pilot went into evasive maneuvers, trying to outrun whoever it was firing at us. I incorrectly assumed it was Luna security, but their jurisdiction ended at the neutral zone. We were under direct attack by Peon craft.

Then suddenly, it stopped as quickly as it started. "We caught a break." The captain came over the speakers again with the sound of relief in his voice. "We ran into a British patrol, and they engaged our pursuers. We'll be out of range before that is resolved for good or bad." Bron and I breathed a sigh of relief as if we had not been breathing through the entire event. "Please stay in your seats while I assess the damage." We sat in total silence. I couldn't help but think about how close we had come to the end of our days since my last day at Melbourne Grammar.

Eventually, the cabin door opened, and a man stepped in. He was an old and scruffy looking, typical stereotype of old cargo hauler captains. "G'day. Sorry about all the buffeting back there, but we're out of danger. I'm your pilot."

"Where are we going?" was the first thing I asked.

"I've plotted a course to Mars, but it's not the optimal time for a Martian transit. It'll take us eleven weeks, instead of the usual six."

I looked about the ship. "There are no cabins. Are we expected to stay in these seats for eleven weeks?"

The captain chuckled. "Of course not. The ship is specifically kitted out with a M.E.T. We'll be uploaded, and for you, it will appear that we arrived instantaneously."

Bron didn't like that idea at all. "Everything I've heard about those things says they're dangerous. People come out of there dead, not at all, or seriously fucked up."

The captain merely shrugged. "All forms of space travel are hazardous, Ma'am. However, you don't have a choice. This ship isn't designed to carry waking passengers. There's nowhere for you to sleep. There'ss insufficient food, and the environmental systems don't cater for long-term air recycling."

"And what do you suppose we do when we get to Mars?" I said snappily, seriously irritated by the situation. The moon was bad enough. I certainly didn't want to go to the Martian colonies.

"With all due respect, Ma'am," the captain responded. "That's not really my problem. My role here is to get you to Mars."

"Make it your problem. I'm not going to Mars. We're going back to Earth." I demanded.

Any smile or cordiality instantly left the captain. "Do you think you're the only one who has a problem with this situation?" he sneered at me, and Taylor tried to stand between us, raising her hands to calm us down. She failed. "We all have families we've left back Down Under. And getting you out while everyone back on that base will, if lucky, only be deported from the moon. You have no idea the sacrifices people have made to keep you alive; frankly, I don't think you deserve it. Now sit down and shut the fuck up."

I complied, but Bron remained standing, looking red with anger. I reached out, grabbed her arm, and pulled her down beside me. The pilot turned to Taylor. "I need to check to see if the M.E.T. is still working and wasn't damaged in that attack. Then we can upload them." Taylor nodded, and the captain turned and walked back through the door, closing it behind him.

"How dare he speak to us like that," Bron fumed. "He's just an employee."

I rested my hand on hers to calm her down and said, "oh, don't worry, Bron. He won't have a job once we get to Mars, but for now, we need him."

The one hour turned into two, and we spent most of it in silence.

When the captain finally returned, my mood had not diminished.

"Okay, we're all set. We have some damage to the ship that I have to work on, but everything is okay to upload you."

"I want transit lock codes implemented," Stepanchikov demanded.

The captain frowned. "Why?"

"Someone back there betrayed Miss Grant, and I'm going to see it doesn't happen again," she said coldly.

"What are transit lock codes?" I asked.

"Means no one can interfere with you while you are in the M.E.T.," Stepanchikov explained. "I'll be the only one who can release you."

"Sounds fair to me," Bron said, and the captain just shrugged.

As we got out of our seats again, we said nothing to the captain as he led us into a backroom. There was a circle on the floor and what looked like a camera pointing down from the ceiling. I looked at it nervously, but not as nervously as when the captain said, "you need to get undressed. No one can be uploaded with inorganic materials unless they've been filtered out."

I stared at him in wide-eyed horror. "Then you better filter them out because I'm not getting undressed, mate."

He sighed impatiently. "I'm rated to operate the M.E.T., but I'm not a M.E.T. tech. No one here has the time or the ability to do that."

"Then you can wait outside," Bron said curtly.

The captain sighed again. "And who do you think is going to upload you? I assure you I've done this a thousand times, and I'm not the slightest bit interested in seeing you unclothed."

That turned out to be untrue. I thought his eyes would pop out as I removed my clothing, and he looked at my body most inappropriately. I was not alone in his leering. He also checked out Bron, who was not a GenMod but was a shining example of the craft of the plastic surgeon and a personal trainer. She stepped on the circle first and stretched out her arms and legs at the captain's instruction. However, I couldn't help but chuckle as she turned her hand and gave him the finger just before he

hit the upload button. A bright flash of light momentarily blinded me, but it was just for a moment, for my ability to recover from such things was, well, perfect.

Bron vanished, and it was my turn, and as I stood in the circle, he hesitated a moment, inappropriately admiring my form. "You fucking pervert," I sneered at him. His smile vanished, and he angrily hit the upload button.

I opened my eyes. For me, no time had passed, but I was not aboard the shuttle. I was lying in a hospital bed. At least it looked like a hospital bed, and it turned out it was. I was in a room that looked sterile and undecorated. I felt disorientated. I looked around, and standing over me was a man in jeans, a tee shirt, and a white doctor's coat over the top. He wasn'tt a bad-looking bloke, but that was the last thing on my mind. "Okay, what the fuck happened?" I said, finding my voice dry and hoarse.

"Well, g'day, Hannah." The young man smiled at me. "First off, you're completely fine, although it was touch and go for a minute there."

"Can you just answer my question?" I responded irritably.

"Now, don't get yourself worked up, mate," he said with a grin. "There was a little problem with your ship. While the captain was trying to do repairs, it went through a major decompression."

"And the M.E.T. failed?" I asked.

111

"Not exactly." His smile faded. "As a matter of fact, it worked better than intended. Now you should prepare yourself, but basically, your craft flew straight past Mars and went into orbit around the sun."

I narrowed my eyes at him, and I sat up. "How long was I out?"

"I'm afraid you were gone for about two years."

CHAPTER THIRTEEN

— • —

UPWARDLY MOBILE HANNAH

I stared at him for a long time, trying to see if I could see deception in his eyes. "You're joking, right?" I said at last.

"I'm sorry, but I'm not." He replied softly, but he still had that whimsical smile on his face that I just wanted to slap right at that moment. "You got very lucky. You went into orbit around the sun, but with each passing day, you moved further and further away from it, reducing the amount of power the solar panels could absorb. That was also good, since the shuttle sent an automated alert when power dropped below levels that could maintain the M.E.T."

"Why didn't the captain call for help?"

"Sadly, he was in the ship when it decompressed and died instantly. I'm sorry."

"Why are you sorry?" I asked, confused.

"The loss of your captain."

I shrugged that off. "Meh. That wasn't a great loss. The man was a pig. So how did I end up here?"

He looked concerned at my flippant reaction to the death of a man, but replied, "well, fortunately, the Japanese got to you before the Peons did. They found you and your friends were still uploaded, but the signal was degrading. They removed the M.E.T. unit from the ship and contacted us."

"Who is us?" I asked, eyeing him carefully.

113

"Oh, I'm so sorry," he said cheerfully. "I didn't introduce myself." he offered me his hand, and I tentatively took it. "I'm Doctor Deacon Cooper of Grant Medical Services."

He looked surprised as I rolled my eyes, but something suddenly occurred to me. "You said you found my friends and me. There were four of us."

He looked a little taken aback by this and said gently, "Damn! I'm sorry to say there were only three viable signals that were retrievable. Anyone else in there had suffered total pattern degradation. The computer system probably simply deleted one, when it realized it had to maintain power. It's a failsafe, so at least some of the crew will survive."

"Are you going to keep me in suspense, Doctor Cooper?" I asked, getting quite annoyed now.

"Oh, please call me Deacon. After all, you're technically my boss." He beamed at me.

At that point, I just totally lost it. "Who the fuck are the other survivors!?"

"Oh, that was Bronwyn Donovan and Emberlynn Stepanchikov. Although retrieving Donovan was a tad more problematic."

"In what way?" I said, hoping that my relief that it was my friend that survived, and not Emily Taylor didn't show.

"Your signals were quite degraded. However, you and Miss Stepanchikov's genetically modified D.N.A. reformed you intact."

"I am not a GenMod," I said automatically out of sheer habit, and he chuckled at that, but it quickly faded as he saw the glare on my face.

He chose to change the subject. "Unfortunately, Miss Donovan was not so lucky and had to undergo multiple surgeries to save her life."

"Is she going to survive?"

"Oh, she'll survive, but we've had to replace some organs and one of her limbs with artificial ones. Getting approval was quite difficult as Australian medical insurance is not exactly valid nowadays."

"Fuck the insurance." I snapped. "You said you were Grant Industries. I'm Hannah Grant, for fuck's sake, and you're going to do whatever she needs."

"Well, a few things have changed since you've been gone," he said softly. "Your mother and sister are officially listed as dead, although it was never confirmed. And last year, you were officially listed as dead too. You have only one living relative, but she's apparently has gone off grid and is also assumed dead."

"Stacey," I said softly.

"Indeed. The last record of her was signing up with the United States Navy, and then she disappeared from all records. It is possible that she is involved in some sort of covert activity, but the chances are that she died somewhere in the line of duty."

It suddenly dawned upon me what he was getting to. "Who owns Grant Industries now?"

"Well, most of your shares have been floated on the stock market and reinvested into the company, but a lot of the corporation was bought up by Drake Tanner. He pretty much controls everything."

"I thought he already did," I said, pulling back the bed sheets and climbing out. I was covered in a hospital gown and looked around for my clothes.

"Oh, previously, he had to get board approval for all major decisions. Now he owns enough stock that he doesn't need to."

"Do you think you can arrange for me to have some clothes or something?" I said like I was addressing a servant. "I don't think I can walk around like this."

"Of course." He clicked a pin on his lapel and spoke into it, asking someone at the other end exactly what I had just asked for.

"What is happening back in Australia?" I asked.

Deacon sighed. "Now, that's not a happy story. It remains occupied and has been officially declared part of the European Union, although obviously, the Pacific Alliance doesn't recognize that. The Peons don't let any news come in or out, but rumors are, we are still fighting back."

I reached up and rubbed my temples between my thumb and forefinger. I had what I assumed was a headache. Never having had one before, I had nothing to compare it to. "My head aches."

"Don't worry about it. We upgraded your nanobots, and your superior repair systems are working overtime. You'll be perfectly normal in a few weeks, and your eidetic memory will return."

I was about to say, 'I'm not a GenMod' one more time, but I realized it was stupid. Of course, he knew. He was a doctor, after all. Someone

115

I had avoided all my life, since I never got sick. "So, nothing in the war has changed, as per usual?" I asked.

"Well, apart from the fact we're losing, no, nothing."

At that point, a young nurse walked in carrying a bag. She smiled at Doctor Cooper and then at me before handing me the bag. I said nothing to her, and she raised a slight eyebrow before walking out. I opened the bag and pulled out a pair of slacks, shirt, underwear, and a pair of runners. They were not exactly high fashion, but they would do.

"I'ill leave you to it." He went to leave, but I stopped him.

"No, don't go. Just turn around," I instructed. I wasn't finished with him. He nodded and did as he was told as I quickly pulled on the garments. As I dressed, I continued to question him. "Where am I?"

"You're aboard the cruise liner, the Twilight Wanderer."

I smiled, for that was pretty much the best ship in the Solar System, not for speed or power, but for the sheer first-class luxury of the place. And, of course, it was owned by the family subsidiary, Grant Leisure. But my smile quickly diminished as I realized the family no longer owned the company. "Can I assume the family suite is still available?" I asked, deciding to see if my name still carried any authority.

"I can certainly find out for you." He replied.

"You can turn back now. I'm dressed." I instructed as I walked over to a mirror to look at myself. Something was not quite right. Sure, my hair was a fucking mess. But there was more than that. I turned back to Deacon. "I look older."

"Your matrix had degraded. You lost about naught point naught, naught, nine percent of your body mass. Your nanobots and healing matrix compensated for the time loss and restructured you. It only added a couple of years."

"You just took away two years of my life?" I looked at him, horrified.

He gave me a quizzical look and a grin. "You're kidding me, right?"

I tilted my head and looked at him with irritation. And he realized I wasn't kidding. "Miss Grant, deny it as much as you will, but you are genetically modified, and as such, cells that die off in normal people are constantly reproduced in you. You won't age beyond twenty-five or six."

I blushed slightly as I realized how stupid I had been. Barring a violent death, I was immortal. "So legally, I'm now twenty?"

"Well, the normal process would be to file for a court order to redefine your age as most people do if they spend a lot of time traveling in an M.E.T. However, you're currently stateless, unless you plan to return to Australia and submit to European rule."

I sighed and let everything sink in. "You know something, Deacon. I think I want to go and check into that suite, get something to eat, and then have a good sit down with a lawyer. Are Jenkins and Bath still our family attorneys?"

"I have no idea. However, I'm not quite ready to discharge you. I'd like you to stay for a couple of days to ensure everything is fine with you."

I just smiled at him. "You're more than welcome to come with me, Deacon, but I'm not staying in here."

"Well, I have other duties, Miss Grant. You are not my only patient."

"You're the ship's doctor. A passenger ship, at that. I'm sure you can allocate someone else to hand out the space sickness pills." I said sarcastically.

"Actually, I'm not the ship's doctor." He replied. "I'm a specialist in M.E.T. related trauma. I was brought on board specifically for you and your friends."

"So, Bron and Stepanchikov are your only patients?"

"Indeed. Although Miss Stepanchikov has already been discharged."

"Well, if you could arrange for someone to escort me to the family suite and let Stepanchikov know where to find me, I would appreciate it."

An hour later, I was in the family suite of the most exclusive spaceship in the Solar System.

What can I say about the Twilight Wanderer, the ship that was to become my home for the next three years? Grant Industries hadn't built it, and it had flown under the banner of an American company for ten years. That was until my grandfather, then head of Grant Industries, bought out the company that owned it.

When my mother took over, she planned to rename it the Marcia Grant, but it had become such an iconic ship that marketing told her it would be a mistake. She was over a mile in length and held the record as the largest ship ever built, which she held until the construction of the U.S.S. Constitution.

She was a leisure cruiser but with a twist. Only affordable by the extremely rich, the ship was filled with the usual elements of exclusive finery. Five-star restaurants, casinos, and the latest in high-tech actual reality gaming suites. It had shopping malls with high-end merchandise and even grocery stores.

You see, unlike the old ocean-going liners that had inspired its construction, the Twilight Wanderer had one aspect that no earthbound ship would ever encounter. The ship would take people to the outer planets, which could take six months to a year to reach the destination, just so the wealthy could look out of the observation domes to see things, such as the rings of Saturn or the red eye of Jupiter. Since no one generally would take a year or two years of vacation, the ship required facilities for the rich to continue conducting their business. Thus, we had suites of offices rented out at exorbitant prices, and rather than cabin rooms, people rented apartments where they effectively lived out their daily lives.

In some cases, company owners moved into the Twilight Wanderer and made it home, as they conducted their business across the Solar System. It was a living, breathing community of around twenty thousand people, including crew. The one major difference being, this little town in space was entirely under corporate control.

It also undertook a second role as a cargo carrier containing vast storage facilities on the lower decks, along with a fleet of shuttles to deliver the cargo to the destinations ensuring no interruption of its billionaire passengers. However, there was one severe restriction in that we couldn't carry any military supplies.

Although the ship managed to continue its activities during the war due to the fact there was a convention not to attack Civilian ships, that rule would be set aside if it was believed we were in any way aiding in the conflict.

The Grant family suite was permanently reserved for us. When not in use, it was closed down, and that's the way it stayed, mainly as my mother rarely left the Earth.

I did, however, find it very strange that my mother, who nearly always favored the modern over the old, had had our sweet modeled on the Palace of Versailles. Everything looked like it was the seventeenth century, with gold inlays, mirrors and all the finery of French nobility. It took up about a fifth of the top deck, which considering the ship was a mile long, is a considerable size. It had

seven staterooms with their own bathrooms, lounges, and offices for work. Of course, it was fully staffed with stewards and company clerics whenever a family member was aboard. Even what would become my office looked like a royal residence. The monitor on my desk was an old knightly gold frame, and my communications device looked like an old 1920's phone. Of course, 1920's phones didn't fit in with pre-revolutionary France, but since they didn't have phones back then, it was a compromise. There was even a kitchen, where a chef could prepare meals for the family, A rather extensive gymnasium, and even a movie theater. You could pretty much live in the suite and be constantly entertained and sustained without stepping outside, which is almost what Bronwyn and I did for the next three years. I rarely had cause to leave.

When I arrived, the place was filled with stewards prepping everything for our use. The head steward was most flustered, since they usually had notice that a family member was to arrive and could do all of this before we arrived. He offered to show us down to one of the lounges on another deck so we could wait until they finished, but I declined. So, instead, he introduced me to Kerry Anthony, a girl not much older than me who was to be assigned as my personal maid or servant, whatever you prefer to call it, who would be responsible for seeing it to all my needs. Of course, this was not unusual for me as I had a similar setup back home in Melbourne and considered it very normal. I was shown into the bedroom that would have been my mother's, and again, just like everything, it was done out like the French Renaissance. A large four-poster bed on which you could probably fit about five people. To my great delight, it was a smart bed that would mold itself around me in the most optimal comfort a human could imagine. They also showed me a large office where I could work from, not that, at the time, I had any intention of doing so. Again, it was large and ornately designed, with a plush carpet that I would soon find out was so delightful to walk on in bare feet that I would frequently kick off my shoes whenever I went in there.

However, despite all this luxury and comfort, it wasn't home, at least, not then. Although in time, it would become so. For the first three years, I totally resented being there, and when we ultimately lost the ship years later, I would come to miss it. However, that is a story for another day and one that I believe my friend, Tabitha Makepeace, will tell you. For now, all you need to know is that this was to become my new home at the base of operations. Although, at the time, I considered it just a place to lay my head, until I worked out a way to get back to the Earth as fast as possible.

CHAPTER FOURTEEN

— • —

THE LEADER OF THE PACK

I must admit my mind was a well of emotions and thoughts. For everyone around me, it had been two years since Australia fell. For me, it was yesterday and was still fresh in my mind. I was not sure what I would do.

I do not know why I avoided visiting Bron. I guess there was a modicum of guilt that kept me at bay. I was reunited with Stepanchikov, who knew little more than me about what was going on as she had only been up a day before me.

The company assigned Luca Ramirez, one of the corporate executives who served aboard the ship, to bring me up to speed on everything happening. I didn't do anything for a couple of days other than watch the news and stuff myself with pastries from the ship's five-star catering service. With my enhanced metabolism, I never put on weight, but usually, I would eat healthily as was fashionably appropriate.

The more I learned about the occupation of my country, the more annoyed I got. Officially Australia had a government still operating in Canberra, but it was no more than a puppet of the Peons. The Pacific Alliance did not recognize it and still considered Australia to be a warzone. I was extremely pissed that the Pacific Alliance had done nothing to liberate the country, at least as far as I could see. Indeed, the Alliance appeared to be losing the war. Mars, which once had colonies from all nations, was now firmly under control of the Peons. Australian colonies throughout the Solar System had been taken over by the Peons or absorbed by the Americans. Any Australian that was not still Down Under was a stateless unwanted vagabond of the Solar System. Many had signed up with other Pacific Alliance countries, predominantly the U.S.A., Japan, and Britain. Australia had become a forgotten country with forgotten people.

I can't honestly say I was a patriot who flew the Southern Cross and sang Waltzin' Matilda over a barbie. But I got increasingly pissed as I became aware of everything that had happened over the last two years.

My mother's company was the only thing Australian still going strong. Grant Industries was still a powerhouse, although now officially registered as an American company, which for me, was intolerable. I've already made it very clear that I had no interest in participating in the family business. But as I saw the company profiting from the war, rather than doing anything to help the nation that gave birth to it, I got angrier and angrier.

When I asked for a lawyer, they tried to appoint me one of the company ones, but honestly, I didn't trust them to have my best interests at heart, especially considering the plan that was ruminating in my head. Finally, I got a good night's sleep, and just like my mother, I rose at dawn and summoned Luca Ramirez to meet with me. It was an old trick of my mother's. Get her people up at the crack of dawn or even randomly during the night. People were more malleable when they were half asleep. Luca arrived, and I met him in my new office in what I will now call my apartment. He had hurriedly dressed and made himself as presentable as possible, but he couldn't hide the tiredness in his eyes.

"I was looking at the stock prices for the company this morning," I said, sitting back and drinking my coffee, of which I did not offer him one. "Share prices have been in decline for the last week or two. Can you tell me the reason behind that.?"

I felt sure I knew the answer, but I wanted to hear it from him, and he shifted uncomfortably in his seat before responding. "Well, Miss Grant. It is because you're back."

I was right, and I allowed myself a smile, but only briefly. "Can you elaborate on that?" Again, I knew the answer, but I wanted confirmation. I hadn't studied business, but I had been around my mother all my life, and she had thought of little else.

"The company has been without a Grant for two years, and people are unsure of your intentions now you're back. No one knows if you'll assume control of the company and remove Drake from office."

Again, I was right, but I now turned to a question I truly had no idea about the answer to. "And what is the stock market's opinion on me doing just that?"

"Well, if I could be completely frank with you, Miss Grant, that's the fear. It's known that you don'tt have a business background beyond your relationship with your mother. The last time you were seen in public, you were just eighteen years old, and whatever the law may say, you're still eighteen years old, at least in life experience."

That was the question I needed to be answered to finalize my decision. I didn't want to take over the company, but I did want it to continue to be successful in putting my plans in motion. I let the silence linger between us to make him more uncomfortable. Again, this was tactic I had watched my mother use. Though obviously, I didn't trust Luca. He was appointed by a man who was probably having a fit that I had just come back from the dead. Eventually, I said, "arrange a conference call between myself and Drake if you would, please."

"Well, it's not really my place."

I raised a hand to stop him. "It's not a suggestion, Luca. If you don't have access to him, find someone who does, and ensure he knows it's in his interest to meet with me today."

As he left the room, I wondered if my gamble would pay off.

"Miss Grant, it is good to see you. We were most delighted to learn of your survival." Drake's image on the vast television screen in my apartment's lounge accentuated every nook and cranny of his face in super high definition. Despite his age, he wasn't a bad looking bloke. However, I wasn't stupid, and I knew that my sudden resurrection was not a delight for him, and I made it clear.

"Please do me the same courtesy as you would, my mother. Spare me the platitudes, and let's be frank with each other." I replied with a mixture of ice and venom.

"As you wish, Miss Grant," Drake calmly replied. "But please, you requested this meeting. I'd like to hear what you have to say."

"First of all, let me say that you need not fear. As long as I get what I want out of this conversation, I will not be coming after the company."

"Oh, Miss Grant, I don't fear that as you don't have the resources to fight us in court. We can drag it out for years, and to be frank, everything you have right now is at the courtesy of the company. You have no money, and as a GenMod, you have no status. The Grant family is dead; you are just some flotsam that remains."

If he had intended for that to intimidate me, he was very much mistaken, for I pretty much already knew that would be his stand. "Oh, my dear Sir. I don't need money to take you to court. I just need to offer a humble one percent of the company stock to any lawyer who wins me control of it, and they will be queuing up from Venus to the Kuiper Belt to represent me for that multibillion-dollar prize."

That took the smug smile off the supercilious git's face. "We can still drag it on for years, and you get nowhere, Miss Grant." He said defensively. "I am offering a generous one-off payment for you to sign a waiver giving up any and all interest in the company."

"Don't insult me, Drake. I am Marcia Grant's daughter, and while I never paid any interest in the company, I did watch my mother. Your stock prices are falling due to the issue of my sudden resurrection. Do you think that would improve or increase if I file litigation against you?"

"We had an agreement to set up a trust fund for you. Do you plan to renege upon that arrangement?"

"Oh, Drake. You fucked that up when you turned me over to the Luna authorities." I raised a hand to stop him as he was about to protest. "No, no! Don't try to deny it. It just makes you look like a bigger moron than you already do."

I'm sure his face went ashen as I watched him, but his smile quickly returned. "I'm listening to your counteroffer, Miss Grant."

"I will settle for ten percent of your stock. a seat on the board and this starship for my personal use. I also want my own company division with no board oversight. I do what I want unwatched and unhampered."

124

He frowned at that last one. "You want the Twilight Wanderer, the largest and most profitable ship in the Solar System, to be your personal yacht?"

"Not exactly. It will continue with its current duties, and indeed Grant Industries will still take the profit from it. However, I'm to be left alone, and there will be no corporate observation aboard this ship. You will see no reports on what happens on board, beyond booking the passengers and arranging the flight plans."

"That is extremely odd. You must agree."

"Odd or not, I don't give a shit what you think," I responded easily. "These are my terms, and they are not negotiable."

"I agree to your terms, but I'm only willing to give you five percent, which is not negotiable." He replied

I rolled my eyes and sighed. "You think you hold some of the cards here, don't you? If I take you to court, the share price will continue to fall. We stand to face a risk of a takeover from a competitor. I don't think you want to risk that, Drake. However, if it helps your ego to think you gain something out of this, I'm willing to drop to eight percent, and that really is final."

"I said five percent, Miss Grant, and I'm not wavering on that. That is still multi-billions of dollars every year."

"I'm sure it is, but it's also a level that I will remain at risk of you being able to have me removed from the board. It would be best if you didn't have that option. Eight percent or this conversation is over now." There was a long pause until I added, "Or I file a claim for one hundred percent and watch Grant Industries burn underneath you."

"You would destroy your mother's legacy?" Drake snorted. "Do you not think she would still be proud of what this company is?"

"Don't go playing the mother card on me, Drake. I don't give a shit what she thinks. However, she wouldn't be proud of it being a company that doesn't have a Grant sitting in your chair. I'm getting bored of this conversation. Do we have an agreement or not? This is really the last time we are going to even discuss this."

There was a long pause, and then Drake sighed. "I will agree, but I have one condition. You'll sign a contract never to try to remove me as chairman of the board."

I pondered that, for in doing so, I would handicap myself. Drake could ignore me forever more. "I would agree with one stipulation. Upon your death, your shares will revert to me, and I'll have control of the company."

"You expect me to leave my family penniless?" he said coldly.

"You have no children, Drake, and I'm fairly certain your wife is set up for life. I hardly see her coming in as the board's new chairman upon your demise. You know, as a GenMod, I'll still be around a long time after you, and I'm simply ensuring my future."

"A GenMod can't 't be chairman without...."

"Leave me to worry about that." I sounded confident like I had a plan to deal with that situation. To be totally frank, I did not and was just ensuring I didn't burn any potential bridges.

"Have Luca send me the details of your attorneys, and we'll get the paperwork done. Well played, Miss Grant. You are certainly your mother's daughter."

As his image disappeared from the screen, I couldn't help but wonder if that was a compliment or insult, but I sat back, feeling quite proud of what I had achieved.

I later engaged the services of an attorney that had absolutely no connection to Grant Industries. That wasn't easy, considering the reach of the company. The guy was young and fairly inexperienced, but I preferred that to someone who would give me a lot of shit over what I wanted to do.

It was a couple of days after I met with Drake, and I was still waiting for all the paperwork to be completed, when Deacon visited me.

"I just wanted to let you know that Miss Donovan is ready to be discharged from the hospital wing."

I had dreaded this. I had literally put Bron out of my mind, not wishing to see her after the injuries he had described. But she was the only friend I had now, and to be honest, I wanted her at my side. I had looked up what happened to the old gang. My mates from Melbourne Grammar. Isla had been listed as dead, as had Patrick. I still hoped that Sarah was alive, but she was listed as missing. It is more likely her body had never been found, or if it had, it was one of the thousands that remained unidentified.

With some trepidation, I headed down to Bron's room in the hospital. When I entered her room, I audibly gasped when I saw her. She was going through a small bag, and she stood beside her bed, and she looked up at me with a start, not having heard me enter. She at once turned away from me. he entire left side of her torso was no longer human. Her arm was missing, replaced by metal and wires of an artificial prosthetic. But what stood out was the metal plate covering the side of her head and about a third of her face.. "You're a fucking robot." I found myself saying. She looked back at me, shocked by the statement, and then, to my surprise, she burst out laughing.

"Go fuck yourself, Hannah Grant." She stepped over to me. "Why the hell didn't you come and visit me?"

I shrugged. "I've been busy."

"Don't give me that. You just didn't want to see this." She pointed to her face and the glowing red eye of the artificial lens that looked back at me. Kind of ironic, but it looked pretty similar to Stacey. The main difference being half of her face was covered in metal.

"Well, there is that, too," I admitted with another shrug. "Sorry, mate, but you're just not cute enough to be in the gang anymore."

She laughed. "You know. Lying here, knowing I'm never going to be prom queen, really makes you think about priorities."

"Well, considering we don't do prom, you'll never be prom queen anyway." I chuckled. "Anyway, this is only temporary. With my resources, we can have all that hardware hidden and have you looking human again."

"That'll take several years of different surgeries, and I'm not sure I want to go through that."

"You want to go through life looking like that?" I said. My vanity finds such an idea horrific.

The smile faded from her face, and she said, "I found out my mom and dad are still alive. Both my brothers are dead, killed fighting back. I'm going back to Australia, mate. I want to be with my family."

"Wouldn't you rather help fight back than just go into what is basically a prison?" I asked.

She narrowed her single eye and looked at me questioningly. "What did you have in mind?"

127

I was about to answer her, and then I thought twice about it. "No, not here. Come back to my apartment."

Thirty minutes later, she was sitting in my lounge. I had a steward make up a room for her, as she agreed to stay with me until she made her final decisions. "I want to help the fight back. I want to do what I can for other Aussies, roaming the Solar System with no home."

"Fuck Hannah, what do you think you can do?" she said, sneering at my idea.

"Quite a lot, I think. I'm back in the family business and have a division that will receive no oversight. I'll be left alone to do what I want."

"And how is that going to help anyone?" Bron snorted derisively.

"Grant Industries is a fucking powerful organization." I snapped back. "Hell, back in Alice Springs, they not only found us but also got us out of there. The company security division is a veritable equivalent of a country's intelligence service. We own half the bloody ships in the Solar System." Okay, that was an exaggeration, but we had a hell of a lot of ships. "We have fingers in every pie. Leisure and recreation, military hardware, high-tech computer systems. We can make a difference by using my division as a front." I paused to take a breath and forced myself to calm down. "If we make the right contacts, we can ship weaponry, communications or any other type of fucking hardware into Australia to those who are putting their lives on the line to liberate our country. We can unite those out here, we'll find them, and find them a new home until we can return to Earth and go back Down Under."

"It's a nice plan, Hannah. You almost convinced me that you can do it, but where do I fit in?"

"You're the only person here that I trust. I want you here at my side. I want you to advise me, and I want you to take care of things."

She rolled the only eye that she could. "You want me to be your personal assistant?"

"No, Bron, I want you to be my chief executive. The only thing I know about business is what I watched my mother do. Hell, I'd have trouble organizing a keg party." I sighed, looking down at my expensive leather patent shoes, and said meekly, "I need you, mate. And that's the honest truth."

A thin smile crossed the side of her face not covered in chrome. "I think you have a deal, mate. Let's see what we can do."

CHAPTER FIFTEEN

— • —

INDUSTRIAL ACTION

The Twilight Wanderer was an ultramodern luxury cruise liner. It was designed with one goal in mind, and that was to fleece the wealthy and powerful of as much money as possible.

It had managed to continue in its career throughout the war, thanks to an unwritten rule of not attacking civilian vessels. I had even heard rumors that the ship would sit on the outskirts of battles, so its passengers could watch the destruction for entertainment. War is stupid.

With Drake's agreement, this vast vessel of opulence was now mine. I had no actual planned use for it other than to live here. The family suite took up one-fifth of one such deck, which was pretty vast, considering the ship was over a mile long. It was more than a residential area. While my living quarters were the size of a luxurious Melbourne apartment, offices, gymnasiums, swimming pools, and other resources were also available.

It's hard to wrap your head around how vast Grant Industries is.

Even the companies we didn't own, we owned substantial shares in. Just enough to stave off a monopolies investigation, but enough to have that virtual monopoly.

So, where am I going with this? The reality was, I was way out of my depth, even running a division of my mother's company.

Numerous Grant Industries executives were aboard the Twilight Wanderer for various reasons, from vacations to overseeing the running of the leisure division, and I summoned them together to perform as some sort of company board.

131

That first meeting was quite uncomfortable. None of the executives had particularly worked together before and came from all areas of the organization.

However, at my request, they managed to put together reports on the resources available to my small company division.

The most senior of these executives was Maxwell Erickson. He was head of the British sports division and was on board as part of a vacation with his family. He naturally took the lead due to his position and headed up our first meeting.

You could cut the tension with a knife as Bron and I entered. Everyone was unsure of what was going on now that the young society girl appeared to be taking over. I readily admit I had no idea myself, as I took a seat at the head of the table with Bron sitting just to the side of me on the adjacent corner.

There was silence as everyone looked at me, and I realized I was supposed to lead the meeting. I quickly passed the buck on that. "I'd like to thank everyone for taking the time to be here. These are interesting times, and I hope we can get organized." I looked down the table at Erickson, who studied me carefully at the other end. "Mr. Erickson, I understand you have a report which will bring me up to speed on everything."

He looked at me for a long uncomfortable moment, before looking down at his tablet, and saying, "I have a basic summary, but it would take quite a while to give you a full inventory, even if that was possible."

"Why wouldn't it be possible?" Bron asked.

Erickson looked at her and then looked at me questioningly. "This is Bronwyn Donovan, who will collaborate closely with me as we move forward," I said, securing her authority. "Please cooperate with her and answer any questions she may have."

"The parent company is dividing resources for reasons I personally do not comprehend, separating eight percent under the direct authority of Miss Grant. Eight percent is still multi-billions of assets throughout the Solar System. It's a project that will take some months to complete, and a lot of legal issues that come with it."

"Understood." I replied, "let's stick with the disposition of our Australian assets for now."

Erickson stared me again, and it was starting to become quite irritating. "There are no Australian assets. Everything that was salvageable from the Australian invasion is now registered within the United States, Japan, or Britain."

"Surely that is just a technicality," Bron said almost sneeringly. "That is literally little more than crossing out the name Australia on documentation and writing in the United States. The assets still exist."

"That is the case for any Australian registered assets outside the mainland, but obviously, we have lost access to our astrodomes and Industries based in Australia."

"Are we just talking to some legal mumbo jumbo here?" I said irritably. "I'm looking for what we have coming in and out of Australia. I'm not interested in the corporate structure."

"Then frankly, Miss Grant, I don't understand the question. Grant Industries is a multifaceted organization structured along many lines of subsidiaries, all of which were reorganized when the parent country was changed from Australia to the United States. Officially we have nothing that is legally considered Australian anymore. Australia is a nonentity." He did not look at all apologetic at my reaction to that statement.

"Oh, Mr. Erickson, I can assure you that we are still very much an Australian company. I don't give a fuck what the paperwork says." I said, much to the shock of those around me.

"I think, Mr. Erickson, that you don't have the ability to follow through with the vision that Miss Grant has for this division of this company," Bron said softly, and honestly, I wasn't sure where she was going with this. But I let it go.

"Considering I don't know what that vision is, Miss Donovan, I think that's a rather strange judgment call."

"And I think you just made my point." Bron looked around the table. "Are any of you actually Australian?"

Just under half the assembled group raised their hands. This was not a surprise, considering most corporate appointments hadn't been made in my homeland.

"With your permission Hannah, I would like to ask all the non-Australians to leave at this point. Mr. Erickson, please leave your report with us."

The assembled board looked at each other and slowly began to gather their things, and headed towards the door. Erickson remained in his seat, staring at Bron and then looking at me. "Do you have any idea what you're doing, Miss Grant?"

Before I could make a response to that, Bron said simply, "your services are no longer required here, Mr. Erickson. Thank you very much for your attendance."

He stared at her again, then slowly shook his head with a patronizing sigh and began gathering his things. As he got to his feet, Bron said, "I asked you to leave your report behind. Please put the tablet back down."

He turned back to us, looked at each of us in turn, then at the tablet, and seemed to weigh it in his hand before placing it back down on the table and walking out.

The six remaining executives were now looking incredibly uncomfortable. "I know this all appears weird and strange but bear with us," Bron told them. "Anything that is now said in this room, stays in this room. After you hear us out, if you wanna walk out that door, you're good to go, and we'll never mention it again." She had their full attention now. However, Bronwyn looked to me to speak, and I frankly had no idea what to say. She smiled and then looked back at the assembled team.

"This division of Grant Industries now has one simple goal. We'll use all our resources to do what we can to aid resistance forces back Down Under. Our only goal is anything and everything we can do to help them."

As she spoke, I studied the reactions of those assembled. Some were concerned, and some looked excited at the chance of some payback. "That is an interesting idea, Miss Donovan." said a young man. "However, we all have our own jobs in various aspects of the company and are only here in an advisory capacity at Miss Grant's request."

"And you can walk out of here right now and go back to those jobs making money for a bunch of Yanks," Bron replied. "Or you can stay here with Hannah and help our people."

"You don't have to decide now," I said in the silence that followed. "Take a day or two to think about it and let us know. However, everything we do here will be classified and secret. Nothing, not even how I like to take my tea, will be reported back to the parent company. I will expect a hundred percent loyalty to this division, and this division alone."

Again, there was silence, and Bron said, "let's meet here again in two days at the same time."

We watched as they filed out, and once the door closed, I looked at Bron. "Bloody hell, girl, you certainly know what you're doing."

Bron laughed. "My family's business may not be as big as yours, Han, but unlike you, I plan to follow in my family's footsteps."

"You know, mate, I think you should be the C.E.O. of this adventure. I honestly have no clue what I'm doing." I said honestly.

Bron grinned, "Are you sure you can afford me?" she said jokingly.

I chuckled, "I have no idea, mate. You tell me." I said with a shrug.

There is one other factor I need to tell you about before we proceed. Emberlynn Stepanchikov would go on to become my most loyal employee. While Bron would go on to run the company division, Stepanchikov became head of my security division and the brains behind our Australian resistance plans. She also became the major reason I am still alive today, but I'll tell you more about that later.

It would turn out that all the Australians who had been in attendance would agree to join us. Bronwyn disappeared into meetings with lawyers to ultimately tell me, but we were now a legal entity known as New Generation Concepts, a division of Grant Industries.

Cargo hauling was about ten percent of our operations, and it became our primary concern, as it was the method with which we could supply Australian resistance forces. However, neither Bron nor I knew the first thing about smuggling or resistance fighting.

I found myself quite surprised when I looked into our security division, and one morning over breakfast with Bron, I said to her,

135

"This doesn't make sense. It virtually looks like we supply mercenaries and private armies."

Bron grinned, "yes, well, we don't use that terminology, as that would be illegal in nearly all countries. But effectively, yes." She paused to take a sip of her tea. "You really don't know how powerful your mother's company is, do you?"

I sh rugged, "I never really took time to think about it, Bron."

"I think we can make a difference back home," she said, her tone now soft and serious. "We just have to ensure we don't draw the attention of either the Peon or even our own Alliance governments."

"But where do we even start?" I said back, almost pouting as I said it.

"I suggest we try to contact Crocker. I don't even know if he's still alive or what's happening, but if he is, I'm pretty certain he'll be pretty established by now."

"Do you have any idea how you can do that?"

"Nope, so I plan to ask Stepanchikov to see if she can track him down. She's not an Aussie, so I'm not sure how much to tell her."

"Trust her," I replied. "She's proven herself."

Bron arranged for us to meet with Stepanchikov that afternoon, while I had to respond to another issue. The captain of the Twilight Wanderer had made numerous attempts to meet with me, and I had been too busy to respond. I didn't realize it would be as big an issue as it was.

Captain Tate was an older man who appeared to me to be past retirement age. One of the problems of being genetically modified and looking like a perpetually young cheerleader, is it is very difficult for people to take us seriously. Tate looked almost startled when he took me into his ready room by the bridge.

"Thank you for taking the time to meet with me, Miss Grant. I felt the need to establish how everything will work now."

"To be quite honest with you, Captain, I didn't see there would be any sort of change."

"Well, the ship is no longer part of Grant Leisure; we no longer receive all instructions from the parent company."

"Surely you must be scheduled for operations months ahead of now?"

"Indeed, we are, but many crew members think this will interfere with their careers and would like to return to Earth and look for alternative employment on other ships now."

I sighed softly. "Why must everybody make things complicated?"

"If I could be candid, Miss Grant, you're an unknown entity to everybody. The last time you were even seen was in a TV show, where people followed you to different parties. It's extremely hard to trust someone who doesn't appear to have any experience in running a corporation."

I snorted at that. "I don't need trust, Captain. I'm not a politician trying to win favor with the public. I do, however, expect obedience."

The captain frowned. "Define obedience, Miss Grant?"

I glared at him, bemused. "I don't comprehend your question, Captain," I said with obvious sarcasm. "If you don't understand the word obedience, I suggest you look it up."

"The simplicity with which you put things shows you don't really understand what you're doing. The Twilight Wanderer operates under maritime law. You may be my employer, but on board this ship, all authority resides with me."

"That kind of contradicts the employer and employee relationship, does it not?" I sneered, not sure if I believed him.

"That may be so. But it has been the way of things with ships for thousands of years. I want to clarify that you won't be running things here."

"Oh, Captain, if that's how you want to do it, that's perfectly fine with me." I smiled sweetly. "The one thing that I am clear of, though, is that I could fire you at a moment's notice and replace you with someone else. So yes, you can have all the authority here that you like, but if you piss me off, then we'll part ways."

"In that case, Miss Grant, with all due respect, you can have my resignation with immediate effect."

***

137

"He can't do that." Mathew Baker was the young attorney I had engaged. It was less than an hour after I had met with the captain. I had hurried back to Bron to tell her our new problem. She had summoned him into a meeting with us the moment I told her about the captain's resignation. "He's quite right about the maritime law," The solicitor told me. "But he also cannot simply abandon his position while in the middle of a cruise. The problem is he is fully aware of this, so I don't know what he's playing at."

"This doesn't seem like some simple whim," Bron pondered. "It seems to me there is more behind this than just a pissed-off ship's captain."

"I think you're right," Baker said. "It seems to me more like someone is trying to undermine confidence in Miss Grant and has brought the captain in on it."

"Are you honestly saying there's some conspiracy against me?" I said with a sigh.

"Well, I'm not totally sure, but it would appear that way," said Bron, and Baker agreed. I sat back and shook my head. "This is the type of bullshit I did not want to get involved in. But hey, someone wants to go to war with Hannah Grant. I'll be more than happy to oblige them."

Rumors of the instability of my division of the company continue to spread. More and more staff aboard the Twilight Wanderer were becoming uneasy. I freely admit that I was in way over my head. I may have been legally twenty on paper, but in reality, I was still just eighteen and had not even graduated high school. My sister Stacey was probably more qualified to run a Grant Industries division than I was.

Morale on board was at an all-time low and started to become reflected in the service provided. So, customer complaints started to come in.

I couldn't help but get pissed off that people were complaining about what I consider to be petty things, but as far as I was concerned, my country had just fallen yesterday. It had been two years for the rest of the Solar System, but for Bron and me, it was still fresh, and we were running out of patience.

Bronwyn met with the captain several times, but he was uninterested in resolving the problems.

I released several statements Bron wrote, assuring people of their jobs and future careers, but to no avail. As the Twilight Wanderer set course back to Earth at the end of its cruise, we were facing the possibility of no longer having a crew and being stranded.

CHAPTER SIXTEEN

RADIO FREE AUSTRALIA

Baker became a constant companion at our breakfast meetings in my suite. It was his answer to a statement by Bron that made me realize who was actually behind this. "I always thought the crew were contracted and couldn't just quit without cause," she said almost casually.

"That's completely true," Baker replied. "But they're not quitting. They're all simply applying for transfers."

"Then why can't we just simply decline the transfers?" Bron responded with a frown.

"Unfortunately, that's where everything is becoming somewhat complicated. They're employed by the subsidiary of Grant Leisure, which this ship is no longer a part of. When the parent company transferred the ship to you, they didn't transfer the crew's contracts."

I couldn't help but grin at the audacity of it. "So, Drake is playing silly buggers."

"Well, not exactly the wording I would use, but essentially accurate," Baker nodded.

"He's effectively going to leave us stranded in port," Bron hissed.

"This is no different than when my mother had to deal with the unions," I said, trying to recall the various issues my mother had dealt with over the years. I then looked up at Baker. "Thank you. I think Miss Donovan and I can take it from here."

The dismissal was clear, and he simply nodded and took his leave of us.

141

Once the door closed behind him, I looked at Bron. "Behind all of this, there must be rabble-rousers that Drake is using. Deal with the rabble-rousers, and any issue may very well go away."

"And how do you propose to do that?" Bron frowned.

"Well, that all comes down to seeing if we have Grant Industries security on our side. I think it's time we had another conversation with Emberlynn Stepanchikov," I said with a smirk, as I poured myself another cup of tea.

Over the weeks, Stepanchikov had become more comfortable in my company, and instead of standing like some sergeant major every time I came in, she was now more relaxed. After all, we did live together in my suite, and she could not stay at attention twenty-four seven.

Her expression remained impassive as we explained the situation with the crewmen. When we finished, she gave a soft sigh. "I can certainly deal with this, but not legally," She said casually.

Bron frowned, "what exactly do you mean?"

"Well, your crew are perfectly entitled to quit or transfer as they please, and there is nothing legally you can do to stop them. However, the remainder generally backs down if you take out the ringleaders." She spoke like she was discussing crew rosters or other mundane ship activities.

"Can you define take out?" Bron said uneasily.

Stepanchikov studied her for a moment. "Miss Donovan, it's clear the hierarchy of Grant Industries is going to great lengths to destroy Miss Grant's credibility. Extreme action may be necessary."

"By extreme, are we talking about killing people?" Bron responded.

"It is not beyond reason to believe Drake will try to take out Miss Grant. We don't have the luxury of being squeamish about what needs to be done." Stepanchikov shrugged.

"Oh, don't worry about that," I said. "I honestly intend to stay alive at all costs, Miss Stepanchikov. Our concern is that such action will be traced back to me."

Stepanchikov nodded. "I understand, and that is why I intend, with your consent, to bring in someone from the outside. Someone I once served with."

"Who?" Bron asked.

142

"An American security expert called Charlotte Kensett. Frankly, she is the best there is. It will take some time to arrange a meeting, but if we get her on board, you can consider your problems over."

"What do we do in the meantime?" I asked.

"Carry on with your plans. It will be at least four months before we get back to Earth and this situation truly hits you."

If you have been following this series in order and read the books by Michael Phelkar and my sister Stacey or even that psychopath Emma Dodgson, you already know who Charlotte Kensett is. The British-born American agent who worked for the United States Outland Security Department when I met her. However, it would be more than a month from the time of our meeting with Stepanchikov and my first encounter with the American spook.

I temporarily replaced the captain of the ship with the first officer. Although he was little more helpful than the captain, he appeared willing to do his job. The ship fell back into a sort of routine, albeit a tense one.

Bron appeared to come into her own as she frequently met with the executives after they signed on with us and worked out the logistics of what was in our control. We had access to multiple resources that could severely help the resistance back in Australia. Weapons, food supplies, clothing, you name it, we had it. The only snafu in our plan was that we had no clue how to do it. Grant Industries was now a registered American company. With no trade between the European Union and the Pacific Alliance, at least not legal, we had no legitimate means to send any of our cargo ships to Australia.

Stepanchikov once more came into her element. "I have managed to make contact with the gentleman you have informed me about, Mr. Crocker," she told us at one of our breakfast briefings. "I have implied we can assist him, but I haven't gone into details as I have not spoken to him directly."

"Is there any way we can set up communication with him? I want to talk to him myself," I asked.

"Well, I can set up a secure line with him, but I honestly don't recommend you speak to him yourself. Nothing can be guaranteed to be private and away from the prying eyes of the Peons. If you are seen communicating with resistance forces, it will put you high on the Peon radar."

I pondered this a moment. I was not one to put myself at risk, but a part of me strongly wanted to be seen as actively helping my people. "I think I'm going to risk it," I said at last.

Stepanchikov looked momentarily frustrated with this. Security people generally didn't like their wards putting themselves in the firing line. "As you wish, Miss Grant. I will see what I can do to set it up."

Two days later, I was sitting in a secured conference room with a couple of Stepanchikov's guards standing outside and one of her technicians monitoring the security of our communications. Mr. Crocker was able to see me but only had sound communication to respond, so I could not see him. "Hannah Grant, well, this is a surprise. I should warn you we have less than fifteen minutes before the Peons will be able to track me. Hopefully, we conclude this conversation in under ten."

"G'day Croc, I will do my best. Good to hear you again. I have come into control of assets that could help you out Down Under. We have food supplies, clothing, and weaponry, which I assume you can do with."

"We most certainly could," Croc responded with surprise. "However, our greatest need is communication surveillance equipment."

At that, I looked at Bron, who sat adjacent to me, and she looked down at her terminal. She nodded. "We can see to that, too," I told Croc. "However, the main problem is getting them to you. I have the ships, and I have the supplies. Locating personnel willing to do it and finding a way of doing it without getting them killed or captured is the problem."

"Well, finding personnel willing to do it is something I can't help with," Croc replied. "However, we can set up drops. Find good enough pilots to fly in and drop off the supplies, and we can provide you with locations that will take the Peons a while to get there. Australia's a big place."

"How are things going down there?" I asked uneasily.

Croc sighed. "Honestly, I wish I could give you good news. We're holding our own but not really gaining any ground. Decent long-range communication systems will go a long way."

"I'll do what I can. We need to find a way to keep a line of communication open, and I want you to work with Stepanchikov if you can't contact me directly. You can trust her."

"This could just be what we need to turn the tide, Hannah. Stay in touch." And with that, he was gone.

"All we need to do now is find out what personnel will be willing to risk their lives making these runs Down Under," I said unconfidently.

"Easier said than done, Han," Bron said with a dejected sigh. "We barely have enough experience to run this division. Hell, we have no experience. We're now talking about running an anti-Peon rebellion."

"That is why you engage the services of people that do have the experience," said Stepanchikov. "I'm already compiling a list of people that had the potential to do just what you ask. We can start in the next few weeks."

As Bron and I headed back out into the corridor, I couldn't help but laugh. "A few weeks ago, I was wondering if I should go all the way with Patrick. Now I'm an armchair warrior."

Bron's face darkened. "That was over two years ago, Han."

My smile vanished. "This M.E.T. oblivion is bullshit. You could go crazy thinking about it."

"I wonder if they're still alive?" Bron said softly as she hit the elevator call button.

"Who?" I asked.

"Isla and Sarah."

I shrugged as we stepped inside. "No idea, mate. Maybe Sarah, but Isla never made it into the bunker."

Something seemed to click in her head. She suddenly said in surprise. "You never fucked Patrick?" she asked a little too loudly, and a crewman passing the closing elevator door shot us a startled look. There was silence as we started going up before we both looked at each other and burst out laughing.

"Not that it's any of your business, mate, but no, I didn't," I said confidently, knowing what was to come next.

145

"You're not still a...?" her voice trailed off.

"Not a what?" I replied in mock innocence, knowing full well what she was referring to.

"You know...." She glanced down at my private area.

I chuckled as the door opened again, "Isn't that a little personal, Bron?" I said, stepping out of the elevator and heading back into our apartment.

"Absolutely." Bron chuckled as she followed me in. "But you're still going to tell me."

"No, Bron, I'm not." The conversation paused as I hit a comm panel and ordered us lunch.

"So, why not with Pat?" She asked, not giving it up.

I shrugged as I flumped down on the sofa. "Not sure, really. I think I just didn't want him to think I was that type of girl."

"But you are that type of girl," Bron sniggered.

I rolled my eyes and gave her the finger. "Fuck you, Bron, fuck you to hell." I grinned.

Seven weeks after we had first talked about it, Stepanchikov informed me that a method of communication had been set up, enabling us to be able to broadcast to the Australian people. They had somehow hacked into carrier waves that went through multiple communication satellite systems throughout the Solar System. It was quite ingenious. Every time we broadcast, it would go via a different route, making us difficult to track. It also ran on a twenty-minute delay, which meant the broadcast would've finished before the Peons were even able to start tracking it. Even if they did, they wouldn't get through many of the relays. They would have to start again with each attempt. It even went through the highly secure communication station that was the hub of solar-wide Peon communications. The impenetrable Phobos communications base. At least, at that time, it was considered impenetrable.

The question finally came, however, who was going to make the actual broadcasts?

I wanted to find out if we had some actor or actress on board the ship but both Stepanchikov and Bron poo-pooed that idea. The less people who knew about it, the better. I wasn't happy when they both suggested me. "You're already a household name," Bron said to me. "It might be good for them to hear a recognizable voice."

I protested fervently, but eventually gave up and agreed. The following day, I went into the office that Stepanchikov had secured, and sat in front of a desk with a microphone. Bron sat opposite me, and, as was her style, Stepanchikov stood to one side. I looked at both of them, my expression showing the irritation I had with having to do this. I then placed the headphones up on my head, and waited to hear the voice of an anonymous Grant Industries security technician informing me that we were ready to go live. A green light lit up, and I took a deep breath.

"G'day day free Australia," I began. "This is the voice of the resistance and the start of the fight back. I'm...." I paused, deciding at the last second that I wasn't going to reveal my name. The name I did come up with in the spur of the moment would go down in the annals of Australian history.

"Lady Kookaburra. I'm speaking to you from a secret location to let you know, you are not alone out there. Throughout the Solar System, Australians are working to help you. We will be supplying support in the form of equipment, weapons, and personnel. We will continue to update you on the state of the war at regular periods. To avoid being tracked, we will broadcast at different times and locations."

I made it sound like we were actually in Australia, but I wasn't actually lying. The Twilight Wanderer was in motion; I would be in a different location every time I broadcast. "Stay tuned to this frequency for more updates every day. Until the Southern Cross flies over Canberra again, we'll be with you, Australia. We're going to send those Bloody Peons back to hell. You have a good day now."

As I switched off the mic, I looked up at Bron, who had a huge grin on her face. "That was bloody ripper, mate. I just hope someone heard it."

Not only did someone hear it, over the next few days, I learned Crocker was distributing the frequency to as many cells as he could. Every group in hiding had someone monitoring the radio frequencies, ready to hear my next message. We started to be supplied with code phrases used by the resistance that were completely meaningless to me.

While giving out news, I would also say things like, "the wallaby is depressed.", "the shrimp has fallen off the barbie." They were passphrases giving instructions to different cells that couldn't be communicated to directly. I would also deliver uplifting news of victories achieved by the resistance forces. Each cell had its own unique name, and to give one example, messages would go out. "The Free Australia medal of valor goes out to the Ned Kelly brigade, who led a successful assault on a Peon munitions camp just outside Adelaide. They managed to liberate hundreds of firearms and other munitions with minimal casualties. Keep up the good work, Ned Kelly. We're out here rooting for you."

I actually started to look forward to my daily transmissions, and unbeknownst to me at the time, the name of Lady Kookaburra had become more famous than that of Hannah Grant.

A few days later, in a meeting with Stepanchikov, I raised the following issue, "I've been thinking about this Charlotte Kensett," I said uneasily. "Why would she be willing to help us?"

"Because you have as much to offer her as she does you," Stepanchikov replied. "You're going to be offering her a foot in the door within the Australian resistance, something the Americans would be really happy with. Charlotte Kensett operates on a quid pro quo basis. You'll be expected to give something up in return for her help."

"Exactly what is she going to want?" Bron asked with concern.

"To be honest, I have no idea, but you can discuss that when you meet with her."

"And when exactly will that be?" I asked, as it had been over a month since we had discussed her involvement.

Stepanchikov shrugged. "No idea. Charlotte will find a way to contact you. I've made her aware of the opportunity, but beyond that, I have no control over what she does or how she does it."

So it was that we started sending in shuttles with supplies. However, we quickly shut down the operation, as we lost two out of every three shuttles we sent in. Fortunately, those shot down were unmarked, and their registration transponders were removed, so they couldn't be directly traced back to me or Grant Industries. We were stymied, and to be honest, I was ready to give up.

148

CHAPTER SEVENTEEN

CHARLOTTE

About a week later, the Twilight Wanderer made a scheduled stop at a British star base to refresh supplies. We were still a considerable distance from Earth. Some of our British crewmen involved with the industrial action took the opportunity to leave the ship. There were few. Bron managed to contact the Spacers Guild to advertise their jobs, and we managed to replace about two-thirds of them.

Bron and I took the opportunity to get off the Twilight Wanderer for a while. Stepanchikov was not too happy about it, especially when I said I didn't want obvious security with me. Of course, she would still send people to watch us, but they would be discreet.

I started to become claustrophobic while staying in my apartment. So, we went into the civilian base. It amused me that Bron now drew people's attention instead of me, thanks to her cybernetic additions. We kept our visits on the down low, with only our security people knowing, as far as we were aware, that we were off the Twilight Wanderer.

Bozeman and Delta is a fairly prestigious employment agency. They usually work with providing civilian crews for commercial vessels like the Twilight Wanderer. Finding people such as ship captains is usually a long-drawn-out process of interviews, second interviews, and even third. However, Bron and I didn't have time for this, and as we explained this to the agent we met with, he grew increasingly concerned.

"Finding the right match for your requirements is not a simple process, Miss Grant," he responded, looking over his desk with wide

149

eyes when I suggested that we wanted to finalize the arrangements that day.

As was to become the frequent occurrence when dealing with business matters, it was Bron who replied.

"Well, if you don't think you can do it, then perhaps, we should take our business elsewhere."

He didn't take that threat too kindly. His company was the premiere in the business, and the loss of one contract would not exactly faze him. "That would probably be a good idea, Miss Donovan."

Bron casually turned to me with a shrug. "It'll certainly delay us, but I'll let it be known that Grant Industries' employment contracts are up for tender."

I didn't even know what she meant by that, and I just nodded, but the agent's reaction was obvious. Bron would later explain that she had effectively just told him that if he couldn't do what we wanted, we were going to pull every single Grant Industries contract. We employed literally thousands. Of course, we couldn't actually do that because I only owned a division and had no authority over ninety percent of the company; however, my name was Grant, and he didn't know the limit of my clout in Grant Industries.

You would have thought with that threat, he would have become helpful and compliant. While he did indeed do what we asked of him, he did so with great reluctance and very begrudgingly.

"I need to make it very clear that finding a captain for a ship such as the Twilight Wanderer is a procedure that should take many months and usually involves the transfer of a captain in high demand. If we want to conclude this today, we are looking at captains that are currently unassigned. And unassigned captains are usually not top-notch."

"Oh, my dear Kelvin," said Bron, for that was his name. "Are you suggesting we keep the Twilight Wanderer at this space station for several months, while we search for this new captain? I really don't believe an officer abandoning his post is a new precedent."

Kelvin sighed. He looked down at his terminal and began tapping irritably. We sat in silence for several minutes as he read personnel files. "I have several available captains. However, I do not consider any of them remotely qualified to captain a ship on the scale of the Twilight Wanderer."

"Mind if we take a look?" Bron said impatiently.

Kelvin turned the monitor towards us as he shook his head in reluctant compliance.

Bron looked down the list, as did I, but in my case, I wasn't really paying much attention.

"This one." Bron looked at me as she pointed to a name and the description of her nationality underneath it. Australian. I smiled softly, realizing what Bron was already aware of. An Australian captain would be more sympathetic to our more illicit activities, and we could probably bring her on board with our plans.

I nodded with a smile.

"Tell me more about number three," Bron said. She turned the monitor back to Kelvin, indicating where the interesting captain was listed.

Kelvin's face turned from irritation to utter bewilderment. "She is probably the least qualified of them all. She's not even applying for anywhere near the scale of the ship we're talking about here. She is looking for a position in command of a freight vessel not much bigger than a shuttle. Six-man cruisers at best. Take her on, and you probably end up crashing into the sun."

"I'm growing exceedingly tired of your attitude, Kelvin," I said with considerable annoyance. "Listen to me very carefully. I don't give a fuck about what you think. Miss Donovan and I have pretty much been in command of that ship for the last month, and we did okay. Now, are you going to be cooperative, or should I go and put a call into Romano & Sons?" I said, naming his company's biggest rival.

"Madam." He responded curtly. "Our company has a sterling reputation. Providing an unqualified officer to command a ship as prestigious as the Twilight Wanderer will reflect badly on us, if she's incapable of performing her duties impeccably."

"Fine!" Bron responded. "Have your legal department draw up a waiver, and we'll sign it. Hannah herself will put her name to it that we won't hold you responsible for anything our new captain does, and that you strongly advised us not to employ her."

His face softened somewhat. "Would you give me some time to make some calls regarding that? It is not something that I've ever done before."

"Be as quick as you can, please. I'm starting to become bored shitless sitting here," I said most unprofessionally, and I got a scowl from Bron.

He was less than ten minutes, and returned to turn the terminal back towards me with a fully prepared contract that negated his company from any responsibilities. I input my signature code, and the deal was done. All responsibility for any problems caused by a captain provided by the company, fell squarely upon my shoulders.

"Of course, you do understand that the captain in question may not even accept the position?"

"Just arrange a meeting with her, would you please?"

And he did. Although he gave us another of his petulant sighs, when I suggested a nice little café to meet at that I had seen on the way here.

He made the call, and the captain confirmed she could meet us immediately. Bron gave Kelvin the details of Baker, the lawyer, to sort out any contract should we decide to engage her. However, as I got out of my seat to leave, I couldn't hold back muttering, "fucking moron," loud enough for him to hear. I got another scalding look from Bron as we left the office.

Twenty minutes later, I was sitting drinking a latte on the sidewalk of the little coffee shop.

She turned out to be a woman of about thirty and looked incredibly unsure of herself when she approached the table and asked if we were who she was looking for. She sat at our table, and I ordered her a coffee.

"I have to be honest with you," she said, as she added some extra sugar to her drink. "I can't help but think this is some kind of wind-up. Are we really talking about the Twilight Wanderer?"

"I assure you this isn't a wind-up," Bron told her. "We have very unusual circumstances, and you're probably more qualified to fill that post than you realize. However, I can't go into that sort of detail until we have a deal. I hope you understand."

She smiled, "I can't say I understand, but I am willing to go along with it for now."

"Fair enough." Bron shrugged. "Tell us about your background."

"Well, as you probably already know, I served most of my career with the Australian Air Force. After Last Day, I was recruited by the United States and served aboard a fighter carrier, where I remained in command of a squadron engaged in the war. I retired last year and have captained several freighters for the last two years, but was made redundant when my last vessel was scrapped several months ago. I have since been looking for a position in civilian service."

"Do you think you have the balls to take on a ship like the Twilight Wanderer?" I asked.

"Honestly, yes, I do. Size doesn't matter as the orders are the same. It's a simple matter of managing a modicum of increased responsibility."

Although I was unsure what modicum meant, I got her point. "What are your thoughts about what's going on back home?"

"Well, if you'll excuse my French, it's all bullshit, isn't it? I just wish I could do more about it."

At that, Bron and I glanced at each other with a smile. Yes, she had the potential to be part of the resistance plans.

"I don't think we need to know anymore," Bron said to her.

She seemed to take that as a rejection and started to get up, thanking us for our time. "Where are you going? We have contracts to sort out." Bron frowned at her.

She looked quite surprised and sat back down. "You mean, you're giving me the job?" she responded with astonishment.

"Of course," Bron responded. "We just need to get the paperwork done, and I'll announce that Trisha McFarland is now the commander of the SS Twilight Wanderer."

As McFarland left, we remained sitting out on the sidewalk drinking coffee and simply just relaxing from the stress of everything that was going on, when a tall, dark-haired woman approached us. She was dressed in a business suit, but what stood out most was her three-inch high stiletto heels.

153

"Miss Grant?" I was unsure if it was a question or a statement, but I tensed. Who could possibly know I was here? "Please do not be alarmed. I do believe we have a mutual interest to share."

Her accent was British, upper class and sophisticated. Uninvited, she sat at the table adjacent to Bron and me. I knew my own security was watching me discreetly. I wanted them around, but I didn't want to draw attention to myself by having them obviously at my side. "My name is Charlotte Kensett. I work for the United States Outland Security Department."

"You don't sound like an American, mate," Bron said coolly.

She looked at Bron and smiled softly. "Expat. I was born and raised in London, but I am now an American."

"How did you know where to find us, Miss Kensett?"

"Oh, my dear Miss Grant, let's not worry about that right now. I want to come straight to the point that we are most interested in. Your planned activities in your homeland of Australia with Mr. Crocker."

I tensed, but I hoped I hid it well. I knew we were expecting to meet with Miss Kensett, but she had taken me completely by surprise, and her knowledge of what we were planning immediately put me on the defensive.

"I haven't been back to Australia in years. I have no idea what you're talking about."

"Oh, dear, we're going to play *that* game, are we? I did so hope we could save some time, but as you wish," She pulled out a tablet that fit in the palm of her hand and withdrew very large glasses from within her jacket. She put them on and began to read something.

"You have been running a division of Grant Industries that has, frankly, been making a loss for the company for several months. No-one in the company knows what you do. However, unmarked Grant Industries vessels have been spotted coming in and out of Earth space and disappearing into the continental mass of Australia. We began tracking those vehicles and are aware that you are transporting weaponry, navigation systems, communication systems, and basically anything you can get past the Peons to assist the Australian resistance forces,"—she looked up at me—"correct, so far?" she said, but I didn't reply. She looked back to the device and continued. "In addition,

154

you have funneled billions of dollars into corporate and charitable Australian organizations."

"How do you know all this already??"

She dismissed the question with a casual wave of a hand that bore exquisitely well-manicured long red nails. "I want to help you. America wants to help you, but also, we want you to help us."

"Well, you certainly are an American," Bron's tone was sarcastic. "Only ever want to help if there's something in it for you."

Charlotte shrugged. "Maybe so. But aren't we all in this together?"

"We weren't in it together when you didn't come and help us in Australia on Last Day. You left us to get our asses handed to us," Bron sniped.

Charlotte seemed completely unfazed, and I would come to realize that that was her reaction to virtually everything. "I cannot honestly comment on that. I work in intelligence, not in the military. Military strategy is a different department from mine. However, I fully understand if you're not interested in hearing me out, even though I'm here at your request."

Something about Charlotte rankled me, and even though I was aware that we potentially needed her, I was unsure if I wanted to get involved in the doings of this woman. Still, I was interested in what she knew about my operations. "I'll hear you out."

"We need to get our people into Australia, but the Peons have spies everywhere. All my attempts have failed. Frankly, I'll be honest, my department leaks like a sieve. However, even though the Peons know your activities, they have failed to catch you. And for that, you can consider me impressed."

"That's not entirely true. We have lost a lot of our people and our ships. However, as far as I'm aware, those haven't been traced back to me. But so far, you've only told me what you want from me, not what you have to offer me."

"We could equip your shuttles with the most up-to-date anti-tracking devices and significantly reduce your failures. In return, at least for now, we ask that you allow our operatives to build those shuttles to be inserted into Australia. Isn't getting that and getting American operatives into Australia to support your resistance cause enough?"

155

"It could be if I knew exactly what they were doing there, but I don't, and I know you're not going to tell me any more, and I'm not going to tell you about our operations. But let me clarify that we're not in this for the Pacific Alliance or the oh-so-great American nation. We're in this for Australia, and Australia alone. You ignored us at our greatest time of need and want us to trust you now?"

"I, Miss Grant, am not banking on you trusting me; I'm banking on you *needing* me. The agency plans to drop experts in guerrilla warfare and will be training resistance fighters. Now isn't that something you can get behind?"

"No, while that's appreciated, I still don't believe that's the whole story. Miss Kensett, trust me when I tell you that you are more likely to get my cooperation if you're honest with me. There are two reasons you would do this. You are getting ready for a counter-invasion, or you want to use Australia as a distraction to keep the Peons busy. And I know America is not ready for that invasion."

Charlotte smiled at me. "How very astute of you, Miss Grant. Indeed, the operation is to cause a distraction. However, I'm sure your own security will tell you your resistance forces are getting beaten to a pulp and stand on the brink of extinction." I couldn't deny this, for they were the reports I was getting from Croc. "You can send them all the weaponry and equipment in the Solar System, but without training on how to use them effectively, they are pretty useless."

I had to agree, but I thought I'd push her a bit more to see if I could get something else out of this. "Let's take this a little further. I want a full partnership."

"Partnership?" Charlotte frowned. "We're not brokering some corporate deal here, Miss Grant."

"Oh, that's exactly what we're discussing, Miss Kensett. I want access to your intelligence and resources. I want to know that when I call on you for help, I'll get it. I won't ask you what you want my people for, and you won't ask me what I want your people for, but together, we can cooperate."

"Agreed," Charlotte said after she pondered it for a moment.

"There's also the matter of the industrial action that will shut us down once we reach Earth," Bron said. "We're effectively going to be stranded in Earth orbit. No crew, no staff."

Charlotte smiled warmly. "That is a minor problem. It will be dealt with. However, you should be aware that one of your executives reports everything you do to the company chairman. I'll need you to take her out before I can deal with the rest."

"Why can't you deal with them if you can deal with everyone else?" Bron asked suspiciously.

"Indeed, I could. However, you want me to put myself and my people at risk, so I need to see that you're willing to do the same and not simply roll over on me when I have done what you wanted."

"You don't trust me, Miss Kensett?" I said softly.

Charlotte chuckled. "Trust is the fastest way to a quick death, Miss Grant. I prefer to be in a position where we cannot betray each other for any reason. Take out the executive, and you give me something I can use to protect myself. It is a simple matter."

"Who is it?" Bron asked, a lot more concerned about the suggestion than I was.

"Melanie Bradford. She hopes she will get a place on the board in return for supporting Drake. I recommend you do it before you leave port; that way, you can put the disappearance down to them abandoning the ship or something. Consider it the signature on our contract." Slowly, she rose to her feet and appeared to be about to bid us farewell when she stopped and pondered a moment before saying, "I will tell you something of interest as part of a goodwill gesture and a test of trust as I do not want this repeated to anyone." Charlotte had a way of drawing in your curiosity. I think it was a method to distract you, and what she said next suddenly did. "Your sister Stacey is alive. She is serving with an elite U.S. Marine unit under the command of a woman called Jenna Plural."

I shrugged. "That isn't really news to me because I guessed as much since there's no record of her death, and she just disappeared. How can you confirm this is accurate and she's not dead?"

"Because, my dear Miss Grant, I have spent the last few years working with her. She's the pilot of the ship on which I serve. I will be in

157

touch, Miss Grant, and I truly look forward to a long and mutually beneficial arrangement." She turned, and with a clip-clop of those expensive heels, she disappeared into the crowds of people.

As we took the shuttle back up to the Twilight Wanderer, we waited until the stewards left us alone, and Bron turned to me. "So, what're your thoughts on this Bradford thing?"

I shrugged. "There's not an alternative, is there? Even if Kensett didn't want us to do something about it, we'd still have to."

"I'll get Stepanchikov to pick her up when we get back."

"That would be too suspicious. I think we should simply invite her to a meeting." I replied.

"You want to be present when it's done?"

I shrugged at that. "Well, it's not exactly going to be the first time we've killed someone, is it, Bron?"

"I guess not," Bron said, sat back, and fell silent.

I put thoughts of Bradford out of my head for the time being, for I found myself unable to put Stacey out of my mind. She was my only living family. I'd never met her; I had never particularly wanted to meet her until now.

I reached out to my security people as soon as we were back aboard the ship, and they investigated further. Stacefield Ellen Grant was alive and serving aboard the U.S.S. Lewis Puller under the command of a woman called Jennacia Plularian. However, that was as much as I found out. I had no idea where she was or what she was doing, and it would be another year before I found out.

However, in the meantime, I had a traitor to deal with.

CHAPTER EIGHTEEN

— • —

A GIRL'S NIGHT OUT

I have often been asked how it is that I've never been prosecuted for the homicides that I had been involved in. The death of Josh and Melanie, among others, have been thoroughly investigated and deemed self-defense. Of course, it is unlikely that that would have been the result had I not been exceptionally wealthy. I am today considered the wealthiest individual in the Solar System with a fortune within the realms of ten digits. Even then, I was in the top five when I owned only eight percent of Grant Industries. Money is power and influence, and I don't apologize for that. Any animosity you have towards me for being so rich and powerful comes simply from the fact that you are not. Were you in my position, I have no doubt you would use it as I do.

Of course, things would change with the fall of the Pacific Alliance at the time of economic strife that would face the losing countries of that war. However, I'll come back to that later.

As soon as Bronwyn and I returned to the Twilight Wanderer, we headed back to the executive suite. I ordered a light lunch. We ate mostly in silence with everything that was going on ruminating in our heads until finally, I tossed my fork onto my plate and said to her, "You know something, Bron. We need a proper break." She looked up at me questioningly at that statement. "Let's go to one of the ship's casinos and blow ridiculously large amounts of money."

"Well, the fact we're both under twenty-one may be a problem with that idea," she said lightly.

I couldn't help but laugh at that. "Ironic that I can legally own casinos but can't legally enter them. However, I find it highly unlikely that anyone will stop me from going there."

"Okay, Han. I think it would probably do us good to get well and truly cooked."

With that decision made, we went online to look at the inventory of some of the ship's high-end fashion stores. We both purchased new outfits. I went for a slutty little short dress with no sleeves and matching shoes. On the other hand, Bron did everything she could to ensure the cybernetic replacements were covered. When we'd changed later that night, she looked in the mirror at the metal plate on her face and let out a long sigh. "I don't think I'm ever gonna get used to this, Han."

"You don't have to," I replied, trying to be reassuring. "Even if you can't restore organic skin over the top of it, you can get artificial replication to cover the obvious areas."

"I'm not a charity case, Hannah. You don't have to cover my medical bills."

I turned on her, quite irritated by this martyr attitude. "Any payment made through Grant Industries, that you bloody well earned, is not charity."

She glanced at me with a smile. "Well, it's not like I'm getting paid."

"I never really thought about that. You can have anything you want and just put it down on expenses."

"I know. It just doesn't feel the same."

"Fine. Allocate yourself a salary. I have no clue what your position is worth, but I'm sure you can work it out."

As I went to put on my makeup, she made as if she was going to do the same, but once again looked at herself in the mirror and turned away. I stopped and looked at her again. "Sit down," I said, indicating the closed toilet seat. She looked confused, and I simply pointed to it again. "Go on." Still looking confused, she complied. "Hold your head up." Again, she complied.

Slowly and carefully, I added the eyeliner over one good eye and made her up over the next twenty minutes. Even with the cybernetic plate and the artificial eye, Bron was quite the stunner, and when she finally got up and looked into the mirror, she smiled, and tears glistened in her eye.

"If you don't stop crying and ruin that, I'm gonna slap you," I said with a grin, as I turned to do my own. She stood and watched me in silence as I completed the task.

Finally, I turned to her with a big smile and said, "Okay, Bron, let's go do this."

There were several casinos on board the ship. There was one that was exclusive to first-class VIPs. Naturally, that's where we went. The pair of us certainly stood out from the crowd. Me, with my artificially designed features and Bron with her visible faceplate and artificial hand. The doorman instantly recognized at least me, if not both of us. "Good evening, Miss Grant. It's an absolute delight that you join us here tonight. What would be your pleasure?"

I smiled sweetly. "Just find us a quiet table for now, if you please."

He led us to a booth set away from the gaming tables, and we took in the sounds of the casino, the calls of the croupier, the rolling of the dice, and the spins of the wheels. We drew many looks and a few murmurings from people pointing us out. However, as we sat quietly with our drinks and I didn't appear to do anything exciting, the attention started to dwindle. I nursed a rather sparkly looking cocktail with a sigh.

"What's the matter?" Bron asked.

"I can't get drunk. I don't have any metabolism inhibitors," I muttered.

"Can't you get some?"

"I guess I could call that Doctor Cooper and ask him."

"Somehow, I doubt you'll get him to supply those. He seems a little squeaky clean to me."

"Meh, I'm his boss. He can't say no." I replied.

Bron chuckled. "While I have no doubt you *could* find a doctor willing to provide you with the legal medications, I highly doubt someone like Deacon Cooper would break the law, no matter who you were."

I was not too fond of this idea. I was starting to enjoy the power and the influence. I could see how my mother had found it the ultimate

161

aphrodisiac, and slowly but surely, the idea that anyone could say no to me was becoming harder to believe. "Maybe so. However, it doesn't help me out tonight, does it?" I said with a sigh and sat back, just as a young man stepped up to the table.

"G'day, Miss Grant, Miss Donovan," he said with a warm smile, recognizing both of us, but I had no clue who he was. Bron, however, recognized him instantly. "G'day, Mr. Barclay."

I looked at her questioningly, waiting for her to introduce me. Bron looked a little embarrassed, "Mr. Barclay is a member of our executive team." In turn, indicating that I should have recognized him.

I was unfazed, for I didn't care whether my inability to recognize him offended him, but I said to him, "care to join us for a drink, Mr. Barclay?"

"Actually, I'm here with a date. I just wanted to say g'day."

"Is it a first, second, or third date?" I asked with a smile.

He looked surprised by the question and said, "we've been dating for some months now."

"Well, in that case, we're not interrupting anything if we say to you, bring your date over here and join us," I grinned.

He smiled at that and replied that he would bring her over. However, as they walked back towards us, Bron gasped, and her single eye went wide. "What's the matter?" I said under my breath, although they probably still weren't close enough to hear me if I had spoken normally.

"His date. It's Melanie Bradford," She replied uneasily.

"The one Kensett told us about?"

"Yeah."

Shit! This was not going to be comfortable. I slid over to make room for Bron to come and sit on my side of the booth, as Melanie and then James Barclay sat opposite. I was staring eye-to-eye with a woman I was supposed to kill.

Bradford was in her late twenties. Maybe even her early thirties. I can't really judge age that well. She was all smiles and fluffy dog sweetness. She totally didn't fit the hard-arse executive persona.

"So, where are you from, Miss Bradford?" I asked as Bron summoned over a drinks waiter to take their orders.

"Oh, please, Miss Grant, call me Mel," she said in a bubbly, singsong voice.

"Okay, and please call me Hannah or Han," I replied casually.

She looked like I had just given her the keys to the vault in giving her permission to be so informal with me.

"Originally, I'm from Sydney, but I spent the last few years living in the American base on Karas. I was heading back to Earth, when Last Day happened."

"What were you doing on Karas?" I asked.

"I was in charge of the outer systems logistics team servicing the planets from Jupiter and beyond."

"That sounds like quite the responsibility."

"It was, but I'm sure I can do much more for the company."

"Well, unfortunately, my division doesn't have quite such high-placed positions to offer, but we are pleased to have you with us," I lied.

She looked a little bit disappointed in my words, and I realized that she had been attempting to open up a dialogue about her future. This made one thing clear to me. If she was advising Drake of everything I was doing and yet still trying to arse crawl to me, her loyalty was to but one thing. Herself.

Bron was engaged in a quiet conversation with Barclay, but clearly much more uncomfortable in the presence of Bradford than I was. Don't get me wrong, Bron will always do what's necessary, but she has more of a conscience about it than I do. The bitch queen I knew from high school was gradually disappearing to become someone more responsible. Her accident in the M.E.T. made her re-evaluate what was important in her life. While she would always remain loyal to me, she would become what I consider to be my conscience. Something I realized I lacked, as more and more time passed.

"So, what do you hope to achieve with the company in the forth-coming year, Hannah?"

It took me a moment to realize that it was Barclay who had spoken. I was too wrapped up in thinking about Melanie. I glanced over at him with a smile. "Oh, let's not worry about company stuff tonight, James. This is a night off. Let's keep the conversation on other things."

163

I looked back at Melanie. "Did your family manage to escape Last Day?"

Melanie looked sad at that question, "I haven't heard anything from my parents, and I don't know if they're dead or alive, but my brother was serving with the Australian Rangers and was off-world. He now serves in the United States infantry, but I haven't heard from him in a while."

"Oh, I know how you feel," I replied untruthfully, for honestly, I gave no thought to the wellbeing of my kin. "My mother and sister have been listed as dead, but no-one knows for sure."

"Do you mean Annabelle or Stacey when you talk about your sister?" Melanie asked me. It appeared to be an innocent enough question, but again my heightened senses went some way to help me to sense some form of deception. The change in her pupil dilation, as she said it, immediately put me on guard. She was fishing for something. I couldn't work out what, and honestly, I held no secrets about my family relations, so I answered her quite honestly. "I refer to Anna. I've never even met my other sister Stacey. She's what one would call the black sheep of the family and has pretty much nothing to do with us."

"Aren't you worried she'll come along and stake a claim in the company?" Melanie asked innocently.

Ah, there it was. Drake probably wanted to know if I had any sort of communication with the only person that had the vaguest legitimate claim of challenging my position. "Stacey has never shown any interest in us, and I'm fairly confident she still won't."

"Surely it's a temptation, though. Even a one percent stake in the company would make her a billionaire."

"It is possible, I guess, but I would deal with it if it happens. Frankly, I don't know if she's dead or alive. She's not exactly in the safest career."

"She was quite a legend back in Australia, I understand. She holds the record for piloting the fastest terrestrial aircraft."

"Does she?" I said, genuinely having no idea what she was talking about.

"Oh yes. It made the news about six months before the fall."

I grinned. "I guess everyone gets their fifteen minutes of fame," I said, using the famous Andy Warhol quote.

"Apparently she was investigated for being a possible GenMod. Her ability to react in an aircraft is considered to be superhuman."

Now that intrigued me. Was it possible that my sister Stacey had undergone some form of genetic modification? Not everyone got the full treatment like me, and there were GenMods that looked and appeared like regular people. Many parents had tweaked their child's intellect more, leaving their physical attributes alone. I had no idea why Stacey and her brother—or rather, should I say, our brother—were estranged from us. The subject was considered persona non grata, and I can't honestly say I ever showed an interest in my older sister.

"Well, she clearly couldn't be," I stated. "The US military would never have accepted her."

"Oh, the US military does have GenMods within their ranks," It was Barclay who said that, and he looked weirdly smugly proud that he had something to contribute to the conversation.

I looked over at him with a wry smile. "Only those born before the Grozny uprising. Not illegal ones. I'm fairly certain Stacey is only a few years older than me." I said. It was rather a stupid response that indicated I knew more about GenMods than the airhead society girl should. He smiled knowingly at me and returned his attention to his drink. I really started to doubt now that anyone believed me to be a regular human being.

"Well, I didn't just come here to sit and chat," Bron suddenly seemed to come out of a quiet stupor. "Let's go see if we could lose some of your money."

I smirked at her. "Didn't we just agree to put you on a salary? You can lose your own fucking money." Barclay and Bradford looked somewhat startled at my use of profanity. However, Bron and I slipped out of our seats and headed to the gaming area.

After losing a few thousand on roulette, I started to get bored with the game, left Bron at the table, and moved on to blackjack. Now, this I found was quite easy. I simply counted the cards as they came out of the six-pack deck and predicted the odds. I found myself winning almost every hand. I was clearly not an expert on the game or the rules. Whilst entirely legal, card counting was against every casino's rules.

However, I was allowed to carry on for quite a while as I put the security people in quite a predicament. I could hardly be robbing a casino that I actually owned. However, I was setting quite a bad precedent, and eventually, the casino manager came up to me and asked to have a quiet word.

She explained to me that card counting was against the rules. That put paid to me playing that game. It's not possible for me to switch off my natural ability to observe everything around me, and that included being able to predict what cards were coming out of the decks. The result was, I was now bored, and after finding out Bron had lost as much as I had won, we called it a night. We went back and bid Barclay and Bradford a good night.

The moment we were back in the corridor heading towards the elevator that would take us back up to our suite, Bron turned on me with considerable annoyance. "Why did you do that back there?"

"Do what?" I replied, genuinely confused.

"Get all chummy with Bradford. Listening to her mention her family and stuff like that. It's only going to make what we've have to do even harder."

"On the contrary, I think she confirmed exactly what Charlotte Kensett is accusing her of."

"Even if that was the case, finding out she's actually quite nice makes me feel sick."

As we stepped into the elevator, I looked at her quite bemused and gave her a shrug. "It didn't faze me, and honestly, Bron, there's no reason you have to be involved in that. Leave it to Stepanchikov and me."

And that is what happened. Stepanchikov was prepared to go much further than the average security officer. I think it was Drake's attack on me for being a GenMod and being prepared to use that against me that had riled her up. We'd never discussed the mutual situation of us both being GenMods. However, I discovered that she was perfectly legal, having been born before Grozny and, therefore, extremely old.

We became close, and a bond formed even though we always remained completely professional with each other.

We discussed the situation with Bradford, and two days later, we were ready to deal with the situation.

CHAPTER NINETEEN

— · —

CORPORATE RESTRUCTURING

We couldn't go through regular channels and have Bradford come to my office. The chances of anyone overhearing such a thing, or her saying to someone that she was visiting with me, would arouse suspicion if she immediately disappeared afterward. Stepanchikov began monitoring her movements on the internal ship's cameras. We didn't have cameras in rooms or apartments, but we did in nearly all the corridors. Stepanchikov was to wait for some time when I was alone in the office, and we could catch Bradford outside her quarters without anyone else. This could happen at any time, so I was prepared to receive Stepanchikov's call at a moment's notice.

It was early one morning, and as I didn't need as much sleep as everyone else, I was already up by four AM. I wasn't exactly working and was slouched down in my night attire, watching some trashy soap from America. When the call came through from Stepanchikov, she used a few simple words. "Bradford is on the move."

I didn't even reply. I just jumped up, went straight into my bedroom, and rapidly got dressed. As discussed with Stepanchikov, this wasn't going to be quick. I wanted to challenge her about what she had told Drake and see if I could learn more about her actions before dealing with the situation.

I headed into my office and switched on the monitor. It was tuned into the same cameras Stepanchikov was following. One of Stepanchikov's aids had stopped Bradford in the corridor, and I turned on the sound.

"Hannah Grant wants to see you in her office for breakfast this morning. Could you go straight over to her?" the aide said. I don't know if he was in on what was going to happen or not, but he seemed quite calm and professional, so I'm guessing he probably didn't.

A wide smile crossed Bradford's face at this invitation. "Yes, of course. Let me go back and change into something more appropriate," she responded eagerly. I can only imagine she thought an invitation to breakfast with me was a positive sign to her career.

"No, Oscar." I heard Stepanchikov say, and it took me a moment to realize that she was speaking into an earpiece in Oscar's ear. "Ensure she goes straight to Miss Grant and don't let her out of your sight, and don't let her go back to her apartment."

"I think you should come with me straight away. I'm already late trying to find you, and Miss Grant is not the most patient person." Bloody cheek! I grinned as he said this. I guess that was kind of true, but I was sure he was only saying it to get her to move faster.

This didn't please Melanie, who was dressed in casual jeans and a tee shirt. However, she wasn't about to miss this opportunity of a lifetime to suck up to me.

I returned to the lounge and found the security guard waiting for me. One of Stepanchikov's men whom she apparently trusted extremely well. It was not uncommon for security personnel to come in and out of the suite without knocking. Stepanchikov regularly had her people run sweeps for listening devices or anything else that could compromise my security. On this occasion, he carried a large, folded plastic sheet. When I looked at it questioningly, then at him, he said casually, "preparing for your office cleaning this afternoon." Although I was confused, I nodded as he headed into my office.

I called down to the stewards to bring breakfast for two and gave them my order. I had a craving for French toast and ordered a double portion. Less than five minutes later, the young aide escorted Bradford into the suite, and I smiled warmly at her, offering my hand. "Come on in. Melanie, it's really good to see you again."

"Likewise, Hannah," she positively beamed at me, clearly ecstatic at this singular honor of a private meeting with the boss.

"I wanted to discuss your future with the company. I thought we could do it over breakfast, if that's alright with you?"

"Oh, it's perfectly fine! I'd be absolutely delighted to have breakfast with you."

I led her into the dining room, where a pot of hot coffee stood prepared on a counter beside the dining table, and I poured us both one. "Cream and sweetener?" I asked her.

"Just a smidgen of cream, please," she said, holding her thumb and forefinger close together. I added the cream and then passed her the mug. "Please take a seat." I indicated to the chair that she'd have to turn her back to me to sit before I joined her in the adjacent chair. As soon as she couldn't see me, I clicked on the small communication device under my lapel, ensuring that Stepanchikov could hear everything that was going on. I then joined her, just as the stewards came in with our food, which they laid out neatly on the table in front of us. "How long have you been with the company, Melanie?" I asked as I poured a liberal helping of syrup on my French toast.

"Oh, it must be about six years now. I came here straight from Uni."

I responded with genuine surprise. "You've risen in the ranks fast."

She positively radiated as she replied, "what can I say, Hannah? I'm extremely good at what I do and have much more to offer in the right position."

I smiled at that and took a sip of my coffee before responding, "indeed. Where exactly do you see that being?"

"Well, of course, I'm perfectly happy to serve wherever you see fit. However, I've always been interested in heading my own division."

"And do you have a preference for your own division?"

"Well, military hardware is really where the big money is. Although I'm fully aware that I'm not quite ready for that," she then paused and smiled, "unless you think I am?"

Oh, she was good. That question immediately put me in a position where I would have to make it clear where I saw her going. However, she had no idea it didn't matter what I said. "Well, that's a possibility. However, we're part of a small division within the company at large. I would've thought, with your ambition, a transfer back to the authority of Mr. Drake would be more in your line."

171

The smile didn't dissipate, but I saw a rapid change in the size of her pupils. "Oh, Hannah, you made it very clear in the first meeting that you expected total loyalty from us. I gave you that. It wouldn't be appropriate for me to seek alternative offers from Mr. Drake."

And it was time to turn the tables.

"Yet my security tells me that you've been having many chats with Mr. Drake or his personnel."

At this, the smile instantly vanished, and a considerable look of panic crossed the young woman's face. "I'm not sure what you mean, Hannah," she said, clearly hoping this wasn't going to go where she thought it was.

"My security informs me that you've been in regular contact with Mr. Drake's office and informing him of everything I'm doing here."

"I have no idea what you're talking about."

Things would have gone very differently if she'd stuck to that story. I was never going to take the simple word of Charlotte Kensett, who I didn't know, that this girl was betraying me. No matter how suspicious I was, without a clear confession, I wasn't going to take her life, even if it meant reneging on the deal with Charlotte.

"Oh, come now, Melanie," I said, doing my best to sound disappointed. "I know the world out there thinks I'm a stupid little high school girl who doesn't know what she's doing, but they've got me wrong. Do not think I'm an idiot. Things will go much better if you're honest with me." I reached out and placed a reassuring hand upon hers. I smiled, encouragingly. "I like you, Melanie, and I can see you going places as part of my team. However, I need you to be completely honest with me."

Although she hesitated nervously, a slight smile eventually crossed her face. "He simply asked me to provide him with details of operations here. I really didn't think of it as anything other than normal operating procedure."

I looked at her understandingly, "I get it. You didn't understand my instructions about not discussing what we did with him."

Again, her pupils changed, and I could see that she saw that I had given her a get-out clause. At least, that's what she thought. "Well, I wouldn't say I didn't understand it; I just didn't realize how serious it was," she lied.

"Fair enough," I smiled. "I think we can forget all about it. I'm so pleased because I do have a position I think you can fill." The look of relief on her face could not be hidden from me as I turned back to my toast and took a bite. With my mouth still full of food, I said casually, "I would appreciate it if you could transmit all the records you have shown Mr. Drake to me, just so I know where we are with him, and then we can go into the office and discuss your future."

"Of course," she smiled and pulled out her handheld tablet from her jacket pocket. As I drank my coffee and ate, she tapped on the device before laying it down on the table beside her. "All done."

I smiled back at her. "Thank you, Melanie."

As we ate breakfast, I knew Stepanchikov would be going through all those files to ensure we had everything we were expecting.

Less than ten minutes later, the security officer, who had brought in the plastic sheeting, came into the room. "Sorry to interrupt you, Miss Grant, but Miss Stepanchikov is in your office. She needs to see you on an urgent matter." That was the signal that Stepanchikov was ready.

I feigned a sigh, dabbed my lips with my napkin, and made to get up. "I'll try to make this not too long, Melanie."

"Oh, please take your time, Hannah," she replied cheerfully.

I headed to the door, then stopped and hesitated. It was all part of the act, for I knew exactly what I was doing. "Actually, Melanie, why don't you come with me? Whatever my head of security wants, I'm sure I can trust you with it."

If I hadn't already secured this woman's trust, I certainly did now. Beaming like a kid who'd just been invited to Disneyland, she jumped up and followed me into the office. The guard escorting us left us at the door. Melanie looked confused by the plastic that covered the carpet from the front of my desk right up to the wall. "They're doing some office cleaning," was my simple explanation. Stepanchikov was standing in the center, and I asked Melanie to join her. It was an odd thing for me to do, for I should've offered her a seat, but she was on

173

such a high that she didn't even think about it and meekly joined my security officer, as I took my seat behind the desk.

However, the smile on Melanie's face rapidly disappeared when she realized that Stepanchikov wasn't talking to me, and we were both looking intently at her.

"What's going on, Hannah?" she asked with concern and looked damn well confused.

My eyes were fixed on her coldly, and I allowed myself a dramatic sigh. "You betrayed me, Melanie. You worked against me. I made it very clear where I stood, yet you decided to play games."

Fear entered her eyes, and I couldn't help but enjoy it. That feeling of power, when someone is afraid of you, is quite intoxicating. Judge me as you will by that, but unless you're in that position, you couldn't possibly understand.

"But we just discussed that. I thought everything was clear," she said, rushing out the words, trying to put everything together with that dim little brain of hers, completely unaware that Stepanchikov had now moved to stand directly behind her.

"Drake is out to destroy me, possibly even kill me. Do you really think I would sit back and take risks with sad little girls who think they can play both sides in order to climb the greasy pole?"

She looked like she was about to protest again but faltered, and, looking down, she simply said, "you were just trying to get me to show you what I showed Drake before firing me, weren't you?"

"You're partly right there, Melanie. I didn't need to know how much damage you'd caused. However, I can assure you I have no intention of firing you."

A moment's relief started across her face, but that rapidly vanished as Stepanchikov reached over the top of her head with a cord in her hand and pulled it back against her neck. Melanie managed a gasp before Stepanchikov cut off her airway, bringing her clenched fists together behind her neck and squeezing tightly. Melanie scrabbled at her throat, clutching at the cord, but she'd have barely been able to defend herself against an average woman. She didn't stand a chance against a genetically modified superior being. Stepanchikov stepped in close to her, still gripping the ends tightly and holding her up as she tried to wriggle and thrash about. But then her eyes started to bulge out of her head, as her face turned red, and I sat back in the chair, crossed my legs, folded my arms, and watched with some fascination. Her eyes remained transfixed upon me, and she slumped into unconsciousness but, with luck, held on.

Apparently, it takes a couple of minutes for someone to die after they pass out from strangulation, and after about a minute, I got bored. I went back into the dining room to get my coffee before returning with it. Melanie lay motionless on the plastic sheet, her eyes staring up at the ceiling. Stepanchikov's assistant had rejoined her, and they both pulled up the sides of the plastic sheet and wrapped her in it. Stepanchikov looked up at me and nodded. I nodded back and took a sip of my coffee before placing it on the desk. Without another word, I headed out to a prearranged meeting with a couple of executives, which would be my alibi should anyone raise any questions. By the time I returned an hour later, Melanie, Stepanchikov and her aide had gone.

We left the British space station that same morning. Bradford's letter of resignation was on file, and the only one to question it was Barclay, but even he was convinced that the flighty young executive had truly quit the company. Although they were dating, they hadn't been particularly close.

We continued our journey back to Earth for our passengers to return to their homes. It would take a couple more months, and during that time, the rabble-rousing unionists became quiet. I don't honestly know what Charlotte Kensett did, but whatever it was, it had clearly worked.

The new arrangement with Charlotte Kensett turned out to work very well. We stepped up our operations Down Under, and while we provided transport for her agents, she supplied an arsenal straight from the United States Department of Defense storehouses. News of increased resistance came in almost weekly.

By the time we reached Earth, we had a full-scale operation running, and I was clearly entrenched as the omnipotent leader of my division. Rumors about Melanie spread, but without evidence, that's all they were. I have no clue what Stepanchikov did with the body, and honestly, I don't care.

I did have one final problem when we returned to Earth. That was Bron, who was considering leaving me.

"I want to go back to Australia," She told me bluntly one evening. "I want to find out what happened to my family."

This was quite the dilemma for me because, as you can probably tell, I knew fuck all about running this company. I pretty much left everything to Bron. However, she was and is the closest thing I've ever had to a best friend, and I was not about to stop her, if that's what she truly wanted, and I wasn't about to let her go without trying to change her mind.

"I can understand that, but hear me out," I replied with genuine concern in my voice. "What do you honestly hope to achieve? If you find your parents alive, great, wonderful, yippee. You find out they're dead, hell, bad. But either way, your story ends there. You'll be trapped in an occupied state."

"I can find Crocker and join the resistance."

"Yes, you can, but what would you be? Just cannon fodder for some guerilla fighting?"

"At least I'll be doing something. I'll be fighting back."

"Bron, you're doing more for the war effort here, organizing everything that is going into helping them. You know full well I can't do what you do. I don't have your skill in organizing this shit. I don't have the patience for it. You are saving countless lives and playing a bigger part than you ever could Down Under."

Bron grinned, "do you really give a fuck about those people down there, mate?"

"What's that supposed to mean?" I replied curtly.

"For you, it's not about the people. It's about the Australia you lost!"

"Does it matter? I want to go home, Bron, just as much as you do. I miss my country, and I miss my life. Whether I do or don't care about the people, I do care about the Australia I once knew."

"Even if you do liberate the country, it's not going to be the same. Countries never are after such events."

I sighed frustratedly, "don't get all fucking philosophical on me, mate. And don't turn this on me. Whatever the reasons, if you want to help Australia, you'd stay here and continue helping me."

Bron pondered this, biting her lower lip. She thought about it and stared into space. "Here's my deal, Hannah. Use some of our resources to find my family, and if they are alive, get them out of there, and we'll carry on as we are."

"You know I can't promise we'll find them, but I promise you, we *will* try."

Bron agreed, but that little crisis was averted.

After disembarking the passengers and some crew rotations, they weren't nearly as bad as had been threatened. We were due for a cruise to Jupiter. I wanted us to continue on that itinerary, but I didn't really want passengers aboard. However, it was pointed out to me that it would be a big red flag if we traveled to Jupiter without the passengers.

I did, however, reduce the number of people that were going to come aboard. Shipboard maintenance was the excuse. I received a letter of complaint from Drake's office, considering I had just reduced the profits of the journey by several million, but neither Bron nor I responded to it.

However, we would never make it to Jupiter because halfway through the journey, something really bad happened.

We lost the war.

Chapter Twenty

Jenna Plural

I was asleep when the announcement came, and Bron burst into my room and turned on the television. I sat up gradually in my bed, cursing her name, but fell silent as I saw the president of the United States on the screen, declaring the official surrender to the European Union. As the day went on, one by one, all the other nations of the Pacific Alliance capitulated. I was in a state of disbelief, but I didn't have time to even think about it. Panic broke out on the Twilight Wanderer as people realized everything about their way of life was gone, and they didn't even know if they had a home to go back to. I met with Trisha, the ship's captain, and agreed to let her maintain control with the use of my security. I lost contact with my off-ship people almost immediately. Everything was in meltdown. I admit I sunk into a deep depression, as I realized I would never be going home again. I would never see Australia again. Even I couldn't turn the Australian resistance into a world resistance. Hell, I didn't even know if the will to fight was still left in the people.

The ship continued on its course towards the Jovian system for the lack of anything better to do.

Several weeks after the Pacific Alliance surrendered, I went down to do my daily broadcast. I had returned to making up the messages. Our supplies to Australia had effectively stopped, and I hadn't heard from Crocker in all that time. I didn't even know if Australia was still receiving these messages, although I would find out much later they were, and that pleased me. "G'day free Australia. We are rapidly approaching Anzac Day and looking forward to remembering the heroes of the past and the heroes of today, I would like..." I stopped, noticing the green light had changed to red. I looked up at Stepanchikov and mouthed the words, "what does that mean?"

She came around to my side of the desk and frowned. "It means we've been disconnected, but I've no idea why," she leaned over me and tried to put in a call to the technician that kept us online, but there was no response. We had no idea what had happened when we left there that day. It would only be when the message came through from Jenna Plural, that we would discover that she had completely destroyed the Peon communications base on Phobos, where transmissions were routed through. Although Radio Free Australia would restart after the Battle of Deep Space, I would not be at the helm, and my broadcasting days were over.

All communications had gone dead, as the Peons blocked everything. After a few days, we received orders from whatever puppet government they had in America to turn in our ship to the nearest American or Peon base.

Unrest among the passengers steadily grew. We had many important people on board who all wanted to contact their families, government department, or companies back home and were growing increasingly frustrated.

Almost two weeks into our isolation, and with no news from outside, the bubble burst.

Until then, I had effectively maintained control with diplomacy and a modicum of Stepanchikov's security, but it wasn't enough. I don't know what the catalyst was, but I received a call one afternoon that about twenty or so passengers were marching on the bridge. McFarland had immediately sealed herself in, and what was initially a show of force became a show of violence, as people started wrecking things, and more people joined them.

I mentioned an emergency meeting with Stepanchikov, Bronwyn, and the lawyer, Baker. I had, by now, kept the entire executive team out of every decision-making process, and they were nothing more than figureheads of the areas they were supposedly in control of.

"Okay, Stepanchikov, advise me," was all I said, as she came in.

"I don't think you have any option left, other than to put down what is a mutiny, on board the ship," She said quite firmly.

I looked at Baker, engrossed, "repercussions?"

"Well, you're probably within your legal rights to put down any mutiny, no matter how extreme. However, if you can do it without casualties, all the better from a PR standpoint."

"Exactly who are we aiming these public relations at? The only ones that can judge us now are the Peons," I said curtly, but he just shrugged.

"Whatever we decide, we have to do it now. We can't sit here debating this," said Bron.

I looked back to Stepanchikov, "you are at liberty to take any and every action to put this down."

And she did. I watched on the monitors as her security division moved in. They used tasers and nightsticks. However, someone pulled a gun, which was a clear signal to my security officer. The resistance rapidly crumbled, after about seven of the protesters were gunned down. The instigators were all sealed in their cabins, and I declared a form of martial law, controlling everything the passengers did from here on out.

We became more like a refugee ship than a cruise liner. Although we had supplies for almost a year, I had no clue how long we would be stranded without a base of operations, so I began rationing food and water. Stepanchikov's security team patrolled the corridors, and we recruited even more from passengers and crew that were ex-military and willing to share their talents with me.

Then, that fateful call came. About three weeks later, a message went out over French carrier waves, with a woman claiming to be Major Jenna Plural, calling out to the Solar System for all free ships to rendezvous, unite, and fight back.

It was a small beacon of hope, and even though this call was going out for military ships, I made sure McFarland set course for this rendezvous point.

As we drew closer to the fleet, she drew my attention to the problem of Admiral Baines claiming rank over Jenna Plural and securing authority over the fleet. However, we then intercepted the communications between Baines and Plural, albeit via Mr. Phelkar.

"This is Michael Phelkar of the U.S.S. Lady Liberty to the U.S.S. Constitution. Do you read me?" The stilted English voice I would come to know asked clearly over the general airwaves.

A woman's voice replied. "This is the U.S.S. Constitution. Please state your designation code. I don't see you listed as a United States vessel."

"Cut the bullshit. You already know we don't have a designation code for the Lady Liberty. She is a spoil of war, all above board and following the Galle Convention. Command was transferred here from the U.S.S. Lewis Puller."

"You're one of Jenna Plural's crew?" The woman sounded quite excited.

"That is correct. I have the privilege to serve under Major Plural, and this is her flagship."

Then, there was another pause. "Um, I have Admiral Baines on the line for you."

"Mr. Phelkar, I demand to speak with Lieutenant Plural!" The admiral demanded.

"Major Plural is currently unavailable. She is in a strategy meeting and cannot be disturbed. However, she demands to know why you're arranging inter-ship communications in a time of war where the enemy can overhear them."

"You insolent ass! As you well know, the war is over, and the military has been dissolved until further notice. And that genetically modified freak you follow is certainly no Major. I have stripped her of all rank until a formal court-martial can be held."

"I'm sorry, Admiral, but what you're saying doesn't make sense. If there is no military, in your opinion, you cannot strip her of her rank. You don't have the authority to do so by your own admission."

"What are you talking about, boy?"

"Unlike you, Mister Baines, the genetically modified freak still recognizes the authority of the United States military." I was sure I heard someone in the background laugh, but it was cut short. "You have made it clear to the entire fleet that you intend to surrender to the enemy. As a result, you have abdicated authority in these matters."

"Is this fleet-wide?" Baines said, clearly no longer talking to Phelkar.

"Umm, yes, sir," the woman who answered the call replied.

"Turn it off, you stupid—" And their end of the line went dead.

Phelkar then addressed the fleet "Major Jenna Plural requests all ships indicate their intent not to turn themselves over to European authority."

I waited patiently for our captain to respond as ship after ship started to transmit its support for Jenna Plural. When nothing happened, I called down to the bridge. "Captain, I expect you to respond to the instruction by Mr. Phelkar. Please do so at once."

The voice of the ship's first officer came back to me. "Captain McFarland is off duty, and with all due respect, Miss Grant, Baines does have authority here. I don't know who this Jenna Plural is, but the Admiral clearly has standing and our best interests at heart."

"I'll be the judge of that. This is my ship!" I snapped. "Baines has made it very clear he's just going to turn us over to the fucking Peons. You start your transmission now, or I'll send Stepanchikov down there to do it with your intestines, am I clear?"

He didn't respond, but I saw that we were signaling our transponder codes moments later. We had chosen a side. It didn't occur to me until later, that protocol should have been for him to wake the captain in these circumstances. Obviously, as I would become aware, he had his own agenda.

Baines's voice burst once more over the communications. "Discontinue these transmissions at once. That is an order."

All across communications, transponder codes broke the silence of space. All but a few had taken Jenna's side.

There were no more direct communications, but we heard that Jenna Plural had transferred her command to the U.S.S. Los Angeles and had met in a virtual conference with the commanders of the military ships. We were not invited. However, within a couple of hours, it was officially announced the fleet captains of the American contingent had elected Jenna Plural to lead them through this crisis.

I considered this a done deal, and both Bron and I were quite hopeful that, at last, something positive was going to happen. However, Baines did not concede, and tensions once more rose within the fleet.

I was woken by the First Officer the next night with the cryptic message that something was happening and I should come to the bridge. This raised my interest and concern, for I rarely ventured into the captain's domain.

As I entered, I looked up at the screen to see a close-up of the U.S.S. Constitution and several ships moving in around it. Unbeknownst to me at that time, my sister Stacey was piloting one of them. "What's going on?" I asked, as I stepped up beside him.

"I could be wrong, but I think those ships are about to attack the Constitution," he replied cautiously.

I stared wide-eyed at the vessels dwarfed by the vast battleship, which looked like it could swat them like flies. "Do they stand the remotest chance?"

The first officer shrugged, not taking his eyes off the screen as he said, "it looks like we're about to see if *your* Jenna Plural can pull it off."

I turned to look at him with a narrow frown, "My Jenna Plural?"

"She certainly doesn't have my support, Miss Grant. We restrict the authority of GenMods for a very good reason."

My eyes widened at that, but I said nothing. Did he not know I was a GenMod, or was he deliberately baiting me? I didn't have time to consider it further, for suddenly, the attack began.

One of the American vessels suddenly swerved underneath and began to release hundreds of troops in space suits with jet packs that carried them across to the official flagship of the United States. Then, there was silence. Nothing was happening, as the little pinpoints of light landed upon the ship's hull, and we couldn't see what was happening inside. Eventually, I gave up watching and returned to my quarters. A few hours later, the all-ship broadcast came online and Admiral Baines officially conceded defeat and was offering his full support to the new Admiral Jenna Plural.

When we finally arrived, I couldn't help feeling that we had made a mistake, for everything seemed to be in chaos. However, within a few days, a man called Michael Phelkar, whom I would come to know quite well, announced himself as the head of civilian affairs. Passengers on my crew started giving him a hard time as they tried to communicate with this Major Jenna Plural, and I got very pissed off when he blocked all communications from our ship because of it. I was effectively cut off again.

I was fully cognizant of the fact that my position was tenuous. All banking transactions based on the American economy had stopped. When your power base is completely incumbent on the flow of money, and that money stops flowing, you can quickly flounder.

At this time, my power was solely based on the Twilight Wanderer and maintained by the heavy hand of Stepanchikov and her security team.

"You once told me your loyalty to me was absolute as long as your paycheck was deposited every month," I told Stepanchikov one morning at one of our breakfast meetings, before the others arrived. "Since I can no longer deposit your paycheck, I thought I'd ask where we actually stand right now?"

Stepanchikov shrugged. "Are you willing to pay interest on my backpay when you can pay it?"

I grinned at that and replied, "Oh my dear, I absolutely promise you seventy-five percent and a bonus."

"Then I think we have a deal, Miss Grant." She smiled.

I had started to include the ship's captain in the daily briefings. After all, my continued authority did not extend beyond the ship's airlocks.

"The fleet has opened up communications with us again," McFarland informed me after Bron and Baker arrived. "It appears everything related to civilian ships joining this fleet is now under the authority of this Michael Phelkar fellow."

I looked to Stepanchikov and asked, "Do you know anything about this Michael Phelkar?"

"Not much," she replied. "He is a British diplomat employed by the Ministry of Defense in England, or rather, was. He served as part of the Royal Air Force for many years as a drone pilot, but was invalided out after a car accident in London. It appears he was recently attached on some mission with the United States Marines, and I can only assume that is how he met Jenna Plural."

"And what do you know about Jenna Plural?" I asked. "The name sounds very familiar to me, but I can't quite work out where I've heard it from."

"Crocker," said Bron. "Back on Oz, he told us that he once served with her many years ago."

"Ah, yes," I said, as I recalled the conversation. "She's a GenMod, isn't she?"

"Indeed, she is," Stepanchikov added. "She is one of the oldest surviving GenMods to predate Grozny."

"Doesn't that limit her authority?" Bron asked.

"Under American law, yes, it does, but does American law apply anymore?" The question was rhetorical, and Stepanchikov continued without pause. "She's had varied careers over the last couple of centuries, but most of it has been serving as a United States Marine. She was serving as a Colonel in the Pentagon when the Grozny uprising happened. She was considered one of the United States' best strategists. However, after Grozny and the limitations were put on the authority of GenMods, she was bumped down to the position of Lieutenant again. She remained in that position for the last seventy years."

"Yet she announced herself as a Major Plural," I stated curiously.

"Yes, that is strange. I don't see how she would have achieved such a position legitimately. I can only make a wild assumption that she's adopted the title for herself."

"If that's the case, how would it be possible for her to maintain authority?" Bron asked uneasily.

"Oh, I can assure you, the Jenna Plural I know is quite resourceful."

My eyes widened in surprise as I looked at my security officer. "You know her?"

"Knowing her is probably too strong of a term, because it's probably been many years since I last worked with her. However, you'll find as the decades pass, you'll come to know most GenMods that are out there. It is the one constant we can count on."

"What do you mean by that?" Bron asked.

Stepanchikov fixed her eyes on her, "you'll grow old and die, Miss Donovan. Miss Grant here will live on. She'll find her time with anyone brief. In a century, you'll be little more than a vague memory. However, other GenMods she meets over the years will live on and become the only constant relationships in her life."

Bron looked deflated at this comment and looked uneasily at me. However, now was not the time to deal with her insecurities. "Do you believe this Jenna Plural has what it takes to lead us out of this mess?" I asked, directly to Stepanchikov.

There was no hesitation in her response. "I most certainly do. I would go as far as saying, had Jenna Plural remained in her position at the Pentagon, this war would have ended many years ago in a Pacific Alliance victory. She's a natural leader and a tactical genius. I would place my trust in her, and I don't say that lightly."

"But we're not a military vessel, Miss Stepanchikov," stated Bron. "How do you think she would deal with the likes of us?"

Stepanchikov shrugged that off. "Exactly as she has done. Pass off responsibility for us to someone that she trusts. This Michael Phelkar fellow must be very close to her and have her ear."

"Do you think I should arrange a meeting with him?" I asked.

"No." It was Baker, the lawyer, who replied. "We really don't know your status until we learn more about what's going on with Grant Industries. Drawing attention to you could ultimately end in you being considered a person without influence. That would be something hard to recover from, even if you re-establish."

"So, I should remain in the shadows?" I asked, not liking that idea at all, although it would later work to my advantage.

"Well, I wouldn't quite put it like that, but keeping yourself off the radar, for now, may be a good idea. Have the captain deal with Michael Phelkar."

And that is precisely what we did, although I listened in on the conversations whenever any communication was made with the U.S.S. Los Angeles, which was now the flagship of this new ragtag fleet.

CHAPTER TWENTY-ONE

DECEPTION

The next communication from the new command was one that was detrimental and not beneficial to us. It made me wonder if I'd made the right decision to join up with Jenna.

Many ships were without supplies, having been on course to return to Earth or whatever destination they had where they would've normally restocked.

The office of Michael Phelkar had contacted us for an inventory of our supplies, and Bron had duly supplied them with such. The result of that was a few days later, and a redistribution order came through. Fleet personnel were going to come aboard and strip our ship of all but immediately necessary food supplies.

After a meeting with the others, we agreed to comply with the order. There wasn't an alternative, considering we had nowhere to go, and we were going to have to rely on this fleet for our very existence. Some cargo hauler was going to get to dine on venison and caviar, amongst other things. This somewhat amused me to think about.

However, this was not nearly as hard on us as the next order came through. Personnel redistribution. The United States and other countries have various levels of national service. In a twenty-year war, it's simply something necessary to continue it. The length of this service ranged from two years to six, depending on the country. As a result, most of our crew were Navy veterans. This time it was from the office of a woman called Claire Addison, who you know to be Jenna Plural's second in command. They set up recruitment stations looking for volunteers to switch from civilian to military service. Many of my crew signed up. What pissed me off the most was they had no consideration for where they were leaving me shorthanded. What made it worse, our new captain Trisha McFarland also took the opportunity to regain her military wings. Turned out she knew this Jenna Plural and immediately transferred to the U.S.S. Constitution. As a temporary measure we made the annoying executive officer captain.

Bron met with a woman called Sakamoto, who was once a member of the Japanese Imperial Guard but, for some reason, now served permanently under Jenna Plural. She was in charge of this reallocation program, and a meeting with Bron was simply a courtesy. Bron explained that the program had left us desperately short of engineers, to which the response was that we had to make do, but contact her should the problem become insurmountable.

However, the following day, she sent over a tech called Paris Sinclair. She collaborated with our engineers, about how going through system shutdown would further reduce their workload. With many passengers also being recruited on transfer, we started moving the remaining passengers from certain decks to shut down the power there. This again caused consternation, as one of the decks we closed down was first class, and we moved everybody into steerage. Wealthy executives now found themselves sharing accommodation, and they were not happy. However, fear of retaliation by Stepanchikov maintained order.

I have to be completely honest. My tension was at an all-time high. Our situation was controlled and secure, but not knowing what the future held and where I was going, both physically and personally, became increasingly frustrating.

One morning, at yet another of our meetings, the captain informed us of something neither I, Bron, nor Stepanchikov, had even remotely envisaged.

"Plural is separating the fleet," he told us. "She's creating two divisions. The fastest and most battle-ready ships, including her own, the U.S.S. Los Angeles, are forming up, leaving behind the slower ships, including us."

"And what do you think that means?" I responded, for I knew even less about military strategy than I did about corporate operations.

"I would hazard a guess that she intends to abandon us here. She's taking the best ships, and leaving those that can't keep up to fend for themselves."

"Bullshit!" Stepanchikov snorted. "While I am aware that Jenna Plural would have no qualms about sacrificing a ship or two if it aided in her strategy. Abandoning thousands of people is just not in her nature."

"You said it yourself that you haven't met with her in over a century. Can't it be that she isn't the woman you once knew?"

"No. Immortality affects the psyche a lot differently than it does mortal people. You strive to make your achievements in a limited life span. As do GenMods for the first hundred years or so, but eventually, we start to view the world day by day, knowing that anything we begin will ultimately end, while we continue on. Jenna Plural established her value system long ago, and surrounded by mortals, she has no one with greater experience to challenge those values," Stepanchikov turned back to me. "I assure you, Miss Grant, she will not abandon us."

"I can understand you having faith in a fellow GenMod, Miss Stepanchikov. After all, history shows that you all band together. I, however, don't have your faith in them."

"Grozny was seventy-five years ago, Captain," Stepanchikov stared death at him. "Get over your bigotry."

The captain appeared unfazed by this and turned back to me. "My recommendation is that we set a course for the nearest American or European base and turn ourselves over, before we run out of what's left of the supplies Plural hasn't stolen from us."

I didn't immediately reply, and I looked at Bron, who shrugged, leaving any decision completely to me. I sat back in my chair and let out a sigh as I pondered the information given to me. I didn't know if what Stepanchikov said was correct. I may be a GenMod, but I was still only eighteen years old and hadn't experienced the immortality she spoke of.

191

"We wait," I finally replied. "We wait and see if she does indeed leave. A few more days is not going to cause any major hardships."

"Presently, that is the case, but what if she starts to decide to start stripping us of our hardware? We have a lot of equipment that can very easily be transferred for military use," the captain said, unwilling to give up on his argument. "She only needs to strip our engines of a few items to leave us stranded here."

Stepanchikov grew angry now, something I had never seen her do before. "Now you are living in the realms of fantasy, Captain. You have now gone from Jenna Plural abandoning us, to actively killing us. If you don't have anything serious to contribute, I suggest you shut the fuck up."

"Okay, let's try and keep this civil, can we?" Bron said, raising her hands to try and calm them down.

"I've said all I'm going to say," the captain said irritably and rose from his seat. "If you need me, I'll be on the bridge, Miss Grant."

I visibly tensed as he walked out without my permitting him to. "I think he's going to be a problem that we will need to deal with," I muttered.

"Unfortunately, we don't have anyone to replace him with," Bron said regretfully.

Another day passed with no news from the fleet, but I monitored their movements very carefully and kept Stepanchikov at my side to explain what was happening with the ships. Even she was surprised when the advanced vessels did, indeed, start moving away from us, accelerating to interplanetary speeds. It appeared the captain had been right, and we were being abandoned.

"This can't be right," Stepanchikov said, and for another first, she sounded doubtful.

"You fucked up," I said irritably, and I stormed out of my office to head down to the bridge, with her following close behind. As I got into the elevator, I called Bronwyn on my radio to come join us, and she said she'd meet us there.

She must have been closer as she was already there when I entered. "Lock onto the course for the nearest American base, Captain. Get us the fuck out of here," I shouted. He positively beamed at that and ordered his helmsman to plot a course from one of Saturn's moons.

However, Bron stepped up to me and pulled me away from the captain to speak to me quietly in the corner. "Something's not right here," she whispered. "When I came in, the helmsman was arguing with the captain, telling him that he needed to tell you something, but I didn't hear what it was. The captain refused, but the conversation ended the moment they were aware that I'd arrived. I think he's hiding something."

I turned back towards the captain. "Belay that last order," I said, stepping up to him. "It has come to my attention, Captain, you're hiding something from me, and I want to know what it is."

He tried desperately to look confused. "I'm telling you everything that I know," he said most earnestly, but again, I watched the pupils change size. The motherfucker was lying to me.

I turned to the helmsman. "Maybe you can be more honest with me."

The helmsman looked up at the captain nervously and then back at me. I saw the captain glare at her, challenging her not to say anything, but she finally said, "it's the Peons, ma'am."

"Shut up, you stupid bitch!" The captain made to move towards her, but I grabbed him firmly by the collar and pulled him back, and he was unable to break my grasp.

I looked back at the helmsman. "What about the Peons?"

"We received a communication from Commodore Addison's office, that a massive Peon fleet is headed our way. They're preparing for battle."

I let go of the captain and glared at him, and he looked at us angrily as he kept his eyes fixed on the young helmsman. "You didn't just lie to me, Captain. You tried to manipulate me, you dumb motherfucking moron."

"You're going to get us all killed with that genetically modified bitch, Miss Grant!" He positively screamed at me. "I'm just trying to save the lives of everybody on board this ship, as is my responsibility."

"Well, there's another genetically modified bitch that isn't finding this acceptable!" I screamed back at him, angrier than I'd ever been in my life. He looked momentarily at Stepanchikov, thinking I was referring to her, and then his eyes widened in realization as he looked at me. "God damn it, you're one of them too?"

I didn't reply, and in my anger, I grabbed him by the collar again and slammed him hard against the wall. I wasn't thinking and, in my anger, didn't pull my strength back. He hit the bulkhead hard and almost instantly fell limply in my hand. As I let go of him, he fell to the floor, and there was a big splatter of blood on the wall behind him. I instantly froze, and I looked down at him staring up at me, and I didn't need to check a pulse to know he was dead. I just stared at him as I heard the sound of the bridge crew scrabbling to their feet in a panic. I barely heard the words of Stepanchikov. "Everyone, stay calm and in your seats."

Bronwyn ran over and crouched down over him. "Holy fuck, Han. You killed him."

I didn't reply. I didn't exactly care that I had just killed this motherfucking traitor. I only wish I hadn't done it in the crew's presence, which would now make things a little awkward. I turned back to the helmsman. "Call the Los Angeles and inform them that we stand ready to assist in any way possible." The communications officer simply nodded and turned back to his console. I looked at Bron and nodded toward the body. "I trust you can deal with that."

Without waiting for a reply, I strode out of the room.

Later, Stepanchikov would inform me that the bridge crew was dealing with the situation. While in shock about what had just happened to the captain, most were extremely pleased that we were not going to turn ourselves over to the enemy.

We were without a ship's captain, but we would follow routines and get by until I could appoint a new one.

When Bronwyn met up with me, there was no discussion about the captain, and she simply informed me that fleet command had requested we operate as a hospital ship and be ready to receive incoming wounded and dead. I immediately called Deacon Cooper up into my office. He had remained aboard the ship at my request to continue monitoring Bron's recovery from her injuries. Although she seemed perfectly fine, I had left nothing to chance.

Although we had a ship's doctor, I didn't really know him, and I wanted someone that I was at least familiar with to head up the preparations for the request that had been made of us.

"To be honest with you, Hannah, I don't have the experience to deal with a major emergency," he advised me with concern.

"Well, if you know someone who is, then please tell me," I replied.

He pondered this a moment before replying dejectedly. "Unfortunately, while I'm not qualified, I'm the closest to qualified you have on board this ship. Most of our senior medics transferred out in the crew requisitions recently. Have they given you any idea of the numbers of casualties?"

I shook my head. He sighed. "Great." He then pondered a moment and said, "I have a limited number of nurses and E.M.T.s at my disposal, so I strongly recommend you put out a call to passengers and crew for anyone with medical experience that can be transferred to me. I'll start working on that, but please let me know whatever logistics you set up to deal with the incoming wounded."

"What are you talking about?" I asked, confused.

At that, he sat down, his eyes widened and looking incredibly concerned. "We can deal with the wounded, but someone needs to deal with how we're going to get them on board and where they're gonna be. You need to set up medical facilities for an untold number of people. You need a procedures to get them off their crafts and onto here as quickly as possible. You've gotta prepare the shuttles to go out there and pick up the wounded flying through space in their suits with no ships."

"How the fuck am I supposed to do that, Deke?" I said, wide-eyed and jaw-dropping to my knees.

"Hey, I have enough of a problem to resolve. That's on you. However, your captain should be well versed in how to deal with it."

I didn't mention we no longer had a captain. "I'll let you know when we have it sorted," I said with a confidence that I distinctly lacked.

After he left, I sat back in my chair for a moment, wondering how to deal with this clusterfuck. Up until this point, I'd relied on other people, and did nothing myself. I pondered palming this off on Bron, but I'd been pushing her too far of late, and the stress was clearly showing.

"Okay, Hannah Grant," I said aloud to myself. "Time to be the leader you've always pretended you were." I reached down and hit the inter-ship com that would be heard in every room throughout the vessel. "This is Hannah Grant. I have to inform you that we are going into battle with a Peon fleet. We have been called upon to function as a first-line medical ship and will be receiving casualties. I want anyone with any form of medical or nursing experience or even first aid to report to Dr. Deacon Cooper in order to assist him. I want all deck handlers, stewards, and non-technical personnel to go to the cargo holds and start preparing them as medical centers. Move the beds out of the staterooms and down there for immediate use. I also want all shuttle pilots to prepare any and all ship's vessels to be able to go out to pick up the wounded," I paused and pondered what to say next. "I know many of you will be afraid. I know many of you will have doubts that we are doing the right thing by not surrendering. I want to assure you that I will do everything within my power, to ensure your safety in this coming battle. Please remember, it is against convention to attack a civilian ship, especially one rendering medical aid. We are unlikely to come under direct attack, but we need to be prepared. Good luck everyone, and I want you to know how proud I am to collaborate with you all in this great endeavor."

Bron would later tell me how amazed she was that I had taken that control. She meant it as a compliment, but I didn't take it that way, although I didn't tell her. I had done nothing other than set the agenda. I had taken none of the risks, but now things were different.

Chapter Twenty-Two

The Medical Ship

My mother had generally treated employees with contempt. Her opinion was that the working class was lazy and required close supervision and a metaphorical stick was needed to beat them. I had no reason or experience to disagree with that ideology, and my confidence in the crew and passengers stepping up to the tasks that I had set for them was not very high. As far as I was concerned, they were all pretty stupid and needed close observation.

Under that concept, I later headed down alone to the cargo areas believing that I would have to supervise everything, even though I had no clue how to achieve the tasks I had set.

So, you'll understand that I was most surprised that everything was working like a well-oiled machine. A chubby little man called Pinner was apparently the chief supervisor of the vast cargo holds of commodities we carried for delivery to the Jovian system.

I was surprised to find him authorizing the dumping of cargo out of the ship.

I met him in one of the larger cargo bays stacked high with supplies. We weren't a cargo hauler, but good business sense meant we used every available space to make extra profit.

He was a cheerful portly man who greeted me quite informally from the control room that overlooked the cargo area. It was locked off from the main cargo area with a large window covering the entire wall and looking down into the storage area. The need to transfer items in space meant you had to be cut off from the area that would quite often be airless.

As I have said, he was overseeing the dumping of cargo, and I grew genuinely concerned about this. "We may need that stuff," I said incredulously.

"Oh, don't worry, I'm making sure we're only dumping stuff we can't possibly need," he pointed out the window at two of his men moving stuff toward the rear cargo hatch. "Take that, for example. They're moving a consignment of toys that were destined for a colony. So, unless we start having children on this ship, we're unlikely to ever need them. The problem is, Hannah, we use every available space to maximize the profits from delivery. In order to set up the medical areas that you want, we need to empty them."

I admit I was impressed at his initiative. So much so, that I didn't even notice the inappropriateness of his informality using my first name.

"Good job," I responded enthusiastically and left him to it.

I intended to return to my accommodation, but I found all corridors leading to it were now blocked by people moving beds and mattresses down to the cargo hold. This turned out to be the case with the elevators, too, and I had no idea what to do other than just stand there. A crewman stopped and asked if they could help me, and I explained my predicament. They led me to a small hatch in the ceiling, and for the first time, I became aware of the emergency ladders between decks. He let me back up two levels, but before we reached the level of my accommodation, I noticed some medics in the corridor due to the smocks they wore in one of the corridors. I had the crewman stop and wait for me, as I went down the corridor and found Doctor Cooper. He was calling out directions and listening to staff call back inventory lists of medications they were stacking up on carts to take down to the receiving areas. He clearly had everything under control. "I'm very busy, Miss Grant, unless it's urgent."

I smiled at him and said, "carry on." I returned to my aide, who led me back into my offices.

Bronwyn was there, receiving reports from various areas of the ship, and she informed me that of our eight shuttles, we had pilots for six.

That would have to do. Over the next twelve hours, each area of the operation reported that they were ready. I then called down to the bridge and instructed our communications officer to inform the fleets that we were ready.

The waiting game began.

Of course, I wasn't involved in Jenna Plural's game plan, and I remained concerned that the best of our ships were still on course to some base far away. As it stood, the ships that the Twilight Wanderer remained with were little more than cannon fodder.

I found it difficult to eat that night. My anxiety about events to come was making me rather nauseous, which was quite a rare occurrence for me as I never got sick.

I finally got a call from the helm informing me that, within the hour, the Peon fleet would be close enough to begin an engagement. Bron and I immediately went down to the bridge to monitor the situation. Although I didn't think of it at the time, I had effectively become the ship's captain. And to my surprise, I found I actually enjoyed exercising my authority rather than passing it on to someone else. The wait was dull and boring as no one spoke while we all sat there in anticipation. I had automatically taken my place in the captain's seat without thinking about it, and Bron quite appropriately sat next to me in the chair that should have been for the first officer.

Even over the communications, all was silent, with the fleet operating on exclusive military frequencies that our equipment was locked out of. However, when the battle began, it would be fleetwide to ensure all the civilian ships participating were well prepared.

When I finally heard the words we were waiting for, my pulse began to race. I can't tell you if it was either fear or exhilaration, as my adrenaline pumped its way through my heart.

"This is the U.S.S. Benjamin Franklin. We can confirm that the Peon fleet is now directly between us and the Addison flotilla. It's now or never, Admiral."

"Thank you, Franklin." This was the first time I heard the American-accented voice of the woman who would become my hero. "Plural to Beta Fleet. This is it, boys and girls. Engage your engines, full thrust towards the Peons. Captain Addison, about-turn, prepare to engage the enemy."

"Aye, Major," Addison replied. "Alpha Fleet one-eighty on my mark."

The Battle of Deep Space had begun.

I had never paid any attention to the war, and watching the ships engage left me speechless. I audibly gasped as thousands of tiny pin-points of light began to depart their vessels. Human beings launching themselves into the void in the hope of boarding the enemy vessels.

I jumped out of my seat as I saw a ship silently erupt in a brief flash of light. "Whose was that?" I demanded.

"It was the H.M.S. Coventry, ma'am. One of ours." The helmsman said dejectedly, and I cursed.

Everything became a blur, as ships exploded all over the void, and I couldn't follow. Comms were a confusing mess until the comms officer filtered out everything except transmissions.

Jenna barked out orders I didn't understand. They were all about maneuvers and strategy, but then Bron and I looked at each other excitedly, as we heard the voice of an Aussie girl. "Admiral, the Chesty is under heavy attack," she said urgently. "Much more than other ships."

There was a pause before Jenna asked, "Are you holding your own, Tomi?" I assumed she was talking to this Chesty the Aussie had mentioned.

"That's a negative." Came the reply, and Bron informed me this was the Sakamoto she had been working with. "We are compromised with Dutch commandos on board. Engines destroyed. We have lost key personnel. I'm losing troopers faster than we can download them. Implementing self-destruct."

"That is a negative, Sakamoto. I repeat, that is a negative!" Jenna shouted back. "You are to abandon ship. Do you read me?"

"That is not protocol, Admiral. My duty is to ensure that this ship does not fall into enemy hands," Sakamoto replied.

"Fuck protocol, Sakamoto. You are of more value to me than that piece of shit ship. They can grow goddamn tulips on it for all I care. I want you alive!" Jenna ordered, and I respected that.

There was a long pause before Sakamoto came back again, "the ship's captain is the last to leave."

"Damn it to hell, Tomi. I'm not going to continue repeating myself. Get off that ship, and that's a fucking order."

"What about the rest of the crew?"

"Evacuate as many as you can in the life pods and eject the M.E.T. Anyone who doesn't make it then tough luck, but I need you, Batty, and Harlow off that ship. No more talking, do it."

"Harlow is already dead, Admiral."

There was a pause before Jenna replied softly. "Get yourself off that ship."

"Yes, ma'am." The line went dead.

The formations began to break up as both fleets' ships entered what was known as the dance of death. Ships of both sides twisted and turned to lock on to the enemy or avoid them.

Jenna came online again, barking out, "Plural to all ships, break protocol now, bring your ships in close to the enemy. They are not trying to board. They are trying to blow you out of the sky. Make sure you stay close, so that they have to destroy their own ships to get to you."

Pinner, the deck supervisor, came on internal communications informing all who needed to know that, "We have our first incoming casualties. Cargo bay six releasing umbilicals for ship-to-ship transfer with U.S.S. Trinity."

"How many?" Dr. Cooper responded.

"Seventy-two, but more ships are incoming with casualties," Pinner advised.

"What the fuck...?" Cooper's voice trailed off before coming back. "I need all hands not engaged in essential work to report to the medical areas."

I sat for a moment before it occurred to me that I was not engaged in essential work, and ordering Bron to keep me updated, I headed down to the cargo bay.

To say I was out of my depth would be an understatement. Little rich society girl getting my hands dirty. Marcia Grant would be appalled. The truth is, the whole experience exhilarated me. I'll be honest

201

with you. I truly believe war is fun, and there is no better thrill than putting your life on the line. Kind of ironic, since I had fled the Earth to escape it.

I expected to see Cooper when I entered the cargo bay, but obviously, his skills were needed more with the patients than giving out instructions. Several other volunteers had turned up along with me, and the young woman supervising everything treated me no differently than the others. At the time, I gave no thought to that, as I looked down into the cargo bay through the large window, seeing that all the beds had already been filled. People were lying on the floor on blankets as Doctor Cooper triaged everyone who came in through the airlock at the side of the main door. I could see through the glass of the cargo hatch, and along the umbilical reaching out to a small scout vessel. Both walking wounded and people on stretchers were being brought out into the docking bay. I couldn't help but wonder how they'd gotten wounded, for they were clearly not combatants. It was only when I later saw a hole ripped in the side of the cutter, when it disconnected and moved away back into the battle, that I realized these were shipboard injuries from explosives those motherfucking Peons planted on the outer sides.

I was interrupted from my thoughts when the supervisor shoved a handful of bandages into my hands and a bag full of stims. She shouted at me to get moving. "They need you in there!"

I will never forget that day. It is indelibly imprinted upon my mind, and if I live for one thousand years, it will always seem like yesterday. As I went down those steps into the main area, all I could hear were the screams of the dying. Dozens of men and women cried out for their mothers,

fathers, and other loved ones. Bloodied, bruised, missing limbs, burned faces. They were everywhere. I stood frozen by the horror of it all, until Doctor Cooper shouted aggressively at me. "Start bandaging people, Hannah! Don't just stand there like a fucking idiot, mate! If you can't do it, get out 'cause you're just in the way!"

I didn't reply, but I immediately went to the bedside of a man who had a gaping wound in his side. I had no idea what to do. I just stood there staring down at him, horrified at the gore, totally unaware that he was already dead until someone told me. I moved onto the next bed, where I managed to bandage a young woman who had a gash in her leg. She cried out in pain, and I pulled one of the stims out and shoved it into her side. I moved on to the next one as soon as it was done. The next hour was an eye-opener for me as I saw untold suffering. I was confused when I saw two men I knew to be stewards lifting people off the bed by their wrists and ankles, until I realized they were moving the dead, which were starting to stack up in a corner. We had barely gotten through half the people there, when a shout went up that another ship had attached the umbilicals, and more were coming aboard.

This was not going to end well, but I had an idea. Doctor Cooper called after me as I ran back up the stairs, clearly disappointed that I appeared to be abandoning helping them. However, when I was back in the office, I hit the ship-wide intercom. "All current passengers are report to the nearest medical bay. Get your arses down here ASAP!" An engineer called back to tell me they couldn't leave their posts, but I replied. "I don't give a fuck, mate. We're not going anywhere. Get your fucking arse to medical bay, or I'll be making damn sure you never work on a ship again."

I disconnected the communications and ran back down the stairs to receive a beaming grin from Doctor Cooper across the room. As the hours passed, I could see the crew becoming exhausted. Stepanchikov and I started taking over the heavier duties, as we could continue on as if we'd only just started. I was surprised to discover that Bron knew a lot about first aid. She had arrived when I put out that all ship call and was helping to splint broken bones. Ship upon ship docked and discharged their wounded and left. Eventually, it began to slow. Someone called out that our ships had started to flash their transponders, and the cheer went up. I had no idea what it meant, and seeing my confusion, one of my crew told me it indicated that the battle was won.

This didn't mean the casualties stopped. However, I needed to find out what was going on, and I told Cooper this, and he nodded understanding. Bron and I headed back up to the bridge, which was vacant. However, the communications were still on.

"The last two Peon cruisers are heading directly for the U.S.S. Constitution. Collision speed!" Jenna was shouting as we entered. I looked up at the screen, and sure enough, two cruisers were heading at incredible speed toward the Constitution.

"Tracker, you have Peon cruisers coming in on you," Jenna called out urgently. "Can you get anything online?" There was no reply. "Addison, disengage now and protect the Constitution."

"Admiral, all ships are in the process of picking up troopers. We've got thousands of shuttles out there in space. If we stop now, we'll lose a lot of our men and women."

"Damn it to hell! I won't lose that ship!" The Admiral then appeared to be talking to someone within her ship. "How good a pilot are you?"

"I can do at a pinch," Came some distant sound in a European voice.

"Get us in there. Get us into the docking bay. Don't spare the thrusters. Carry on, Addison, disregard my last order."

I watched, captivated, unable to do anything, as I saw one of the ships get closer and closer to the Constitution. I sat back in the captain's chair, trying to keep myself calm, frustrated at my inability to help.

Then as if out of nowhere, I saw another ship heading towards them. I slid to the edge of my seat and watched in great anticipation, wondering what was going to happen next. I gasped audibly as the ship collided directly with the Peon cruiser. It was only half its size, but it did what was intended as both ships began to break up

"For Harper and Wagga, you fuckers!" I recognized the voice of the Australian that I had heard earlier. In the background was the sound of grinding metal and explosions, and I was convinced this young Australian was not going to get out of this. But when I thought it was all over for her, her voice came online again. "Okay, you pack of rabid dingoes. Time to disembark this joy ride. Abandon ship, I repeat, abandon ship. Move it, you shits, that's a fucking order."

"Stacey Grant, I love you!" Jenna's voice came on again, and she was laughing. "Don't die, or I'll bring you up on charges."

However, I was not. I jumped out of my seat, staring at the screen in disbelief at the name I had just heard.

"Ahh, you only get all kissy-kissy when I save your genetically designed arse from hot water," my estranged sister responded comically. "Love to chat, but I gotta get these arseholes moving to the escape pods." The line went dead.

"Addison, make picking up Stacey's escape pod a priority," Jenna ordered

"But Admiral..."

"Just do it!" Jenna snapped irritably. "And send out as many troopers as you can to board the Constitution."

"On it, Admiral."

I stood there staring at the screen as a tear ran down my cheek. I had just heard my sister for the first time in my life.

CHAPTER TWENTY-THREE

BIRTH OF THE CONFEDERATION

"Did I just hear right?" Bron said, sounding almost as surprised as I was. "Did she just say Stacey Grant?"

I didn't answer her as I stepped over to the helm control. I looked desperately around for some method of scanning for life pods. As you can probably guess, I was fucking clueless. However, I did know how to activate the internal ship's communications. "Will the bridge crew all return to their positions immediately?" I said, sounding a little desperate.

It was probably only a few minutes, but it seemed like an eternity before the helmsman came onto the bridge. There were no perfunctory greetings, and I said quite authoritatively, "can you scan for life pods?"

She nodded and returned to her seat as I stood behind her and leaned over her shoulder. "I need you to find one carrying an officer called Stacey Grant."

She looked up at me uneasily as she said, "well, ma'am, there are literally hundreds of life pods out there, but none of them indicate who's in them."

I muttered a few situation-appropriate profanities as I stood back upright and stared at the screen at the fleet that was scattered all over the vicinity. As the communications officer came in, I turned to her immediately. "Are you able to scan comms to find out if anyone is picking up life pods?" I asked her.

"I can, but in this situation, there's quite a lot of chatter. Is there anything specific you want me to look for?" she said as she took her seat.

"Yes, I want you to find out if anyone has picked up an officer called Stacey Grant."

She nodded and placed an earpiece in her ear. Several minutes passed until she finally looked up with a smile. "The H.M.S. Manchester has picked up a Lieutenant Stacefield Grant. She has minor wounds and is being shipped out to the U.S.S. Constitution."

I let out a sigh of relief and smiled at her. "Thank you."

Bron and I headed back to our quarters. "What are the odds that in this vast Solar System, you would run into your sister?" Bron said, sounding amused.

"Probably higher than you'd imagine," I replied. "Considering all military vessels that aren't captive of the Peons are heading here to become part of this fleet."

"Are you going to give her a call?" Bron asked.

I shook my head. "We've never met. She's my half-sister. I don't even know what she's like. She left with her dad before I was born to go live in Wagga."

"So? She's still your sister," Bron said incredulously as we stepped into the elevator.

"What am I supposed to say to her?" I said wearily, leaning back against the wall and folding my arms. "G'day, Stacey. I'm Hannah. Sorry you grew up with nothing, while I had a silver spoon in my mouth?" My tone was sarcastic. "No, she won't want to meet me."

"Fuck. If I had the chance to meet any of my family right now, I'd kill to do so. She's all you have left, mate."

"I've got you." I smiled, but she saw straight through it. Not the fact I saw her as family. That was without doubt. She could tell I desperately wanted to know this estranged sibling of mine. I don't even know why. As I am sure you have come to realize, I struggle with any form of empathy and hadn't even grieved over the loss of Annabelle, the sister I grew up with.

"Yeah, mate, we're besties forever, but she's still your sister. Go meet her," Bron smiled knowingly at me as we entered our apartment once more. I shook my head again and allowed myself to collapse into a heap on the sofa with a resigned sigh. "Look, before you decide, let's find out some more about her."

She pulled out a handheld tablet. "Access Grant Industries security files. Give me all the data on Stacey Grant, United States Navy, Australian citizen."

"No records found." Came the cheerful reply from her device.

"I've already tried that a while back. There are no records because she's in some sort of covert ops."

"Yeah, but you can bet now that she's resurfaced, our intelligence files are already being filled up. After all, she seems good mates with this Jenna Plural woman."

"Then try her full name, Stacefield Ellen Grant."

Bron nodded. "Access all files on Stacefield Ellen Grant, United States Navy, Australian citizen."

"One matching file. Stacefield Ellen Grant is twenty-eight years old and currently serving as a lieutenant in the United States Navy. She's attached to a covert United States Marine unit known as Theta squad, under the command of Lieutenant Jennacia Plularian. Known aliases are Stacey Grant, Gillian Bale, and Anna Roshanko. Her current position is the chief pilot of the U.S.S. Lewis Puller. She is the only person in history to be the recipient of the Australian Victoria Cross and the United States medal of honor. She is considered by both the European Union and the Pacific Alliance as the best pilot in military history. Parents are Marcia Grant, deceased, and William Grant, deceased. She has one immediate living relative, Hannah Grant."

As the voice stopped, Bron looked at me and saw me staring at her wide-eyed. "Shit. She's a fucking war hero."

"Looks that way," Bron grinned. "Do you wanna meet her now?"

I mulled this over in my mind before replying, "I do want to meet her, but not like this. There's bad blood between her side of the family and mine. My mother ditched her and her father and deliberately ensured he would never succeed. She totally fucked that guy right up. I don't want to throw it in Stacey's face that I am the heir of Marcia Grant. Something that should rightfully be her position as the eldest child."

209

"You're not gonna do something stupid and hand her your share of the company, are you?"

I laughed at this. "I might feel bad about the situation, but not that bad. I really like my lifestyle too much to let anyone take it from me," I got serious again. "However, when I meet her, it's going to be on common ground."

"How exactly are you proposing to do that?"

I smiled at her with a bemused look on my face, "I have no clue, Bron, I really don't."

As it would turn out, there would be little time to even think about Stacey, let alone do anything about it. Although the battle was over, things didn't exactly slow down. Doctor Cooper still had bays full of wounded, and more were still being brought in, as people were picked up from disabled ships or on life pods.

Jenna Plural now had a new task. She didn't have to just turn this fleet into a battle-ready, capable military force, but as more ships began arriving every day, she had to turn it into a living, breathing community. We had no planet or moon we could call home. The birth of the Solar Confederation existed entirely in the void of space.

I still didn't know how I felt about everything, but for the lack of an alternative, I went along with it. That was about to change just two days after the Battle of Deep Space. I was alone in the apartment with both Bronwyn and Stepanchikov helping Doctor Cooper organize the transfer of those who were able back to their own ships, or to new ones, in the case of those that had completely lost theirs. I was making myself a snack in the little kitchenette when I heard my T.V. come on. This only happened in the event of someone transmitting an emergency override, and I headed back into the living room to watch it.

The bridge of the Constitution was displayed, although I didn't realize that was what it was until partway through the proceedings.

A tall attractive man appeared at a podium dressed in a sharp suit and tie and immediately began to address the camera. "This is Michael Phelkar, speaking to you from the bridge of the U.S.S. Constitution. I present to you the new leader of the allied resistance forces, Jennacia Plularian."

The camera turned, and stepping through the doors, I saw Jenna Plural for the first time. She wore a black uniform I didn't recognize, but would later learn this was to become the officer's uniform of the soon-to-be-announced Solar Confederation. She was strikingly beautiful and bore a confidence about her I could only dream of emulating.

Phelks stepped away from the podium but remained by her, just over her shoulder as she took his place. She indicated for the crew, who had stood up when she entered, to resume their seats. She then looked directly at me. At least, that's how it felt as she turned to face the camera grimly. "I pray that I come to you today, as a beacon of hope." Her voice was soft and warm, and reassuring. "I have assumed command of the loyal remnants of the allied forces. You should have already heard about the great victory over the Europeans in the Battle of Deep Space. We emerged from it stronger and more committed to the cause of freedom than ever before, for I say to you now, as clear as I can be." I almost jumped, as she slammed a leather-gloved fist upon the podium, and her tone switched to anger. There was venom in those beautiful, large blue eyes. "We completely and utterly reject the surrender of the leaders of the Pacific Alliance! We won't roll over like a dog under the tyranny of the European Union! We won't hide. We won't run. We won't capitulate. We didn't ask for this war!" Spittle flew from her mouth. Her voice softened again as she said, "I did not ask to sacrifice the lives of our young. I don't love war." She paused, then shouted, "I love freedom, and I will fight, bleed, and die to see that restored!" Again, her voice lowered, "It is not going to be easy. You are bloodied and bruised, but we have shown the Europeans that we will be masters of our destiny. I say to you all," She raised a clenched fist and shouted once more. "Rise up! Rise up and be counted as a hero! Rise up and turn on your oppressors. We will be out here, growing in number every day. Taking the fight to wherever a European cowers and hides. We are battered, but we are unbroken. We will strike at the very heart of European domination. We will destroy every ship. We will destroy every base. We will destroy every European we encounter until no more Europeans are left." She paused and took a breath before continuing. "We will take no prisoners. We will pursue the enemy with our hearts filled with a vengeance for the loved ones we have left

211

behind on Earth. I dedicate myself and ask you to do the same, to the total eradication of the European Union. I don't bring you victory today, but I do bring you the promise of victory tomorrow. It may take months. It may even take years. I promise you, with everything that I am, we will prevail! And to you Peon scum out there. I am coming for you. The day will arrive when the European Union is no more than a footnote in the history books. This is total war, and we are coming home." At that, the screen went black.

I felt my heart pounding in my chest, and excitement rose within me as I listened to the woman who brought hope back into my heart. It was amazing. She really made me feel like we had a chance. She made me believe we could win and that it wasn't over.

I did a happy dance around the room, only stopping when Bron burst through the door excitedly. "Did you hear it, Hannah?"

I grinned stupidly at her. "Oh yes, I heard it. We're going to win this, Bron. She's going to take us back to Oz."

Chaos followed the broadcast as all over the ship celebrations broke out, and I would later be informed this was happening all over the fleet. Bron and I, however, had no time for celebrations, for the restructuring of the fleet, and the organization of the newly announced Solar Confederation took up all our time. Later that day, we received news that the Twilight Wanderer had been seconded into military service.

I didn't know what this meant for me, so I called together my little inner circle.

"So, what exactly does this mean for us?" Bron asked Baker before he had finished sitting down at the table.

"Well, it's certainly not good. Typically, it means that the military will come in and take over the running of the vessel. In normal circumstances, we would get compensated with a nominal rental fee, but these aren't normal times, and Admiral Plural isn't just trying to put the fleet together but an actual working community. We are likely to get nothing from it if they take over."

"You said 'if.'" I said, picking up on his wording.

"Well, I have an idea, but I honestly don't know if it would work. It's never been done before," he said quite meekly.

212

"Just tell us, Eric. At this stage, we have nothing to lose, and you may have something," I replied impatiently.

"Well, the new Solar Confederation is trying to start its own system of economics. In doing that, they will need private corporations, and I don't see Jenna Plural adopting a socialist model. Indeed, she'll want to separate civilian life from the military as much as possible."

"Get to the point where any of this will help us," I said irritably

"Quite simply, you need to convince the authorities to retain the Twilight Wanderer as a civilian vessel and recognize Grant Industries as a valuable asset in establishing a robust commercial system."

"And just how do you propose we do that?" I was getting irritated with the man, but it was Bron who replied.

"The military isn't going to want to implicate themselves in crossing the line between the civilian sector in the military sector," she said quite confidently. "I think it's quite possible that they would jump at the chance of having us run things from here as a third-party contractor to the military. They lost a hell of a lot of personnel in the last battle, and replacing them isn't easy. Give them a chance to let us run this for them as a civilian operation. I think they'll go for it."

"Do you think we can negotiate that, Bron?"

"Yes, but you will still have to be present. It'll be quite insulting to them not to have the head honcho at the table."

I shrugged, "I don't see a problem with that."

They would arrive the next day. It would be a team of lawyers, military personnel, and members of Michael Phelkar's ministry of civil affairs. It looked like they were ready for some big corporate battle, believing we were going to try and challenge their authority.

Representing the military was Captain Remus, formerly commander of the U.S.S. Houston but now working as part of Jenna Plural's administration. With him was a young woman called Abigail Thompson. Although she was dressed as a civilian, I could tell that she was military due to her bearing. Along with them were several lawyers and other clerical staff whose duties I would never find out.

I invited them up to my executive suite and the little boardroom where I usually met with my own people. The tension was incredibly high, and it was clear they were expecting us to offer them stiff resistance. They were let in by Stepanchikov, and after the perfunctory greetings and shaking of hands, we took our seats at the table, them on one side, with Bron and Baker up on my left and right.

"I'll get straight to the point, Miss Grant," Captain Remus said firmly. "Admiral Plural is extremely pleased with how well this ship handled the Battle of Deep Space. We are very grateful for the many lives you saved. However, we are going to need a full-time medical facility, and it's been decided that the Twilight Wanderer is the perfect ship for that to happen. I understand this will be hard on you, for, unlike normal circumstances, we can't compensate you for it. However, needs must be, and we have no alternative. We will, of course, find alternative accommodation and—"

"I'm sorry to interrupt you here, Captain," Bron said quietly but firmly. "Would you be willing to listen to a counterproposal?"

Remus sighed. "There's really nothing you can do to stop this happening."

"Oh, we have no intention of stopping this from happening, Captain," I said with the warmest smile that I could muster, although, in reality, his defensiveness was quite irritating. "Jenna Plural has the full support of myself and my team. We simply want to offer an alternative way of managing this situation that would be mutually beneficial."

His eyes narrowed suspiciously, but he said, "I'm listening."

"Twilight Wanderer is a vast ship that takes up a lot of resources and requires a lot of personnel to run it. Correct me if I'm wrong, but that is something you have a severely short supply of?"

She waited for him to answer that, but all he said in response was, "go on."

"Grant Industries is, without a doubt, the most successful corporation in modern history. Our logistical capabilities are second to none, and if you forgive me for saying so, exceed even your own within the military services. Given that we're also hoping to have a robust economy to make this truly a community rather than some socialist oligarchy, we feel that this would be better off in the private sector."

"I'm afraid the decision has already been made, Miss Donovan," the captain said, sitting back as if the conversation was over.

"Please give us the courtesy of at least hearing us out before we walk away from here," I asked him.

He gave a reluctant nod, and Bron continued. "We propose that the military contract us to do it for them, rather than take over the ship. We'll be responsible for supplying all your medical needs, and yes, we certainly have experience with that. We can also put the ship to use for other commercial ventures that will be beneficial to the community. This effectively means one less responsibility for your superiors to worry about. Our company has several generations of experience running these things; frankly, the military does not. We can turn this into so much more than just a military ship at a minimal cost to you in both finance and personnel."

She stopped and waited for his response.

There was a long silence before he said, with a sigh. "As I said, the decision has already been made. I'm just here to see that it's carried out and that you are informed of what's going to happen."

I felt my heart sink down into my stomach. It had been a good damn try, but we clearly were going to lose this one.

"Just a moment, Captain," the young redhead, Abigail Thompson, said softly, and I noticed that she was studying me with curiosity. "I personally think this is an excellent idea. The Ministry of Civil Affairs wants a newfound confidence in the economic system we hope to set up. A name like Grant Industries is going to really help boost that. Miss Donovan also has a fair point that our personnel resources are extremely limited. Keeping the Twilight Wanderer as a civilian vessel contracted to the military and therefore under the Ministry of Civil Affairs will reduce an incredible burden."

"Well, I'm not here to make any sort of decision, but if you want us to take it back to the higher-ups, we can do so."

We felt some relief as we saw them back off onto the shuttle, but we didn't get our hopes up because the decision was still up in the air. However, it wouldn't be for long. Less than twenty-four hours later, Bron and Baker went into a closed virtual meeting alone with a few of our executives and advisers to discuss the offer she'd made. I paced around the apartment while they negotiated the deal, to emerge three hours later, with a contract that Commodore Claire Addison signed on behalf of the military and Mr. Michael Phelkar, on behalf of the civil administration. Grant Industries were back in business.

Chapter Twenty-Four

—·—

Resurrection of Charlotte Kensett

In the next few days, I probably worked harder than I had ever worked in my entire life. While Bronwyn was supremely competent at setting policy and giving us direction, neither she nor I had any experience running a corporation's day-to-day activities. Especially one contracted to serve the military, so with great reluctance, I started to bring back the executives I had so far done without.

We had to deal with a few issues at our first board meeting before we could get their agreement to come back on board. Technically they had never left, and I had continued paying their wages, but with financial transactions from the United States now stopped, their first concern was their salaries.

"If you can't even pay us a wage, what's the point for us to even make an effort here." I can't remember who said that, and it doesn't really matter, for it was clearly what everyone was thinking.

"It's only a matter of time before the new Solar Confederation introduces its own form of currency and a banking system. I assure you that you will be duly compensated when that time comes," I informed them from my position at the head of the table.

Another executive smirked at that and said, "then perhaps we should come back when that happens. Right now, Miss Grant, you have absolutely nothing to offer us."

I fixed my eyes upon them and shrugged casually. "You're welcome to leave whenever you wish to." Then, as he rose from his seat, I added, "do you require the stewards to help you pack?"

217

He stopped and looked at me. "What do you mean?"

I snorted derisively. "We are no longer a passenger ship; even if we were, you couldn't afford the fee. No-one can remain on the Twilight Wanderer who isn't working. I'll send the stewards to help you pack. However, please bear in mind that, as I understand it, you're only allowed to take one case on board a refugee ship."

I'm quite certain he turned absolutely white, for rumors were that the refugee ships were packed to capacity with people who had lost their own vessels and had been unable to obtain positions on other ships. They were little more than homeless camps, relying on the charity of other ships.

"Maybe I was a little premature," he said, as he made to sit down, but I shook my head.

"Oh no, sir, you've already made your decision and made it clear you had no intention of working with us. You clearly have no loyalty to Grant Industries, and we'll be better off without you, so goodbye, mate."

He made a protest, but Stepanchikov stood up and very politely, but firmly stated, "I will show you the way out."

Bronwyn would later berate me for losing quite a competent executive, but I clearly needed to make a point to everyone else sitting there, and it did, for no one else made any complaint from there on out.

We went on for about three hours, going through the contracts and analyzing everything that we had agreed to provide Jenna Plural. We then discussed who had the best experience in dealing with those responsibilities. By the end of the meeting, we had effectively set up separate departments to deal with everything from medical services to cargo handling. As everyone funneled out, I was looking forward to my lunch. When it was just myself, Bron, and Stepanchikov left, I made to get up, but one of the clerks came in to inform me that I had a visitor. Tired and hungry, I snapped at her, "who is it?"

"It's Charlotte Kensett, Miss Grant."

Now that got all our attention. "Send her in, will you? And make sure no-one is in the office when I meet with her, including yourself. You can go to lunch."

I soon heard the familiar clip-clop of those expensive heels approaching the door, coming to an end when she stepped in and onto the carpet of my boardroom.

Dressed in one of her business outfits, she looked more like an executive than I did, as she smiled warmly at me before greeting Stepanchikov first, "Good to see you again, Emberlynn. It's been a minute." With an extremely rare smile, Stepanchikov rose to her feet and offered her hand to Charlotte.

"Good to see you're doing well for yourself."

Charlotte raised a questioning eyebrow saying, "really? And how is it you know how well I'm doing?"

Stepanchikov chuckled, "Oh my dear Charlotte, you're not the only one who has friends in certain places. I heard you were now Jenna Plural's internal security head."

"That I am," she smiled, but I noticed something in her eyes that told me she didn't really like Stepanchikov having that information, or at least, not knowing how she got it. Charlotte turned to me. "It is good to see you again, Miss Grant, Miss Donovan."

"Likewise, Miss Kensett. Although I must admit, I had assumed you were dead."

Charlotte smiled as she indicated a chair, and I nodded for her to sit. "Well, I hope my resurrection doesn't displease you, my dear," she said as she made herself comfortable.

"Not at all. I'm seriously hoping you're here to tell us that we can resume our operations in Australia."

"I am working on that," she said, sounding genuine. "To be honest with you, which I readily admit is a rare thing for me, I've lost contact with many of my operatives on Earth. After Jenna took out the primary communications hub for the Peons, they're trying to make up for it now they have access to the former Pacific Alliance communication systems. The result is that I no longer have secure lines to Earth, and my agents would be foolhardy to try to communicate with me, and be caught doing it. So, no, I can't promise you that we can resume activities in the near future."

"So, for what reason do we have the honor of your presence?" I asked, unable to hide the disappointment in my voice

219

"I want to ask a favor of you. Not a major one, but one that would help me out incredibly."

"Name it," I replied.

"I want to set up offices on the Twilight Wanderer. Make it my base of operations."

"I don't have a problem with that, but I am curious as to why?"

"On military ships, all comings and goings are recorded, and there's no way around that."

"They're also recorded here. We don't just let people come on board and leave," said Bronwyn, although she wasn't being antagonistic to the idea.

"Indeed, that is so. However, there are ways around it aboard a civilian vessel. I need the onus to prove that I shan't be tracked."

"Consider it done," I replied. "However, I also have a favor to ask of you."

This didn't seem to faze Charlotte, whose expression was one that considered that to be fair. "If it's within my power, consider it yours."

"Actually, this is of a personal nature," I said, and she looked intrigued as I invited her to sit with me in the lounge.

"Have you ever told Stacey you've worked with or even met me?" I asked her once we were situated more comfortably.

"Well, that is a surprise. It didn't even occur to me that you wished to speak about your sister. But no, my relationship with you is purely professional, and I don't discuss my professional activities with anyone who doesn't need to know. Stacey falls into this category, even if she is your sister."

"Has she ever mentioned me?" I asked uneasily. "Is she likely to be aware of who I am and what I'm doing?"

Charlotte pondered this studiously. "Hmm, to be totally honest, I have no idea. She's never mentioned you to me, but then, we're not exactly friends." I have to admit, I found it hard to believe that Charlotte would actually have any friends. "However, if you're asking for my professional assessment, I don't think she knows, and I don't think she cares."

"So, you don't suppose she would've followed me in the media or anything like that when we were back Down Under?"

Charlotte chuckled. "Oh, I certainly don't think Stacey watches reality TV. She only watches anime, old movies, and porn." Behind me, Bronwyn stifled a laugh, but I wasn't as amused. "If you don't mind me asking, Hannah, where are you going with this?"

"I want to meet her, but I don't want to have to be aware of my connection with Grant Industries. This means I want a favor from you."

Charlotte frowned and crossed her legs almost defensively. "Oh, my dear Hannah, you're talking about a close personal friend of the Admiral. Involving me in any shenanigans relating to Stacey is really more than just a favor."

I grew irritated with the look of contempt on her face at my suggestion. "So, you don't think that Jenna Plural will want the resources of Grant Industries on her side when it comes to our operations beyond our legitimate contracts?"

"Oh, my dear, I seriously hope you're not suggesting that you're going to back out of your current arrangements with me?" Her tone was now quite intense and unpleasant, while not openly threatening, the possibility was present.

"Absolutely, I do," I replied, unintimidated. "Because that arrangement is with the United States of America, which is now under the control of the enemy. I never agreed to be part of Jenna Plural's rebel Alliance or Solar Confederation, as it's now called."

"So, you're going to ask me for a little favor involving your sister, and in return, you will ensure that Jenna Plural has access to the resources of Grant Industries?"

I smiled patronizingly at her. "Oh no, I'm going to ask for a few favors, but I assure you Jenna Plural gets my utmost loyalty if she continues the fight back."

Charlotte pursed her lips and folded her arms. "Very well, what is it that you want?"

"I want the record changed within your systems listing me as a refugee from Oz. Give me a position in your military. I don't care what rank and make it airtight. I want anyone within this fleet, who looks me up, to see that I'm no longer the rich kid from Melbourne."

Charlotte mulled this over. "I can certainly do that, but why on Earth do you want me to?"

"Oh no, that's my business," I said dismissively.

"Oh no, no, Hannah, that won't do," Charlotte shook her head and stared at me over her large, framed glasses. "You are effectively asking me to infiltrate you into Jenna Plural's military structure. My first loyalty is to her, and I wouldn't take that risk without an extremely good reason."

"Fine." I relented. "I want to meet my sister on equal ground. I don't want our pasts to be an issue. That's all there is to it."

Charlotte sighed disparagingly. "Well, I can't say that's a good reason, but it's a safe reason, and I don't see how it could hurt anything," she paused, staring off at some invisible spot on the carpet before shrugging and looking back up at me. "Sure, I'll do it. However, you should be aware that I have a remit from Jenna Plural to extend the protection of the intelligence services to certain people in her inner circle. That includes your sister. While I'm not overly fond of her, I take my duties seriously and want to clarify that I will be coming for you if any harm comes to her by my doing this."

I smirked back at her, indicating her attempt to intimidate me was a complete waste of her time. "Have no fear, Charlotte. All I want to do is meet my sister. Where it goes from there will be entirely up to her."

And that, as they say, was that.

I was surprised at how quickly Charlotte managed to get everything in order. The Battle of Deep Space celebrations were not even over, and she had a shuttle transfer me to the U.S.S. Constitution. It was a clear sign of the amount of power and influence Jenna Plural had bestowed upon the woman that would become known as the Hand of Jenna.

Bronwyn was not too happy about the plan. I was going to be away for some time, and during that time, we weren't going to be in communication. I would simply disappear. This was a military-grade deep-cover setup.

Charlotte and I met in, what I would later discover, was one of many hidden offices of hers throughout the fleet. Indeed, she had several offices in various parts of the Constitution alone. There was some intelligence strategy to her moving around from office to office, but I couldn't understand it for the life of me.

She had prepared a detailed cover story that would pass muster if I were looked up on records. It was simple, really. I was one of many refugees having fled Australia four years ago after Last Day. I was signed up in the United States Air Force as a mechanic and aspired to become a pilot, but was held back because I was not an American. Sounded good in principle, provided Stacey didn't want to discuss aircraft mechanics. However, Charlotte went one step beyond. She assigned me two of her operatives to pose as my mates. Both were Australian.

Billie and Eleanor were well-versed in the art of subterfuge. I never found out much about their backgrounds, and would later discover, never even knew their real names. How they came to be in the employ of someone like Charlotte Kensett is anyone's guess. Like most Australians who didn't recognize the puppet government in Canberra, they joined the Americans.

Most Aussies that escaped Australia on or after Last Day were either refugees or had joined the military of one of the Pacific Alliance countries. Although they were known as the Australian Free Forces, that was little more than a token, for there was no command structure behind that fabricated organization. It was simply intended as a morale booster to give Australians the idea we were independent.

Of course, all that was lost in the new Solar Confederation, which promised to end the national boundaries and form a new interplanetary nation. I was never really sure if that was little more than propaganda, but time would show me that truly was Jenna Plural's plan, although I would later stand in direct opposition to her over it. But that is a story for another day. The plan was that we would set up a chance encounter. Apparently, my sister frequented various clubs and bars, and the plan was to run into her randomly. We were supposed to be these Aussie refugees working aboard the U.S.S. Constitution.

My background was to be that I was an Air Force mechanic, something I probably couldn't pull off over a duration, but since we intended only to do this for one night, they taught me enough to wing it. Of course, it turned into a complete clusterfuck, and I would have to play the role for much longer. They say that hindsight is 20/20. I suppose that, with hindsight, I had totally taken the wrong tact here.

I'm not exactly someone who lacks confidence in oneself, as I'm sure you should know by now. However, I clearly didn't think straight when it came to Stacey. She was the last living member of my family. Not only that, but she was also my family's estranged last living member. Hiding the fact that I was still a very wealthy and established individual, I think, came from several positions. Indeed, there was the fact that I wanted to meet with her on equal terms, and her not be judgmental about the separation of our social class. Also, there was part of me that was scared she would lay claim to the estate of our shared mother. It wasn't that I would be opposed to bringing Stacey into the family business. I just wanted to make sure it was on my terms. Of course, this was futile, for Stacey would never have any interest in the family company. In fact, I don't think it even occurred to her just how wealthy she could've been, had she chosen that way. I must admit that Stacey is not the brightest person I have met.

I even decided to dye my hair black. For the life of me, I don't know why. I guess I was caught up in this cloak-and-dagger world. It wasn't like I would hide who I was with a fake name.

Celebrations of the Battle of Deep Space continued throughout the fleet. Admiral Plural allowed this to continue, coinciding with her ultimate announcement of the new Solar Confederation, combining all the nations of the former Pacific Alliance, except for Japan, which wouldn't join for another year.

The Battle of Deep Space sent a message to the Solar System that we were not just a ragtag desperate bunch of guerrillas going down fighting, but a cohesive force, capable of taking on the European Union.

Everyone was on a high, and parties sprang up everywhere.

I kept tabs on Stacey's movements using Charlotte's agents and my company security department. One thing I quickly learned was where there was a party, Stacey wouldn't be far behind.

In the quarters I had sequestered through Charlotte Kensett aboard the Constitution, my operatives tried to predict where Stacey would turn up. We got it wrong a couple of times, turning up to parties in the hope that she would appear, but she did not, but a couple of days into that, we got lucky.

We went down to a mess hall for one such event, my two agent best buddies alongside me. We had a couple of drinks. I found the music loud and overbearing and was about to give up, when one of my colleagues nudged me and nodded toward someone. I looked up in that direction. It took me a moment before I noticed Stacey pushing her way through the crowded mess hall, making her way up to the bar

"We should wait until she finds a seat," I said softly. "Any ideas on how I should approach her?"

However, before either of them could reply, I noticed she was heading in our direction. The place was packed, and there was barely any seating anywhere. Stacey had noticed the empty chair near us and headed towards it.

"Mind if I sit here, mate?" She asked the agent I knew as Billie. I have to admit we were all taken off guard by this turn of events. We had rehearsed approaching her, not the other way around.

"Yeah, sure. Go ahead." Billie told her, and she leaned over to me and whispered, "how do you want to play this?"

"How the fuck do I know? I'm not the cloak and dagger girl," I whispered harshly back.

"Is there some sort of problem?" Stacey asked with a scowl, and I realized the three of us were sitting there like morons, staring at her.

Billie smiled up at her. "Are you from Down Under?"

Stacey smirked and raised her glass to us. "Fucking oath, mate. Good to see another fellow countryman."

"Where from?"

"Wagga."

"No shit. I'm Billie from Alice Springs. This is Eleanor from Sydney and Hannah from Melbourne. What's your name?"

"Stacey. If you don't mind me asking, you all look a little too young to have been serving in the military when we lost our country. How'd you end up on the Constitution?"

"We weren't in Oz when she went down," Billie responded, thinking quickly. "Except for Han over there. Our parents worked for the mining consortium out on Io. Ellie and I are civilians. I'm working in logistics. Han, she's Air Force."

And that's when our eyes met. I felt a lump in my throat and a knot in my stomach. She was much shorter than me, and while not completely uggo, she was fairly plain. Her over-large front teeth protruded to the degree that her mouth was never completely closed. I tried to comprehend her expression, which was clearly one of curiosity. I gave her the best smile my nerves could muster. Why the fuck was I feeling intimidated? No-one intimidated me. NO-ONE!

Yet here I was, feeling awkward, in the presence of my previously unknown sister.

CHAPTER TWENTY-FIVE

STACEY

"Are you a pilot?" She yelled out, trying to be heard over the music.

I chuckled at this, not intentionally but due to my nerves. "Oh, I wish. Unfortunately, I'm just ground crew, nothing really exciting. I'm just a maintenance engineer."

"Don't sell yourself short," she responded with a frown. "Maintenance engineers are the lifeblood of the Air Force. Pilots wouldn't have the first clue if it weren't for you making sure their kite was flying."

I laughed again. "You almost sound like you're Air Force yourself." Of course, I knew full well she was a pilot.

"Sure am," oddly, she quickly changed the subject. "What d'you sheilas say to a round of shots and a jug of brew?"

"Let me get them," said Ellie. "It was my round anyway," and she headed to the bar.

"Do you know many other Aussies around here?" Billie asked her.

"Nah, mate," Stacey replied. "To be honest, I just got posted here after my last ship was destroyed in that last battle."

She seemed somewhat coy about her role in this war. "So, what is it that you do?" I asked.

She glanced away and shrugged, saying, "oh, I'm between postings right now,"

Before I could pursue it, someone bloke came up and asked Billie to dance, and as she accepted. His buddy went to ask Stacey, but she waved him away with a shake of her head, and he asked Ellie instead.

227

Alone with Stacey, there was an awkward silence before she said, "have you ever thought of going through flight school?"

I looked at her sadly. "Unfortunately, it's not an option. You have to be a commissioned officer to be a pilot, and Australians don't get commissions in the United States Air Force, unless they've already got some skill or another that the Yanks decide is useful."

"Maybe that will change now," she shrugged. "Did you hear Jenna Plural's speech?"

I grinned, and it was genuine admiration for our new leader. "Did I ever! Isn't she just amazing? She makes you feel like our flag is already flying over Brissy again. And she's so beautiful that she looks like a GenMod. She's perfect."

An unexplained grin crossed her face before she responded. "Well, the military will no longer be based on national lines. The new fleet is going to be completely integrated."

"You know, I hadn't thought about that." It was the truth. I hadn't thought about it; honestly, I didn't care. "You have a point, and I have the grades to take the aptitude test. But will there even be things like flight schools? We're now just this big, ragtag fleet of ships. We no longer have a homeworld or a place to land a ship."

Billie came back without her dance partner. "What happened to the hunk?" I asked her, as she sat back next to me. I was slightly annoyed that she had interrupted us, since we had broken the ice.

"He had an issue with his ability to control his hands," Billie snorted, playing her part like an Academy award winner. "I told him I'm not that kind of sheila. I hope the slap I gave him leaves him with a nice big handprint across his face tomorrow."

My sister and I laughed at this, and the mood started to relax as we chatted about home.

I was surprised about the amount of alcohol that Stacey could consume. While she is usually quite adept at holding her liquor, that night, she seriously drank to excess, and I had no problems keeping up with her, considering I hadn't taken any metabolism suppressors and the alcohol had no effect on me. My two companions had a harder time remaining sober, and the group got quite merry, with all of us remaining in character. By Stacey's own admission in her book, That Girl from Wagga, she didn't get suspicious at all.

She was very different from the people I was used to. She was coarse and crude, but incredibly likable. Despite my better judgment, I found myself relaxing and generally having a good time with her.

Around two a.m., she started to look the worse for wear and excused herself to go to the bathroom.

When she didn't come back, I grew concerned. Billie offered to go look for her, but I decided to do it to myself, as it would possibly give me an opportunity to talk to her alone again. I went into the bathroom, which was fairly busy, but there was no sign of Stacey. I hung around for a bit, wondering if she was in one of the cubicles, but as people came and went, she didn't appear. There was one cubicle that had remained closed for quite a considerable amount of time, so I went over and looked under the door to see Stacey lying there, dead to the world.

The door was locked. I turned round to the other women in the room and asked casually, "does anyone have a nail file or anything like that? My mate is passed out drunk in there."

After a quick search of bags, someone handed me a small metal file. I inserted the tip into the emergency lock release outside the door. Passing it back, I pushed it open and slipped inside. I knelt down on one knee and winced as vomit stench came out of the toilet. I flushed it and covered my nose and mouth with my hand until the offending stench diminished slightly. I pulled off some toilet paper and wiped some remnants of the vomit from her face, and she moaned softly, but didn't open her eyes. Carefully I sat her up, and briefly, her eyes flickered, and she smiled at me. "Is it my round?"

"Oh, I think you've had quite enough, Stacey," I chuckled. Making sure the cubicle door was shut behind me, I lifted her to her feet. Something that was, while not impossible for an unmodified person, was certainly not as easy as I had just done it. I placed her arm around my shoulder and guided her out of the stall. While she was able to take steps, I was virtually carrying her entire weight, unbalancing me. As we left the bathroom, my two companions saw me and came rushing over. Billie, taking the other side of her, we led her out of the bar and down the corridor. As soon as we got to a private corridor, I turned her around and heaved her arm over my shoulder in a fireman's lift.

My companions looked startled, even though they knew that I was a GenMod. Billie took the lead, going ahead to ensure no-one saw me. We got into the elevator and took her up to her quarters. Outside, I turned my back to the door so Stacey was facing it. I carefully lifted her hand onto the palm pad to open the door.

"I can take it from here, ladies," I told the others, and they departed with little more than a nod. The lights came on automatically as we entered, and I was surprised about how sparse it was. There was no sense of personalization. I was expecting it to be some big mess, with dishes and laundry scattered over the place in keeping with what was clearly her chaotic personality. I took her into the bedroom and laid her down carefully on the bed. She curled up, looking quite content as she began to snore. I sat by her on the bed for about half an hour, just looking at her and wondering. She was my sister; yet so little about us was the same. Eventually, I reached forward and brushed the hair out of her eyes. I was startled as the artificial eye turned to look at me. I thought for a moment she was awake, but then realized it was an automatic defense system assessing me as a potential danger. However, even that wouldn't wake her up in her current state. Then, I got up and headed out the door, ordering the lights off as I went out.

As I returned to the room assigned to me that night, I wasn't feeling that good about events. I don't know what I was truly expecting. I just wanted to get to know her better. I don't even know if I intended to reveal myself to her during the course of the night, but it is something that should've come to an abrupt end. I had nothing in common with her, and I had only played along with what she considered fun. Standing on the table with her singing Waltzin' Matilda and pretending to be drunk was, frankly, humiliating. As I prepared for bed, I decided that I would simply return for the Twilight Wanderer and put this all behind me.

One of the problems of my new persona was that I literally had to fend for myself. I tried to cook myself some eggs and bacon for breakfast and actually started a small fire. This, of course, alerted emergency personnel, who rushed to my quarters and had me sitting there, filling out various forms and informing me that I was going to see a reprimand from my commanding officer. With hindsight, it was quite amusing that my cover had been so effective, but it didn't occur to anyone that I wasn't who I said I was. However, the result was that I missed the early shuttle over to the Twilight Wanderer. Charlotte gave me clear instructions that I wasn't to reveal my identity at any time while on board the Constitution. As a result, I had to book another regular shuttle, just as anyone else would. I couldn't help but feel that was ironic, since I *owned* the bloody shuttle. However, I found myself stuck in my little room with nothing to do.

That was, until a young officer came to my door and ordered me to report to Captain Grant.

I must admit this took me by complete surprise and left me with some trepidation. Had she found me out? What could she possibly want to see me for? Wasn't I just some woman she'd met in a bar, just like she'd probably done many times before? I changed into the uniform Charlotte had provided, and following the young officer's directions, I headed off to Captain Grant's office.

As I made my way there, it occurred to me that she had never identified herself as Captain Grant, and the young mechanic I pretended to be would've had no idea that she was an officer. I would have to look surprised when I saw her and react appropriately. In my younger days, I may have been a drama queen, but I was no expert on the dramatic arts, and I entered her office with a considerable amount of weird unease.

There was a small reception, and a young man sat behind the desk. He was in uniform, but I don't recall his rank and position. I told him who I was and that Captain Grant had requested to see me.

"Ah yes, she's expecting you. Please come with me," he led me through to her private office, where she sat tapping away at a computer screen. "Hannah Grant, Captain." The young airman introduced me.

I did my best to look completely surprised when she looked up and smiled at me.

"Come in, Hannah. Take a seat," She beckoned me over.

"Hey, Stacey, I mean, Captain Grant," I felt myself become strangely nervous again, and my face grew hot.

231

"I'm not big on formalities. Stacey's fine, mate," she said, sitting back.

"You failed to mention that you were an officer last night," I said with mock admonishment.

"Well, it would've kinda ruined the night, don't you think?" She shrugged. "I just wanted to celebrate our victory with a couple of sheilas from Down Under," she grinned.

"I can understand that," I replied and decided to throw it out there. "It's funny, but I have a sister called Stacey Grant. I've never met her, but I know she's an officer in the Air Force."

She just sat there staring at me with a wry grin on her face. I immediately realized she knew full well who I was. I looked at her coyly and played along, "Stacey?" She nodded. "Oh, fuck me!" I exclaimed in mock surprise, causing her to chuckle. I tried to figure out how long it'd been since she'd discovered it. "Why didn't you say anything last night?"

"I only found out myself a couple of hours ago, when I pulled up your personnel file."

She pulled my file? What the hell did she do that for? As I've said, I was just a chick she'd met at a party. "Why were you looking at my personnel file?" I asked with a frown. After all, even fake Hannah would find that unusual.

"For a position working with me that I wanted to discuss with you. So, I want to be clear, what I'm about to talk to you about has nothing to do with our relationship."

"Okay," I said uneasily. This was not what I had anticipated.

"I'm starting a new squadron, and I want you to be part of it," she said it like she was inviting me to a boutique store.

I tried to think quickly. I was hardly going to be able to be her flight mechanic. I didn't even know how to inflate the tires on a car. "I'm not due for transfer for another year. I really don't think they'll let me out of my current position."

She smiled. "Don't worry about that. That's my problem. I was hoping you could move over to my team as soon as possible, although it may be a couple of weeks before we get everything in order. The position is voluntary. You're not obligated, nor am I ordering you to come over to us."

"I really appreciate it, but I'm in line for promotion to a mechanic position. I don't want to miss out on the opportunity."

"I'm not recruiting you to be a mechanic. You said you wanted to fly, and the only thing stopping you was the fact you're Australian. Like I said last night, that doesn't apply anymore."

Holy fuck! What had I gotten myself into here? "Oh, are you serious?" I smiled.

"Well, I have to get permission to start teaching new pilots, but I don't think I'll have a problem with that, and you'll have to begin training as a gunner. If I think you have the chops, we can start working on flight training."

"Oh my God, that would be amazing!" I said excitedly, while my brain turned somersaults as it looked for an exit strategy.

"Don't get too excited. As I said, I need permission first. However, I can tell you that you'll begin gunnery training as soon as your transfer is approved. So, what do you say, Hannah? You wanna join me?"

"Absolutely," I said.

"Then let's make it happen. Leave the paperwork to me, and when the time's right, you'll hear from your C.E.O. about your transfer."

It was a dismissal, and I got up. "Thank you for this opportunity," I responded and headed toward the door. I was going to call Charlotte to get me the hell out, but something stopped me. I realized she'd gone out of her way to help her 'down-on-her-luck' sister. Yet she was the one with nothing. That was special, and it hit my usually lukewarm heart. I turned back to her. "Would it be inappropriate to say that I'd like to get to know you as my sister?"

"Why would that be inappropriate?" She shrugged.

"Well, you're an officer and all that. And well, there's our obvious family issues," my voice trailed off. I hadn't intended to mention the family issues, and it just slipped out

"Well, I don't think it'll be the first time someone outranks their sister, but they can still share a prawn or two on the barbie," She replied, ignoring my comment about the family.

"Let's do lunch sometime. Can I call you?"

"Anytime you want, sis," she replied with a warm, infectious smile.

CHAPTER TWENTY-SIX

FAMILY MATTERS

I wasn't supposed to contact Charlotte Kensett unless it was an absolute emergency. I hadn't considered Stacey wanting to train me as a pilot. It was one bloody emergency like no other. I couldn't call her directly, but I had a little device that would send her a signal, and she would contact me. I certainly didn't expect her to turn up in my little room like she did.

I slowly and carefully explained what was happening and, for the first time, saw a look of frustrated disbelief on her face. "What's going to happen when she contacts my C.E.O. and finds out they don't exist?" I said it almost in a panic.

"Oh, it's much worse than that, Hannah," she said with a frustrated sigh. "He *does* exist. He just doesn't know that you do."

I looked at her incredulously. "Why the fuck did you use a real person?" I snapped.

"Seriously, Hannah," she replied irritably. "Do you think I could create files for every person your fake persona may have come into contact with? Be realistic!"

"Fair enough," I responded, completely deflated now. "However, I've gotten in way over my head. I need you to get me out."

"And what? Simply go ahead and disappear?"

"If I must, yes!" Clearly, I wasn't thinking straight.

Charlotte rolled her eyes and shook her head. "Oh, my dear Hannah, you've gotten yourself in way too deep for that. Now Stacey knows who you are, at least some form of you. If you were to disappear

235

suddenly, she would tear this fleet apart, looking for you. Trust me, I know her. It wouldn't take her long to discover that you are, in fact, the wealthy executive of Grant Industries, which would put me deep in the shit with Jenna. No, Hannah, you're going to have to ride this one out."

"Don't be ridiculous, Charlotte. I don't know a fucking thing about aircraft or spaceships!" I shouted in frustration. "Don't you think Stacey might notice when she has to show me how to put on a fucking seatbelt?"

Charlotte looked at me over those large librarian glasses and said in a very calm, yet condescending tone, "well then, perhaps you should give some serious thought to telling her the truth on your own terms, rather than have her find out. Stacey Grant will be severely pissed off if she finds out another way. She is more likely to forgive this situation if you just be upfront with her."

I sighed softly, my anger spent. "Perhaps you're right, but I do still want to get to know her."

Charlotte placed her long, manicured hands upon her hips, "You should be aware that she is probably one of the most obnoxious women you could ever know. I don't see this ending well. The pair of you are multiple social classes apart."

"She's still my sister. Can you understand that?" Charlotte didn't reply, and I realized she really could not understand it, making me wonder about her past and family.

She sighed and said, "I will set up an intercept for any communications Stacey sends to your C.E.O. and respond on his behalf. Hopefully, she won't try to call him directly, but even then, hopefully, I'll be able to deflect the calls and make excuses for his absence."

"Thank you, Charlotte. I owe you one," I said softly.

"Oh, you owe me more than one," she said, leaving me to my thoughts.

The following day I received the message that my transfer had come through, and I would have to attend a briefing about becoming a pilot. However, it didn't prove as difficult as I thought it would. I played the part of the shy girl who didn't want to interact that much with my other new recruits to Stacey's squadron, and fortunately, it was classroom-based, and I could sit quietly at the back, not understanding anything they talked about.

However, it quickly became clear to me that Stacey was avoiding me. She barely made eye contact when standing at the front of the class, addressing us, and would leave quickly and arrive late, so there was no time between the lessons for us to interact. This aroused my suspicions, but I did nothing about it. That was, until a call from Charlotte asking me when I was going to deal with the situation on my end.

As you probably realize from everything I have told you here about this situation, my mind was going back and forth, with part of me wanting to meet Stacey and get to know her and the other part of me wanting to run away. The indecision was killing me. However, not knowing why she was avoiding me became a serious itch that I couldn't scratch. I decided to bite the bullet and go see her. However, I wasn't going to challenge her in her office. So with resolve, I waited until I thought I would catch her coming home from work and headed over to her quarters.

No answer came when I knocked at the door, but I decided to wait instead of leaving. It was almost an hour, and when she came around the corner and saw me standing there, she was visibly startled.

I was standing back against the front door, legs crossed and arms folded, glaring as she stood there looking at me with a dumbfounded look upon her face. "If you don't want to see me, I want you to tell me," I said snarkily. "If that's the case, I'll never speak to you again. Hell, I'll even ask for a transfer."

"Well, I'll deny the transfer," she grinned awkwardly, but I didn't find it funny.

"You're my Captain, so should I stand and salute you now?"

"I don't expect anyone to do that, even when we are on duty," She said unusually meekly. "Do you wanna come inside?"

"That depends. Do you want me to?" I said churlishly.

She made me stand aside and opened the door indicating for me to enter. "Wow! You certainly keep it bare for big and fancy officer's quarters," I commented as I saw the lounge as sparse as her office.

"I lost everything I had on board the Lady Liberty, when it was destroyed. I just haven't gotten around to getting anything. To be honest, there's nothing I really want," she shrugged as she slipped off her jacket and haphazardly tossed it on a chair.

"Nothing? Nothing at all?" As someone who accumulated things as virtually a way of life, I really couldn't comprehend not wanting anything.

"Not really. I lost a picture of my best friend and me that meant a lot to me, but I can do sweet fuck all about that now."

"Can't you take another?" I said. It was a throwaway comment, and I had no idea of its importance.

"No. She died." Stacey responded like it was nothing.

"I'm so sorry," my concern was genuine, and I turned back to face her. I almost lost Bronwyn in the M.E.T. accident, so I kind of understood what that felt like. "How did it happen?"

She shrugged and, in a tone of clearly fake unimportance, replied, "four years ago on a mission, but I can't talk about it. It's still classified."

"I understand," I replied but couldn't help but wonder what classified even meant now we were no longer nationally aligned.

Stacey opened a small drinks cabinet. "Want a drink? I got scotch, and I've even got Portobello brandy."

Now that surprised me. Portobello was a brandy produced by Grant Wineries back in Australia. It hadn't been available since Last Day. "Seriously? I've never even tried the stuff," I said as I stepped over to examine the bottle.

"How come?" She asked me like that was the dumbest thing in the world.

I shrugged, "I just turned eighteen the day before Oz fell." In her book, That Girl from Wagga, Stacey says I said I was sixteen. I don't know why she said that, but I'm guessing she got confused. Legally I was twenty-two when we first met, but thanks to my two-year timeout in the M.E.T., I was twenty.

"Eighteen, and you hadn't started drinking? Are you sure you're a Grant?" she chuckled.

238

I laughed and gave her a cheeky wink. "Well, I never said that. I just didn't have access to Portobello brandy."

"I guess your life is very different than mine," she chuckled as she opened the bottle.

That turned my stomach. I really didn't like these feelings of guilt. I was so not used to them. "I'm sorry, Stacey. I know that Mum was a shit mum to you," I muttered.

"Was? Is she dead?" she asked, almost sounding eager.

"To be honest, I don't know. I didn't see her on that last day. I was in school when it happened and never went home." I was getting too close to reality and quickly corrected my course. "Do you mind if we don't talk about this?"

"Not a problem." She said, giving me a glass with almost five shots worth of brandy in it. "I grew up in Wagga. Dad never remarried and died when I was sixteen. I was shit broke. My brother, or rather our brother, tried his best to support me but was killed during his national service. So, I lived on the streets for a couple of years until I joined the Air Force. After the Battle of Cape York, Jenna recruited me, and I've been working with her ever since."

I had almost forgotten her relationship with our leader, and of course, I wasn't supposed to know. I feigned surprise as I asked, "you've worked alongside Jenna Plural?"

She laughed at my reaction, "Take a seat."

We both sat back in armchairs. "So, what's she like to work with?" I asked.

"To be honest, she's one of the finest people I have ever met," she smiled.

I admit I found the idea that my sister worked with Jenna Plural quite exciting. "I bet she is. And you're actually friends with her?"

Her face fell at this. "I thought I was, but I haven't seen her since she assumed her new position," she shrugged. "I think she's far too important for the likes of me now."

"Well, I'm sure she's very busy with all that's going on now. When I saw her and heard that speech, I knew we'd found the right leader to get us out of this mess," I said, expressing my honest opinion.

239

"Now, that is something we can agree on," Stacey raised her glass in a toasting gesture. "I honestly wouldn't trust anyone else." Then she sighed. "However, I do miss hanging out with her, though," She said regretfully.

I looked at her, deep in thought. I had considered my wanting to meet her as simple curiosity, but now I felt a strong connection with this coarse, badly educated strafe from the streets of Wagga.

"Stacey, I just want to say I'm sorry about what happened with the family."

She was instantly dismissive. "No worries, mate. I got over that years ago."

It didn't take my genetically enhanced senses to tell me she was lying. "Please be honest with me. I don't know what happened. Growing up, the subject of you and our brother was off-limits."

She sighed, looking uncomfortable as she downed the remains of her drink. "I didn't fit into her perfect world. In her eyes, I was flawed, which simply wouldn't do for Marcia Grant," she fixed her eyes on me coldly. "And that, my dear little sister, is why she replaced me with a GenMod."

I tensed and fell into my automatic, instinctive response as I looked away, surprisingly intimidated by her glare. "I'm not a GenMod. They're illegal. At least any that were designed after the Prague Convention."

The coldness disappeared as she chuckled. "You asked me to be honest, and yet you won't do me the same courtesy?"

Oh my God, she did make me feel bad. Feelings I had never experienced before and did not like. However, I glared back at her before I could check myself and snapped, "well, your story can't get you killed. Mine can."

She dismissed that notion. "Not anymore, little sister. Jenna Plural is in command now. She has no issues with GenMods."

I already knew this, since I knew she was one. Stepanchikov had told me about her. However, I couldn't help but be concerned that if Stacey became aware that I had intimate knowledge of a woman, who until recently had never been heard of, she may be suspicious.

"Jenna is accepting of GenMods?" I said with the best wide-eyed surprise I could muster.

"Born and bred in a tank just like you," Stacey laughed. "Albeit in a time when it was legal."

"You mean I no longer need to live a lie?"

Stacey grew quite grim. "While you're never gonna be free of the prejudice, and I assume the laws are still in place back in Australia, which would mean you'd lose your citizenship, I can assure you as long as Jenna prevails, you are as safe as safe can be."

I found myself reflecting on all the fear I endured when questioned about my existence and the rumors about me. Then I looked at my sister again. I wondered why my mother had decided she wasn't good enough. "If you don't mind me asking, what was supposedly so wrong with you that our mother did what she did?"

She laughed sneeringly at my question. "Ironically, it turned out to be a totally fucked up misunderstanding. I was a klutzy kid. I could never sit down and be quiet when there were so many things to do and see. I like to talk, and I like to interact with everything around me. My mother didn't think this was normal. She said I was hyperactive, and that was a problem. She took me to see a specialist, a pretty dumb one," She got up and poured herself another drink, and I declined when she offered one to me. As she returned to her seat, she continued her story. "They made me take this test. There were shapes on the screen, and I had to press this button every time one came up. I was eight years old, and it was just boring as fuck. So, I made it more entertaining when I pressed the button. I made little exploding noises," She suddenly grinned, then laughed. "I guess even back then, I was considering a career in the military. Well, after what seemed like an eternity, the medical dickhead came back in. She gave me this little pill. I can still see it, a little blue one, but I had trouble swallowing it. It tasted like shit. She then made me wait a while, sitting there on my own, before coming back in and asking me to repeat the test. This time she didn't leave. I felt so uncomfortable. In fact, I was pretty well scared stiff because I didn't really understand what was happening. This time I concentrated harder on the test because she was watching me, and I didn't wanna do anything wrong. Her conclusion was the little blue pill had calmed me down when it was the fact that she scared me shitless."

Was that it? I thought, absolutely horrified. It was nothing. It wasn't like she was schizophrenic or something. "So, what happened?

"Well, I'm sure you're aware of Mother's desire for that perfect public family. I didn't fit in with that, and when my father objected to her medicating me, there was a fight about it. He took me away rather than have me medicated. This embarrassed her. It was okay for her to leave her partners, but it wasn't okay for her partners to leave her. She used her power and influence to ensure my father wouldn't be successful in any career. She started legal proceedings to get me back, but then suddenly, she stopped. Six months later, you were born. The perfect Grant."

I stared in disbelief as I listened to her. I knew I was a bitch, but I had nothing on Marcia Grant. Yeah, I admit I'm more than happy to fuck over the next person to get what I want or for some payback, but not family. Never family. This was her daughter, for fuck's sake. My sister.

To my incredible embarrassment, I felt a tear run down my cheek, and I quickly wiped it away. "I'm so sorry this happened to you. If it makes you feel better, my life with our mother wasn't pleasant. I was more a prize pig on display than an actual daughter. Everything was about appearances; my father left when he discovered we weren't genetically related. She had told him she was using the D.N.A. of herself and him to create me, but she didn't. I have no clue who my father is other than he's some genetically superior donor, maybe even a GenMod himself. I doubt I will ever find out, and to be honest, I don't really care." I slid forward in my seat, putting my glass on the side table and resting my elbows on my knees. It was time. I was going to tell her the truth about me. The whole truth. "Stacey, we come from a pretty fucked up family, but you and I are still family, and I want to get to know you as my sister. I want to be part of your life." However, before I could continue, and much to my frustration, the door buzzer went off.

Stacey looked more irritated by it than I did. "Don't worry. I'll get rid of whoever it is, and then I'll take you to the officer's mess, and we'll have one of their fancy dinners." She paused, then shrugged with a grin, "well, it's fancy for me."

I heard her talking to a woman but couldn't determine what was being said. Moments later, my world exploded. I will admit that contrary to our later much publicized fights, I would be president of the Jenna Plural fan club, if such a thing existed. The last thing I expected was to meet her, and most certainly not in the humble quarters of my big sister.

I jumped out of my seat, and remembering I was supposed to be a grunt in her air force, I gave her a sharp salute and instantly felt stupid.

"Careful there; you might pull something," Jenna said in that soft American voice that just invited you in. She was the same height as me, making Stacey look even shorter as she stood barely above our shoulders. She was even more stunning in person, and I would go as far as saying she left me looking quite plain.

"Yes, ma'am. Sorry, ma'am," I replied, my embarrassment complete as my voice shook slightly.

Stacey poured her a drink and said casually, "Jenna, this is my sister Hannah."

CHAPTER TWENTY-SEVEN

FINE DINING AND VEGEMITE

Jenna smiled and offered me her hand. "Nice to meet you. You're Stacey's family, and I don't expect pomp and circumstance when we're alone."

I stood rigidly on the spot, not sure what to do or say. "For fucks sake, Han. Sit down, you drongo," Stacey laughed at my expense. Being made fun of was also not something I was used to, and I felt a tad resentful as the both of us retook our seats.

"I have to be honest," said Jenna. "When Addison gave me the list of your recruits, and I saw the name Grant, I was curious enough to look up and see if there was a relationship. Though, I'm sorry it looks like I'm interrupting you tonight."

I was concerned that Stacey would agree and that Jenna would leave, but once more, making fun of me, she said, "I'm sorry, Boss. My sister appears to be having an attack of hero worship."

I was mortified, but I couldn't deny the truth of the statement. "I'm sorry. It's just when I heard your broadcast...Well, it was so inspiring, and I really became convinced that we're truly going home...." I felt myself blushing. I decided it was probably a good idea if I got out of this situation. "I'm sorry. I'm sure you two want to be alone. I'll get going."

"No, it's me that's intruding," Jenna replied

"Oh, for fucks sake," Stacey interceded. "Will you two knock it off and sit the fuck down? Whatever Jenna is, she's still just a person. But

245

I can guarantee you, there are only two things she'd judge you on – your patriotism and your ability to kill Peons."

Jenna laughed, "I can't deny this. Tell you what, have you eaten yet?"

"We were about to go out to the officer's mess and get some dinner," Stacey replied.

"If you don't mind, may I take you up to my mess and get you both dinner?" Jenna asked.

I looked to Stacey hopefully. "You planning to pick up the bill?" She said. "Hell, I won't say no to a free feed,"

Vanity always being my curse, I asked. "May I be permitted to go change quickly?"

"Sure," Jenna smiled. "Tell you what, you go change, and I'll have one of my people come down to escort you up to the command section."

I jumped up and stupidly found myself saluting again. Jenna grinned and, following the protocol of an officer always having to return a salute, got up and did so.

I hurried back to my quarters, pulled out one of my more formal outfits, and quickly changed. I then checked my hair and makeup, ensuring I was as presentable as possible. With excellent timing, there was a knock at the door just as I finished, and a young, uniformed man escorted me up to the command rank officers' mess. As we entered, he led me over to a large table that was occupied just by Jenna and my sister.

"Airman Grant, present as ordered, Ma'am."

He gave Jenna a sharp salute, and she stood up and returned it, but she replied to him quite curtly, "I asked you to escort her here, not place her under armed guard. She is my guest, not my prisoner."

"I'm sorry, Ma'am."

"You are dismissed, Lieutenant." She then smiled at me. "I'm sorry. Come and take a seat, Hannah."

"Yes, Ma'am," I went to sit by Stacey, but Jenna indicated to join her.

"Hannah, I want you to think of this as a family dinner. We're off duty in an informal setting. So, while we're here, please call me Jenna."

At the time, I didn't know what a privilege that was. One thing she was extremely strict about was who could or could not address her informally.

I managed to relax a little as the evening drew on, and we enjoyed a fine meal with wine and good company. I was pleased that the subject of my past and current situation never came up. Lying to Stacey was one thing, but lying to Jennacia Plularian was another. During the meal, she commented on how she would trade the fine dining for some vegemite any day.

When we left, Stacey invited me to stay the night at her place, and I agreed. She had a steward bring a cot to set up in the lounge, as she only had one room and a single bed.

She poured more drinks and then got me a slice of her favorite dessert, New York Style cheesecake.

We chatted about nothing special, and I really felt relaxed now around her. I wanted to do something to show my appreciation for her. I came up with an idea that would surely piss off Charlotte Kensett.

As you know, I don't need much sleep, so after Stacey went to bed, I headed back to my little quarters, and I completely broke protocol by putting in a call to the Twilight Wanderer.

"What's wrong?" Bron responded, full of concern, as soon as she heard my voice.

"I need you to do me a favor, mate. I want you to get me a jar of vegemite."

"For fucks sake Hannah, it's two in the morning," Bron whined.

"It's important, or I wouldn't be asking you."

"So important that it couldn't wait until morning?" she sighed and said, "I'll make sure there's some on the next transfer shuttle for you."

"I want it before breakfast," I said sharply.

"We have no shuttles going over there before midday," she replied irritably.

"Seriously, I don't give a shit how you do it, but I want a jar of vegemite before breakfast."

"What the fuck, Hannah! You don't even like vegemite."

"Yeah, I'd rather eat shit, but I'm serious! Bron, get me that damn vegemite. "

"Do you have any idea of the cost and logistics involved in that? I'm going to have to get a pilot up and schedule an emergency transfer flight plan. All for a fucking jar of vegemite!"

"Don't give a shit about that. Just get it here," I said.

"It is going to cost a fortune."

"Still not giving a shit, mate."

Stacey Grant waking up is an experience. It's a cacophony of coughs, grunts, groans, and profanity. I could hear her clearly in the other room. I smiled to myself as I popped the bread into the toaster. I had emptied out most of the jar. The rarity of the stuff would look as suspicious as a homeless man drinking Portobello brandy on a sidewalk. The smell of it had made me gag and retch.

"You have vegemite?" Stacey hurried out of her room, having smelled the vile goop.

"I have vegemite," I smiled at her, holding up the small jar.

"I will give you a thousand dollars if you make me a slice of vegemite toast, and I'll chuck in a fifty for a cuppa."

I laughed, extremely pleased with myself as I passed her a plate.

She lifted the slice of toast like it was the most precious commodity in the Solar System. Carefully she took a bite, closing her eyes and savoring it. "Bloody hell. Now, if that's not a little slice of heaven."

"It's all I have left. I only have a scoop or two."

She dropped the slice and looked embarrassed. "I'm sorry. I don't wanna pinch your vegemite stash."

I grinned, handing her a coffee, "I got it out for you."

"Why?" She said, looking confused.

"Because you're my sister. Go on, keep eating. It'll make me happy," I said honestly. "Just think of it as nineteen years of birthday presents I never got the chance to give you."

"Oh, you can't do that," she said with a smirk.

"Why not?"

"Because I can't afford to find nineteen years' worth of presents that could possibly equal vegemite on toast."

248

I faked liking the stuff so as not to make her suspicious, but I wanted to throw up after every bite.

"I'm probably gonna to be going away for a few days," she told me. "Jenna has an assignment for me. I have no clue what it is, but I don't usually get called on for anything that doesn't involve flying, so I'm guessing I'll be leaving the fleet for a while."

My first concern was who would be covering her briefings with the squadron. It could easily be someone who put considerably more interest in what I did or did not know. "Stacey, I was thinking about requesting some time off myself. I haven't had a break in over a year, and since you're going to be away, maybe now is a perfect time?"

"Sure," she said casually. "I'll sign you off for a couple of weeks. How's that sound?"

"That would be perfect, Stace." I smiled.

She did indeed ship out the next day, for a mission that she wouldn't have told me about, even if she had been able to.

Of course, it's no longer classified at the time of writing this, and her mission was to deliver that psycho Emma Dodgson's team to Enceladus.

I took the opportunity to return to the Twilight Wanderer. Bron reported that everything was going well, and I attended a board meeting with her, but I wasn't paying any attention to it. My interest in Grant Industries had waned somewhat. I took the opportunity to have a long bath with my oils and sweet-smelling stuff that I enjoyed and so missed on board the U.S.S. Constitution. It was so nice to eat decent meals again, but I was certain that I would never get the taste of vegemite out of my brain.

And once more, sleeping in my form-fitting king-size bed made me realize how fortunate I was. I asked Stepanchikov if she could find out when Stacey returned, and she said she could, but I didn't ask her how. So, I enjoyed my time with Twilight Wanderer while waiting for Stacey to return. Bron slowly drew me back into the company's activities, which had rapidly increased upon the announcement of the new currency exclusive to the solar federation being put into circulation in the coming weeks. After a while, I started to grow concerned that Stacey had not returned. Not that concerned about doing anything about it, even if I could. I had no idea what she was doing or where she even was. However, one night Stepanchikov came into my room and woke me. "I'm sorry to disturb you, but I thought you'd want to know at once."

"What is it?" I said, climbing out of bed and pulling on my robe.

"Stacey Grant has gone missing. She was last reported flying away from Enceladus after dropping off a marine assault team. A search has begun in the surrounding area, but the ship is generally believed to be destroyed. I can't get more details on that because it's very hush-hush."

"We will see about that." Without getting dressed, I hurried out of my apartment with Stepanchikov close behind me. My night bridge crew looked startled as I ran into the room and shouted at the communications officer. "Get me a line to the U.S.S. Constitution."

Seconds later, a voice came over the communications. "This is the U.S.S. Constitution. How can we assist you today, Twilight Wanderer?"

"I want to speak to Jenna Plural, and I want to speak to her now!" I snapped sharply. I didn't care about anything else. To hell with my pretense. To hell with everything! My sister was missing, and I wanted to know damn well what was going on to find her. There was a long pause at the other end. "I can't do that, Twilight Wanderer, unless I know the reason and who I'm talking to."

"I'm Hannah Grant, sister of Captain Stacey Grant, and I need to speak to Jenna Plural now!"

"Hold the line." That was an infuriatingly long pause until a voice that wasn't Jenna Plural's came online. "This is Commodore Addison. How can we help you, Twilight Wanderer."

"With all due respect Commodore, I asked to speak to Jenna."

"I am aware of that, Corporal Grant, but as I am sure you were aware, we're not in the habit of putting enlisted personnel through to the Admiral, even if they are related to Stacey. I'm just giving you the courtesy of responding to you, due to who your sister is. Now, you can either talk to me, or we can end this call right now."

"Fine." I snapped back. "What is going on with Stacey? What are you doing to find her?"

There was another long pause before Addison replied suspiciously, "what makes you think there is anything wrong with Captain Grant? She is off on an assignment."

"I'm not playing games here. I want to know where she is. She has been reported as missing."

"Will you hold for a moment, Twilight Wanderer?" There was another interminable pause.

"What's going on, Hannah?" The unmistakable voice of Jenna Plural came back to me.

"Admiral," I said imploringly. "I need to know what's going on with Stacey."

"Fine," she replied coldly. "As a courtesy to her, I will tell you that she went missing while on mission. We can't trace her vessel, but we are doing everything we can to find it. However, I want an explanation as to how you know about this situation."

"I just heard a rumor, that's all," I heard what sounded like a sigh of relief coming from Stepanchikov.

"This is highly classified, and there is..." she stopped suddenly, and I could hear a voice in the background. "Admiral, we have an incoming call from Lieutenant Dodgson on Enceladus."

"Patch it through to me," she instructed, then turned her attention back to me. "Hannah, I have to go. Just be assured, I'm doing everything I can." Before I could respond, the communications officer advised me she had cut the line.

There was nothing more I could do, so I returned to my apartment. I paced around the room for I don't know how long, but a couple of hours later, suddenly, a loud klaxon went off, and Lieutenant Bourke, the ship's helm officer's voice barked, "All ships crew prepare for emergency maneuvers. Report to your posts, I repeat, all ships prepare for emergency maneuvers."

This time I pulled on some clothes before I ran out of the room. At the same time, Bron came out of hers. "What the hell was that about?" I asked.

"It means the fleet is preparing to move, and we're receiving instructions," she said curtly. "You would know that, if you hadn't been

251

off playing little sister while we were going through all the drills and preparations for situations like this."

"Oh, fuck off, Bron," I snapped. "You had everything under control, and honestly, I just get in the way."

"That is most probably true, Hannah Grant," she said angrily as we raced down to the bridge.

I immediately looked up at the screen as we entered. The ships of the fleet were lining up for some form of maneuver. Bourke had already powered up the engines, and I was starting to see that he was moving us away from the civilian vessels. "Why the hell are you taking us into the military flotilla?"

"Because we are military now, shit for brains!" Bron snapped at me.

"Stick it up your ass, Bronwyn," I replied. Yes, it was totally unprofessional behavior in front of the crew. However, it's easy to forget we were still only twenty years old, and while we had aged very quickly in the circumstances, there was still an element of the bitchy teenager in both of us.

"Navigation system is receiving course instructions from the U.S.S. Constitution. Plotting them in now," Bourke informed us.

"Where are we going?" Bron asked him.

"Give me a moment, please, Miss Donovan?" he instructed calmly.

About a minute later, he advised us. "We have received orders. We're going into combat with a French fleet around Enceladus. We are to prepare for heavy casualties."

As soon as the communications officer heard that, she opened up internal communications. "All personnel prepare for enemy engagement and heavy casualties."

I then heard Deacon Cooper giving orders over the internal comms for his medical staff. Slowly but surely, the fleet powered up and began to accelerate. We would be behind the fleet. Quite a long way behind, considering we didn't have the speed of a military vessel. The battle would already be underway before we arrived.

To be honest, I didn't really care. All I was concerned about at that time was what was happening with my sister.

CHAPTER TWENTY-EIGHT

— · —

WHATEVER HAPPENED TO MR. PHELKAR?

I was almost going to give up, when the communications officer informed me that she was picking up unusual chatter on a Peon carrier wave that I might be interested in. I got her to put it on the loudspeaker.

"This is Stacey Grant making an emergency broadcast. I repeat, this is Captain Stacey Grant making an emergency broadcast. I'm in a stolen V8 Interceptor with Peon markings on a Peons transponder code. I'm heading back to the fleet, but I'm being pursued."

I laughed out loud and hugged a surprised Bron, who just grinned at me.

"Please do not approach the fleet until you have transmitted the appropriate codes," came the official fleet response.

"Can't do that, mate. They've been trying to get the codes from me, and I don't know if they're listening in right now. I'm not in an American vessel."

"Do not approach the fleet. You will be fired upon."

My joy turned to fear as I heard those words. "Can we intercept her?" I asked Bourke.

"No, Ma'am. This is happening back where the civil fleet is. We're not in range."

"Put me through to Jenna Plural, now," Stacey was insisting.

There was a long pause. "You expect me to put you through to the Admiral?" Control said disbelievingly.

253

My sister laughed. "I'm Stacey Grant. I'm supposed to be a fucking legend or something. Yet, I get the one moron in the Solar System who doesn't know who I am? I'm that girl from Wagga, you drongo."

"Ma'am, you're coming in too close. Send the codes or turn back. We will open fire on you."

"If you won't put me through to Jenna, put me through to Addison or Tracker or even that bitch Kensett."

"Hold the line, interceptor," the fleet officer said.

On the bridge of the Twilight Wanderer, we all held our breaths until we heard the voice of Claire Addison. "Please repeat your identity," she said.

"Oh, for fucks sake, you're taking the piss now!" Stacey shouted irritably.

"Yes, that is Stacey Grant," Addison sighed. "What happened, Stacey? We had ships out there trying to find you. Dodgson reported that you left Enceladus safely, but then we heard nothing from you."

"Got captured. Long story,"

"Well, you'll be pleased to know Dodgson's mission was successful. We're moving the fleet to the Enceladus base. However, there is a Peon flotilla waiting for us."

"What can I do to help?"

"Dock with the Los Angeles. It still doesn't have a commander. Take command of it."

There was a long silence. "Are you serious?"

"No. I'm crazy, Stacey, but I need that ship flying ASAP." Addison growled back at her.

"At your command, Addy," Stacey responded.

"Saints preserve us," I heard Addison mutter before the line went dead.

As it turned out, there was to be no battle. Upon our arrival, the French fleet had already been decimated by ground fire from the Enceladus base, and rather than engage us, they chose to flee, and Jenna let them go.

Later that day, it was announced that the Enceladus base was now part of the dominion of the Solar Confederation and would become its new base of operations.

Bron immediately went into counsel with the executive team to find out how this would affect corporate operations. Much to her chagrin, I said I would remain on the bridge to find out more about what was happening with Stacey.

The Twilight Wanderer moved into an outer orbit around the moon with many of the other ships, as the rest of the fleet headed out to join us. Of course, I was only interested in the U.S.S. Los Angeles, which arrived several hours after the announcement that the moon was taken. I imagine Stacey would have been pissed about missing out on the action.

I put in several calls requesting for Captain Grant to call me back, but I received no response. Indeed, the whole fleet was once more in a state of reorganization.

It would be several days before I got to see her again. However, the ever-resourceful Stepanchikov managed to find the whole story. She met with me in my office. "Apparently, your sister was intercepted by Americans that are still working with the Peons. She was taken prisoner, along with the First Minister of Civil Affairs."

"Michael Phelkar?" I questioned with surprise. "What was he doing on her mission?"

"Unfortunately, I don't have the answer to that. However, unlike your sister, he didn't escape, and he's currently a prisoner of the European Union."

"That's an unfortunate loss. I understand he was doing quite an exceptional job managing civil affairs." I said with little interest.

"Actually, it is a little bit more serious than that," Stepanchikov imparted. "He is part of what has become known as Jenna's inner circle, and the Peons are going to make a big show of having him prisoner. Most likely, a big public trial for treason against his country, in not accepting the surrender. It could be quite embarrassing for Jenna Plural."

"Embarrassing, yes, but he is really just another casualty of war," I shrugged.

"You should be aware that Stacey was interrogated. According to the reports I've seen, she was quite severely beaten and suffered an incredible amount of torture."

I sat up with this, concerned. "Is she going to be okay?"

"She appears to be fine. She has taken control of the U.S.S. Los Angeles and is carrying out her duties."

"Do you have any idea why she's not returning my calls?"

"None. That is a personal matter and not something I can answer. I can't really investigate without actually asking Stacey Grant herself; however, at a guess, I would say she is extremely busy."

I didn't know what to make of the silence from my sister, but that would change the following day, when I was sent orders to transfer to the U.S.S. Los Angeles. I say me, but it was Corporal Hannah Grant, my fictional persona. I had thought that game was over, but I wasn't about to pass up the opportunity to see her again.

However, before I could depart, a major issue came up. Bron came to see me to discuss it.

"We have received a request from the office of Jenna Plural. I say request, but it's just a polite form of an order. The administration wants us to transfer our headquarters to Enceladus. They seem to think it would go some way to helping enshrine confidence in the moon being an actual territory of the Solar Confederation. It's time to say goodbye to the Twilight Wanderer."

I had listened very carefully to what she had to say, and I knew she wasn't going to like my response. "I'm not going."

Bron's eye narrowed, "I don't think you realize the importance of this issue."

"You don't need me. I want to get to know my sister, and that's what I'm going to do. You already run the company without me. I'm just a figurehead. And to be honest with you, I never really wanted to be involved with this business. Give me whatever papers to sign, but I'll make you head of whatever you need to be."

Bron rolled her eye at me. "I'm already the head of everything, Hannah. The only one that can override me is you, and that's because you're the owner. If you are determined, then this really *is* goodbye."

"Don't think of it like that. We'll still be in contact. I still own the business, and you'll still have to apprise me of what's going on. But, it's your show now, and truly, honestly, it has been from day one. I love you, Bron. You are as much a sister to me, if not more, than Stacey is. You'll always be my family and always my BFF."

Bron gave me a stupid grin, stepped up, kissed me hard on the forehead, and gave me the tightest hug. "I love you too, you dumb bitch."

Later that day, I transferred to the U.S.S. Los Angeles and was issued quarters in the listed staff deck, finding out I would share with someone else. Sharing! Not something my side of the Grant family was used to.

I was virtually unpacked when a call came for me to visit the captain.

I had worked out what I was going to say, but when I first greeted her, and it was going to be something warm and pleasant. However, as I stepped into her office and saw her, all that came out of my mouth was, "Holy fuck, they sure messed you up."

Her face was swollen and black and blue, and even her two front teeth were missing. She laughed at my reaction and then winced in pain. "Don't make me laugh. It fucking hurts."

"Hey, at least you're not the good-looking one out of the two of us now," I grinned at her, and she laughed again, followed by an intense wince of pain. She picked up some folder on her desk and threw it at me. I chuckled as I ducked out of the way. "Okay, Stacey, I have to call you Captain in your office, and I don't want to catch up with my captain. I want to catch up with my sister. Can we get the fuck out of here and go somewhere more comfortable?"

Fifteen minutes later, we were in her captain's quarters, and I feigned being impressed by its size. It was insignificant next to mine on the Twilight Wanderer, but would impress a young corporal in the shared accommodation of a squat bunkroom.

"Want some more Portobello?" she asked me as she went straight to the drinks cabinet.

"I'd love some, but really, Stace, it's wasted on me unless I take metabolism inhibitors. Got any wine?"

She stared at me as if I had just asked her to eat shit. "Wine? Fuck no!" But then she shrugged. "Guess I can order some." She stepped up to the intercom. "Galley, this is your extremely gorgeous Captain calling. Can you send up a bottle of wine?"

"That's an affirmative, Captain. Any particular type?"

"Fuck knows. Just make sure it does not taste like piss, mate."

"Um, I'll do my best, Captain," he replied uneasily.

We spent the night like a couple of schoolgirls having a sleepover. We talked about shit like boys and growing up in Wagga and Melbourne. Silly stuff. However, the mood quickly changed when I said, "Why is there such a big deal about this, Michael Phelkar? We've lost so many people in this conflict, but rumors are going around about plans to rescue him."

The smile suddenly disappeared from her face, and I believe it was the first time I saw despair in her single bright eye. "Well, they keep it on the down-low, but Phelks and Jenna are an item. And we really miss him."

Once more, my ability to notice even the slightest reactions came into play, and I realized my sister's relationship with Michael Phelkar was beyond merely professional. I was determined to find out whether that meant good friends or more. I gave her a knowing grin and said, "*we?*" My grin widened as she colored up slightly. "Looks like you have a thing for him too."

When her eye started to glisten, my smile was replaced with concern.

"We were involved." She said softly, looking away.

I leaned forward in my seat and placed my hand on her knee. "He dumped you for Jenna?" I asked.

She gave a sneering fake laugh at that. "No. He saw me again after he became involved with Jenna. Although I didn't know they were involved at the time."

Now that got me pissed. "Oh, my God! The man's a pig."

"Therein lies the real problem," she chuckled at my reaction. "He really isn't a pig. Sure, that was a fucked-up thing to do, but I don't think he intended it. In every other way, he's probably the nicest guy I've ever met." And with that, I realized she still had feelings for him.

"You're in love with him, aren't you?" I said.

Tears now welled up, and she looked away, embarrassed. "I wish to fuck I wasn't," she said barely audibly.

I moved to sit on the couch, wrapped my arm around her, and pulled her close. "Hey, sis. You're going to get him back. I don't know how, but I promise you that you will get him back, if I have anything to do with it." It was a dumb thing to say, for as far as she knew, I had the power of an insect in the grand scheme of the Solar Confederation.

Four hours later, I was back on the Wanderer and in the fancy new office which I afforded Charlotte Kensett.

"What are we doing to rescue Michael Phelkar?" As I asked the question, Charlotte Kensett's eyes widened, and then she wrote down: Phelkar.

"Absolutely nothing," she replied. "It would be a waste of resources, and even if it wasn't, I have specific orders not to get involved."

"You always obey orders, do you, Charlotte?" I shot back irritably.

She smiled at this. "When your boss is Jenna Plural, you generally don't want to piss her off."

"That's Jenna's orders?" I asked, most surprised. "I don't get it. I'd heard that he was fucking her."

Charlotte momentarily looked a little disgusted by my choice of terminology but replied, "it's all politics, Hannah. Jenna is new to her position, and while the people trust her, she is still in her honeymoon period. Michael Phelkar is currently the most secure prisoner within the European Union, and a lot of lives and resources would have to be expended on his liberation. As much as she wants to, she can't do that for something that is purely personal."

"Yeah, but you're a spook, Charlotte. Can't you do something under the radar?"

"It's very hard to do something under the radar to rescue an individual that, not only went out of their way to make themselves have a public profile, but just appeared on interplanetary televisions in a high-profile trial. You have to accept Mr. Phelkar is lost to us."

"Yeah, I'm sorry, but I'm not willing to accept that. What about if I bankrolled any rescue effort? Would you help me then?"

"Hannah, although I am loath to admit it, I don't even know where he is. Most of my contacts back in London have gone to ground, and let's just say my relationship with the British government was less than cordial, even before they capitulated to the enemy."

"What if I was to go there myself?"

She laughed at this until she saw that I was deadly serious. "Please tell me that you're kidding, Hannah? You are talking about infiltrating the United Kingdom, which is under Peon control. While I can get you in there, once you are there, I will be able to do nothing to help you."

I sighed. "Fine. If you're not willing to help me, I'll have to find another way. Personally, I thought you would liked the opportunity to have someone able to re-establish the links with your agents in the field."

Charlotte chuckled again. "Oh, Hannah. You know my weaknesses well. Indeed, I would." She stared into space for a moment before looking back at me. "You're sure you're serious about this?"

"Absolutely," I said with resolve.

"This would have to be completely under the table. It cannot be linked in any way to the Solar Confederation. If you are successful, the credit must be solely with you or Grant Industries. The political fallout of Jenna Plural spending resources to get what is, effectively, her boyfriend out of custody could have serious ramifications."

"I'm doing this for Stacey. Honestly, I don't give a shit where the credit goes."

"Very well. However, it would be foolhardy for you to go alone. I'll reassign you my two agents that helped you in your meeting with Stacey, as they are untraceable and not on the books," she paused and pondered something. "They're good agents, but I think you also need someone that has a more direct relationship with the Peons and thus, keep you out of the Peons' hands. If we can persuade her to go with you, she's possibly one of the best combat veterans I know."

"If she sided with the Peons, how could you possibly trust her?" I asked incredulously.

"I trust nobody, Hannah. You don't always need to trust people. You just need to control them. Leave me to worry about that. However, you must understand this. Once I have you inside the United Kingdom, you are entirely on your own. I won't even have a method of extracting you, and you'll have to work out your escape from there.

You should also know that I have literally no idea where Michael Phelkar is. He could have already left the planet."

"Right! Just get me in there."

"There is one other thing you may not like," she said. "But it is not negotiable. I cannot let this prisoner just walk out of here, and I certainly cannot be seen to be involved in her escape. In fact, there can be no involvement by anyone within the Solar Confederation. Her escape must have an excuse that covers me, my department, and, more importantly, Jenna Plural herself. You need to break her out."

"So, you're basically saying I need to take the fall for her escape," I growled.

"Exactly."

"That'll leave me looking like a traitor. My sister won't be thanking me. She'll want to kill me."

Charlotte shrugged. "Look at it this way. If you return with Michael Phelkar, literally anything you have done will be forgiven and understood. If you don't return with Michael Phelkar, you will most likely be dead anyway. So does it really matter?"

"Do you have any family, Charlotte? Dying with the idea that my sister will hate me forever for betraying her and Jenna Plural is not exactly a woohoo moment for me."

"Well, get over it because that is non-negotiable. It really doesn't matter to me one way or the other if you bring back Michael Phelkar. If you wish, you can get up right now and walk out of this office, and I will completely forget this conversation ever happened."

"You know, Charlotte, you really are a complete bitch."

That small smile crossed her face again. "I don't know why people keep calling me that. I wouldn't do what I did if I didn't care about them."

"Personally, I think you get off on it, mate," I muttered.

"Well, I do enjoy my work, if that's what you mean."

"Not exactly, but whatever."

CHAPTER TWENTY-NINE

THIS SCEPTERED ISLE

Charlotte Kensett suddenly worked fast. Twenty-four hours later, my two party mates arrived at my humble quarters on board the U.S.S. Los Angeles. It turned out that their names were actually Allison and Kylie. At least, I think they were. As I think about it, they could have been just new fake names. Who knows!

They had apparently worked with Australian Intelligence before Last Day and were quickly snapped up by Charlotte Kensett to collaborate with the Americans. However, they did bring someone else that I was not expecting. It was a tall, gaunt man in his forties, and he gave his name as Liam Carter. Although I can't honestly tell you if that was his real name, either. Apparently, he was a Brit and had a military intelligence background. Charlotte had put him in charge of the operation.

"The shuttle that is going to be waiting for us off the port bow," he told me. "While we work off the books, there's a small chance we can be traced back to Miss Kensett. This means the three of us cannot take any actions, in any way, aboard the U.S.S. Constitution. You are going to have to liberate Myers alone."

"How the fuck am I supposed to do that?" I replied, looking at him like he was completely mad.

"Well, to help you, we have arranged for a system of failure to counter security measures within the bridge area. You will need to use a card swipe rather than retina or palm prints. However, we need you to be clearly seen on the cameras."

263

"Why?" I said suspiciously.

"Because if you are seen, it will be simply considered that you are a traitor. It will reduce the chances of opening an internal investigation."

"And you've somehow authorized my I.D. card to open up the cells?"

"Not exactly." He reached into his pocket, pulled out an I.D. card, and handed it to me.

My eyes widened as I looked at it then I stared back up at him. "How did you even get this?"

"I simply took it from your sister's quarters."

"You went into my sister's quarters while she wasn't there?"

"Not exactly. She was asleep."

"Great," I said with annoyance. "I'm working with a creepy arse fucker who sneaks into my sister's bedroom at night."

"It is all about plausible deniability. Losing a security card is a serious offense, but she is forgiven for not believing she needs to secure it from her sister, which is the most obvious one you would take."

"You all seem more concerned about covering your asses than the actual mission."

"This mission is ad hoc. All we know is we are getting you into England, but everything is played by ear after that. Now, if you quite finished bellyaching, are you ready to go?"

The jailbreak was not exactly an amazing high-security affair. The nature of space travel meant resources were rarely spent on maintaining any sort of prisoner population. It was even smaller than the little jail cell I spent the night in back in Alice Springs. There was only one guard on duty, for there was, in fact, only one prisoner. As I stepped through the door, the guard on duty started to raise his hands before I even pulled out a weapon. "Idiot," I muttered. He was clearly working for Charlotte or had been paid off in some way. I couldn't help but wonder about that, but if indeed he was paid off by Charlotte, she would also see him as a potential security risk, so his days were probably numbered. We went through the motions of removing his cuffs and tying him to his desk.

There were only four cells with transparent glass doors, and McKenna Myers was not exactly hard to find. "I was starting to think you weren't coming," she said irritably with a clear southern drawl.

"I didn't know we'd specified the time, mate."

Her eyes narrowed as I swiped the card and opened the door. "You're Australian?"

"And you are an American. With introductions over, shall we get out of here?"

We casually walked back out into the corridors. I made that way as unsuspiciously as possible across the ship to rendezvous at an airlock with the rest of the team. "So, what exactly is going on?" McKenna asked me.

"You don't know?"

"All I know, is that bitch Kensett gave me an offer I couldn't refuse. I'm supposed to get some kid called Hannah Grant into the United Kingdom."

"That's me," I said casually.

She shot me a look, "any relation to Stacey Grant?"

"My sister."

If looks could kill, I'd be dead. Clearly, there was no love lost between McKenna and Stacey. "I take it you have a problem with my sister?"

"We used to be good buddies, but we both went down different sides after the surrender , but forgive me for saying, that bitch of a sister of yours is why I'm locked up here."

"Well, my sister is a patriot."

"Fuck you, Miss Grant. There is no bigger patriot in the Solar System than me. It all depends on what you consider to be a patriot."

"That's easy, Miss Myers. A patriot is someone who doesn't side with the Peons as you did."

"I chose what was in America's best interests, and ending this war was the best interests."

"No-one loves peace more than me, Miss Myers, but not at any price."

Before she could respond to that, we turned the corner, and Allison was standing there waiting for us. "G'day, mate," she said cheerily to Myers.

Myers turned to me. "Is this entirely an Australian operation?"

"I can assure you, Miss Myers, that this is entirely an independent operation with no national boundaries," I replied.

"Well, if you ladies have finished standing around chatting, we need to get a move on. The others have already crossed over. Come on." Allison let us into the airlock. They were very professional and started putting on EMU suits while I fumbled with mine. Myers was watching me.

"You're not military, are you?"

"Not even remotely," I replied as she stepped over with Allison to help me.

"I really hope someone is going to explain to me what is going on."

"Don't worry, Miss Myers," Allison told her. "Everything will be explained once we're on board the shuttle."

I can't say my first and only spacewalk was ever fun. Fortunately, I was attached to Allison and Myers, and they took me to the shuttle. We didn't use any kind of jet packs. They simply jumped with me into the void of space and let the momentum carry us to the craft. The outer door and the shuttle airlock was already open, and Kylie stood there dressed in an EMU suit, ready to catch us and pull us in.

The outer door closed behind us. Everyone waited for the airlock to repressurize before we removed the EMU suits. I felt the engines' hum and the craft's forward momentum before we'd even finished. Once we were unsuited, the inner door opened, and we stepped into the shuttle.

I'm reliably informed that the shuttle was a spoil of war commandeered from the Peons. Honestly, I can't remember the nationality, but the intention was to reduce attention to us When entering Peon airspace.

I was introduced to our pilot, who I'm sure you already know from the writings of Mr. Phelkar and my sister. Neville Batty was a sweet guy who, unbeknownst to me until long after this mission, was both a friend and colleague of my sister. I have no idea how he became involved in the shenanigans of Charlotte Kensett and myself, but he was a competent pilot.

He took us out of the fleet without incident, and we were quite far away when he reported the fleet had gone on alert.

"They have discovered your escape," Carter advised Myers. "Kylie, Mr. Batty, they may send people after us."

"Oh, I don't think so, Mr. Carter. This shuttle has an imaging repulsor field. They have no idea what direction we've even gone in."

The journey was not going to be fast. It would take us several months to get to Earth, and I was about to face what had become the biggest fear in my life. I felt chills down my spine, as Mr. Carter said. "If you're absolutely sure, Mr. Batty, I see no reason why we can't immediately upload to the M.E.T."

I was so afraid of the damn thing, that stripping off was not an issue to me this time. Mr. Batty took control of the M.E.T., and we went off into oblivion one by one. It is always quite bizarre how instantaneous the scrambling devices were. That simple flash of light momentarily blinded me, only to see the little pilot still standing there. "Welcome back, Miss Grant," he said with that cheeky little smile, as I grabbed my clothes out of the locker and quickly got dressed. As he shut down the M.E.T. system, I looked up at him, "are you not downloading the others?"

"They've already been downloaded, Ma'am. They're waiting for you in the main passenger area."

"Please call me Hannah," I told him, following him through to the others.

They'd been downloaded much longer than I had, for Kylie was serving a hot meal and handing out plates. It was not like there was a table or anything, and everyone sat down in a seat with their food on their lap. I slipped into a chair beside Allison, and took the plate from Kylie as she handed it to me. "How long were we out?"

"Almost three months," Liam told me. "We're a day out from Earth."

"Any idea how we're going to get in?"

"I've been trying to contact our operatives in London, but I'm not getting any response. The result is I've not been able to set up any form of cover to enable us to get through security. We're going to have to land outside of any established community."

"The Peons are simply going to let us do that?" I responded disbelievingly.

"Of course not," Liam said irritably with a mouthful of food. "We are going to have to rely on Mr. Batty's flying skills to avoid being blown out of the sky. I'm sure Miss Kensett told you about our difficulties on this mission. It is highly unlikely we're even going to succeed in finding out where this Mr. Phelkar is. Indeed, it is looking highly unlikely we'll even make it to London."

"Fine," I replied irritably. "You can just drop me off and go home."

"You wouldn't last a day. You stand out like a sore thumb," Myers shot back at me. "GenMods aren't exactly designed not to draw attention to themselves."

"I am not a GenMod," I said automatically, and everyone got a laugh out of that, except for Myers, who rubbed her neck and stared at me.

After the meal, we reclined in chairs and got some sleep. It may seem like we're asleep in the M.E.T., but you come out in exactly the same condition as when you went in and with the stress of spacewalks and fleet escapes, we were all pretty tired.

As we entered what was called Earth space, he started to pick up chatter over the comms. "Everything is in bloody French. It is weird not hearing any English."

"Has anyone tried to contact you? "

"No, the image impulses are still affected, but the closer we get, the more sophisticated your satellite system is. We'll be detected."

About two hours later, the radio burst into life, blathering something at us. Batty ignored it and kept going on course. Another hour later, a Peon fighter patrol started to follow us as more urgent calls came over the radio. Truth be said, I was waiting for us to be blown out of the sky. And indeed, as we entered near-Earth orbit, they opened fire. Batty may not have been of the same standard as my sister, but he was still a very competent pilot. He dodged and weaved, and while we were struck a couple of times, we, fortunately, did not go up in smoke, or otherwise, I wouldn't be here telling you this story.

More craft started to join those in pursuit of us, but I could no longer watch, as Carter took us out the back, and we put on cold weather gear and military-caliber D.E. belts. As we came down over England, he opened the back of the craft, and I stared out into a foggy day, unable to see the ground, as first Allison, then Kylie jumped.

I hesitated, but not for long, for Carter pushed me out, and I began to plummet to the ground. I then made probably one of the most foolish mistakes of my life. We were using good old-fashioned parachutes, which were always maintained for emergencies and covert operations like this where there was an atmosphere. For that same reason, Michael Phelkar didn't use a D.E. belt when he was ejected from the shuttle back at Virginia Beach, just before he met Jenna. The belts generate energy that can be detected, so using them for infiltration, or, as in the case of Phelkar, to escape attack and capture, was to be avoided.

However, as Carter had pushed me, I panicked, and instead of waiting for the chute to open of its own accord, I found the rip cord and pulled it almost immediately. This ejected it right in front of the shuttle's port engine, which immediately sucked it in and jammed. To my absolute horror, I was hanging from the shuttle like a ragdoll in a child's hand. I was in a literal panic until I heard the voice of Neville Batty coming over the radio. "Release the ropes, Miss Grant," he called out as he slowed the vessel and started to circle the area so we wouldn't get away from the others.

"But that's going to kill me. I don't want to fucking die, Mr. Batty!"

"You have a second emergency 'chute in there. It's really your only option. I can't land with you there, and no one can get to you."

"How do I release the ropes?"

"Pull the red tag on the side of your pack and hurry up about it."

I tried to turn to see the red tag, which only caused me to spin around, so I felt for it instead. I found a tag of some sort, and for all I knew, it was the washing instructions, but I pulled it hard anyway, hoping it was right. I screamed as I suddenly plummeted away from the shuttle and saw it disappearing into the fog. I felt what I believed would be my ultimate doom until, suddenly, the second emergency chute opened, and I breathed a sigh of relief. "Thank you, Mr. Batty," I said once I had caught my breath.

"Radio silence, Grant," Carter demanded with obvious irritation in his voice at my idiocy. I don't know why he was holding me to the standard of his military. I had barely received instruction, let alone any training for this sort of thing. As I floated down, I pondered whether I had just made the biggest mistake of my life coming on this mission. Clearly, I was way out of my depth.

Everything around me was a dense white mist, and I waited to feel myself splatter into the ground. But the belt automatically activated, and my descent began to slow. If I'd realized how high we were, I would've probably been terrified, but something about not being able to see takes away that fear. However, I did land face down in a muddy field.

"Everyone, stop moving. Follow my signal." I looked down at the device strapped to my forearm, and the map came up with a red bleep to which I was to head. This was Carter. I ran blindly through the mist, only able to see a few feet in front of me. I already felt the cold of my wet clothing beginning to chill me. I could only imagine what the others felt like, considering I was able to withstand environmental issues much better than they could. I could suddenly make out a figure ahead of me, and I mistakenly thought this was Carter, and I sped up to reach him. It was only at the last moment when I realized he was in a foreign uniform. One I didn't recognize, so he wasn't French or German. He was holding a big fucking rifle, and it was aimed at me. I slipped down to the ground as he fired, and I rolled as I pulled the snap pistol from my holster, and coming up again, I shot him squarely in the chest. He staggered back a few paces but remained standing. Bloody body armor. I fired again, this time at his face, which was clearly a lot softer since he went down instantly. "Grant!" I heard Kylie calling.

"Over here," I called out, and she appeared out of the mist, and although it wasn't necessary, she helped me up. Myers then also appeared.

"We're surrounded by fucking Peons," she said urgently. "Come on. We gotta get moving."

Suddenly, the noise of a hail of bullets rang out. Just in front of me, McKenna went down. I stood rooted to the spot, absolutely terrified, but as soon as Kylie returned fire, I began to as well. To my surprise,

McKenna climbed quickly back up to one knee, and with her weapon pressed against her abdomen to steady it, she returned fire into the fog. Cries and shouts went up as we found our targets. When it fell silent, I looked at McKenna questioningly. "Fortunately, they hit my body armor but didn't penetrate," she muttered, clearly embarrassed that she had been taken by surprise like this. "Come on, let's get moving. The gunfire is going to draw the attention of everyone here."

Heading off at a brisk pace, I stayed close behind McKenna, with Kylie bringing up the rear. Suddenly several more figures appeared, and once more, gunfire erupted. I felt a stinging pain in my abdomen, but it wasn't until after the action that I realized I'd been shot. We returned fire, but suddenly one of the figures jumped upon McKenna, bringing her to the ground, and I saw a glint of a knife coming out of a sheath at his thigh. I don't know if I was being brave, or it was just some instinctive reaction, but I quickly stepped up to where he lay on McKenna, placed to boot on the back of his neck, and pulled his hair back with all my genetic strength until there was a sudden crack and he lay limply on top of my companion. She pushed the body off as I turned back to Kylie, and we continued to fire into the fog once more. Suddenly I fell to my knees, the pain in my abdomen becoming quite unbearable. Quickly Kylie was at my side and down on her knees, pulling up my shirt as McKenna stood over us, guarding us. "Fuck!" Kylie muttered. "It's quite a deep wound. I'm sorry, Hannah, but I don't think you're going anywhere." She pulled out a patch of sealant from the pouch on her belt.

"Don't count me out yet, mate," I muttered back. "I'm a GenMod. My nanobots are state-of-the-art." As this sealant dried, stemming the blood flow, I got up. Kylie looked most surprised, while McKenna looked like she had seen this all before. Soon, there would be little more than discomfort from the bullet that was still lodged within me, but not enough to impede my progress. Kylie clicked on her radio and tried to call Carter and Allison, but no response came.

We continued heading towards Carter, but suddenly more gunshots rang out, and looking down at the map on my wrist, the red light blinked out.

"What the fuck does that mean?"

271

"It means he's dead," Kylie said. "Come on. We need to go in a different direction." We half ran, half walked across this field, eager to gain both distance, and equally eager to be cautious. McKenna was in the lead, with Kylie at my side. I could hear the shouts of the Peons talking to each other, which gave us our bearing to head away from the voices. We finally reached a drainage ditch on the side of a road and jumped across with no idea where Allison was. Kylie then took the lead. "We need to go to ground and find somewhere to stay in hiding until nightfall, or until they stop looking for us in this area."

"How long before they give up?"

"They're not gonna give up," McKenna responded. "They'll expand the search until we're found. However, they don't know how many we are. At least, I don't think so. If they got Carter and Allison, maybe they think it's just them."

"We can chat about it later, ladies, but right now, we need to keep moving," Kylie said urgently and raced across the country road to the other side. We followed, and I could just make out an old barn.

"Why don't we hide in there?"

"Because it's the most obvious place to search," Kylie replied, and as she broke into a run, we followed, and we soon came to a thicket of trees and Kylie stopped us. I thought, at first, this was where we were going to hide, but she was just trying to get her bearings. "We need to put as much distance between us and this place as humanly possible," she said urgently, and she stared at the map on her wrist.

"We're in a place called Shropshire," said McKenna, mispronouncing the name of the place. She, too, was looking at some map and then looking around. "Thank God for this fog," she muttered. "We would have been dead before we even reached the ground."

"We can also thank God they weren't carrying infrared goggles. At least I assume not, because they can't find us." Kylie suddenly stopped talking as we could hear distant voices coming our way. Without another word, we headed off again. We continued onwards for several hours, crossing over roads or avoiding them entirely. Finally, my companions started to get tired. We hunkered down in a cow field behind some bushes that were grown to act like a fence. "I wish I knew what happened to Allison."

"Can't you call her up?" I asked

Kylie shook her head. "No, that's probably how they tracked Carter. While it could be possible, they could've just run across to him. We can't take the risk. Get some sleep. One of us will stay on watch until nightfall, and then we can carry on."

"You go ahead. I'll keep watch. I don't need to sleep for many hours yet."

Honestly, I don't think I could have slept anyway because, quite frankly, I was terrified. Kylie and McKenna, however, didn't appear to have a similar problem, as they lay down in the wet grass and were quickly asleep.

CHAPTER THIRTY

— · —

OLD LONDON TOWN

I sat silently for the next hour, with every sound that came my way scaring the life out of me. Halfway through my second hour, I saw a figure hidden among the mist coming our way. I kicked McKenna as I drew my weapon, and she was up at my side in a second, her weapon drawn. She was about to fire when my keen eyes realized who it was, and I quickly pushed her arm aside. "It's Allison."

"Well, g'day, you turkeys," she grinned at us as she walked up to the group. By this time, Kylie was awake, and she was up at her side, and for the first time, I saw some emotion from her as she grinned happily at seeing her friend. "What are you guys doing hiding down here?" She teased. "I got us a ride."

We all looked at each other in surprise and followed Allison to a road where a nice little compact car awaited. I probably wouldn't have been as cheerful to see it if I had known that she had killed the driver to get it. That was something I didn't find out till long after the mission. Allison climbed into the front with McKenna riding shotgun, while Kylie and I climbed into the back. "Please ensure you fasten your seat belts." The car told us, and we complied.

Allison switched on the navigation system and simply said, "London."

The vehicle's automated system powered up, and just like we were tourists in the country, the vehicle took us onwards at a steady pace, keeping us within the speed limits and from attention. We soon cleared the fog, and I could see the fields of England clearly now. I

275

started to relax a little bit. It had been four years since I had been on a breathable planet, and despite the cold, I rolled down the window and enjoyed the smell of the country air. Twilight Wanderer is a beautiful ship, but nothing is more beautiful than Mother Nature, but it wouldn't last as we eventually entered the grime and grit of the city of London.

"Okay," Kylie said, becoming all businesslike. "Kensett had me memorize a list of contacts and addresses of agents who worked for her, but she has since lost contact. We should try each one of them until we get lucky."

"What if we don't get lucky?" McKenna said most snarkily. "What if the first one simply turns us in?"

"We're not going to go to their houses, mate," Kylie replied sarcastically, "I'm going to call them first." She pulled out a small cell phone and tapped in a number. She switched on the loudspeaker as it rang. A man's voice answered with an English accent. "Hello?" The boy sounded nervous. I assumed the number Kylie had called was exclusive to Charlotte's operations. "G'day, mate," Kylie said cheerfully. "The sparrow has left the nest."

There was a long pause at the other end of the line before he replied. "Nothing personal, but I don't trust the old passwords. The government is now working with the Peons, and I honestly don't know if our operations have been revealed to them."

"Do I sound like I'm from the British government, mate?" Kylie said snarkily.

"Tell me the name of your handler?" Came the response.

"Come off it, mate. It works both ways. I'm not giving away the name of my handler. Do you think I'm a complete Charlie?" I didn't realize it at the time, but she revealed our handler's name, for Charlie was a reference to Charlotte Kensett.

The man on the other line gave a little laugh. "The sparrow is hungry."

Kylie grinned as she looked over at Allison, who was also smiling. He had given the correct passphrase response. "We are looking for a home base for an immediate operation," Kylie continued. "Can you assist?"

"Can you make it to Romford?"

"We are about an hour out," Kylie said as she checked on the GPS. "But we are in a stolen car and don't know if the Peons have gotten onto it yet."

"Can't you ditch it and get another one?" Our contact suggested.

"Our mission is time-sensitive. We'll take the risk but don't worry, we'll dump the car a mile or two from your location. Transmit your address now."

The address was transmitted to the car, automatically updated its navigation, and changed direction. As the call ended, Kylie put the phone away and rested her head back on her seat.

"How come my mission is time sensitive? We don't even know where Mr. Phelkar is," I asked.

"The Peons aren't gonna give up looking for us. The faster we move, the faster we can keep ahead of them," Allison replied.

About an hour later, we arrived in the town of Romford in the suburbs of east London, just on the border of the County of Essex.

Allison pulled over the car, and we climbed out. We removed our weapons from side holsters to ones hidden under our jackets, and we walked casually for about half a mile until we came across an old house that must have been a couple of hundred years old. It seemed kind of weird that we just rolled up the path and rang the doorbell. A man in his late fifties opened the door. "You never said there was four of you," he grumbled.

"Is that a problem?" Allison asked him.

"It just draws more attention to you," he said, looking around at his neighbors' houses. "Quickly come inside." We followed him one by one, and he led us into a small cramped, musty-smelling living room where an old lady sat by a fire. "Don't worry about mother," the man muttered. "She doesn't even know her own name these days." I looked at the old lady, who smiled up at me with a vacant expression in her eyes. "Take a seat. I'll make you some tea, and then you can tell me what's going on."

I sat down in an armchair while the other three sat on the sofa. A few minutes later, the old man returned with a tray and a teapot with various unmatched cups. "I have to be honest with you. I assumed it was game over and that I would never hear from Miss Kensett again."

"Don't worry, mate. It certainly isn't over," Allison told him. "There's a new leader in charge, Jenna Plural, who will turn things around." McKenna snorted at this, but we ignored it.

"You're with Jenna Plural?" he looked quite pleased. "I heard her broadcast."

"So, her message got through," Kylie grinned.

"Indeed, it did, and it certainly brought a ray of hope to many people here," he said, laying down the tray and taking a seat. "We don't have much faith in the Americans these days. In fact, we haven't for a long time, but she seems to be a Yank we can get behind."

"She certainly is," I said with a smile.

"I hope you don't mind if you get straight to business. We don't have much time. The Peons know we've landed, and the hunt is on," Allison told him as she took a cup of tea from him.

As he finished handing out the drinks and went to grab himself a chair from his dining room, he sat down and said, "how can I help you?"

"We need to find a man called Michael Phelkar. He's a prisoner of British authorities, albeit through the Peons," Kylie informed him.

"You don't need to explain to me who Michael Phelkar is. The media was full of him for weeks. I watched his sham trial and listened to the Peon propaganda through the BBC. There's probably not a person in England that doesn't know the names of Michael Phelkar and Jenna Plural. However, finding him is an altogether different matter. The Peons are expecting this Jenna Plural to try to liberate him and keep a very closed mouth about his location."

"Are you telling me there's absolutely no way we can find out where he's being held?" I asked, starting to feel this whole endeavor was now useless.

"Now, I didn't say that, did I?" He smiled softly at me. "I'm not saying it's impossible. I'm just saying it's extremely hard. I will have to call in a lot of favors to find out that information for you. Our network isn't as secure as it once was 'cause some of our agents are, frankly, pleased the war has ended. Who I can and can't trust is very shaky right now."

"Kensett has deemed this mission a priority. Whatever the risk, we have to find Michael Phelkar," Kylie said firmly.

The man paused and pondered this before getting up out of his seat. "Let me make some calls."

The gentleman came back about thirty minutes later. "Okay, one of our operatives is going to meet with you. She has some information."

"Why couldn't she give you the information over the phone?" Kylie asked.

"Just paranoia. Since the capitulation, we have lost contact with quite a few of our agents, and we don't know if they have been captured or just gone native."

"Fine. But only two of us are going," Allison said. I looked at her questioningly. "I'm paranoid too, and for all I know, this nice gentleman here is sending us into a trap. Kylie and I will go. You and McKenna can stay here."

"And if it is a trap, that means you've left McKenna and me sitting here twiddling our thumbs," I replied. "She's the muscle, I'm the passenger, and you are the agents. We can't risk losing both of you."

"She has a point," Kylie said. "Me and blondie will go."

"Now, I might have something to say about that," McKenna said firmly. "My orders are to not move away from Miss Grant."

"You don't get a say, Myers," Allison replied dismissively. "Our orders are flexible due to circumstances on missions like this."

"I must now assume that that delightful Miss Kensett did not explain my part in this," McKenna reached up and tapped her neck. "You see, Miss Kensett did not particularly trust me. Inside here is a small device that, in the event of the death of Miss Grant, will release a toxin into my bloodstream. Therefore, if you separate me from Miss Grant, I'm gonna have a really bad day."

"So, you're here by force and not voluntarily?" I said disbelievingly.

"Give the GenMod a gold star," McKenna responded sarcastically. "When you broke me out of jail, did you think I was in there for drunk and disorderly, or I was helping for the love of Jenna Plural?" She looked at me like I was stupid.

279

This didn't appear to phase either Allison or Kylie, making it clear to me that this was not as unusual as I thought, and it must have been something they had experienced before."Fine." Allison said. "Then the two of you go."

"Seriously?" I stared at her wide-eyed.

"I don't see why not. You're just meeting someone, getting some information, and coming back. We'll be in touch with our communicators at all times."

And so it was. About an hour later, the man in the house drove us down to Romford station. He never did divulge his name, so for purposes of relaying the story to make it easier for me, I am just going to call him Fred.

Allison had given me legitimate British payment cards. I purchased two tickets to Liverpool Street Station, one of the four main terminals for rail transport into the city, before one had to rely on the underground.

We also had fake identification cards, which Charlotte had promised would pass muster, but all the same, I hoped and prayed we wouldn't be asked for it. It was also recommended that if we were stopped, I should do the talking. While not that common these days, an Australian in London was more likely than an American. However, we didn't have to go far; our contact was to meet us in the Maccas at the top of the escalators just outside the station. We took our seats at the table by the window described to us and waited.

"So, what's your story?" I asked McKenna.

"You mean, how is it that I'm not on the side of Jenna Plural?" She replied, and I nodded. "I was close to Jenna Plural once. I was actually working with her until about two years ago. I was the second in command of her team until I got transferred. However, when the war ended, all I wanted to do was go home back to Alabama. However, she chose to continue the war, and every American had to decide, and I decided to follow my chain of command. That's all there is to it, really."

"So, did you know my sister well?" I asked.

"Stacey?" McKenna's almost sad look crossed her face as she said, "yeah, I knew Stacey." She smiled. "She was one of my best buddies

280

for a long time. We worked together for three years, but I chose duty over friendship, and we now stand on opposite sides."

"I have to be honest. I can't understand your choice. I want to go back to Australia more than anything, but I want my country to be my country," I said quite arrogantly.

"You haven't spent the last ten years of your life fighting a senseless war, watching your friends get killed and killing people you never knew," McKenna said defensively. "I'm sick of it. This war should never have begun. It is a war of greed, Miss Grant. It's about who can gain the most resources, and we're sending generation after generation to their deaths every year."

"We didn't start this war," I replied curtly.

"Oh, my dear Hannah, take the cotton balls out of your ears. So much propaganda is flying around, that I think the truth of who started this war will be forever lost."

"The victors write history. America will be branded alongside Australia as the aggressors. In defeat, we become the bad guys," I chided.

"I'm not a philosopher, Miss Grant," she sighed and sat back in her chair. "Nor am I a historian. I'm just a country girl who got called up to do her national service and stayed on because I once believed in the cause."

I studied her carefully. She was not being wholly honest with me. As I've told you before, I can pick that up easier than most people. "There's something about this you're not telling me, something very important to you," I said.

She looked startled for a moment and then grinned. "Can't keep anything from a damn GenMod, can you?" She sighed and continued. "Would it surprise you for me to say that I'm engaged?" She didn't wait for me to respond, and honestly, I didn't care enough to be surprised about anything. Curiosity is a wholly different thing. "John Anderson. He served with me on board the Lewis Puller, and we got transferred around the same time. He is a technician. We served together for a year on the Potemkin, but then he got posted back to Earth. I haven't heard from him since the surrender," she then looked back at me. "So I'm sure you can understand that I want to find out what happened to him and hopefully reunite."

I pondered this and said, "first of all, call me Hannah. Second, let me make a deal with you. If I can find a way to remove that thing in your neck and you continue to help me with this mission, we'll leave you behind. You can turn yourself in to the British authorities or find your own way back to the US. Because quite frankly, I don't think Charlotte will let you go once we return, even if she promised such."

McKenna looked surprised. "You would trust me to continue to help you without this thing in my neck?"

"I trust that you want to go home and that you're a woman with some integrity. If you try to stop us all, turn us in, then Allison and Kylie will kill you. I trust that your desire to return to America and your home in Alabama is a stronger consideration than stopping us from rescuing a man with no strategic value."

Before she could respond, a little old lady walked to our table and stated the passphrase we'd been told us to expect. I counter-replied, and she sat down with us. She played with a small device the size of a cell phone on the table in front of us. "Just a sound distorter. It will garble whatever we say should anyone be listening to us with any devices," she said. "We still need to be brief, however. Michael Phelkar is currently being held in the Isle of Man prison."

"Where is that?" I asked.

She looked at me with raised eyebrows. "It is on the Isle of Man in the Irish Sea. Very remote, very impenetrable. At least not without a full-scale attack."

"That's not an option. We need another," I said insistently.

"Oh my God, girl, will you just shut up and listen to me?" The old lady said irritably. "I told you I don't have much time. The penal colony transport H.M.S. Parkhurst will take off from Stansted Airport in three days. It will fly to the Isle of Man and pick up Mr. Phelkar for transport to the penal colony on A117."

"Where is that? I asked.

"It is one of the lesser moons of Jupiter. It's a hard labor camp. They're mostly political prisoners of the Peons. However, we may be able to get you aboard that ship as service workers. You simply need to wait until they pick him up, and then it's up to you how you get him off the ship once it's in flight. I will meet you again at Stansted in three days." Before I could say anything else, she stood up and started walking away. I looked up at McKenna, and McKenna looked at me, but we said nothing as we finished the rather bland burgers before heading back to the train.

CHAPTER THIRTY-ONE

H.M.S. PARKHURST

We stayed with Fred and his mother for those three days in quite uncomfortable conditions, for he only had two bedrooms, and his mother had one of those. He slept on the couch, and we took turns sharing the bed in his room.

The morning came fast when we were to drive to Stansted Airport, which was out in Essex. After calling in a neighbor to watch after his mother, he drove us there. Apparently, the old lady had been in contact with him, and we were to meet a few miles away in an old FedEx truck.

It was like something out of a movie, for we drove straight into it. When we got out, we saw it was stacked with various equipment, including clothes rails. The old lady and a young man with her pulled out various uniforms for me to try on. How on Earth she got our sizes is beyond me, but the stewards uniform provided to me fitted perfectly. However, I was about to throw a spanner into the works. I looked at the old lady and said, "with all this equipment here, do you have anything that would remove an explosive microdevice?"

Everyone except McKenna looked at me suspiciously. "Indeed, I do. Why on Earth do you need it."

"I want you to remove such a device from this lady's neck." I indicated to McKenna.

"Now, just wait a minute," Allison said sharply.

"I promised her we would leave her behind," I said sharply.

"That isn't part of the plan. My orders are clear. She comes back with us."

285

"Frankly, I don't give a fuck about your orders, Allison. Once we're aboard this vessel, McKenna gets to walk."

"Hannah, I have no clue where you get the delusion that you're in charge of this mission," Allison snapped with considerable annoyance. "You may be bankrolling it, but that doesn't give you authority here."

"I don't expect authority here," I scowled. "However, McKenna is not coming back with us. That leaves you in a position where you either remove the device from her neck or leave me with her. Was the option of leaving me here with her given to you by Miss Kensett?"

"No," Allison simply said. "I do, however, have the option to shoot her at any time I choose should the need arise."

"She's going to be executed anyway, and you know it, and she knows it. I don't think that's fair payback for helping us."

"I don't know what's going on here," said the young man. "But we're running out of time. And you're not making me feel very comfortable right now, ladies."

Allison sighed. "Fine, go ahead, but you're taking the fall for this with Kensett when we get back. Is that clear?"

I nodded to the old lady, who shrugged and went and found a small gun-shaped object from amongst a big pile of what appeared to be randomly stacked equipment and stepped over to McKenna. She placed it against her neck, and with a click and a gasp of pain from the woman, she stepped back. "All done."

"Can we now get a move on?" Allison said curtly.

"Kensett has managed to get us I.D.s to replace the ship's crew," the young man stated. Again, I have no idea about his name, but a few minutes after this interaction, I would never see him again, so it hardly matters. "They're already expecting two new recently employed crewmen who no one would recognize."

"Only two?" Kylie asked with concern.

"Yes, I'm afraid two of you won't be leaving with the Parkhurst," he said, like there were no consequences to this. I couldn't help but think how cold-blooded spooks were. I'm no golden heart, but still...

"Well, McKenna is not leaving anyway," I said. "Is there any way you can put her in touch with the Americans to get her out of here?" and the old lady nodded to me. "I should probably stay, too, as both

Allison and Kylie are much more prepared for this. Somehow, I'll find my way out." Thoughts of finding my way back Down Under stirred. It was a dumb suggestion and said in the excitement of the situation. Fortunately, they didn't agree.

"As much as I like that suggestion, Hannah, it's not an option," Allison replied dismissively. "Charlotte made it a prime directive of the mission that you come back alive."

"Why?" I asked honestly, unaware why Charlotte was so concerned for my welfare

"Charlotte doesn't exactly explain herself, but if it makes you feel better, you can think that she likes you," Allison managed a grin. "But it's probably more likely she doesn't want to lose the resources of Grant Industries." Indeed, that was more likely.

"Okay. Kylie, you go with Hannah," Allison said, becoming all business again. "I'll go with McKenna. Let's see if we can get out of the U.K. to America. I'm more likely to find a way back to the fleet that way."

Kylie, clearly not happy, said nothing in response to Allison's statement and nodded as she finished fastening the buttons of her tunic. Allison turned to me and offered me her hand. "Good luck Hannah. It's been... interesting working with you."

"Let me assure you of this, Allison. Those resources of Grant Industries that your boss favors so much will be turned to making sure that you get out of here." She said nothing in response to that but smiled. She stepped aside to briefly talk to Kylie privately as I got back into the car with Fred, and Kylie soon joined us. We pulled out of the truck, and I looked at McKenna and Addison as they waved us off as the door started to close.

Fred drove us into the airport just like it was another working day, the two young girls working on his majesty's prison service.

I would have probably shown my nervousness if I'd been ordinary. However, as I followed Kylie to the service entrance and we showed our I.D.s, no one had the faintest idea that inside, I was at almost panic levels.

I managed to relax somewhat when security handed back my I.D. and waved me through. I wondered how a couple of Aussie sheilas would pass off as government employees, but as we entered the terminal that would take us out to the Parkhurst, I was surprised when Kylie spoke in a perfect British accent. She gave them the fake name on the I.D. card, and we were shown through to the supervisor. He was a tall, burly guy with a friendly face and a welcoming smile. "Glad to have you aboard! We've been running short of staff for about three months now. Let's get on board, and I'll show you around the ship."

We went through some large doors and got onto a bus, with what I assumed was the rest of the crew. Twelve in total. There were lots of hellos and welcomes, making me nervous about what we would need to do to achieve our mission. I really hoped I wouldn't have to hurt any of these people who were so warm and friendly. I kept as quiet as possible, although I was already preparing a story about being an ex-pat Aussie who had moved to England before the surrender.

The H.M.S. Parkhurst was a small personnel carrier that had been retrofitted as a prisoner transport. It was military green and looked like a giant beetle, all curved and rounded. Fitted with an M.E.T. device, they could potentially take at least a hundred prisoners at a time. Although Gordon, for that was the supervisor's name, told us that we would only be transporting one special prisoner, though he didn't name him. "We take turns to be on duty with most of the crew being uploaded in the M.E.T. Not everyone is uploaded, just in case there was some sort of system failure. We don't want the prisoner to be downloaded onto an empty ship." He chuckled at this, and you really couldn't help but like this chubby guy. "At least three of us always remain on duty. It's quite a cushy number, actually, as you only work for five weeks but get paid for five months each way." We disembarked the bus, walked up the ramp, and into the old ship. Gordon led us through to quarters that had two bunks which were shared between five people. Three of which would be in the M.E.T. at any one time. It didn't look like a prison ship, because there were no cells or anything like that, just a few quarters, a dining room, a recreation room, cockpit, and an engineering section. Kylie and I were the only ones with no technical skills to speak of. Our job was to prepare meals and maintain the ship, which meant a lot of cleaning. Something I had never done before.

I have to be honest and tell you I didn't exactly know what the plan was. I was the fifth wheel throughout this mission. I just continued to follow Kylie's lead, but she didn't say much, and I think it was because she hadn't been comfortable about leaving Allison behind. I don't know how long they had worked together, but it had clearly been for a long time.

Of course, I could remain silent forever, but no one questioned my story about being an expatriate Australian who now had British citizenship. Of course, these were just rank and file of the British Home Office prison service. They had little more than a school education and a desire to have the exceptionally good health benefits of working in the prison service. I wondered at the time why there was no one more official on board, considering the status of the high-profile prisoner they were taking. Everything was low-key because they didn't want to draw attention and thus divulge how and when they were moving Mr. Phelkar.

Obviously, that plan failed, or we wouldn't have been sitting in the takeoff seats as the H.M.S. Parkhurst lifted up from Stanstead. We made a three-minute flight over the Irish Sea to land on a small docking pad barely five hundred yards from the prison. I stood looking out of the window nervously at a mixture of both British and Peon security lining up between us at the entrance of the infamous place of incarceration.

It was only about forty-five minutes later, and I got my first actual look at Michael Phelkar. He looked vastly different than when I had seen him standing with Jenna Plural on screen. He was dressed in a gray prison one-piece tunic. His hands were manacled in the front, and so were his legs. He was flanked all around by four more guards, and it took quite a while for them to come down the pathway, as he had to shuffle due to the restrictions the manacles gave to his stride. Eventually, he disappeared from my view, and I heard his footsteps on the ramp. I went to the entranceway to see, but Kylie came beside me. "Don't look so interested," she said softly. "The crew isn't supposed to know who we're taking."

However, the crew was not stupid. The fact that we were only taking one prisoner, a rather expensive way to transport someone, drew the crew's attention. Michael Phelkar came up the ramp. He didn't look worse for wear and seemed to be in good health and even seemed to be in a fairly pleasant mood. He looked up at the eyes staring at him and studied everyone in turn. When he looked at me, his eyes narrowed slightly as if he had recognized me. Automatically I smiled, and he smiled back before the guard behind him shoved him in the back, and they turned off towards the engineering section with the M.E.T. equipment. The door closed behind them, and several minutes later, we saw the flash of light from under the door frame, which indicated the prisoner was on board.

A few minutes later, the voice of the pilots came over the intercom system. "The prisoner is aboard. All crew to take up positions. We lift off in four minutes." Gordon moved to close the hatch door, but someone from outside suddenly shouted at him, and he waited. Two people came on board, a man and a woman. They showed I.D. cards to Gordon, and he frowned. I can't remember what they said to him, but it was inconsequential beyond being aware that one spoke with a French accent and the other with a German one. The ununiformed officials almost literally screamed out 'Peon spooks." I wanted to find out what these European intelligence officers were doing there, for the crew had clearly not been expecting them, and that was the intent, which is why they boarded at the last moment. "We're gonna need to take them out first," Kylie said to me as we returned to our quarters. "We need to make our move when we're at the closest point to the confederation fleet. I went through crew rosters, and we're not on the same shift patterns. If we don't take control of the M.E.T. somehow, we won't see each other until we arrive at our destination, and any opportunity will be long gone."

"Oh, surely whoever is out here can get the other one out of there when the time comes?" I responded.

"That sounds fine in principle. But according to the schedule, you'll be out here when that happens. What experience do you have with operating an M.E.T.?"

"None, but is it really that hard?"

"In theory, no, but I can't show you how to do it without arousing suspicion. I'm fairly confident that one of the Peon officers will always be awake." She opened our locker, grabbed a bag, and pulled out a small bottle marked headache relief. "Put this into whoever's drink, and you'll knock them out. However, there'll still be three other crew members to deal with." The door suddenly opened, and Gordon was looking none too happy. "I know you are newbies, but when the pilot tells you to take your seats for takeoff, I expect you to do it. Come on."

We followed him out and took our positions, strapping ourselves into the seats in the back row of the lounge with the other crew. We felt the nausea of the compensators being activated and started heading vertically up into the air.

It wasn't long before we once more saw the darkness of space. I expected the jostling and shaking that accompanied an Earth takeoff just like it had my first time. However, it was smooth and comfortable, and it took me a moment to realize the reason behind this. There were no longer weapons and probes aimed at us. No one was trying to take us out, not just because we were on a Peon ship.

The Pacific Alliance had had just as much artillery in Near-Earth orbit as the enemy. It was because, on Earth, the war was over. The Peons controlled the entire world. It sounds very silly telling you this, but this was the first time I truly became aware of what was at stake. Of course, they quickly returned to their defenses after the Martian events a few weeks after I returned to the fleet, but right then and there, it was totally surreal. There was no-one left in Earth orbit that offered a threat to the ship. It was no more than twenty minutes when the pilot released us from our confines.

The crew was cheerfully chattering away as we headed to the M. E.T. I tried to join in to avoid arousing suspicion as we all undressed. Then in a flash, it was literally three months later, and I was on board the ship without my co-conspirator.

It was the German woman that was on duty when I came out. I had expected her to be intimidating, but she was actually quite pleasant. One of my supposed crewmates showed me my duties. Break times were taken in the dining area, where Heidi Keller spent most of her day looking at a computer screen on her laptop. Since we all took our breaks at different times, it was hard to avoid being alone with her. "You are Australian, yes?" she said to me in a thick German accent.

"True blue," I said it automatically, and when she stared at me confused, I laughed lightly and said, "I was Australian. I got British citizenship about five years ago."

"You miss Australia, do you not?" she asked pleasantly.

"Not really," I lied. There is nothing more that I wanted in this world than to go back to a free Australia. "I miss some things, but I'm quite happy living in England."

Keller sighed, "I miss Deutschland. It has been two years since I've been home."

"Where in Germany are you from?" I asked.

"Well, I was born on Mars but raised in Dusseldorf," she replied.

"What was it like living on Mars?"

"Meh, I do not remember it well. I was a small child when we moved back to Germany," she sighed again and sat back in her chair. "I am glad the war is over, and we will soon get back home again." She then glanced at me. "I am sorry the war ended the way it has. I would have much rather we had found peace with a mutual understanding."

"It is what it is," I shrugged. "No point in worrying about it now, and are we really at peace? Apparently not everyone has accepted the surrender." I'm not entirely sure why I brought this up. I think it was just my insatiable curiosity to be able to sit here and talk with the enemy and hear their point of view.

A look of disgust crossed Keller's face. "If you are referring to Jenna Plural, she is no more than an irritant. People will soon realize not to trust a GenMod. They are an aberration of nature." And with that, any sympathy I was starting to feel for her rapidly disappeared. She may have noticed that I was a GenMod, but I'd had to stop taking care of my appearance since starting this mission. I wore no makeup, and I no longer brushed my long hair. Of course, that didn't make me any less attractive, but the perception of GenMods was that we looked perfect all the time, and I took full advantage of that misconception.

Chapter Thirty-Two

— • —

Michael

The days were long and arduous, and I found out that I really didn't like cooking and cleaning and was no good at either. The crew certainly would agree with me on the cooking part, even though it was little more than reheating pre-prepared meals that were stored in the kitchen M.E.T.. However, it did help me become familiar with the basic operations of such a device. At the end of the week, I was re-uploaded, and Kylie came down, but we were never alone for more than a few minutes before I was sent off into nothing again.

I continued this way for about three months, and I was two days out from being re-uploaded, when the date of the most optimal distance from Jenna Plural's fleet arrived. If we didn't do it now, we would be moving further away again.

To say I wasn't nervous would be a lie, but as I prepared breakfast that morning, I slipped the mickey into Keller's tea and served breakfast. My other two crewmates were humble technicians. I didn't believe I would have any problem with them when the time came. We were on autopilot, and no-one was helming the cockpit. I dished up my own breakfast and sat down to wait. No-one noticed that I was not joining in with the conversation this morning.

I felt revolted by the two British guys chatting and laughing with the German. One was even flirting with her, and she appeared to be reciprocating. The irony of war where people could go from multiple enemies to allies. However, they were about to get a shock, and I was to get an even bigger one. I was expecting Keller to fall asleep, but she suddenly started convulsing in her seat and trying to stand up, only to collapse over the table, appearing to have some sort of fit. I stared in disbelief, as my two colleagues started to panic and tried to hold her down. I was shouting for someone to do something. No-one was a qualified medic, but I heard one of the men shout at me to go to the M.E.T. and download someone called something or other. This was my chance. As I raced to the engineering section, I managed to get my head around what was happening and realized that Kylie had lied to me. I hadn't knocked out the European agent; I had poisoned her.

The M.E.T. was much more complicated than the device I down-loaded bacon from, but it only took me a couple of minutes to bring up Kylie's fake name on the computer console, and then it was all a matter of hitting the download button. I forgot to close my eyes as the flash game, and it took me a moment to see Kylie standing before me. "Is everything going according to plan?" she asked if she went to a locker to retrieve her clothes.

"No, you sadistic motherfucker, why didn't you tell me I was going to be killing her?" I snapped back angrily.

"Would you have done it if you had known?" she said, looking up at me casually.

"Honestly, I don't know, but I would have liked to have that choice."

"And that's why we didn't tell you. We can't afford the luxury of your conscience. Why should you consider what is in the best interests of a fucking German?"

"Not all of them can be so bad!" I snapped.

I was startled when she spun upon me, her face filled with blood-red anger. She pointed her finger at the wall beside her. "Go tell that to the millions of dead back in Oz, Hannah Grant! Stand over the mass graves of men, women, and children and tell them there are nice Peons. Tell it to those who lost their arms, legs, or even their eyesight. Tell it to the people still starving in labor camps, because their cities lie in ruins. Not everyone had their Mummy's company to save their pretty genetically designed waste of space, arse, Hannah Grant! Then, tell me there are good fucking Peons." I made to reply, but she moved the finger to point it directly in my face. "No," she said, no longer shouting, but still, the hatred in her voice was clear. "Don't say a word. We don't have the time to get into a blue. Just know this. Jenna Plural is right. There will be no justice until every last Peon is dead."

"Including the children?" I said softly.

Her face faltered, and her hand fell to her side as she turned away from me. "If that's what it takes to stop them growing into Peons, then yes. Whatever is necessary." She pushed me aside and stepped up to the M.E.T. device, scrolling through the names. "Downloading now."

I was expecting to see Mr. Phelkar appear, but I saw the middle-aged pilot instead. He smiled at us, but it didn't last long as Kylie said to him, "this vessel is under the control of the Solar Confederation and the jurisdiction of Jenna Plural." She reached into the breast pocket of our tunic and handed him a piece of paper she'd prepared before she'd been uploaded. "You will change the course of this ship to these coordinates. If you don't, I will erase everybody within the M.E.T."

To my surprise, his eyes widened, and he looked quite calm. "No need to make a threat, darling," he said almost cheerfully. "I'm not exactly friends with the Peons. Just tell me how I can help, and I'm with you."

"That's appreciated," said Kylie. "But I'm sure you can understand I can't simply trust you once we're back to the fleet. We can discuss where your loyalties lie."

"I understand."

She moved to the door with him, but I stopped her asking, "aren't we gonna download Mr. Phelkar?"

"Only once the ship is securely in our control. Unless you're telling me that you took care of the two other crewmen."

"I didn't, but can we try to avoid killing them if possible? They're Brits, not Peons."

"That will be up to them, Hannah, not me."

We headed out, and the two crewmen were sitting at the table staring at the dead body of Heidi Keller, who would never see Dusseldorf again. Foam still ran down from her mouth as her body expelled the toxins. When they saw the pilot come out, they stood up. "Relax." the pilot said, waving them back down. "They're with Jenna Plural."

295

They almost looked relieved, and we realized this would be easier than we ever thought possible.

"Is there anything we can do to help?" said one of them, as the pilot disappeared into the cockpit.

"The only thing I need from you is to come quietly with me so I can upload you," Kylie said in a reasonably friendly tone. "I can only hope that you understand that I can't simply take your word that you're willing to assist us. However, once we get back to our fleet, our superiors will assess your loyalty." We took them back into the engineering section and uploaded them.

Then the moment came. She scrolled through the names once more, and when she found it, she hit the download button, and Michael Phelkar appeared in front of us.

We stood there dumbly and stared at each other for a few moments. "Well, hello there," he said, staring at me with widened eyes. "If this is to be, my interment will not be as bad as I thought. Or maybe I have died and gone to heaven."

I raised a quizzical eyebrow at him and said, "g'day mate. I'm Hannah Grant, and this is Kylie..." I hesitated, realizing I didn't know her surname. "We're here to get you out of here."

"Grant, did you say?" It was his turn to raise an eyebrow. "Any relation to....?"

"Stacey," I said, cutting him off. "She's my sister."

His eyes narrowed into a frown as he looked me up and down before saying very disbelievingly, "seriously?"

"Yes, seriously," I scowled. "What would I have to gain by making that shit up?"

"Now you certainly sound like Stacey," he smiled.

I glanced down at his body and then looked back up at him. With wide critical eyes, I said, "do you want to put some clothes on, mate? Your dick is starting to look happier to see us more than it should on a first meeting." Although I said 'us,' he had not taken his eyes off me for a single moment since he had appeared.

The big idiot glanced down to where I had been looking and turned away, embarrassed. "I'm not entirely sure where they put my clothing, but I'd appreciate it if you'd help me out of this situation."

Kylie snorted and rolled her eyes, "I'll leave it to you to acclimatize him, Han." She muttered something like, "Oh my God, what a creep," as she headed out.

I had no idea which locker they had stored his clothes in any more than he did, but I turned around and began to open them, pulling out various garments and judging the size. I simply tossed to the floor anything I didn't believe would fit him until I found a passable pair of shoes, trousers, and a shirt. I forewent the undergarments because, ew, gross, who wants to wear someone else's undies? I turned away as he began to dress.

"Is Stacey here?" he asked as he pulled on the trousers.

"No, she's back at the fleet." I turned back to face him as he indicated it was safe to do so. "This isn't exactly an official mission."

"What exactly do you mean by that?" he asked, as he pulled the shirt over his head.

"Jenna Plural was unable to authorize a rescue operation. So, I came myself."

"Why?" he asked suspiciously.

I shrugged at him. "For my sister."

"I never even realized Stacey had a sister. I knew she had a brother who was killed in action."

"She has two sisters, as a matter of fact," I replied, indicating for him to follow me out the door once he was ready. "Although I should probably say 'had' as it's more than likely that Annabelle is dead after all this time."

"How long was I in the M.E.T.?" he asked as we stepped out the door.

"Just a few months," I replied but looked up at him when he suddenly gasped. We had entered the living quarters, and he was looking at the dead body of the German officer lying down on the table. "Yeah, sorry, we haven't really had time yet to dispose of that."

He stepped over to her and lifted her head by her hair so he could get a look at her face. "It couldn't have happened to a nicer young lady," he muttered.

"You knew her?"

He sighed softly, "Oh yes, I knew her. She spent the last few months tormenting me for no reason other than she appeared to get off on it."

"Really?" I said, surprised. "I found her to be quite charming," I said, extremely pleased that Kylie was not there to hear him, after her tirade back in engineering.

He let go of her hair, deliberately letting her head fall with a thud against the table. He turned back to me. "Yet you killed her?"

I shrugged and said, "she could have been as virtuous as a fucking nun, but she was still in my way."

"Do I correctly assume that you're also a veteran of the Australian military?"

I laughed at that, "I am as civilian as they come, mate. I run a business. I have never served a day in my life."

Before he could respond to that, Kylie stepped out of the cockpit. She looked up at Michael for a moment, studying him carefully before smiling at him and saying, "Are you hungry, Mr. Phelkar? I can make us all some lunch."

He smiled at her, "Oh my, two very beautiful rescuers, and Australian at that. Is this an entirely Australian affair?"

Kylie looked at him noncommittally when she replied, "Dunno about an Australian affair, mate. Since Last Day, I've worked for the Yanks and now for Jenna Plural."

"I see. What branch of the military are you in?"

Kylie shook her head as she stepped over to the small kitchen area and started to make a coffee. "I'm not military, mate. I'm with intelligence."

I noticed Michael's smile disappear for a moment as he said questioningly, "Charlotte Kensett?"

She looked back over her shoulders, appearing surprised that he knew about Jenna's head spook. "Yeah." She indicated the coffee and asked us both if we wanted one. Michael said yes, but I declined. I sat at the table away from the dead body and watched them both with interest. "How is everything back on the fleet?" Michael said as he joined me.

"Well, it's a little bit chaotic as we make the move to Enceladus."

298

Michael looked surprised. "Emma Dodgson was successful? My my, I can't say that I really believed she would succeed in that."

Neither Kylie nor I knew who he was talking about. Soon, Dodgson would become an indelible blot on my family's history. "Oh, I'm sorry," Kylie said. "I forgot you wouldn't know anything about that. Admiral Plural has declared Enceladus the temporary capital of the Solar Confederation, although the provisional government remains ensconced aboard the U.S.S. Constitution."

"Yet Jenna didn't authorize this rescue?" Michael sounded a little disappointed.

"No," I replied. "As I've already told you, this is entirely an independent operation."

Michael gave me a wry smile. "Ah, by that, you mean Jenna is officially unaware of what is going on?"

"No," I responded again irritably. "I mean that Jenna is entirely unaware that this is going on."

His eyes narrowed, "I find it hard to believe that Charlotte Kensett would go out of her way for my sake."

"She didn't," Kylie replied with a smirk. "You entirely have Hannah here to thank for this one. I don't know any details, but I'm fairly sure Hannah and Charlotte negotiated a deal that is very much in my boss' interest."

Michael turned his eyes upon me questioningly, and I replied, "I am trading a lot of resources within Grant Industries to pull this off."

"Grant Industries?" His eyes widened as he took the steaming coffee cup from my companion.

"My company," I said.

He looked at me like a deer in headlights. "Oh, I certainly know what Grant Industries is. I just had no idea that Stacey was associated with it. I knew that she had a wealthy side to her family, but I didn't realize she meant those Grants."

"Yeah, well. Stacey got the shit end of the stick. My mother was a bitch, and now she's dead," I said as if it was a simple matter.

A look of realization appeared to cross the Englishman's face. "This is why you've done this, isn't it? You feel guilt at how your sister was treated, and you were doing this for her."

It sounded silly when he put it like that, and I merely shrugged, "my reasons are my reasons. Does it really matter?"

"Not really, my dear Hannah. Stacey and I are very close, and she means a lot to me. "

I snorted at that, but didn't elaborate. He was momentarily startled and then looked somewhat embarrassed. He now realized I was aware of the unconscionable triangle between my sister, himself, and Jenna Plural.

"Perhaps you could tell me if there's anywhere I could possibly take a shower," he said, turning his attention back to Kylie. "The facilities where I was imprisoned were not particularly pleasant."

"Sure," Kylie said, jumping up. "Come on. I'll show you."

CHAPTER THIRTY-THREE

A BITCH CALLED PRIDE

I sat back as the two left the room, trying to work out what I thought of this Phelkar. It was less than a couple of minutes when Kylie returned with a huge grin on her face. "Damn, that guy is hot." She said, slipping back into her seat.

I looked at her with disdain. "You think so?"

"He sounds like some sort of English Lord."

I snorted. "He sounds like a stuck-up pig to me."

My response startled Kylie. "What makes you say that?"

I sighed. "I guess you could say I'm biased. The bastard fucked my sister while he was dating Jenna Plural. To me, he's a big sleaze bucket."

This seemed to intrigue Kylie even more. "Wow, he certainly likes his women to be high profile."

I frowned. "Sure, with Jenna, but Stacey?"

Kylie looked at me like I was retarded. "You really have no idea what a legend your sister is?"

I laughed at that, but it quickly dissipated as I saw that Kylie was being serious. "Oh, come on, you are bullshitting me for sure."

"Stacey Grant was already a legendary name even before she pulled that stunt at the Battle of Deep space. She has the bloody Victoria Cross, after all."

Yeah sure, of course I heard it and I guess it was impressive to other military. Did it really matter in the real world? I had thought so, but if Kylie was right then apparently people did consider this shit a big deal.

301

It wasn't something I would have ever remotely considered. Sure the military had their place but surely they weren't part of my world?

"Her maneuver at the Battle of Deep Space, where she took out that French frigate with the Lady Liberty, has cemented her name in the annals of history. She will be remembered like von Ribbentrop of World War One and Mahoney of the Martian conflicts. Your sister is a bloody hero, Hannah."

I stared at her for a long moment as she fell silent. "I had no idea about that." I eventually replied.

I had never really paid much attention to the war, as I have said several times in this chronicle already, and had never paid any heed to what my strange sister was doing. I had spent much time with her over the last few months, but she never really liked talking about her life back Down Under. Sure, there were silly little things like how she liked to surf on Bondi Beach and the occasional story about a wild party. She even talked a lot about her best friend, Harper, but she never spoke about the war or her part in it. The fondness I had developed for her was undoubted in my heart but believe it or not, I felt a pang of jealousy at this new revelation.

Growing up, I was always the center of attention within my family and among my peers. Of course, this all seemed perfectly normal, and I never really thought about it until after Last Day. I was nobody's center of attention anymore. Unless, of course, you counted Drake, who appeared to be obsessively interested in destroying me. The Solar System had changed, and me with it. I loved my sister, and to be quite honest, she was the first person I truly had those feelings for. But she had something all my money could never buy... the respect of the ordinary people. It really wasn't fair.

Kylie excused herself, saying she was tired and wanted to get some sleep before we re-uploaded ourselves for the journey back to the fleet. "You should get some sleep, too. It'll be good if you're refreshed and awake when we arrive there," she told me, and I couldn't help but find that amusing. M.E.T. travel is so weird. If I were tired when I went in, I'd be tired when I downloaded three months later. Time is literally nonexistent!

Pride can be a bitch and seriously make you make some dumb decisions. I was annoyed at myself that I was jealous of the sister who had nothing and continued to have nothing. But she had something I had never had. She had the respect and admiration of the people of the Solar Confederation. It wasn't something I could possibly achieve. People don't hang pictures of corporate executives on their bedroom walls. Well, not unless they're complete weirdos. I realized Stacey had something I desired, and I was used to getting anything I wanted. But one can't simply buy respect.

However, as Michael Phelkar came back into the room, I realized there was something I *could* take from her. And I smiled up at him warmly. "Oh, that feels so much better," he said. Then, noticing the absence of our companion, he asked where she was.

"She's gone to have a rest," I said gently, indicating the seat next to me. "Sit next to me. Let's get to know each other," I said in my softest voice. He looked a little confused but quickly complied as I sat up and crossed my legs, allowing one to brush his purely by 'accident'.

"I must say, you don't look much like Stacey," he said, glancing down at my legs, which, unfortunately, were clad in prison guard overalls.

I placed my elbow on the table and rested my chin in my palm as I looked into his eyes. "Oh, I do so hope you're not disappointed," I said innocently.

He looked momentarily flustered but came back quickly, "Oh my dear, I most certainly am not. However, you remind me more of Jenna Plural than Stacey."

"That's because I've been genetically modified to be pleasing to the eye," I said, with more syrup than Canada could produce in a year. "You do find me pleasing to the eye, don't you, Michael?" I said, making sure that I sounded like I would be disappointed if he didn't.

"Oh well, I'm..." he said, all of a fluster. "I assure you, Hannah, you are exceedingly beautiful, and no mistake on that. However, I am surprised that you're a GenMod. May I ask how old you are, if it is not impolite of me?"

"I'm twenty-one, Michael," I said, using my legal age rather than my actual age after my two-year stint in the M.E.T..

303

He looked a little confused. "It was my understanding that Gen-Mods haven't been made for nearly fifty years."

"What can I say? My mother was Marcia Grant, and Grants get what they want," I traced my finger along his arm.

He laughed at this, confusing me. I frowned but in a cute, pouty way. "Is there something amusing about that?"

"Oh no," he said, still chuckling. "You just reminded me when someone said something similar to me not so long ago."

I kept my eyes fixed upon his longingly, until he had just that right amount of discomfort. I reached up and ran the back of my finger across his cheek. "Oh well, it is clear to me that not everybody has to be genetically modified to be attractive, Michael."

He stiffened, probably in more ways than I could see, and looked quite flustered. "Well, Hannah...." but his voice trailed off. I pulled my chair closer to him, my knee now resting on the calf of his leg. He didn't move it away, indicating that there would be no resistance to my intentions.

"You have beautiful eyes, Mr. Phelkar," my tone was now one that would cause Canada's syrup supply to run dry. "I can see what my sister saw in you." It was no simple accident that I brought up Stacey's name. This was all about sating my jealousy. Should he continue in the direction I intended, I wanted it to be clear his mind that I was taking something from her. If I were right about him, the guy wouldn't care about fucking his ex-girlfriend's sister.

"Well, that's certainly nice of you to say so," he fumbled.

Oh my fucking God! The man was so awkward I didn't understand why he wasn't still a virgin. I guess some moron could see an innocent charm and sweetness in that. But I like men to be men. I know that's supposed to be outdated, but I like men who knew what they wanted and took control. With Phelkar, it was clear that I would have to do all the work. There was no doubt I had him. The way his eyes fixated on mine, he was clearly lost. "I know you like GenMods, Mr. Phelkar, and you get the best of both worlds with me. The perfection of Jenna and the sassy Australian girl." I giggled shamelessly as I saw his pupils dilate and his breathing rate increase. He struggled to speak, and with a huge grin, I let him off the hook as I leaned in and kissed him. Gently at first, then harder, and, of course, there was absolutely no resistance on his part as he reciprocated and let his hands fall down to my hips. I moaned softly, but to tell you the truth, it was all fake. I didn't have the slightest attraction for this man. It was all about the conquest, and while that could make me horny, it was much harder when you felt nothing but revulsion for the man. I pulled back, lowered my head, and looked up at him, submissively biting my lower lip before saying, "Let's go to my cabin." I stood up, taking his hand, and he followed like a lamb to the slaughter. I was utterly disgusted that he hadn't rejected my advances. That would've been the decent thing to do.

The door to the small, cramped room was barely shut when he started grappling feverishly at the zipper on my overalls. I could've stopped him there and left him frustrated and still have my victory. However, amidst my pride, there was also curiosity as to what my sister found so good about this man. As he kissed me, I reached down to check out what he had to offer. A decent length and a fair girth, but nothing to brag about. He let out such a gasp as I touched him that I thought he was going to blow his load before we'd even finished undressing. Now that would have been awesome. I would've relished in his humiliation, and there would've been none of this bullshit about, "it's alright. It could happen to anyone. I don't mind, honestly." It would have been more along the lines of utterly degrading him for such a schoolboy reaction.

His eyes widened as my overalls fell away, and he stared down at the artistry of my genetic designer. Oh my God, he looked like a schoolboy who had just caught his hot teacher undressed. It was hard for me not to give up and walk away, but I persisted. I was on a mission. No-one ever got one up on me, and if that meant letting Michael Phelkar get one up in me, then all was fair in love and war. He reached up and grasped my breasts. His hands were coarse and rough, something I wasn't used to. The guys I associated with back home lived soft lives, never having done a day's work with their hands in their life.

As his clothes came away, he pushed me back towards the bed ever so gently. Stacey describes him as a very giving lover, but I have to disagree. He didn't seem remotely interested in foreplay. I pushed down on his shoulders, indicating that I wanted him to pleasure me orally. Shit. I needed something to get me wet, so it wouldn't hurt. He did so but with incredible impatience and lack of enthusiasm, but I held him in place by wrapping my legs around his shoulders until he did a satisfactory job. Oh my God, it was such a struggle. Even closing my eyes and thinking of my rockstar crush back in high school or old boyfriends of mine couldn't arouse me with this fumbling idiot. My contempt for him was making it even more difficult to fake it.

When I finally released him, he scrambled up like a pathetic, desperate virgin who'd never been with a woman before. I managed to restore my cute inviting smile. "I want you inside me," I muttered passionately, wanting to hurry this up and get it over and done with. To say it hurt when he entered me is an understatement. I had completely failed to become aroused, and it was hard not to wince and maintain that look of ecstasy that I wanted him to believe. "Oh my God, Michael," I cried out in feigned passion as he thrust himself into me.

I pulled his head down over my shoulder so I wouldn't have to maintain that look, as he grunted and groaned on top of me. I continued to make all the appropriate sounds, and he was none the wiser. As his grunts and groans grew louder, I increased my passionate cries. As he climaxed, I tensed my body as if it was also happening to me. As he allowed his body to collapse upon me with exhaustion, I immediately pushed him away, and he rolled over. He made to turn over and hold me, but I immediately got up. I wanted to shower and get as much of him out of me as was humanly possible.

"Hannah?" he said with his voice filled with concern. I turned to look up at him as I pulled on my overalls. "Is everything OK?"

"Everything is just hunky dory, Mr. Phelkar," I said snarkily, as I buttoned up the top and hid the breast he was still staring at.

He looked at me, most confused. "Did I do something wrong?"

I snorted. "Why don't you ask Jenna and Stacey that?"

"I really don't understand. It was you who instigated this, not me."

I shrugged at him dismissively as I sat down and started to tie up my shoelaces. "Well, for a start, you should have said no. I'm your ex-girlfriend's sister, for fuck's sake! And to be honest, I really just wanted to know what Stacey found so good about you."

His response took me by surprise, "and did you?"

I stared at him in disbelief. "Oh my God, you are so full of yourself, Michael! No, I didn't. That was possibly the worst fuck I've ever had. You are a lousy lover, and it was beyond bad. You are the most contemptible piece of shit I have ever met and scraped off my boot! I regret rescuing you. You fully deserve to be in a penal colony as some bitch for a big guy called Bubba. So go fuck yourself, Michael. I can't imagine why anyone else wants to."

The look on his face was priceless, and I will save it till the day I die. I didn't wait for a response, even though he didn't have one, as I turned away and walked out of the door, slamming it behind me.

As I have told you, Mr. Phelkar asked me to write this chronicle, so no doubt you are surprised I included this encounter in my story. It will not surprise me if he tries to get this censored before publication. However, something tells me that Jenna Plural, who is probably as hurt by him as much as Stacey, will let it pass. Some people have questioned my actions in this, saying that I behaved inappropriately. To be honest, I don't care. I am Hannah Grant, and I always get what I want.

CHAPTER THIRTY-FOUR

THE RETURN

As I re-entered the living area, having showered and changed, I saw Kylie sitting at one of the tables. The body of the German officer was now gone. "I thought you were getting some rest?" I asked casually, stepping over to the counter and grabbing a coffee.

"Yeah, like anyone could sleep with that noise going on," she said so snippily that I turned to look at her. She glared up at me.

"Sorry about that," I said. It was clear that I was not.

"That was quite a bitchy thing to do," she said as I sat down at the table next to her.

"What was?" I inquired disinterestedly. I was still thinking about Michael Phelkar. Actually, it was more about me. The whole thing made me think about my own personal relationships. Or rather lack of them. I hadn't dated anyone in almost two years. To be honest, I hadn't really been interested. There's not much time when you run a corporation that's also a cover for what was essentially an Australian smuggling ring.

"I made it very clear that I was interested in him, and you made it very clear that you weren't. So what the fuck was that about?"

"Hmm?" I looked up as Kylie drew me from my thoughts. "Oh, sweetie, I can assure you he's fully available. That guy's a complete slut."

"Apparently, he's not the only one," she said quite venomously.

309

But I just grinned. With an ego like mine, it's very hard to offend me. It was the first time I had seen her drop her austere professionalism. "Had to find some way to kill time," I grinned at her.

As I am sure you're probably aware, this encounter with the First Minister of Civil Affairs made for an uncomfortable situation for the creep. There were few places to avoid another on board this small, cramped piece of shit ship. Not that I tried. I positively relished in his discomfort.

However, for the next few hours, the big idiot tried to avoid talking to me. Whenever our eyes made contact, he would look shifty and look away. Personally, I was just highly amused by the discomfort I was causing him. I may have done what I did out of some jealousy I felt about my sister, but I did care about her, and he had screwed her over. Literally and figuratively. However, there was a journey of several months ahead of us in order to return to the fleet, and none of us intended to stay awake for it. I certainly didn't want to look at that pompous pom's face more than I had to.

After getting a final meal, we headed into the M.E.T. room. Kylie asked me to go first, but I declined. I'm not sure why, but I wanted Michael to be gone before I was. I couldn't help but notice the look of disappointment on her face and realized she'd hoped to get rid of me and be alone with him. I pondered for a moment about giving her that opportunity, but then the thought of bringing joy to Michael Phelkar made me decide against it. As he stepped up to the circle, he gave me the most contemptuous look. I smiled cruelly at him and shook my head disparagingly, turning away as he disappeared. I undressed and quickly stepped onto the device. "See you on the other side," I said to Kylie.

I'm not a religious person, but I said a prayer that I wasn't going to disappear into the other side of the Solar System and wake up a hundred years later or whatever.

And then it was three months later.

Life with M.E.T. can be most disorientating. For me, I'd only been away for several weeks. However, I had been gone for the better part of seven months. As the H.M.S. Parkhurst closed in on the fleet, Confed fighters were dispatched, but they peeled off and returned long before they reached us. Kylie had transmitted her intelligence codes, and Charlotte Kensett had informed the authorities that we were indeed a friendly craft.

We received instructions to land on the U.S.S. Constitution.

As we entered the flagship of the Solar Confederation, I was sitting up front with Kylie and the pilot, and I saw many people had come out to welcome us. I scanned the crowd to see if I could see Stacey or even Jenna, but I couldn't, and that concerned me for a moment.

However, our little adventure was now over, and the cover I had made up for Stacey was probably wide open.

As for Jenna Plural, I was unsure if she would thank me or arrest me for organizing this little mission.

When we landed, I found Mr. Phelkar cleaning himself up. He had found suitable clothes from the crew's lockers so that he wouldn't exit the ship in British prison gray. Finally ready, we headed to the door. Slowly it lowered, turning itself into the ramp that would take us down onto the deck of the Constitution.

Kylie hung back. I turned to look at her questioningly. "There's fleet media down there. It's hardly the place of an intelligence agent to appear in the tabloid press. I'm going to stay on board until the docking bay is clear."

I nodded understandingly and indicated the opening. "After you, Michael," I said quietly.

As he stepped down, a round of applause went up. I stared once more around the sea of faces, looking for anyone I recognized.

A young woman in a pristine United States Marine uniform with her hair tied in a long red braid over her shoulder stepped up with a beaming smile and offered him her hand. I would later come to know this woman as Lieutenant Emma Dodgson, who would make her mark on my family in a way I would never expect.

They spoke briefly, but I couldn't hear what was said, and Phelkar disappeared with her into the crowd of people gathering around him. No one paid me any attention, and I unusually enjoyed that.

I stepped down the ramp and headed towards the door, unsure where I was going. I merely wanted to avoid attention as I didn't do this for myself. I did it for Stacey, and she wasn't here. I wanted to know why.

"I must admit I didn't think you would succeed," I glanced over my shoulder and smiled as Charlotte Kensett came up behind me.

"To be quite honest, Miss Kensett, neither did I."

"Kylie sent me a report while you were in transit. What on Earth made you let McKenna Myers go?"

"I guess I'm just an old softie," I shrugged. "It's not like she can do any harm to us where she is."

"Indeed not. However, she was one of the best combat veterans I've ever met and she would have continued to be useful for a while longer."

"People generally don't perform their best when doing it under duress, Miss Kensett."

Charlotte shrugged this off. "Maybe you're right. But next time, check with me before you make such a decision."

"Next time?" I positively laughed at that. "Ah, Miss Kensett, there isn't going to be a next time."

"I will see about that, Miss Grant," she smiled knowingly at me.

"Can you arrange a shuttle to take me to the Los Angeles? I want to see Stacey."

"Well, actually, there's no ship called the Los Angeles anymore." I shot her a look, my face filled with concern, but I felt relief as she continued, "the ship is now the R.A.S. Wagga Wagga."

I laughed again. "That sounds like my sister."

"Also, she's not aboard the ship. She is currently here on the Constitution," she informed me, making me wonder even more why she hadn't come to meet me.

"If that's the case, I'm surprised she was not down here to meet Mr. Phelkar," was what I actually said.

"Well, I can't comment on that. Trust me, keeping track of your sisters' various shenanigans is really hard and I'm an expert at keeping track of people. However, she has been temporarily relieved of command and is right, at this moment, getting very frustrated with doing desk duty about the ship."

"Relieved of command? Why?" I frowned.

"Again, it's not my place to discuss the personal issues of the crew outside the remit of my position."

"Are you allowed to tell me where I can find her?" I said sarcastically, and she gave me the directions.

I left Charlotte and went two decks up and to the other side of the ship. I finally found a small office. Her reassignment was clearly a long-term one, since they had placed her name up on the door as Captain Stacefield E. Grant. I knocked on the door, and a weary voice called out, "come in. It's not exactly locked."

As I stepped in, I saw Stacey seated behind the desk. She looked up at me, surprised as her face turned grim. "Well, g'day to you, sister." I didn't need to be genetically enhanced to hear the curtness in her voice as she said the word sister.

"Hey, Stacey, I'm back," I smiled, but was caught a little off guard by her attitude.

To my surprise, she merely shrugged. "So? What the fuck do you want me to do about it?"

To say I was confused is an understatement. "I brought back Mr. Phelkar."

"So, I heard. Thank you for that," she said, although her tone did not change. "Is there anything you wanted? I may be flying a fucking desk, but I'm still busy."

I frowned. "Stacey, would you just tell me if I've done something wrong?"

She struggled to stand up, but she did so awkwardly, having to push her chair far back before she even tried. My jaw dropped as I looked at her swollen belly and uncomplimentary maternity uniform. "Holy fuck, you're pregnant!"

"Well, it's good to see your genetically superior eyes are working," she said sarcastically.

"Stacey, what the hell is the matter with you? I thought you'd be pleased that I got Mr. Phelkar back."

"Oh, I am pleased about that, Hannah," she said, shuffling around to the front of the desk. "But you fucking lied to me. You played me for a dumb cunt."

313

I swallowed hard. She clearly knew the truth, but how much I didn't know. "I don't know what you mean."

I felt it before I realized what she had done. A hard untempered slap around my face came my way. It stung, and I stared back at her in disbelief. "You told me you were a mechanic. A poor little refugee from Down Under. You even got Charlotte Kensett to change your personnel files to back up your story when I checked. Yet it turns out you are, in fact, our mother's daughter. You've spent the last two years sitting in your ivory castle above the Twilight Wanderer, profiting from the fucking war. You make me sick. I'm ashamed for anyone to know I'm even related to you."

I stared back at her. I wanted to tell her what Bron and I had been doing these past two years. However, I don't know if it was pride or stubbornness, but I didn't feel I should have to explain myself to my sister. "I simply wanted to meet you on a level playing field. I didn't want you to see me like you would our mother."

She snorted contemptuously. "So, you decided how I would react before you even got to know me? Maybe I wouldn't see you as the stuck-up little bitch daughter of my mother. I don't fucking know now because you took that choice away from me. I appreciate what you did getting Phelks back, although I don't know why you did it, and whatever you say, I probably won't believe you. I really don't want to have anything to do with you."

"You can believe me or not, Stacey," I said defensively. "I did it to make up for the way my side of the family treated your side."

Stacey snorted again. "I never saw it as being on any side. That's where you and I clearly differ. My problem is squarely with our mother. It wasn't with you. Ever. If you took the chance to get to know the real me without pre-judging my reactions, you would know I would judge you on actions, not ancestry. However, your actions give me a clear picture of who you are. You're no different from my mother. You think you know better than everyone and make decisions that affect other people's lives."

"I just thought…" I started to say, but she interrupted me.

"No, Hannah, you didn't think. You didn't just lie to me. You came up with some fucked up crazy plan," she said, her voice rising and her

314

face reddening in anger. "I just spent the last seven months thinking you're fucking traitor. I was left wanting to see you dead. I only found out the truth a few hours ago, and fuck you, Hannah, but it's just not acceptable. You broke my heart. I thought I had a sister, but I just had this web of deceit instead," she sighed and calmed herself, as she was want to do when she'd had a tirade. Stacey always struggled to stay angry.

"I got you Mr. Phelkar back," I said, as if that should put everything right.

"And I said I appreciate that, but what exactly did you expect to happen, Hannah?"

I did not reply to that, but to be perfectly honest, I never really thought that far ahead. She continued, "did you think we would get back together and settle down and raise a family? The guy cheated on Jenna and me, Hannah. That ship has sailed. Yeah, I still care about him, and yeah, I'm over the moon that he's alive, well and back with us, but it changes nothing for me."

I didn't respond, but I glanced down at her belly and then back up at her and asked, "is he the father?"

There was a long silence as she stared at me. "Does it matter?" she eventually replied.

I shrugged noncommittedly. "Am I not allowed to be concerned about the welfare of my niece or nephew?"

She looked a little startled, and I realized she hadn't considered that I was related to her unborn child. "Trust me on this. You'll have nothing to do with her. We're done, Hannah Grant. That's all there is to it."

I felt a knot tie my stomach. I was surprised at how much those words hurt. At that moment, I realized Stacey had been the only thing I had ever learned to truly care about. And even though it was only a few minutes before I learned of the impending arrival of my nephew or niece, I felt an instant bond with her. You see, I can't have children. My body rejects what it would consider inferior D.N.A., and my body's defense systems go to work at once to destroy any imperfect semen straight away. The only way I could have offspring was if I was to breed with another GenMod, and we were extremely rare.

Stacey and I were the last of the Grants. Should misfortune befall me, and I died, the company would end with me as the last family member. There was no way my fiery little pilot of a sister would give up her guns for the executive chair. Inside Stacey, was my heir and the future of Grant Industries.

Part of me wanted to protest. Part of me wanted to fix this abominable situation, but as I saw that look in her one eye, I knew it was hopeless. Seeing the contempt on her face, I sighed, and my mood turned to resentment. Fuck her. She could go to hell. I had just put my life on the line to save the man she claimed she was in love with, and this was the thanks I was going to get?

"Stacey?" I said softly, albeit with a determination to hide my hurt and anger.

"What?" She responded snippily.

"Go fuck yourself." I didn't give her a chance to respond, as I turned around and headed out the door.

As I headed back down towards the shuttle bay and my ride back to the Twilight Wanderer, I felt a mixture of sadness and anger, but by the time I reached it, only the anger remained. I put myself out for Stacey, something I had never done for anyone before, and now I realized, it had all been a big mistake.

The only thing that truly mattered in this world now was me. I didn't owe anyone anything, and I was an idiot for thinking I did. It was about time I grew up and accepted my responsibility to no-one but myself.

A few hours later, I was back aboard the Twilight Wanderer.

CHAPTER THIRTY-FIVE

LOOSE ENDS

B ronwyn was there to meet me when I landed back aboard my ship. She smiled, until she saw my grim expression as I descended the shuttle ramp.

"It's good to see you again, mate. What's the matter?"

I managed to smile. "Absolutely nothing," I said as I followed her out into the corridor heading back towards our suite. As we walked, I responded to the various staff members that passed us welcoming me back.

"How is everything going?" I asked her.

"Got to be honest, much better than even I expected," she replied with a small laugh. "Business is flourishing, and we pretty much have every military contract tied up. We have various production facilities set up on Enceladus, and now pretty much control every commercial venture within the fleet. We only have one real competitor."

I glanced at her. "I'm not a big fan of competition. It complicates things. What do we plan to do about them?"

"Well, it's rather strange, really. They're not even a legitimate company." With that, she had my full attention, and any thoughts of Stacey disappeared from my mind as we stepped back into the apartment.

"What the hell is that supposed to mean?" I said as I dropped myself into an armchair and called for a steward to bring me some iced tea.

"It's the New York Fraternity. They're a criminal cartel that flourished throughout the United States and the Solar System. It appears Admiral Plural has engaged their services. They basically provide her access to their normal legitimate sources, and security turns a blind eye to their more criminal activities."

"Are they services that we could provide?" I asked casually.

"Only if you want to get into the business of drug dealing, prostitution and things like that," Bronwyn laughed but suddenly faltered, when she realized I wasn't trying to be funny. "You're serious, are you, mate?"

"If Jenna Plural thinks it's going to help the war effort, then honestly, I don't see a problem with it," I said dismissively. "Set me up with a meeting with the person who runs this organization. Let's see how we can get our share from it."

When the polite request came through that I should meet with Jenna Plural, it was clearly not a request. It was also quite clear that a virtual meeting was not acceptable. So it was that I had to go through the three-hour procedure of transferring from the Wanderer to the Constitution. She did, however, do me the courtesy of having one of her aides waiting for me when I landed. He led me up to her office by the bridge, where I sat and waited impatiently in the outer office, with only a young lieutenant behind a desk for company. When she came in about thirty minutes later, the warm friendliness I had encountered the night we had gone out to eat with my sister was clearly gone. She barely glanced over at me as she came in and headed straight for her office. "Come with me, please, Hannah," she said quite coldly. I took my time getting up and following her in. As much as my heart was now beating, I wasn't going to show her that I was intimidated. You have nothing to worry about if you've done nothing to cross Jenna Plural. She has your back as much as you have hers. This doesn't stop her from being an imposing figure. She may have looked like she was a college cheerleader, but when those eyes were fixed upon you, they could break the will of the strongest person.

"Take a seat, Hannah." She indicated to the chair in front of her desk as she walked around it to sit on her own. I complied, crossed my legs, and sat back. She studied me for a moment before saying, "I have quite a quandary, Hannah. I need to either praise you or file charges against you. I haven't decided which yet."

"Well, if it helps, I prefer the first option," I said with a smile.

She did not return it. "I have known your sister almost five years now, and to be honest, I will never understand that Australian sense of humor. I find literally nothing amusing in this situation, and I don't understand how you can."

"To be completely honest, Jenna, I don't see why you have a problem. I've returned your first Minister of Civil Affairs, and no harm has been done. Considering your relationship with him, I thought you would've been pleased," I said incredulously.

"Whatever relationship I had with Mr. Phelkar is irrelevant to this conversation, and I'm not about to let it become so. What is a matter for discussion, is that you say that no harm was done. Do you really believe that?"

"I most certainly do," I responded defensively. "I also believe that in liberating Mr. Phelkar, I have effectively humiliated the European Union by taking away their prize prisoner. This is entirely a win-win situation."

"I beg to differ. You engaged in an activity that lost me a shuttle and a valuable prisoner."

"McKenna Myers is probably dead. My one regret is leaving her and the agent behind. I honestly don't understand why you would have a problem sacrificing her for Mr. Phelkar."

"McKenna isn't dead," Jenna said softly. "She has made it back to the United States, and she's retired. According to the reports I've received, she's even getting married to a man called Anderson."

I smiled. "At the risk of upsetting you, I have to say I'm quite pleased by that news. She may have taken a different side, but she's not a bad person."

Jenna shrugged. "I regretfully have to agree with that assessment. However, it doesn't change the fact that you broke a prisoner out of lawful detention upon my ship."

"The end justifies the means, Jenna. I'm genuinely sorry if it upsets you, but I won't apologize for something necessary to complete my mission."

"Your mission?" Jenna raised an eyebrow. "Let's get to the point of this meeting, Hannah. You didn't have a mission, at least not one that was authorized. You acted independently, although you did utilize my resources. You also went to great lengths to deceive me."

"I can assure you, Jenna, but I had absolutely no intention of deceiving you. I had personal reasons that I didn't want my sister to have knowledge of my position."

"Oh, I know all about that," she chided. "You don't need to go into it. Charlotte Kensett has told me everything. My problem is the lengths you went to in order to stage your little game with Stacey. I consider it a severe breach of my security that a civilian could pose as a member of my military. That gives me my concern."

"Honestly, I didn't think it a problem considering that Charlotte Kensett went along with it," I said, throwing Charlotte under the bus, but after all, if she had told Jenna everything, she had tried to push me first.

"As I understand it, you threatened to withdraw the support of Grant Industries with our endeavors. You pretty much left Kensett without a choice."

"It was a bluff, and it worked. The one thing I can assure you of, Jenna, is that you have not only my support, but also my absolute loyalty."

This startled her, and I could tell she was not expecting that response from me. "Can you?"

"Absolutely. I genuinely believe that you're our only hope of liberating my country. To that end, the resources of Grant Industries are completely at your disposal."

"And you can speak for the entire company? From my understanding, you just control a small independent division."

"To be honest, Jenna, that is true, but I assure you, I will have control of the entire company in a very short amount of time. That is, if the Solar Confederation intends not to recognize the restrictions of the genetically modified as laid down in the Prague convention."

Jenna smiled at this and replied, "I don't think the Prague convention is in either of our interests. You need not worry about that. We won't have an issue if you are working for me."

"Oh no, Jenna, it's not going to be like that," I shook my head. "I am a Grant, and I answer to no-one. Not anymore and never again. I may have submitted to your authority before, but I'm awake now. I will run my business as I see fit. You have my full support, but I am nobody's bitch."

Jenna studied me for a while, and I thought she would flip out, but a grin suddenly slid across her face. "You remind me of your sister."

"How disappointing," I said before I could stop myself.

The smile then faded. "I understand the two of you are having an issue over the situation."

"No offense, Jenna. Whatever is going on between Stacey and me is a personal matter, and I'd like to keep it that way. She has set the boundaries of our relationship, and I have accepted that. I have nothing more to say on the matter."

"Fair enough. Just know if I can help in any way, you only need to ask. Stacey is very dear to me and has always been there for me, and I will always be there for her." I didn't respond to that and just sat there expressionless. "Well, I think I've said everything I have to say. Thank you for the reassurance that Grant Industries will back the Confederation. All I ask, is that you don't go off on any other adventures without consulting my office and either me or Commodore Addison."

"Understood, Jenna," I stood up and stretched my hand across the table. She took it and gripped it firmly in a handshake, and I returned to the Twilight Wanderer.

Many things had changed in my absence. Bron had done a sterling job of getting my division of Grant Industries up and running again amid the fall of the US. It turned out that once again, Drake escaped the fall of a country and somehow made it through to a company-owned station orbiting Venus.

For me, I had learned a lesson. My mother had always been right. Fuck Stacey and fuck everything she stood for. Fuck everybody.

No one is worth sacrificing yourself for. I would continue supporting Jenna in the war effort because it was in my best interests. The re-establishment of Grant Industries as the biggest company in the Solar System and the power that came with that would now be my only concern, along with the liberation of Australia. I wanted to go home, and I wanted to go home as soon as possible.

I spent the next few days getting acclimatized after everything that had gone on. I had many meetings with various executives and potential suppliers from third parties. In time, I would either absorb these third parties into Grant Industries or eradicate them. After all, why pay a third party when you can do it yourself? Of course, these meetings would probably be even more boring for you than they were for me, so I will just gloss over them. However, there is one meeting that would probably intrigue you.

I spent about three days working on my vision for Grant Industries. I did this alone without consulting Bronwyn. Something she wouldn't be too happy about when I revealed it. As a result, when I was not in meetings, I spent a lot of time alone. One such morning when I was working in my office, I received a very unusual call.

"Hello, Miss Grant. I hope I have called you at a convenient time. My name is Doctor Michelle Decker, and there is an important matter that I would very much like to meet with you and talk about."

The only doctor I knew was Deacon Cooper, so I immediately assumed she was connected and the issue would be related to his work. "Is this something about Bronwyn Donovan?" I asked.

"No, that name isn't familiar to me. No, this is entirely related to your sister, Stacey Grant."

My interest immediately waned, except for a lingering curiosity as to what this was about. "I really don't see what any medical condition Stacey may have as any of my business," I replied curtly.

"Well, I wouldn't exactly say condition. I'm her obstetrician." Now that got my attention immediately, for I was indeed concerned about the welfare of my niece or nephew. "There is quite a serious issue I'd like to discuss with you."

"Go ahead."

"No, I'd rather do it in person. Fleet communications are still not entirely secure, and this is a very private matter that I do not wish to breach the confidentiality of my patient."

"You're welcome to come aboard the Twilight Wanderer anytime," I responded. "I will arrange for one of our shuttles to pick you up."

322

So it was that an appointment was made for the following morning, and I spent the next twenty-four hours mulling over what could possibly be the issue that would involve me.

Decker turned out to be a tall, pleasant-looking African woman from the Gambia, who I would place in her early fifties. She sat opposite me at my desk. She was a cheerful and pleasant woman but got straight to the point. "There is a problem with your sister's child. She has quite a severe condition that could hamper her ability to navigate the world effectively."

"Go on," I said, handing her a coffee and stepping back to my seat behind my desk.

"It is a rather delicate matter, and what I'd like to discuss with you, I hope that I can be assured, will be kept private."

"Well, it's rather difficult to promise to keep something quiet when one doesn't know what it is they're going to be told, but I assure you that if it doesn't cause any detriment to me, it will not be discussed outside this room with anyone."

"Fair enough," Decker smiled back at me. "Tests have shown that your sister's unborn child has a condition known as fetal alcohol syndrome."

I'd never heard of that, and I waited impatiently for her to get to the point. "This is caused by the severe consumption of alcohol early on in the pregnancy where the fetus is damaged."

Now, this seriously concerned me. "Are you seriously telling me that that stupid bitch continued to drink after becoming pregnant?"

"Yes," the doctor replied, looking quite startled by how I had referenced my sister. "But I don't think knowingly. While it is wholly inappropriate for me to even discuss this, I think you will understand why when I get to the point. Your sister is an extremely heavy drinker and did so before she was aware of her pregnancy."

"I don't think you're exactly giving away a secret here, so please carry on."

"Well, she overcomes her drinking by using the anti-intoxication pills, Alcorin, which has exacerbated the problem."

"Doctor Decker, I don't have all day. Please get to the point, will you?" I said as I spooned several helpings of sugar into my coffee. "How exactly does this syndrome affect my niece?

"Generally, the symptoms are very similar to a mild to severe form of autism."

I felt my heart sink and my stomach turn over as the idea of my niece possibly succeeding me started to vanish. However, she had still not come to her point. I assumed that she was about to ask me to subsidize the cost of some form of treatment. "How much do you need?" I responded, for there was no way I was going to turn my back on my niece, even if I did so with my sister.

Doctor Decker looked confused, "Oh, Miss Grant, I'm not here to look for money. What I want is your D.N.A.."

A silence hung between us, as I was too surprised to respond at first. "What on Earth for?" I asked, quite bewildered now by the whole affair. "From what I can see, Stacey is about to pop. I'm no geneticist, but I'm fairly certain that any such treatments need to be done at the embryonic level."

"That would be ideal, and I'm not saying this procedure is without risk. However, genetic science has advanced greatly, and we can try to fix these issues. However, the treatment can only enter the child via the mother, so if we are to do this, it must be before she gives birth."

"I'm not totally sure I understand. Why exactly do you need my D.N.A.?"

"If you forgive me for saying so, since I'm sure you probably do your best to hide it, you're a GenMod. We want to replace the faulty D.N .A. with yours. This will cause the child to rewrite itself retroactively."

"But why me? There are other GenMods out there?"

At least the doctor smiled. "Indeed there is, and we have already tested Jenna Plural for compatibility. Unfortunately, it wouldn't work, and we're hoping that your familial relationship with Stacey will give us a better result."

"My D.N.A. is barely a match for my sister. Only about fourteen percent of it matches our biological mother."

"We understand that. We don't even know if it *will* work or if the child will have many side effects. This science is still somewhat unpredictable. However, the standard of life this child will have without the treatment has a high risk of being very low indeed."

I pondered this and the ramifications of the decision I would make. "If this works, how will this affect her? Will she be a normal human?"

The doctor sighed. "Not entirely. She will be genetically modified, and depending on what areas of your D.N.A. take, she could turn out like yourself or Admiral Plural, but most likely to a lesser extent."n

Once again, I sat in silence, pondering this before I replied. "I agree, but with one non-negotiable condition." It was a bluff. I was going to help my niece no matter what the cost. "I don't want my sister to know that I've agreed to this."

"Are you asking me to lie to my patient?" Decker frowned.

I shrugged that off. "I'm not asking you to do anything. I'm simply telling you that my condition is anonymity regarding this matter. My sister may feel indebted to me, and I don't want a fake relationship with her," I then corrected myself with a nonchalant shrug. "Actually, I don't want any sort of relationship with her." I arched my fingers and stared coldly at her. "This is about my niece and not her. You can take my D.N.A., but she isn't ever to know I provided it. Is that understood?"

The doctor stared at me, not too happy with this situation, before replying. "Well, if I'm permitted to discuss this with Admiral Plural, who has taken a vested interest in this awkward situation, I'm sure she will agree to your condition and have her name on the record as the D.N.A. donor. However, we have already told Stacey that they're not compatible."

"Just tell her that you made a mistake." I snorted. "Stacey isn't exactly the brightest ember on the barbie. She isn't going to question it."

"Very well," the doctor said reluctantly. "For the child's sake, I will agree to your condition, even though I'm not at all happy about it."

"Well, it's a good thing that your happiness isn't the primary concern here," I smirked. "Do you want to do this now?"

And with that, she removed a small kit from her shoulder bag and took blood from me then and there. I then added my signature code to various documents on her tablet, permitting the use of my D.N.A. in the treatment of Stacey's unborn child.

As the doctor left, I couldn't help but smile to myself. Even if it didn't show, my niece would be a GenMod just like me. However, in this case, a perfectly legal one.

In the meantime, I had a legacy to protect for her.

"You know, Bronwyn. I think it's time we absorbed the rest of Grant Industries under our control. We'll never get anywhere with our hands tied as a small division restricted from trading in certain areas so that we don't crossover the departments controlled by Drake." I was no longer content with just running a division. The time had come for me to take my place as chairman.

"It can't be done, Hannah," Bron told me as I discussed my ideas with her. "You signed a binding contract that you wouldn't try to take over from Drake."

"Not quite," I said calmly, sitting back behind the desk and arching my fingers. "I said I wouldn't take over the company while he was alive. I think it's time to change that situation."

Bron narrowed her eyes at me. "What are you getting at, mate?"

"I want Drake dead," I said bluntly. "Is that clear enough for you? I want him dead before the end of the month and the immediate announcement that I am taking over as head of the board."

Bronwyn looked incredibly concerned with this. Although it was likely she was more opposed to the idea out of some high-minded ethic, than she was concerned about us biting off more than we could chew. "Honestly, I don't know who I could trust to do that. I can pretty much tell anyone within our security department to take out anyone ....but their own chairman. It's unlikely I'll get an agreement."

"Charlotte Kensett will see the benefits of having me in complete control of Grant Industries. I suggest you talk to her."

"Are you sure about this, Hannah?"

"Bron, I tried to do what I thought was right. It came back and bit me. I realized now that I was wrong. I've woken up. Get this done for me."

Before she could respond to me, there came a knock at the door. As Stepanchikov came in, I jumped up to greet her. She gave me a beaming smile which I returned. "Good to have you back, ma'am."

"It is good to be back, Emberlynn," I said, shaking her hand warmly. "Come sit down."

As she sat, she addressed Bron out of the habit of directly answering to her for the last seven months. "We just started picking up a transmission over the company's most secure communication lines. It was significantly unusual and directly related to Miss Grant here that I felt it necessary to bring it to your attention immediately."

"Put it up on the screen," I instructed, swiveling my chair around to face it. The screen lit up with a grainy image of a skinny woman in her mid-twenties. I recognized the uniform at once. Standard issue Peon POW wear.

"Can anyone hear me? We've broken out of Peon custody. There's a full-scale fucking riot going on here." The accent was Australian. "We are trying to take control, but the Peons are shutting down the environmental systems and bugging out. We need help. If anyone can hear us, please come to our aid," she stopped momentarily as an explosion rocked her room. "Shit, fuck and double damn!" She cried out as shrapnel flew over her, and she had to duck down. "It's hopeless," she sighed, looking down at the table in front of her in despair before looking up. When she spoke again, it was in a softer, dejected voice. "Look, I don't think anyone is gonna get here in time, but please try. If this is the last time anyone hears from me, please get a message to Stacey Grant."

She stopped for a moment and just stared at the screen as if the fires around her were nothing more than a television show, then she steeled herself with some last resolve and said, "tell her that I love her. I always have. I always will. And tell her to have a beer on me when the Southern Cross flies over Canberra once again." And with that, the line went dead. I sat there staring at the screen before turning back to Stepanchikov.

"I thought I would check with you before passing that message on." The security officer said.

"Did you get an ID on the woman?" Bron asked.

"We did, but to be honest, it makes no sense."

"Explain? "I demanded.

"The woman on the screen was listed as killed in action five years ago. She was working on a mission with the Americans alongside your sister, Captain Grant. We don't have the details on the actual mission, but Admiral Plural led it."

"What was her name?" I asked, but I was certain I already knew.

"Lieutenant Harper Davis of the Australian Air Force. She was a gunner before the fall of Australia and flew with your sister."

Bronwyn looked down at her terminal, pressed a couple of buttons, then turned to look at me. "Whoever is routing that call is a tech genius," she said. "It's bouncing off multiple relays both Peon and Alliance all the way from the outer solar system. Our best ship out there is the SS Victoria and it's heavily armed with munitions and a complement of our badass security forces. If I send the instructions now, they could triangulate the origin in about six hours and change course."

I just sat there with the best disinterested look I could purvey. "Does this have any relevance to company business?" I said softly.

"No, I just thought...." Bron started to reply awkwardly as she realized what I was going to do. Or rather, what I wasn't going to do.

"If it doesn't have anything related to the company, then frankly, I'm not in the least bit interested," I stated.

"Hannah?" Bronwyn looked confused. "Are you okay?" she asked with concern

I smiled at her, "Oh, everything is perfectly fine, Bron. I've just woken up."

But before she could reply, I turned back to my terminal, feeling quite satisfied that I had just damned probably the one thing that would bring joy to the life of that bitch I no longer considered to be my sister.

I had finally woken up to the reality of the universe. There was no reward for putting yourself out there. You would get no thanks for taking risks on behalf of others. No, all that mattered to me was that I was about to become the head of the most powerful organization in the Solar System, second only to Jenna Plural in influence. I would take over her authority in time, but that's another story.

As the silence hung in the room, I looked up from my terminal and said, "So, what is the next order of business? Come on. We have a business to run."

EPILOGUE: FIVE YEARS EARLIER

REPORT BY LIEUTENANT HARPER ELAINE DAVIS

Not far from asteroid 2 Pallas

My eagerness to go on the Starborne mission with Stacey would become one I'd long regret. As I climbed into that gunnery position on board the French fighter, I was excited by its vast array of weaponry. It proved to be probably the finest craft I'd ever flown in.

We easily took out the squadrons that pursued us as we escaped Pallas.

My gunnery position was very comfortable, and all the panels performing glistened with newness. As usual, Stacey was performing her usual flight maneuvers with the skill that I had come to expect as her tail gunner over the last year.

"Doing a forty-five on starboard," she called out from the cockpit.

"Roger on that, Stacey," responded Trisha, and she immediately opened up with her guns, and we ripped into his fuselage even as he tried to pull up. She then launched a dumb-dumb into his soft underbelly, and he disintegrated. "Got any idea how many bogies we took out?" Stacey called out.

"Fourteen. You broke your record, Stacey," I called back with pride.

"Does it really count if we're not in one of our own ships?" Trish asked. She was sooo jealous of Stacey's long-standing top-dog position.

331

"I'm sure it does. I'm certainly going to count it," I responded, much to the amusement of Stacey.

We had lost one of our thrusters and couldn't outrun the remaining bastards, but neither could they catch up with us. Eventually, they'd have to turn back for lack of fuel.

Then my world turned into the biggest pile of horse shit you could ever imagine.

"Ahh, Stacey!?" I cried out as I saw the big bastard of a fighter slowly catching up. "Another Starbourne is coming in on us."

"I can see it," she said as she pulled off to port.

A sudden volley of missiles launched from the incoming craft, and I released some ineffective countermeasures. I was suddenly startled when the open canopy above me suddenly shut. I looked about and almost panicked as I heard a long hiss and was concerned that air was escaping. It was not. The Starborne had an advanced defense response system we did not know about. It could analyze incoming attacks, calculate the outcome, and respond to protect the crew inside.

The system had just predicted such an outcome from the missiles coming in. To my utter bewilderment, there was a blast of jets that instantly fell silent as soon as I found myself detached from the Starbourne at a rapid speed that pushed me back into my chair and spun me around like a ride at the Disney Down Under theme park.

No longer being connected to the main ship and unknown to little old me, the internal comms were no longer working, and I was cut off from voice communication with Stacey and Trisha. Maneuvering thrusters came on to slow down my spin, and by the time I got my head together, both Starbournes were already far away. "What the flaming fuck!" I exclaimed as I turned in my seat to see nothing but the flare of the engine trails from the two ships far away engaged in combat. "Stacey, I appear to be detached from the ship," I said, but no response came, for indeed, she couldn't hear me. "Stacey," I said louder as if that would help, and I felt a knot tightening my stomach when still no response came. "Trisha?"

Again, no response. Had I been left alone, I'd probably have worked out to activate ship-to-ship communications, but out of the window ahead of me, I saw the squadron of Peon ships change course from pursuing the Starbourne and heading directly for me.

My heart sank, "oh fuck me!" I sighed softly.

I looked down at my weaponry controls, which were all bloody useless since I was no longer connected to any weaponry. I didn't even have control of this thing. Everything was automated. Suddenly the little escape pod shuddered, and I looked around frantically to find out what was wrong before realizing one of the Peon fighters had filed a grapple into my side. I was suddenly tugged out of the automated direction the craft had chosen, and the tug of war began between my thrusters and the fighter. After a brief minute of hope that I may break free, I realized the only thing this would achieve was to cause me to break up. After a quick search, I found the controls to deactivate the thrusters and the automated systems and was pulled along by the Peon fighter. I wondered what fate awaited me as I returned to Pallas.

Jenna Plural will return in

The Angel of Phobos

May 2023